I0640745

# CROSSING IN TIME

## The 1ST Disaster

# CROSSING IN TIME

## D. L. ORTON

*Between Two Evils Series*
*The 1st Disaster*

ROCKY MOUNTAIN PRESS

Copyright © 2015 D. L. Orton.
All rights reserved.

*Between Two Evils Series*
www.BetweenTwoEvils.com
Published by Rocky Mountain Press (USA)
Rocky-Mountain-Press.com
ISBN: 978-1-941368-01-5
Paperback First Edition (v2.3)

Written by D. L. Orton (dlorton.com, @DL_Orton)
Edited by David S. Taylor (thEditors.com)
Illustrations by Micah McDonald
Cover by Andreea Vraciu (platinumbookdesigner.com)
Book Layout by Fernando Urbina
Proofreaders: Sheila Fuller, Keith Moser, David Martin,
Julie Lynn Newland, Rachael Taylor,
Fernando Urbina & Richard Taylor.

*Crossing In Time* is a work of fiction. Names, characters,
places, and incidents are the product of the author's
imagination or are used fictitiously. Any resemblance to
actual persons, businesses, events, or locales is coincidental.

This book contains adult content and is for mature
audiences only. No animals were harmed in the publication
of this manuscript.

The text was set in Adobe Dante, a serif typeface
originally cut for use on a hand printing press.

ALSO BY D. L. ORTON

# Between Two Evils Series

*Lost Time: The 2<sup>nd</sup> Disaster*
Coming Winter 2015

∞

*Dead Time: The 3<sup>rd</sup> Disaster*
Coming Spring 2016

∞

*Out of Time: The 4<sup>th</sup> Disaster*
Coming 2017

∞

*End of Time: The Final Disaster*
Coming 2018

TABLE OF CONTENTS

**Crossing In Time** . . . . . . . . . . . . . . . . . III

*Front Matter*
COPYRIGHT . . . . . . . . . . . . . . . . . . . . IV

ALSO BY D. L. ORTON . . . . . . . . . . . . . . V

DEDICATION . . . . . . . . . . . . . . . . . . XIII

EPIGRAPH . . . . . . . . . . . . . . . . . . XV

**Prologue**     *A Few Years from Now* . . . . . . . . 1

**Part One**    *Ten Months Earlier* . . . . . . . . . . . 9

CHAPTER 1   *Isabel: Falling for Him* . . . . . . . 11

CHAPTER 2   *Isabel: Not in This Universe* . . . . . 17

CHAPTER 3   *Diego: The Fire & the Furry* . . . . 24

CHAPTER 4   *Matt: People Will Die* . . . . . . 41

CHAPTER 5   *Diego: Handle My Weapon* . . . . . 47

CHAPTER 6   *Isabel: Playing With Fire* . . . . . . 53

CHAPTER 7   *Diego: If I Had Any Patients* . . . . 59

CHAPTER 8   *Matt: It's Classified, Doctor* . . . . . 65

CHAPTER 9   *Diego: In a Pickle* . . . . . . . . 75

CHAPTER 10 *Isabel: All the Facts* . . . . . . . . 81

CHAPTER 11  *Matt: The Magic Kingdom* . . . . . 84

CHAPTER 12  *Diego: Wait for Me* . . . . . . . 94

CHAPTER 13  *Diego: The Long Way Home.* . . . 101

CHAPTER 14  *Isabel: Right As Rain* . . . . . . 107

CHAPTER 15  *Diego: Second Chances.* . . . . . 115

CHAPTER 16  *Diego: Get in Line* . . . . . . . 120

CHAPTER 17  *Isabel: Out of the Blue* . . . . . . 133

**Part Two**  *The Magic Kingdom* . . . . . . . . 147

CHAPTER 18  *Diego: I Wouldn't Do That* . . . . 149

CHAPTER 19  *Isabel: It Rings True.* . . . . . . 152

CHAPTER 20  *Matt: The First Peep.* . . . . . . 158

CHAPTER 21  *Isabel: Gone to the Dogs* . . . . . 163

CHAPTER 22  *Diego: The Peeping Tom* . . . . . 169

CHAPTER 23  *Isabel: Lost in the Blizzard* . . . . 172

CHAPTER 24  *Diego: Did You See the Blood?* . . . 176

CHAPTER 25  *Isabel: He's Dead* . . . . . . . 183

CHAPTER 26  *Diego: Tenpins With the Devil* . . . 187

CHAPTER 27  *Matt: Pretty Nasty Stuff* . . . . . 196

CHAPTER 28  *Isabel: Heads or Tails* . . . . . . 202

CHAPTER 29  *Diego: Out of Time* . . . . . . . 206

CHAPTER 30  *Matt: If I'm Wrong* . . . . . . . 217

CHAPTER 31  *Isabel: Precious & Few.* . . . . . 222

CHAPTER 32  *Matt: Top of the List* . . . . . . 229

**Part Three** *La Isla, Another Universe* . . . . . . 235

CHAPTER 33  *Isabel: It Beats Taking the Bus* . . . 237

CHAPTER 34  *Isabel: I Was Misinformed* . . . . . 242

CHAPTER 35  *Tego: I'm Not Going Anywhere* . . 251

CHAPTER 36  *Matt: Shell-Shocked* . . . . . . . 267

CHAPTER 37  *Tego: Around Her Finger* . . . . . 278

CHAPTER 38  *Isabel: Alone in the Dark* . . . . . 289

CHAPTER 39  *Tego: In the Moonlight* . . . . . . 291

CHAPTER 40  *Matt: Throw in the Towel* . . . . 295

CHAPTER 41  *Tego: Crazy for You* . . . . . . . 300

CHAPTER 42  *Isabel: You Have No Idea* . . . . . 308

CHAPTER 43  *Isabel: Drowning in Regrets* . . . . 314

CHAPTER 44  *Matt: Signal to Noise* . . . . . . 317

CHAPTER 45  *Tego: Rip Your Heart Out* . . . . 322

CHAPTER 46  *Tego: In My Wildest Dreams* . . . 332

CHAPTER 47  *Isabel: All Is Lost* . . . . . . . 346

CHAPTER 48  *Matt: We're Domed* . . . . . . . 359

CHAPTER 49  *Tego: Over My Head* . . . . . . 363

CHAPTER 50  *Isabel: One Last Time* . . . . . . 368

CHAPTER 51  *Isabel: Left for Dead* . . . . . . 371

CHAPTER 52  *Tego: To Hell & Gone* . . . . . . 374

**Epilogue**      *Don't Stay Away Too Long* . . . . 377

**End Matter**

ACKNOWLEDGMENTS . . . . . . . . . . . . i

ABOUT THE AUTHOR . . . . . . . . . . . . v

LOST TIME: THE 2ND DISASTER (PREVIEW) . . . . . . vii

# CROSSING IN TIME

*D. L. Orton*

To my husband, Fernando,
and my sons
Tristan, Stefan, & Cedric
without whom this book
would have been finished in half the time.

∞

In the vast and wondrous expanse of space-time,
you guys are the best.

He thought of the woman.
All hopes of eternity and all gain from the past
he would have given to have her there,
to be wrapped warm with him in one blanket,
and sleep, only sleep.

*Lady Chatterley's Lover*
D. H. Lawrence

## PROLOGUE
### Front Range Rockies
### *A Few Years from Now*

T he chubby gun trader shifts his weight and looks up at me, one eye squeezed shut. "What sort of firearm you lookin' to purchase, ma'am?" He's enthroned on a maroon chintz armchair in front of a burned-out Walmart.

"Handgun," I say. "Something easy to aim and shoot."

Behind me, a handful of men mill about a few meager stalls. I can feel their stares pecking against my back, an un-armed woman traveling alone. I force down a flood of disturbing memories and focus on the task at hand: protecting myself in a world gone all to hell.

"You come to the right place, little lady." He glances down at my hiking boots and then drags his gaze up my torso, his top lip curling. "I got a Walther P-22 I might be willin' to trade."

I've never heard of Walther, and I have no idea what a P-22 is—for all I know, it could be a water pistol. I stand there staring at him, unable to get my brain to engage.

The King of Walmart takes off his sweat-stained baseball cap. "Well, lady?" His sunburned skin is covered with grime, and his matted hair is thinning. He leans over the torn fabric and spits into the dirt. "You here to buy somethin' or just gawk at my goods?"

There are snickers from behind me, and my fingers curl around the pepper spray in my pocket.

*C'mon, Isabel, you can do this.*

I cross my arms and set my jaw, bringing up the image of Ripley facing down the Alien, and then sweep a razor-sharp gaze over the rubberneckers.

Heads turn away.

*At least they have some humanity left.*

I meet the gun trader's bloodshot eyes. He replaces his cap, no longer making an effort to hide his amusement. "Whatcha got to trade?"

"Black pepper and cinnamon—and a bit of dry mustard, if you want it."

He leans sideways to see how big my pack is, his boots teetering on one of a dozen milk crates snaking around him. "That all?"

I glance over at the stall next to us. A gaunt man and his two teenage sons are attempting to trade a laptop computer for a half-dozen eggs. I turn back to the chubby gun dealer. "You could swap them for meat."

He kicks a basket full of what I belatedly realize is handmade jerky.

"Or—" I can feel my face flush. "You could trade them for rice?"

He guffaws and eases back into the chair. "I'm not much for Chinese food."

I turn away, irritated with myself, but absurdly relieved by his rejection.

*God, I hate guns.*

On the other side of the parking lot, a bearded old man is selling walnut-sized potatoes from a double-wide stroller. Rip Van Winkle nods, and I return his greeting, wondering how long the world can survive on seed potatoes and discarded baby gear.

"Still..." The gun trader waits for me to look at him. "I s'pose I could use some fancy flavorings on my venison."

I regard the only overweight man in a sea of famine, disgusted with the whole human race and embarrassed by my own full stomach. "Let me see the gun, please." The nicety slips out before I can stop it.

*Good grief, Isabel. Get a grip.*

"Lemme see the pepper."

I unzip the main compartment of the pack and hold the flap open so he can see the plastic bottles inside. "All of them are sealed and within their expiration date."

*God, I must sound like an idiot.*

"Well ain't that just hunky-dory."

Despite the biting wind and overcast skies, my face feels impossibly hot.

He slides a plastic tray off a crate and pulls out a black and silver handgun. "This here Wally's semi-automatic and already broke in." He offers it to me butt-first.

I take a step closer, and the reek of wood smoke, sour sweat, and charred flesh accosts me. I force down the urge to vomit and reach for the pistol.

"B series," he says. "Fires right or left handed. Loads and discharges smooth as Scotch whisky, and it's got a ten-round magazine."

I wrap my hand around the cold metal, and a shudder creeps up my spine. There are few things I find more repulsive than a gun.

"I'll trade you the Wally plus ten rounds of ammo for the

whole backpack."

I set the firearm down on the crate. "The pistol and a hundred rounds. And I keep the pack."

He tips his head to the side. "Handguns are a dime a dozen, missy, but I got hollow-tip Stingers, and you can bet yer lace panties they ain't gonna be making more anytime soon." He takes a slow breath. "Fifteen."

I hook my thumbs in my pockets and glance over my shoulder.

"Now see here, lady." His voice has lost its obsequious tone. "One bullet'll stop a mountain lion or a ten-point buck." He aims at a child in mismatched pajamas. "A hundred are worth more pepper than a goddamn camel can carry." He runs his gaze over my chest and onto my crotch. "Unless you got somethin' else to trade."

*Bastard.*

"See, I could sell you some cheap, unreliable shit—excuse me, ma'am—but you don't want to be shootin' some rapist and have the gun misfire, now do ya?" He pulls the trigger, and it makes a sharp click.

"Fifty," I say. "No backpack." I glance down at his ample belly. "And I'll throw in a five-pound sack of sugar for your camel."

A smile spreads across his leathery face. "Make it forty plus a couple bags of jerky, and you got a deal."

I set my pack down next to the pistol, willing my damn hands to stop shaking. "Let me see the bullets." He spends a minute rummaging in a crate and then holds up a clear plastic case. The label says fifty, and there are ten missing. "Okay, I'll take the gun—assuming the bullets work."

He laughs. "Yeah, them bullets *werk* just fine. I'd be happy to give you a little demonstration, if you like—using one of yers, a'course."

I nod, anxious to see that I'm not being swindled.

He tosses me two bags of jerky and then bumps an empty crate with his boot. "Put yer stuff in there, and I'll show you what this little fella can do." I set the sugar in the bin and dump the spices in on top, watching him load a round into the magazine, insert it into the weapon, and pull the slide back and release it. I stuff the jerky into my empty pack and stand up. "You ever shot a semi-automatic pistol?" he asks, offering me the remaining bullets. He taps the butt of the gun against his palm and looks up.

"No. But I've fired a rifle." *A BB gun, actually. At summer camp. When I was ten.*

"Then you know to expect a kick." He stands and addresses a gaunt teenage boy leaning against the blackened door-frame of the store. "Hey, music man, come watch my stuff while I show this lucky lady my *pistol*." He snorts at the crude humor. "I'll buy you a potato for yer trouble."

The kid emerges from the shadows, a beat-up guitar slung over his shoulder and plastic grocery bags wrapped around his feet.

The gun trader gives him a disgusted look. "And don't you be gettin' no dirt on my chair."

The youth inclines his head but doesn't meet the guy's eyes.

I watch the paunchy man lumber off, trying to decide how stupid it would be to follow him.

"I don't think he'll try anything, miss." The teenager plops down on a crate and stares up at me, his eyes a stunning blue. "Not with all these people around, anyway."

"Thanks," I say. "I hope you're right." I hurry after my gun.

The side lot is littered with dirt-filled plastic bottles, old tires, and other trash. A stray dog is curled up amidst the detritus, and beyond the rubbish is a giant mass of tumbleweeds trapped like some desiccated monster in a barbed-wire fence.

5

The charred frame of a four-story building looms in the distance, and behind it, the Rocky Mountains poke up into the sooty haze. I stop and glance over at the man, his neon orange jacket garish against the browns and grays. "This is as far as I go."

He nods. "Here, boy." The dog lifts his head and looks at us. "Come on, buddy." The man pats his leg and whistles. "I got a treat for ya."

The pet thumps his tail and struggles to his feet. He trots across the pitted pavement, his head down, but his tail still wagging. He's a golden retriever, scroungy and emaciated, but still bright-eyed—and still willing to trust the idiots who got him into this mess.

The gun seller waits until the dog is six feet away, then he steps sideways, clicks off the safety, and fires the pistol.

The animal collapses like a sack of potatoes, a pool of bright red blood spreading across the cracked asphalt.

The man lowers the gun, and I wipe a fleck of gore off my lower lip, my heart racing.

Faces peer around the corner of the building. They gape at the dead animal and then at us, and then they disappear.

"You paid for the bullet, ma'am, so I guess that makes the carcass yers. I'll clean and skin it if you give me half the meat." He hands me the pistol butt-first and then grins. "Hell, we could have ourselves a little dinner party. Hot dog and mustard." He snickers. "Afterwards you could earn yerself an extra bullet or two." He grabs his crotch and makes a vulgar noise.

I stand there staring at the dead animal, feeling sick to my stomach. "No, I don't want it."

"Now that's mighty kind of you, ma'am. I told you this here firearm was in perfect working order, and as you can see, the ammo is live—even if the dog ain't." He snorts. "You sure you don't want to join me for a little backyard barbecue?"

"No." I take the heavy gun and shove it into my pack, my hands shaking so hard it takes me three tries to get the zipper closed. Then I turn and trudge back around the monstrous cinderblock ruin, the loud retort of the gun still reverberating in my ears.

"I'm saving a handful of them Stingers for next time," he calls after me.

The skinny kid is playing the guitar as I walk up. He nods at me but doesn't stop singing:

♪ *When will they ever learn? When will they ev-er learn?* ♪

I take a chocolate bar out of my pack and offer it to him. *Supporting the arts.*

He snatches it out of my hand, rips off the wrapper, and shoves the whole thing into his mouth, his eyes shifting back and forth like a wild animal.

I wait for him to finish. "That's the only one I have, so don't follow me."

"Yes, miss. Thank you. God bless you."

*If there is a God, he's got one messed-up sense of humor.*

I trudge back across the decaying blacktop and up the old highway, periodically glancing back to make sure no one is following me. As soon as the Walmart is out of sight, I vomit all over my gore-spattered boots.

*Oh my god, Diego, what have we done?*

## Part One
### *Ten Months Earlier*

*More than at any other time in history,*
*Mankind faces a crossroads.*
*One path leads to despair and utter hopelessness,*
*The other, to total extinction.*
*Let us pray we have the wisdom to choose correctly.*

Woody Allen

# Chapter 1

## *Isabel: Falling for Him*

I'm brooding over the bloodbath with Dave's divorce lawyers when the heel of my left shoe catches in a metal grate. My ankle twists painfully out of the pump, and I stumble across the crowded sidewalk, my folio spilling onto the concrete.

A hand steadies my arm. "Easy there. Those exhaust grilles can be treacherous." The voice sets off a spark of recognition, but I'm too embarrassed to meet the man's gaze.

"Thank you." I straighten my skirt and reposition my scarf, hoping Captain America will take the hint and continue on without embarrassing me further.

But he doesn't let go. "The pleasure is mine."

There's a hint of amusement in his tone, and I feel another flush of chagrin. Well-dressed professionals—most of the women wearing sneakers and smug expressions—brush past us. I rarely wear high heels, and given the three cups of black coffee I had for lunch, the shellacking I took in the frigid law office, and now the sweltering afternoon sun, I'm feeling queasy.

I teeter on one foot, trying to decide how I'm going to retrieve my shoe while sporting a short skirt, a single high heel, and a twisted ankle.

Captain America releases my arm, steps around behind me, and a moment later, sets the scraped pump in front of my foot. "Careful, hun. The heel feels a bit loose." He reaches for my portfolio.

A strange tightness forms in my chest, and, for a moment, I can't breathe. I stand there like a plastic flamingo, watching his strong, agile hands collect my papers.

*Who is this guy?*

His thick, dark hair is flecked with gray, and he's wearing a tawny sport coat over tan slacks. Although I haven't seen his face, I'd guess early forties, same as me.

I swallow hard, smooth my skirt against the back of my thighs, and squat down, trying to keep the weight off my throbbing ankle. "Thank you. Again. You're very kind."

"You're welcome again." He doesn't glance up, but I can hear the smile in his voice.

I stare at the smooth olive skin on the back of his hands, my heart in my throat. "What I mean is, you needn't pick—"

He collects the last sheet of paper and then looks at me for the first time, a grin spreading across his face. "You haven't changed a bit."

I crouch there with my mouth stuck open, balancing on one wobbly shoe, and look at his face for the first time. "Diego?"

"At your service." He takes my arm and helps me stand. "How long has it been? Fourteen, fifteen years?" He kisses me on both cheeks. "How are you, Isabel?"

The sound of my name on his lips causes my brain to freeze, and the scent of his aftershave ambushes my heart. I stand there gaping at him like I've never spoken an attractive man before.

He smiles. "Damn, it's good to see you."

I blink a couple of times. "What are *you* doing in downtown Denver?"

The corner of his mouth twitches. "I could ask you the same thing."

Office workers continue to brush past us, hurrying home for the long weekend.

I take my papers and then force my foot back into my shoe, ignoring the twinge of pain. "I'm sorry to have troubled you."

"It's my pleasure, Iz. Really. Can I buy you a cup of coffee? Let you rest that ankle for a bit."

My heart is pounding in my throat, remembering how over-the-top, crazy good it was to be with him.

*And how badly he hurt me.*

"I've already had three dreadful cups, but I appreciate the offer."

He takes my hand in both of his. "Then have dinner with me." He strokes my palm with his fingertips. "Please?"

I bite my lip, my body responding to his touch. "I've sworn off men, Diego. All they do is eat my snacks, hog my remote, and leave my toilet seat up." I try to pull my hand away, but he doesn't let go.

"Since when did you own any sort of remote?"

"It was a figure of speech."

"Okay," he says. "So it's just dinner with an old friend, sex unspecified." There's a twinkle in his eye. "Say yes, Iz."

I bite my lip and scan the thinning crowd, trying to think over the voices in my head yelling: *Oh my god, it's him!*

"I don't need any more drama today," I say, still not looking at him.

"Oh, come on. Drama is just life with the dull bits cut out."

"Well, I'm ready for a long patch of boredom."

He laughs, deep and resonant. "We can order cheese pizza, lite beer, and vanilla ice cream. What do you say?"

I gaze at his soft, full lips and then meet his eyes. "Don't you have to be someplace?"

"I was supposed to meet a client, but his flight was canceled." He places my hand around his arm. "So I already have dinner reservations for two. And I promise, no drama."

I stare at him, unnerved by the intense emotions he stirs up in me.

"It's not far," he says, "just past the Brown Palace Hotel, and we have plenty of time to walk. But if you're unsure about your ankle, we can snag a cab—"

"It's fine, Diego. I have a medical degree, remember?"

"Yeah, I do. Could have been a doctor but didn't have the patience." He winks and then places his left hand on top of mine. "Shall we?"

I notice he's not wearing a wedding ring, and despite my determined attempt to suppress it, a wave of relief washes over me.

*Even after all these years, I'm still in love with him.*

And then I realize that he could be married but doesn't wear his ring. The thought is like a hot coal in my chest.

He looks over at me, his expression concerned. "Are you sure you're okay?"

"Yes, Captain America." I take a tentative step, determined not to show the least bit of weakness, but he sees right through me.

"You want a piggyback ride?"

I glare at him. "That would definitely involve drama."

"You're only saying that because it always has."

I laugh. "God, I've missed you." It tumbles out before I can stop it.

He stares at me for a moment, his eyes glossy. "Ditto."

The sun disappears behind a tall building, and a light breeze flits down the narrow street. I turn and take another step, leaning against him as we navigate the busy sidewalk.

The Brown Palace is closed for renovations but is sponsoring a Humane Society "adopt a pet" event in the rear lobby. As we stroll along, I gaze at puppies and kittens romping in the displays behind plate-glass windows. When we reach the end of the block, we stop and watch a black kitten attack a stuffed animal twice her size. When she sees us, she trots over to the glass, dragging the dinosaur with her.

I lean over and tap on the glass. "Hey, kitty girl. Nice work slaying the beast."

She steps on the T-Rex's toothy head and gives a silent meow.

A door at the back of the display opens, and a man lifts the kitten up, strokes her head, and then places her into a cage in the back.

Diego glances at his watch. "They must be getting ready to close for the night."

I nod. The display looks dreary without the kitten, and a lonely sadness creeps into my heart. I retake Diego's arm, grateful for his physical presence. "I wish I could take them all home with me."

"Well, I don't know about all of them, but I'd be happy to buy you the kitten. By the looks of it, you two have a lot in common."

I lean my head against his shoulder. "Thanks, but I can't have pets where I live."

"I see." His arm tenses. "You married Dave, didn't you?"

"Yes," I say. "Two years after you and I broke up."

"But you don't wear a ring." His voice is flat. "Even though you're married."

"As of an hour ago, I'm not. Although Dave and I haven't lived together in more than a year, I didn't get around to divorcing him—and his three lawyers—until this afternoon."

He chuckles. "That explains the bad coffee."

"Yeah, I definitely should have brought my own latte—and my own attorney. I pretty much signed over everything except my patents and my underwear."

"I imagine he'll be back for those."

"My underwear or my patents?"

"If I remember correctly, both."

I blush, and then clear my throat. "So how about you? Married? Passel of kids? Dog named Sparky?"

He stops and opens a heavy glass door. "Here we are. Elevators to the left."

I walk in and gaze at the cavernous marble and glass lobby of a mailbox-shaped skyscraper. "We're having dinner *here?*"

"Yep. It's a hotel, and there's a restaurant at the top. The guy I was supposed to meet is from Chicago, and I thought he'd enjoy the view."

I give him a dubious look. "That sounds expensive."

"I was planning to order from the kid's menu."

I roll my eyes.

"Come on, Iz. I can afford it." He steps away, pushes the elevator button, and then offers me his arm. "And no, I'm not married. Never got over the last girlfriend."

## CHAPTER 2

### *Isabel: Not in This Universe*

W e're seated at a small table next to floor-to-ceiling windows. The setting sun peeks out through wispy, silver-lined clouds, bathing the Mile High City in golden light. A volcano in Yellowstone has been spewing ash for weeks, and despite the impact on the air quality, the Rockies look stunning, their snowy peaks airbrushed in rich orange hues and their lower flanks splashed in shades of purple.

"Wow," I say. "Nice gloaming. And it *is* an amazing view."

"You know, Iz, you're the only person I know who says shit like 'gloaming.'" He holds up his hands. "But you're right, the Rockies put on an excellent show—almost as good as La Isla Beach."

"Well, I'd love to see the sunset that can beat this."

He sets his napkin in his lap. "Okay. I'll take you there."

I stare at him for a moment and then glance away, feeling a familiar but painful tug on my heart. "This is not a date, Diego."

He reaches across the linen tablecloth, dodging a lit candlestick, repositioning a goblet of ice water, and sliding a dessert spoon out of the way. "I've played *futbol* teams with a weaker defense than this table." He slips his fingertips underneath mine. "Thanks for saying yes."

"I didn't. But thanks for asking."

He caresses my hand, his eyes downcast. "Did you have somewhere you needed to be tonight?"

"I should say yes, but the truth is, not only did you save me from the Exhaust Grate of Doom, you rescued me from an evening of Swamp Biome Hell—matching alligator genomes with a box full of loose teeth, sharp claws, and desiccated skin."

"I hope he won't mind too much," he says. "I wouldn't want to make a man-eating reptile jealous."

I roll my eyes.

"Although now that you mention it, I'm pretty sure I met that guy the first time I asked you out." He shrugs. "He obviously didn't age well."

"Right."

"But you haven't aged a day."

I pull my hand away. "Liar."

"Cynic."

"You always were too sentimental, Diego."

"And you're too pessimistic, Iz. That and goddamn impatient." He takes my hand again. "Not to mention obstinate, arrogant, and a royal pain in the ass. Just my type."

I glare at him.

"Well at least I didn't eat all your chocolate or leave the toilet seat up."

"Yeah," I say, "you're one in a million."

"Did I mention how much I've missed you?" He tips his head, his eyes dancing across my face. "The way you roll your eyes when you don't believe me, and the way you bite your lip when you're thinking, and especially the soft sigh you make when I kiss you."

I turn away. "Diego, don't."

He strokes my cheek, his touch electric. "And I love it when you blush. It reminds me there's a vulnerable woman inside that warrior exterior."

I stare at my hands, still trying to get my emotions back under control.

"Did you hear about the silkworm race?"

I glance at him, frowning, but unable to resist.

"It ended in a tie."

I laugh and try to turn it into a scowl.

"Iz." He pulls my hand up to his mouth and kisses it. "What do you say we call it a tie? Start over, and see if we can make it work this time?"

My breath catches in my throat, all sorts of conflicting emotions raging around inside my head.

"And you *do* look beautiful." He moves his lips across my fingers. "I can't believe I found you."

A deep longing fills me, but I force it right back where it came from. "So. How *did* you find me?"

"I was sitting in a coffee shop, waiting for a call from Mr. Chicago, when I saw you come out of the building across the street. I couldn't believe my eyes, so I followed you. And when I saw you teetering along in those high heels, I knew it *was* you."

"Damn pumps. I don't know what I was thinking when I put them on."

"I always did prefer you naked," he says, "but I can understand how that would be inconvenient when meeting with divorce lawyers. No place to stick your shark gun."

I roll my eyes again.

He strokes the back of my hand with his fingertip. "By the way, congratulations on winning the Gruber. I read about

19

it last week."

I glance down at where he's touching me. "Since when do you pay attention to obscure genetics awards?"

"I don't. But I think that makes you the most decorated biome expert in the world."

"I'll try not to let it go to my head." I pull my hand away, but he doesn't let go.

"How about a bottle of champagne to celebrate?"

"No. But thanks."

"I insist." Without letting go of my hand, he catches the waiter's attention and orders a bottle of Dom Pérignon. I give him an exasperated look, and he raises his eyebrow. "What?"

"For a guy who spends all his time in a T-shirt and jeans, you seem very relaxed ordering expensive wine in a lavish restaurant."

"Well maybe I've changed a bit since the last time we went out. It's not our abilities that show who we really are, it's our choices."

"Nice British accent."

"Come home with me, Iz."

I stare at him.

"This is the point where you blush and say yes."

"No, it isn't." I jerk my hand away. "You said no drama, and this is definitely drama."

"I'm asking if you want to come home with me, drama optional. You know: naked bodies, sweaty wrestling, sultry sighs—all of it nice and boring."

"Hah."

He leans forward. "Didn't you ever miss that? What we had together? Did you ever find that with anyone else?" He glances back and forth between my eyes. "Because I didn't, and believe me, I tried."

"I'm not interested in getting hurt again, Diego."

"What about all the good times, Iz? The day at San

Gregorio beach, and the polyester party, and the first night I made you chocolate cake, remember? We wrestled on the couch until we were both laughing so hard we couldn't breathe?"

"Yeah, I remember. And I remember that you made me fall in love with you and then hopped on a plane when I needed you most." I let the old anger leak back into my voice. "For weeks after you left, I cried every time I walked by your office, or smelled your aftershave, or heard someone say your name."

His smile fades.

I look away, tears in my eyes. "So maybe *you* can jump right back into the wild sex part, but *I* can't."

He leans back and crosses his arms. "You mean, unless it's with some guy you just met."

"What did you say?"

"That night with Dave was a betrayal of everything I felt for you, Isabel, and you know it. After you told me, I thought it would be easier to die than endure the pain." He shakes his head. "And you couldn't understand why it made me so angry, why I couldn't just forgive you right then and there and move on."

I can't breathe.

"I was in love with you, Iz. Crazy, over-the-top, raving-lunatic in love with you, and you threw it all away for one cheap fuck with a guy you just met. And all because I had other plans."

I push my chair back.

"I'm sorry," he says. "I shouldn't have said that."

I take a ragged breath, forcing back tears. "For your information, we didn't have sex. I told you I *slept* with him, and I meant exactly that."

"Christ, Isabel, what did you expect me to think? You *wanted* me to assume you had sex with him. You were trying to make me jealous."

"It was a mistake, okay? Perhaps the worst mistake of my life. But you were out with another woman!"

"No, I wasn't. I was having dinner with two friends, and you damn well knew it." He takes my hand in both of his. "Whether or not you had sex is irrelevant. You knew I felt betrayed." He looks up, his face pained. "Couldn't you have given me a couple of days to sort out my feelings before you cut me off forever?"

I stand up. "I can't do this again, Diego." I turn away, but he grabs my wrist, and I let out a startled cry. The people at the tables around us look over, and he releases his grip and takes my hand.

"I loved you, Iz, and I was desperate to find a way to make it work between us. But you wouldn't give me a chance. You hung up on my calls and ignored my texts. You refused to answer the door when I went to your apartment and pretended I didn't exist at work—even told my boss I was harassing you."

*I had forgotten about that.*

"I'm sorry. That was wrong of me."

He shuts his eyes for a moment and then exhales. "It killed me every time I watched you leave work with Dave, knowing he was your new lover." He looks at me. "So don't go lecturing me about how rough it was on you, because there's not a single day that goes by when I don't wish it could have turned out differently."

"Well it was no picnic for me either." Tears spill down my cheeks, but I don't wipe them away. "When I found out you were leaving, I followed you to the airport, hoping I could apologize, explain things, and convince you stay. But when you saw me, you turned and walked away."

"Yeah, well, I was fed up with playing your games and being treated like I was sh—"

"I was pregnant."

The blood leaves his face.

"I found out the night before."

"Christ, Isabel, why didn't you tell me?"

I pull my hand out of his. "I just did."

"Shit. I'm sorry. If I'd known—"

"Yeah. Well, it's a bit late for the guilt and pity treatment."

The waiter appears with the champagne, opens the bottle, and pours it while we sit in painful silence. He nods at Diego. "Are you ready to order, sir?"

"Give us a few minutes, please."

"Take your time." The waiter sets the bottle in a bucket of ice and disappears.

Diego runs his hand through his hair. "You should have told me, Iz." He rubs his face with his hands, the muscles in his neck jumping, and then forces himself to look at me. "So what did you do?"

"I had an abortion. Dave canceled a trip to Europe so he could take me. He stayed with me at the clinic, paid for everything, and when I finally stopped vomiting, he drove me home and held me while I cried all night." I squeeze my eyes shut, the memory still harrowing after all these years.

"Christ."

I take a ragged breath and wipe my face on my napkin. "And before you say it: No, he didn't talk me into it. It was my decision."

He turns away, his face contorted with anguish. "I don't know what to say."

I stand up. "I'm sorry, Diego, but we're just not meant to be—not in this universe anyway. Whatever chance we had, died when you got on that plane."

He doesn't meet my eyes.

I grab my purse and the goddamn divorce folio, and try not to limp as I walk out.

## CHAPTER 3

### Diego: The Fire & the Furry

I sit and stare at her untouched glass of champagne, feeling exhausted and adrift.

*Why didn't you tell me, Iz?*

When the waiter comes over, I let him know there's been a change of plans, and we won't be staying for dinner. He has the good grace not to look annoyed. "Not a problem, sir. Shall I recork the champagne?" I nod and he goes to get the check.

I take the napkin off her plate and lift it to my face, breathing in the scent of the woman I have loved since the first time I held her in my arms.

*Why didn't you give me a chance to make it right, Isabel?*

I peer out into the darkening sky, feeling miserable, my vision blurry.

*I would have come back in a heartbeat—even if you hadn't been pregnant. All you had to do was ask.*

Even this afternoon, it's like everything I do gets turned

into some sort of elaborate screw-up: my help embarrasses her, my restaurant choice is too expensive, my compliments are false, my apology too little, too late. It's almost like being with her is a convoluted and never-ending test. One that she makes sure I fail.

I pinch the bridge of my nose and close my eyes.

*Why are you so determined to make me be in the wrong, Iz?*

And then it all becomes painfully clear.

*She's so afraid of rejection that she jumps ship before anyone can push her overboard.*

"I am such an idiot."

I stand up, determined to go after her and make things right—make things work—and there's a loud *boom*. The whole building shudders and then starts swaying. Almost in slow motion, the ice bucket tips over, and a puddle spreads out around my feet.

"Oh shit."

I stare at the sea of swaying tablecloths, and a mental image of the collapse of the Twin Towers pushes up panic in my chest. The restaurant is forty-one stories above the street, enclosed in massive panes of glass.

*Isabel. Christ, I hope she got out of the building.*

On the other side of the restaurant, a woman shrieks, "Oh my god! Someone's blown up the Brown Palace Hotel!" A few blocks away from us, a massive cloud of dark smoke rises into the fading light. Flames shoot out the windows of the distinctive triangular landmark, and I notice that a handful of other nearby buildings are on fire too.

*Isabel is out there alone in those goddamn heels!*

An alarm goes off in the restaurant lobby, and eighty people turn as one. Two young guys in expensive suits jog toward the exit, followed by what appears to be the kitchen staff. A moment later, there is a panicked herd pushing toward the elevators.

25

A woman in back waves her arms and yells, "I'm staying across the street from the Brown Palace, and my son is there with a babysitter! Please! Let me through!" The frightened crowd ignores her.

I jump up on my chair and almost on cue, the alarm goes silent. I whistle with my fingers and the crowd turns. "Please calm down! We don't seem to be in any immediate danger—at least not enough to justify someone getting crushed to death or shoved down forty flights of stairs."

Out in the lobby, the elevator bongs, and the doors slide open.

The young mother repeats her plea, and then a deep and sonorous voice calls out, "Come on, people. Let her through." A murmur passes over the crowd, and it parts for the frightened woman. A tall black guy is holding the doors. He nods at me and then adds, "Anyone who can't make it down the stairs goes with her."

An elderly man with a cane, a gangly teenager on crutches, and a pregnant woman come forward. The guy in the lobby motions toward their companions. "You folks too. Hurry up now. You can help them get home. Anyone with young children?" A couple with toddlers steps through, and the elevator fills up. "Room for one more. Any doctors or emergency responders?"

I consider lying, but can't bring myself to do it, so I step down off the chair and help organize the rest of the evacuations as quickly as possible.

Seventeen long minutes later, the elevator doors open on a lobby full of irate hotel guests and their pajama-clad children. The air smells smoky, and panicked voices fill the cavernous space. I step out and push my way through the agitated mass of humanity, avoiding a fallen tree, two large golf bags, and a child asleep with his arms around a giant Stitch.

I stare down at the sleeping toddler, my insides all twisted up.

*You should have told me, Iz.*

The moment I get out the side door, acrid fumes accost me. The night sky is glowing orange, and sooty flakes fall out of the darkness, a surreal snowstorm. The fire has created its own gale, and great billows of smoke roll down out of the darkness, filling the space between the tall buildings with noxious gas.

I get my bearings and then start retracing our steps. Isabel must have parked near the law offices, somewhere close to the metal grate where she lost her shoe. Or did she take the light rail?

*Go to where you first saw her and take it from there.*

I start running, fear pushing me forward.

The streets are packed with vehicles, some half on the sidewalk, some going against the flow of traffic, some abandoned in the middle of the street. Motorcycles maneuver through the gridlock, weaving between people running every which way. I narrowly avoid getting hit by a white Lexus that runs a red light.

When I turn the corner, I see a gang of teenagers throw a heavy metal trash can against the window of a jewelry shop. The glass cracks, but doesn't give, and a moment later, the alarm goes off. The guys glance over at me, wondering if I'm going to intervene, and when I look away, they hoist the can up for another try.

I cross to the other side of the street, jogging toward the center of the chaos.

When I get to where we saw the kitten, I stop and look around. The explosion happened on the other side of the building, and this end is still locked up tight. I run down to the end of the block and around the corner of the hotel, my side aching and my heart pounding in my throat, and then I come to an abrupt stop.

The front of the hotel is littered with piles of rubble, and more fire trucks than I can count are spraying water into it and the surrounding buildings, but the flames are spreading fast. Police cruisers and ambulances are everywhere, their rotating lights filling the smoky air with eerie flashes of color.

Crowds have formed around the emergency equipment, people stacked ten deep watching the buildings go up in flames. Someone with a bullhorn is attempting to get the hordes to disperse, but he isn't having much luck. A van from the local TV station is filming the chaos, and all around it, revelers are laughing and waving.

I try to decide what Isabel would have done, but come up empty. The skyscraper across the street—the one with the treacherous sidewalk vent—is ablaze too, only the flames are half-way up the tall building. Just as I'm wondering how *that* fire got started, there's the sound of breaking glass, and flames shoot out even higher up. A moment later, the congested street is showered with shards of plate-glass windows, and all hell breaks loose.

I force myself to think.

*She hates crowds, and she'd be smart enough not to get caught up in this one. Shit, I hope I'm right.*

I turn in a circle, taking in as much as I can. "So where the hell is she?" I pull out my phone and scroll through my address book, knowing that the chances of her number being the same are zero. Still, I push the call button, but the cell towers are so jammed that my phone shows no service.

*Maybe there's wi-fi at the Starbucks across the street?*

I try a text message:

> **Isabel? Where are you? Please tell me
> you're okay.**

I push send and wait to see if it goes through. When it doesn't, I jab the retry button and shove the phone into my pocket.

*Now what?*

I glance back the way I came, trying to make some sort of decision.

*She probably saw the fire and turned around, looking for a way to avoid the chaos. Probably.*

There's a muffled explosion inside the Brown Palace, and I feel a belated shudder of regret for the pets that are trapped in the back. Isabel's spunky black kitten is probably dead from smoke inhalation.

*I hope it was quick.*

I start jogging back the way I came, trying to push the image of the dead animal out of my brain.

*Wait a sec... She wouldn't be THAT stupid... Would she?*

I stop running, a cold fear forming in the pit of my stomach. I replay Isabel's earlier interaction with the kitten.

*Goddamn it.*

I charge back to the front of the hotel and then run along next to the building, searching for a door or window that might have been used to break in.

It takes me less than thirty seconds to find it.

The glass panel in a side door has been smashed, and smoke is pouring out through the opening. I can see the rock she used inside on the floor, and next to it are two pale pink chunks of plastic. The heels from her shoes!

*Oh you stupid, stupid woman.*

Without thinking, I reach through the hole in the glass and turn the handle. The hot metal jerks out of my hand and the door whips open, slicing my arm. I recoil as a giant blast of super-heated smoke and ash surges out.

*Shit.*

I step back and take a quick look at the cut. It's long, but not too deep. I apply direct pressure to the worst part and then remember Isabel's napkin in my pocket. I tug it out and wrap it tightly around the gash, tucking in the end to hold it in place. Blood soaks through, but not a lot.

I kick glass shards out of the way, pull my jacket over my head, and crawl into the smoke-filled hallway. But I can't go more than a meter or two before the heat and fumes are too much, and I have to back out.

*Great job, Superman. Next idea?*

I stand up and force the door shut.

*Find an entry closer to the animals.*

I turn and race down the block to the entrance nearest the kitten. It's locked, and the foyer is dark, but thin wisps of smoke are leaking out of the roof overhang. I kick the door, but the old brass locks are well made, and the wood is solid.

"Damn it all to hell."

I hurry back to the kitten's window, ignoring the stitch in my side, and put my palms against the thick glass.

It's warm, but not as hot as the door handle. I peer into the shadowy interior, but I can't see beyond the empty display.

*If she's not in there, I'm gonna get myself killed for nothing. But if she is…*

I stand there with my hands on my hips, breathing hard, and look around for something to break the glass. The sidewalk is empty except for the trashcan on the corner.

I jog down and put my arms around the huge bin. It's made of heavy steel and one of the legs is bolted to the concrete. I can't even get it to wiggle.

A desperate idea forms in my brain, but it's too absurd to take seriously.

*Right, convince a pack of looters to drop the goods and help me rescue a crazy lady who broke into a burning building to save a cat.*

Still, I gaze down the street at where I saw the kids smashing the jewelry store window. Shadows are moving in and out of the streetlight in front of the shop.

"I must be a lunatic."

I start jogging toward the light when the cell phone in

my jacket pocket vibrates, and desperate hope wells up inside me.

*Isabel.*

I stop and take it out, staring at her name. "For fifteen years, she's been one button press away."

I swipe the screen and read her text message:

> **Diego? The atrium wall collapsed and we're**
> **trapped inside. I can hear a dog barking,**
> **but the smoke is getting bad. If you're**
> **serious about starting over, you better**
> **effing hurry.**

She sent it twelve minutes ago, and it just now arrived!

I tap in 911 and stab the call button, but my phone won't connect.

"Shit."

I press reply and type in:

> **I'm coming.**

And then add:

> **Marry me?**

I hit send and start running.

*Most guys get down on one knee and offer a dozen roses, but Diego Screw-up Nadales sends a goddamn text.*

*I just hope I'm not too late.*

I don't know if it's the panic in my voice, or my threat to kill every one of their girlfriends if they don't help me, but a couple minutes later, the five looters and I manage to wrench the heavy trash bin off the sidewalk and throw it through the kitten's window.

Smoke leaks out at the top, but no alarm sounds.

"You sure she's in there?" one of the looters asks me.

"Yes," I say. "And a bunch of puppies and kittens in cages."

One of the guys starts kicking out the remaining shards of glass, but he stops when we hear muffled barking and then a faint cry from deep inside.

31

I jump up into the small display and yell out, "Isabel? Is that you?"

There's coughing and an indistinct cry, and then more coughing.

"Hold on! I'm coming!"

The leader grabs my pant leg. "Cover your face with something wet, or you'll die from the smoke before you get a chance to save her."

I turn and stare down at him, uh, *her*. She's thin and Asian, and her hair is cut short. In the dark, I hadn't noticed her small breasts and beautiful almond eyes.

She glances around at her gang. "From the sounds of it, the pets are just inside. What do you say we try to get them out—or at least let them out of the cages?"

There's a murmur of assent, and one of the guys asks her, "Did you bring your stuff?"

"Yeah." She takes a wrinkled bandanna and a spool of string out of her back pocket. "You guys?"

There's a chorus of assent.

She motions with her chin toward my bandaged arm. "You can use that cloth, but piss on it first."

I narrow my eyes. "What?"

"Get it damp, you halfwit mooker." She nods at one of the guys, and he crumples the bandanna in his hand, urinates onto it, and then hands it back to her. She ties the damp rag over her nose and mouth like a bandit.

I try not to cringe as I watch the others do the same.

She hops up next to me, amused by my look of disgust. "Haven't you ever been in a fire before?"

I shake my head and then follow her example.

She waits for me to tie the cloth over my face and then says, "Okay, let's go!"

I step across the display and jump down into the murky room. The smoke is thick, but nowhere near as bad as it was

32

up front. Still, it's impossible to see more than a foot or two into the gloom.

"Isabel?!" I shout and then listen. All I hear is feeble barking.

*Please let her be alive.*

I half-expect the gang to go back to their looting, but they don't. When I drop down on my hands and knees, they follow me into the burning building.

A minute later, my head strikes something sharp, and I recoil. "Crap." I put my hand up to my forehead, and it comes away wet.

The girl crawls up next to me. "Use the light on your cell phone, Sherlock." She shines her light on my forehead. "Doesn't look too bad, but you'll probably need a couple of stitches. Who are you trying to save anyway? Your wife?"

I wipe my hand on my pants. "Actually, I just asked her to marry me fifteen minutes ago."

She laughs. "I hope she didn't run in here after you popped the question."

I take out my phone and use it as a flashlight. Bright red drops of my blood are visible on the newspaper lining the bottom of a metal cage. A small tongue reaches out and licks them off the faded headline: *War and Peace in the Baltics.* I shift the light and see a black and white puppy lying on a thin, ragged towel. The girl puts her hand on the cage and peers inside. "Yo, Tolstoy. We'll get you out of there in a minute."

His tail thumps once.

I shine my light around. The black kitten is on the same cart with Tolstoy. She gives a squeaky meow when I reach up to her. "Could you make sure that black kitten gets out too, please? She's going home with me."

"Will do. We'll get out as many as we can before the smoke gets too bad."

Another guy comes up next to us, adding his light to the

search. "These are some damn lucky pets, if you ask me."

I pull a thin plastic sign off the kitten's cage and use it to fan the smoke away.

Golden eyes glow back at us out of the gloom. There must be fifty cages stacked on five or six rolling pallets.

*At least they'll be easy to get out.*

I call out to Isabel again, but there's no response.

The leader wraps kite string around her shoe and then holds the spool out to me. "Here. Take this with you. It's tied to the trashcan outside."

I hesitate.

"You're going to look for your fiancée, right?"

"Yeah." The word catches me by surprise, but I like it.

"Put it in your pocket and keep unrolling the string. You know, like Theseus in the labyrinth."

"Ah. Right." I take it out of her hand and stick it in my jacket. "Thanks."

She starts searching for wheel locks on the cart. "We'll get the beasties out. If you need help, yell and tug hard on the string."

"Okay." I notice that she has her cell phone wedged in her bandanna so that her hands are free, and I copy her. "Thanks again."

"You're welcome, Sherlock. Stay low and keep the bandanna wet. And you better hurry." She looks up at me, keeping her light out of my eyes. "On the bright side, if you manage to get her out of this, she'll have to say yes."

"I hope so."

I edge around the cages and crawl deeper into the building, paying out the string as I go. When I come to a wall, I try to remember which way the voice came from, but my sense of direction is shot. "Damn it."

I force myself to calm down.

*We must be in some sort of conference room off the atrium.*

*Find the doors.*

I turn right and drag my hand along the wall. The smoke becomes thicker until my eyes are stinging. When I come to a corner, I stop and follow the wall back the way I came, grateful when the smoke thins out again.

A minute later, I find the door and press my hand against it, testing to see if it's hot.

It's not, and I feel a surge of hope.

I reach for the door handle and discover that there are two doors, and the left one is already open. I crawl through, pulling the string behind me.

The carpeting gives way to a marble floor that is damp and gritty beneath my hands, but the smoke isn't quite as thick.

*I must be in the atrium.*

I take a deep a breath and call out, "Isabel?! Can you hear me?" I force down a cough and listen for a reply.

A distant roar is coming from the far side of the building along with the faint whine of sirens. I can hear the pop and crackle of flames spreading far above me, but no voices or coughing.

And then I hear notes played on a piano.

*What the hell?*

I rush toward the sound of someone still alive, scrambling over piles of metal railings and plaster rubble, spooling out the string and searching for that damn piano.

And then I see it. On the other side of the atrium, the legless black behemoth has been flattened by a massive piece of fallen staircase. A single foot is sticking out from beneath it, the rest of the body crushed by the immense weight.

Panic closes off my throat until I realize that dead people don't play Beethoven.

*There must be someone else.*

I scramble closer and shine my light into the dark triangle

made by the fallen staircase. There's lots of rubble covered in a thin layer of white dust. And then I see bright red blood seeping out from beneath the piano.

"Oh god, no!"

At the sound of my voice, the rubble shifts, and I realize that someone is lying next to the piano. "Isabel? Is that you?" I grab my phone and search more carefully, looking for signs of life. "Can you hear me?"

The long, delicate fingers of a disembodied hand give a feeble wave, and my heart rate surges.

"I can see you, hun!" The sudden intake of breath causes me to start coughing. "Hang on, Iz. I'll get you out." I choke back tears. "Everything's going to be okay."

*God, I hope I'm right.*

I look back over my shoulder and pull the cloth away from my mouth. "Help! We need a paramedic in here!" I give the string a couple of hard yanks and then turn back to Isabel.

Just in the few minutes I've been in here, it's gotten hotter, and the smoke is worse. Sweat, or maybe blood, is running into my eyes, so I wipe my forehead with the damp cloth and then tie it back over my nose and mouth. I start shifting debris away from her, moving as quickly as I can to clear her face.

A minute later, I can see that she's curled up in a fetal position next to the piano keys, her arm protecting her head. She came within millimeters of being crushed by the staircase, saved only by the indestructible craftsmanship of the piano case—and her nearness to it.

There's not much room to work in, but I manage to push a heavy chunk of masonry off so I can free her head and shoulders. She blinks up at my light, her silk scarf wrapped snugly around her nose and mouth.

Those gorgeous green eyes are the most beautiful sight I have ever seen.

She tries to speak, but starts coughing.

I sweep the hair out of her face. "Shh. Don't try to talk. Are you seriously hurt?"

She shakes her head no.

"Good. I'm going to pull you free."

She nods.

I clear debris until I have room to drag her out, and then I sit down, take hold of her shoulders, and pull hard, pushing with my legs. The exertion makes me cough, but she only moves an inch or two. Something is caught or jammed.

I let go and move over her again. "Can you tell me what's stuck? Is it your clothes?" Her eyelids flutter shut, and my heart jumps into my throat. "Isabel! Don't leave me. Please."

A light flashes across us, and three firefighters in hardhats and gas masks come up behind me. The first one hands me a mask and then steps around me and fits one over Isabel's face.

"Using the string was an excellent idea, sir. We followed it right to you." The voice is muffled, but understandable.

*Those kids saved Isabel's life—and probably mine too.*

I pull down the makeshift bandanna, tighten the mask over my head, and breathe in, feeling the cool rush of oxygen into my lungs. The firefighter taps my shoulder. "Is there anyone else in here?"

I glance at the foot sticking out from under the piano and then shake my head no.

"Okay. We need to get both of you out fast. Can you walk?"

I nod

"Good. Go with Ripley." Another firefighter takes my arm.

I shake my head and then start to take the mask off so I can talk.

"Leave the oxygen on, sir." The voice is female. "We'll get your wife out."

"I tried to pull her free," I say, "but her clothes are caught on something." My words come out as a muddle, but she gets the idea. "I'm not leaving without her."

Ripley speaks into her headset and then pulls on my arm again. "You can stay. But step back so I can get through."

I follow orders and watch the firefighters clear more debris. One of them squeezes in next to Isabel, reaches behind her, and uses a knife to free her. A moment later, they pull her out.

Her whole left side is soaked with blood!

*Please let it not be hers.*

Ripley leans over Isabel and flashes a light in her eyes. "Can you wiggle your fingers and toes?

I shift around so I can see Isabel's response and then let out a breath I didn't realize I was holding.

"Let's go!" Ripley takes my arm as the other two lift up Isabel, one carrying her crossed legs over his shoulder and the other with his arms around her torso. I grab onto the kite string with my bleeding hands, and using the firefighter's powerful light, we exit the smoky building in less than a minute.

Outside, the scene on the street is chaotic, but the gawking crowds are gone.

Isabel is placed on a gurney and lifted into an ambulance, but I refuse the bed offered. "I'll be okay, the cuts are all superficial—but I want to go with her."

"I'm sorry, sir, but unless you need immediate medical attention, there's no room in the ambulances. We're still transporting victims with multiple lacerations and severe blood loss."

"Sure. No worries. Which hospital?"

"UC Med." The paramedic takes my arm and leads me over to the fire truck. "Sit here and keep using the oxygen, I'll be back in a few minutes to check on you."

I sit down, feeling exhausted. "Do you know what happened to the guys who brought the pets out?"

"Didn't see them," the paramedic says, "but we can check with the Battalion Fire Chief when I get back." He disappears into the crowd of emergency responders.

I breathe in the cold, dry oxygen and look around. The fire has spread to other buildings—lots of other buildings. I watch Isabel's ambulance leave and another take its place. Five or six people are loaded in, and it disappears too.

Across the street, I see the animal cages. People are moving around them, but the group of kids who saved our lives are nowhere to be seen. I peer down the street, looking for the jewelry shop, but the whole block has gone up in flames.

There's a loud screech of bending metal from behind me, and I turn just as the ceiling of the atrium collapses, sending a huge cloud of smoke and debris out the broken window I just exited. Flames erupt from the newly formed gap in the sky.

"Damn, that was close."

I stand up, set my mask down on the fire truck, and make my way toward the cages stacked on the grass.

Most of the pets seem to be okay. I switch on my phone light and scan the cages until I find the black kitten. She squeaks when she sees me, her eyes glowing in the dark.

"Hey, kitty girl, you want to come home with me?"

My heart falls when I notice that the cage below hers is empty. Tolstoy's torn newspaper is still in there, but the puppy is gone. I scan the grassy area, but don't see him anywhere.

"What happened to your friend?"

The kitten wrestles with the towel in her cage, and I notice there's an envelope lodged underneath it. I pull it out and read the name scrawled on the outside:

*Sherlock*

I laugh out loud.

Inside there's a note on jewelry shop stationery:

*We took Tolstoy home with us, and Lucky seems to be fine. Take care of the missus.*

*—The Hole-in-the-Wall Gang*

I tip the envelope up and two gold wedding bands fall out in my hand. I smile so big it makes my lips crack.

*Propose by text message and present her with a stolen ring. Classy, Nadales, classy.*

I stick everything in my pocket, scoop the kitten out of the cage, and start jogging toward the hospital.

# CHAPTER 4
## *Matt: People Will Die*

I shiver and pull the jumper tighter around my neck, trying to ignore the fact that tons of dirt and rock are hanging above my head. I don't like enclosed spaces, and this hollowed-out mountain is about as bad as it gets.

For the tenth time, I pick up my empty coffee mug and attempt to coax out one last drop. Sixty seconds tick by. I glance at the locked door.

*What the hell is going on?*

The fan at the back of the room kicks on, and cold air blasts against the back of my neck. My phone says it's not yet five a.m., but I'm done waiting.

I push my chair back just as the conference room door flies open. A man who earlier claimed to be Mr. Johnson scowls at my "Make Cupcakes Not War" jumper. Mr. Undoubtedly-Not-Johnson is wearing a nondescript black suit, white shirt, thin gray tie, and get this: mirrored sunglasses.

*Nitwit.*

He might as well be wearing an "I Killed ET" button.

He takes off his sunglasses. "Having a little nap, are we, doctor?"

That's it. I slam my hands down on the fake wood table. "What the hell is going on? I've been pried out of my bed in the middle of the night, stuffed blindfolded into the back of a hulking SUV, frog-marched into the bowels of a man-made cave, and bullied into waiting in a locked closet with nothing but a bloody awful cup of coffee." I bump the mug and it scoots across the table. "And if that wasn't enough, I've been told absolutely nothing, except that if I don't cooperate, *people will die.*"

I place my elbows on the table and let my head fall into my hands. "Merlin's pants! Who the hell would have died if you let me sleep for a couple more hours?"

"Are you done now, doctor?"

"I'm not a doctor." I look up. "I'm a physics professor, and I've had just about enough of this cloak and dagger shite."

The alleged Mr. Johnson raises his eyebrows and then dims the lights—as if I had just mentioned that the juice and biscuits were running low. "What you're about to see was recorded by a security camera six hours ago, doctor."

"Please stop calling me that! For chrissake, I can't even put a sodding plaster on without written directions."

The government agent leans against the wall and crosses his arms, his eyes on a flat-panel display.

Up on the screen, the cone of a street lamp slices through the gray and black murk. Lurking behind it, bombed-out buildings poke up into the night sky, broken walls standing at odd angles and smoke billowing up into the darkness. The stark infrared image gives the scene a sinister feel of things turned inside out.

*Bloody hell.*

I study the security camera recording. The distant

skyline seems familiar, but I can't place it. At the bottom of the screen, a *Warning! No Trespassing!* sign hangs askew on a sagging chain-link fence. I tip my head sideways in a useless attempt to straighten it.

*This is absurd.*

And then I recognize the mailbox-shaped skyscraper in the background. "Denver. And that's the famous hotel that burned to the ground a couple of weeks ago, right?"

Mister ET-killer glances at me, his lips tight, but doesn't answer.

"I'll take that as a yes."

From the left of the screen, three teenagers bob into view, skulking around past curfew. They swagger down the sidewalk, followed by a black and white puppy, and then stop and look around, unaware that anyone is watching. The tall, skinny kid gives an unconscious tug on his sagging pants, an act as contagious as a yawn, and the other two follow suit. A moment later, two more hooded figures join them, and all five scramble up the chain link fence, the chubby one knocking the crooked warning with his foot. The sign clatters silently to the ground, and the puppy jumps back. The boys leap down on the other side, one of them landing with his pants around his thighs.

*I always wondered about that.*

The trespasser hikes up his jeans, bends up the bottom of the fence to let the puppy through, and they all slink off into the smoking ruins.

The timestamp in the corner of the video freezes, and then the screen goes black.

I yawn and rub my eyes. "You broke down my door in the middle of the night for that? Or did I miss a secret message encoded on the guy's boxer shorts?"

He ignores me. "This next clip was recorded by one of the suspects. It was recovered from his portable cellular device less than two hours ago."

*Portable cellular device, my arse.*

But before I have a chance to respond, an amateur-looking video appears on the screen.

Two guys are looking at something in the burned ruins of the hotel. They lean over and accidentally bump their heads, and the camera guy chuckles. The picture bounces as he moves closer, and a shiny object the size of a basketball comes into view.

"What the hell is that?" The voice behind the camera is a whisper.

The taller guy reaches out, but the other one slaps his hand away. "Don't be a dumbass. It could be dangerous." He looks off camera. "Hey, Lani, we found something!"

The kids gather around the metal ball, and the camera zooms in. The object is glowing like a full moon, eerie and ominous.

The leader of the group, a slight Asian kid, touches the sphere and then jerks his hand away. "Shit! It's still hot! It must be solid metal and worth a fortune. Let's see if we can pry it out."

The voice sounds odd—and then I realize that the kid is actually a girl—and she is obviously used to calling the shots because the other guys get right on it.

Three of them bring back a long piece of steel pipe and wedge it under the sphere, resting the middle on a huge chunk of broken concrete. Then the four of them attempt to pry the object out while the voice behind the camera calls out encouragement. I can see the pipe bend with the applied force, but the sphere doesn't budge.

They rest for a moment, and the chubby guy hikes-up his pants, looking impressed. "That sucker's heavier than a dead preacher. What do you think it is?"

The camera operator coughs. "A bomb."

The tall kid starts backing away, his hands covering his crotch, but trips and falls on his bum.

"You halfwit mooker." The skinny girl wipes her mouth on her sleeve. "If it was a bomb, it would have exploded by now. This whole place was a furnace a week ago, wasn't it Tolstoy?" She kicks the metal ball with her boot to demonstrate her point, and a dog barks.

"Yeah, sure." The guy scrambles back to his feet. "I knew it wasn't a bomb."

The girl looks over at the camera. "Put that thing away, Spielberg, and come help us."

A moment later, the screen goes blank.

Mr. Johnson—who I have decided to call "Agent Dick" in honor of his congenial personality, flamboyant wardrobe, and tasteful pseudonym—flips on all the lights. I sit for a moment, waiting for my eyes to adjust, and attempt to suppress the headache forming in the back of my exhausted brain. Then I open my lab book to a blank page, smooth the paper, and write the date at the top.

Agent Dick peers over my shoulder. "I have orders to get through this as quickly as possible, doctor."

I ignore him and start writing:

*Spherical, dense, metallic, reflective, still hot after more than a week.*

I underline *hot* twice. I consider some common alloys, trying to decide which one fits the description.

*Steel? Titanium? Possibly a gallium alloy?*

He taps his foot and then clears his throat. "Powerful people are waiting to make critical decisions based on your analysis, Dr. Hudson."

*Does this guy go home at night and practice being an arse?*

"Well then bugger 'em. If you expect me to figure out what the bloody hell that is, then belt up and let me do my job." In the notebook, I draw a circle and inscribe a hand so I

45

get the relative size correct. I pencil in the steel pipe the kids used as a lever and the concrete fulcrum, using them to estimate the force applied by four teenagers. I write:

*Diameter = 24 cm? Mass > 440 kg?*

"How much is that?" Dick asks.

I snap the notebook shut, yawn, and stretch my arms. "I'm guessing that metal sphere weighs five times as much as you."

He looks suitably impressed.

As I'm wondering what those kids found in the smoking ruins, the door behind Agent Dick opens and a younger guy steps in. "It's here, sir. They're waiting for us to bring it in."

He's wearing *exactly* the same outfit as Johnson.

*Maybe they got the glasses on a Blue Light Special.*

Agent Dick turns to me. "Let's go, doc. You're not going to believe what those delinquents found."

That's the first thing he's said all night that rings true.

## CHAPTER 5

### *Diego: Handle My Weapon*

The moment I hear the shower start, I pull the shell and note out of my pocket. The traffic *was* bad today, but that's not what made me late to Isabel's place. I had an errand to run, and when I put my new purchase in the glove box for safe keeping, a white sock containing a note and a seashell fell out.

*God only knows how they got in there.*

I turn the shell over in my hands. Striking bands of orange radiate out from a dense, milky-white interior and burst into sharp spines. I found the shell at the beach on La Isla when I was nineteen, and it's been sitting on my desk at work for years.

*Why would someone stuff a seashell and an ominous note inside a sock and hide it in my glove box?*

Lucky jumps up on the couch to investigate, and I pet her soft fur. She's been living with me for the three weeks since the fire, but I know she'd rather be living with Iz. Both of us would.

"It's just too weird."

She lets out a squeaky meow and flops down in my lap. I set the shell down and unfold the note, still spooked that it's in my handwriting.

*Prepare for the worst! When things are darkest, give Isabel the shell and let her go. With Einstein's help, you will meet again. Tell no one or risk losing everything!*

I consider showing it to Isabel, but something about the warning stops me—that and the fact that I've already started preparing for the worst, and I don't want to worry her.

In the three weeks since the fire, Isabel and I have spent every free moment together, and I still can't get enough of her. I slept in a hospital chair the night of the fire, and in the morning, she suggested that we move in together. I have been working to make that happen ever since.

Although we had originally planned to buy something in town, with the way things are going, I asked the agent to find isolated properties up in the foothills, and this afternoon I'm taking Isabel to see one.

The doorbell rings, and Lucky bounds out of my lap. I stuff the note and shell back in my pocket and then stand up.

It's probably just the FedEx guy, but it's Isabel's digs, and I don't want to ruffle any feathers, so I open the bathroom door and peer in. She's singing as she runs her fingers through her soapy hair, and I listen for a moment, enjoying the sweet timbre of her voice.

"Hey, Iz," I call out. "Are you expecting company?"

She peeks out the shower door. "No. Why?"

I gesture with my head. "Doorbell. Want me to get it?"

"Yeah, sure." She gives me an amused smile. "No need to ask next time."

"Okay."

The doorbell rings twice more.

She runs her gaze down my chest. "Or you could just ignore it and hop in the shower with me."

I laugh. "Believe me, I'd love to, but the doctor said no physical activity for eight weeks, and you have thirty-four days to go."

"A shower does not qualify as strenuous exercise, Diego."

"With you, it would."

She laughs and steps back behind the glass. "I hope this remote cabin of yours is worth the trip, Captain America."

"It is. You're going to love the view." I watch her slide her soapy hands across her breasts and down her torso, the translucent glass obscuring the details but not the intent. She starts singing again, something about "hunger for your touch."

There's a loud banging on the front door, and Lucky skitters down the hallway.

"Okay, okay. I'm coming." I close the bathroom door and then stride across the living room, my cock definitely up for taking a shower with Iz.

*Down, boy. We've got five more weeks of torture.*

"And it's not as if she's trying to make it any easier."

I open the front door, still thinking about Isabel's wet, naked body—and stare into an older version of the face I regularly see in my nightmares. It's been fifteen years since I saw him last, but I would recognize that asshole anywhere.

It's Isabel's ex-husband, Dave.

He's wearing an expensive suit, but his hair is thinning and that six-pack he was always showing off has gone a bit flabby. His eyes get wide when he sees me. "Sandwich man! Fancy meeting you here. Didn't take you long to come sniffing after my leftovers, did it?"

"Go fuck yourself, Dave."

"Thanks for the warm welcome, Domingo. Hey, what happened to your forehead? Looks like plastic surgery gone wrong." He scans the living room. "Izzy-Bee around? I need to talk to her."

"No." I block the doorway with my arm and then notice the Tesla SportX parked out in front. There's a platinum blonde sitting in the passenger seat, typing on her cell phone. She doesn't look a day over twenty, and if the carpet matches the drapes, I'm Elon Musk.

She glances up at us and calls out, "You left your phone in the car, cupcake."

I laugh. "Cupcake?"

"Get out of my way, dickface." He shoulders past me. "That her in the shower? Damn if I don't have perfect timing. She always was a good fuck—even if I could never get her to shut that smartass mouth of hers."

The shower turns off.

I stand there trying to decide if I should hit him with a lamp, stab him with the fireplace poker, or just knee him in the balls.

Isabel peeks out of the bathroom, her damp hair tousled. "Who was it?"

"Hey, doll." Dave steps between us.

She recoils. "What the hell are you doing here?"

"Came to see you, of course." He turns to me. "How about you do us a favor and go make lunch? Mommy and daddy need to talk."

I take a step toward him, my fists clenched.

"Don't take the bait, Diego." Isabel steps out of the bathroom wearing only a towel. "He's not worth the effort."

Dave lets his gaze slide down her body, the corners of his mouth twisting up. "How about a quick fuck for old time's sake?"

Isabel lets out a disbelieving huff. "Wait in the living room, Dave. And don't touch anything."

"Your loss, doll."

She steps into her bedroom and then glances back at me. "Could you make sure he doesn't steal anything, please? I'll be right out." She locks the door.

Dave strides past me and peers into Isabel's office. "Nice place she's got here—for a rental. Any idea where she keeps her laptop?"

"No." I pinch the shoulder of his suit jacket and pull him toward the living room. "Out."

"Yeah, okay." He walks past me, pausing to straighten a photograph of Isabel with the scientists at Frozen Ark. "Maybe you could convince her to sign over her research and her patent portfolio. If she does, I'll throw you a bone so the two of you can upgrade." He turns and gives me a once-over, as if he's actually seeing me for the first time. "My prototype biodome has more class than this rabbit hutch."

"Don't you mean *Isabel's* biodome?"

"That's not what it says on the label, amigo, but in any case, it sure beats this shit."

I step forward and grab him by the lapels.

"No offense." He holds up his hands. "I'm sure you're rich enough to buy her a mansion." He pulls away from me and strolls back into the living room. "Probably just driving that piece of junk parked on the driveway to fool the tax man."

I shove him backwards. "Get out."

"Whoa there, sandwich man. This ain't your battle."

"It is now, you clueless prick. Get out or I'm calling the police. And won't that bimbo in your car be impressed when they slap a restraining order on you."

"That bimbo earns more in a day than you do in a year."

"Who knew sleeping with the boss paid that well?" I pick up the fireplace poker and point it at him. "Now get the hell out, or I'm going to get blood all over that pretentious suit of yours."

"Okay, okay." He backs up to the door. "Just tell Isabel

that I came to get the release papers. If she knows what's good for her, she'll sign them before things get nasty."

"She's not giving you anything, you bastard." I take a step toward him, brandishing the poker. "And in case you hadn't noticed, things have already gotten nasty."

He opens the door and slips through. "Fucking wetback."

I walk over and lock the door. "Pompous ass."

"That was impressive."

I turn around, still wielding the poker.

Isabel is leaning against her bedroom door with Lucky purring in her arms. "I see you handle your weapon well."

"I have been known to keep my tip up."

She gives me a sad smile. "I'm going to have to give him what he wants, Diego. He's run all his competitors out of business. If I want my research to do any good, I have nowhere else to turn."

"We'll worry about that tomorrow." I set down the metal rod and put my arms around her. "Right now, let's go see the cabin. Lucky wants to live with you, and so do I."

## Chapter 6

### *Isabel: Playing With Fire*

I slip in behind him while he's brushing his teeth and wrap my arms around his waist, my lips resting against his shoulder blade. I study him in the mirror, the only sound the soft rap of rain on the dark cabin windows. "Do you have any idea what day it is?"

He rinses his mouth, sets his toothbrush down, and meets my eyes. "Friday?"

I glare at him and then slide my hands across his chest, over the muscles in his arms, and onto the waistband of his jeans, letting my gaze follow my touch. "Guess again." I undo the top button and slip my hand inside. "Pro tip: It involves the number fifty-seven."

He closes his eyes, a smile flickering on his lips. "Um... National Ketchup Day?"

I pull my hand away, but he grabs my wrist and looks at me over his shoulder. "And we have a lot of *catching-up* to do." He turns in place, sets my hand back on his chest, and pulls my hips against his. "Starting tomorrow. By my count, you're one day short of the doctor-ordered eight-pack."

"What are you, the number police?"

"I suppose I could let you off with just a warning—assuming you plan to behave. In any case, I need to take a shower before we play spin the ketchup bottle."

I flick my fingernail across his nipple. "And what if I can't wait?"

He grabs my hand and kisses it. "Don't get saucy with me, miss. I'm afraid you'll just have to mustard the courage."

"Oh my god, that was awful." I push him away. "Go take your shower. But you'd better hurry or I might have to misbehave."

"I would relish it."

I laugh and lean against the sink, watching him languidly undo the buttons on his jeans. "God, you look hot."

He wiggles his butt as he takes them off, and then swings his underwear around his index finger and tosses it into the laundry basket.

I laugh. "Very sexy."

He flutters his eyelashes. "I'll take that as a condiment."

"You would."

He reaches into the shower and turns on the cold water, adding just a hint of hot, and then steps behind the translucent glass. I watch him run his hands across his shoulders and chest, looking forward to doing the same.

Exactly eight weeks ago tonight, I was in the ER, hugging Lucky to my chest and watching Diego get stitches. The whole time the doctor was sewing up his forehead, and then his arm, and finally his hand, the nurses were teasing him about saving me—as if he planned the whole thing just to get my attention—but they were all swooning over how romantic it was too. After Diego got a tetanus shot, he pulled out the gold rings, told everyone the story of how he got them, and then proposed to me.

When I said yes, the whole place erupted with applause.

I exhale and walk over to the bed, twisting the golden band around my finger. Lucky is curled up on the foot of the bed, and I run my hand across her silky fur. "He saved us both, kitty girl."

She lets out a contented squeak.

"My sentiments exactly."

I gaze over at the gorgeous man in my shower, wondering how I survived so long without him. While I have been practicing breathing without coughing, Captain America has been transforming our secluded cabin into a self-sufficient fortress. This morning, he was up on the roof wiring up the new solar panels, and then he spent most of the afternoon connecting them to a row of car batteries in the basement. The guy's ordered reinforced windows, on-demand hot water heaters, a rainwater filtration system, and high-efficiency appliances. He even asked me about buying a gun, but I flatly refused. If things get *that* bad, there won't be any bullets, and I'd have to be an idiot to fill up my basement with incendiaries.

I watch him glide soapy hands through his hair, humming to himself. When he picks up his razor and begins shaving his face, a lush wetness forms between my thighs. It's been forever since I felt such a compelling desire to be with a man, and I've been suffering through the eight-week exercise ban just as much as he has, perhaps more.

I pull off his old sweater and crawl under the down comforter, looking forward to being in his arms.

A minute later, he slips in behind me, cuddles up against my back, and slides his hands around me. I inhale the intoxicating scent of bar soap mixed with his sandalwood aftershave. "Mmm, you smell good."

He tickles the back of my neck with his nose and then

kisses me. "I can't believe you're actually here in bed with me, living with me. It's a dream come true."

Kitty girl meows and we both laugh.

He moves his fingertips up my thigh and across my hip, drawing lazy circles. "Do you think there's a universe where we didn't break up the first time, Iz?"

I snuggle against his chest. "And had two kids who jumped on the bed and dressed up the cat and made us so happy we cried?"

"Yeah, something like that."

"I don't know, Diego. I wasn't ready to have kids back then." I trace the outline of his hand. "And we couldn't figure out how to make things work between us."

He's quiet for a bit, stroking my skin and hair. "Well, I can't imagine a universe where I loved anyone *but* you. So somewhere, somehow, I think we got it right."

I take a ragged breath, tears filling my eyes.

He props his head up with his hand and kisses me on the point of my shoulder. "Did you hear about the insomniac who swallowed a spoon?"

I give him a dubious look.

He bumps his hips against me. "He hasn't stirred since."

"Hah."

He hands me a tissue from the nightstand. "Have I told you recently that I'm madly in love with you?"

I take a deep breath and then wipe my face. Even in my darkest moments, he is able to bring me back to the light, make me believe that his love is enough to sustain us both. "How do you remember all those terrible jokes?"

"I read *Increasing Your Brainpower* by Sarah Bellum."

I laugh.

"But speaking of spoons, I feel obligated to inform you that spooning often leads to forking, and forking can lead to, ah, *storking*, so maybe we should talk about birth control."

I shift over onto my back and pick up his hand, playing with his matching ring. "I haven't had a regular period in over a year, Diego, so the point is moot."

He lets out a disbelieving snort. "Given what you told me eight weeks ago, I would have to be an idiot to fall for that one, Isabel."

"Well it's the truth, Captain America. And besides, it would be a whole different story if I got pregnant now." I stare at him for a moment, and then look away.

"Yes, it would be." He rolls over to face me. "And I brought it up because I don't want to get you pregnant by *accident*." He taps on my stomach with one finger. "I've been thinking about the possibilities too, but I think we should hold off for a while."

"Don't tell me we're going to play Scrabble all night because you're worried about getting me pregnant."

"No. I'm concerned about your health, Iz." He pulls me over on top of him and takes my head in both his hands, glancing from my eyes to my mouth and back. "There are condoms in the drawer, but maybe we *should* play Scrabble tonight."

I sit up, straddling his hips. "Does that mean you don't want to have sex with me?"

He picks up my hand and kisses it. "It means I want to be sure you're back to one hundred percent before we start wrestling over who gets to be on top, or who has to come first, or who wants to fuck all night because she's too worked up to go to sleep—"

I feel my face flush. "I told you, I'm fine, Cap—"

He puts his finger against my lips. "Shh. Just listen for a second. Please."

"Since when did you get so bossy?"

"I want to be sure we're making the right choice here, Isabel, and considering what I had to go through to get you to come home with me, I don't want to lose you again."

"Thanks for saving me. It was extremely hot."

"Yeah," he says, half-smiling, "you always did like to play with fire."

I run my fingers across his chest. "Well, if it makes you feel any better, I'll let you call the shots tonight, do all the heavy lifting as it were."

He smiles. "Now that's an offer I can't refuse."

"But no gloating."

"Shit. I should get that in writing."

I smack him on the chest. "You're gloating."

"I am not. I'm enjoying the possibilities." He takes hold of my shoulders. "Are you sure?"

"About having sex or letting you be in control?"

He pulls me down on top of him. "Come here."

## Chapter 7

## *Diego: If I Had Any Patients*

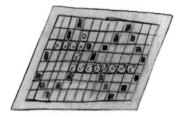

I tease her—kissing her on the mouth but refusing to let her kiss me back—until she pushes me away and sits up on my hips. "That's it. You're fired."

I slide one fingertip across her lower lip. "You're not going to win this one, hun."

"Because you don't want to kiss me?"

"Yeah," I say, chuckling. "I can't believe it took you this long to figure it out."

She smacks me on the chest, but I grab her wrist, and then leisurely kiss the palm of her hand. "I have been dreaming about this for years, Isabel, and I want to take it slow." I glance up at her pinched expression and stifle a smile. "And I know that's going to be difficult for you—but I intend to make it worth your while."

"What if I fall asleep on you?"

I laugh. "I'll take my chances."

She twists up her mouth. "Well then, what if I *like* to be

in control?"

"So what's new?" I take her shoulders, pull her against my chest, and then roll over on top, supporting my weight with my elbows. "Not that I'm complaining."

She slides her fingers roughly into my hair and pulls my head down. "I think you should kiss me now."

*Shit, I've missed her.*

I place my lips against hers, teasing her again, but the moment she tries to push me away, I kiss her with my whole body, wanting to please her, wanting to be the one *she* can't live without.

She moans softly, and the sound reaches down and twists up my insides, making me ache to have more of her. She entwines her legs with mine, pressing her hip against me, and we become lost in the compelling need of that kiss.

When I try to pull my mouth away, she tightens her grip, and I smile, our lips still touching. "I'm not going anywhere."

She grabs onto my shoulders and attempts to push me over.

I raise an eyebrow. "Got a cake in the oven?"

"No, but I wish *you* did."

"I'll make you one tomorrow, hun." I lift her wrists and place them above her head. "Assuming that I survive the night." I hold down her hands and kiss her arm and shoulder. She struggles against me—and then suppresses a cough. I rest my forehead on her collarbone and exhale slowly. "Or we could play Scrabble." I release her wrists. "That way I won't have to worry about hurting you."

"You are not hurting me, Diego." Her voice is defiant.

"I already told you, Isabel, the moment you start coughing, we're done. So either you let me lead, or we wait for another night."

She gives an annoyed huff.

"Take it or leave it, Dr. Sanborn. The game board is in the

top drawer."

Anger flashes across her face. "Fuck you."

"Yeah, eventually." I stifle a grin, and she rolls her eyes. "I'll take that as a yes." I go back to kissing her shoulder. "And profanity isn't allowed in Scrabble, as I'm sure you know." I move my lips up her neck, taking my time. "So you'll have to try a bit harder if you intend to win."

She lets out a sigh of pleasure.

"Which I'm sure you do." I slide my mouth up to her ear and exhale gently—and then wince when she grabs my hair, her body tense with anticipation. I smile, my lips still touching her. "Nine letters. X, Q, ends in TE." I kiss her ear, and she wraps her body around me, her fingernails pressing into my back and her breathing audible.

I move my lips across her cheek, "Mmm, I've missed you," and then lift up her chin and kiss the hollow of her neck. "Exquisite. As in 'You are exquisite.'"

A moan forms deep in her throat, and then she takes my chin and pulls my mouth up to hers until our eyes meet. "Where have you been all my life?"

"Right here waiting for you to let me lead." I kiss her, soft and wet, the exhilaration of being with her filling me with heat and light. When she breaks the kiss, I move my mouth down her body and slip my hand around her breast, enjoying the feel of it resting in my cupped palm. She watches me, her lips parted.

I move my mouth across her silky skin, and she lifts her torso, pressing her breast up to my lips.

"Two Vs, one L, ends in T," I say and glide my tongue around her erect nipple and then take it into my mouth.

Her breath catches in her throat. "Oh god, that feels good." She rubs her hip against my hardness and then reaches down and wraps her fingers around me. "Velvet—over steel."

The double pleasure is too intense, and I pull her hand

away, trying to stay in control.

But the moment I let go of her wrist, she slides it back down. I maneuver my hips to block her and then take my mouth away from her breast. "Patience, hun."

"Yeah, well, if I had any patients, I would have been a doctor, remember?" She presses her nipple up to my lips, gazing down at me, her mouth open, and then moves her tongue slowly across her top lip at the same time she slides her fingertip around the head of my cock.

"Christ."

"Profanity! You lose your turn." Her voice is gleeful.

"You cheated."

She stares at me, her eyes dark and serious. "No matter what happens, no matter how bad it gets, don't walk away from me, Diego. Okay?"

I scoot up and kiss her on the nose. "Okay. I promise." I slide over next to her and glide my fingertips across her alabaster skin. "God, I love to touch you. I can't believe you're actually here with me."

"And that I'm letting you call the shots."

"I wouldn't go that far. I enjoy the wrestling as much as you do, Iz. But not tonight. Not until you're better." I move my hand down between her thighs and stroke her with my fingertips.

She presses her hips against my hand, trying to get my fingers inside.

"You're so wet. Shit, that makes me hard." I move back over her. "Three letters, alternate spelling, starts with C." I slide my mouth leisurely down between her thighs.

"Oh no you don't!" She tugs on my shoulder, but I ignore her. She smacks me on the arm. "Damn it, you never listen to me."

"Uh huh." I place my mouth against her and move my tongue in a wide figure eight, slowly decreasing the arc until she grabs my hair and makes me stop.

I kiss her very gently and then lift my mouth enough to speak. "Is that too intense?"

She takes a shaky breath. "No. Yes! Please stop."

"Let me make you come."

"Not tonight. Not like that."

I take a deep breath, hold it for a moment, and then let it out. "When I was twenty-five, I didn't know what to do with you when you got like this." I move back up next to her. "But even then, I couldn't understand why the sex never seemed to satisfy you—and yet you refused to let me even *try* to make you come."

Her eyes get big.

I finger a lock of her hair. "Just so we're clear, I don't plan to make that mistake again." I give the curly strand a gentle tug. "So I'm not coming until you do. Period. End of conversation."

She turns away.

"Iz? Talk to me. Tell me what you want, what you like."

"It's not something I'm comfortable discussing."

I take her chin and wait until she looks at me. "You mean you don't want to come? Or you don't like oral sex?"

"I don't want to talk about it. Period. End of conversation, Captain America."

"So teach me how to make you come with my hand."

Tears form in her eyes, and then she glances away again. "I can't."

"Hey. No worries." I pull her against my chest and kiss her hair. "We'll figure it out together, okay?"

She buries her face in my neck. "Don't you ever leave me, Diego Nadales. I would rather die than lose you again."

I put my arms around her and roll over onto my back, taking her with me. "There will be no need."

She lifts her head and looks at me, her eyes glossy, and

then she runs her hand down the side of my face, leaving one fingertip pressed against my lips.

I take it into my mouth, wanting more of her—all of her.

"Make love to me, Diego. Like you've been dreaming about it your whole life and are afraid you might never get another chance."

And I do.

# CHAPTER 8

## *Matt: It's Classified, Doctor*

I walk through massive blast doors into the pre-dawn chill. The air smells of burnt plastic, and the summit of the snow-capped peak behind us is lost in a sooty haze. To the east, giant plumes of black smoke obscure the city spread out below us.

*How did all those fires get started?*

"Let's go, doctor." Agent Dick's voice breaks my frozen trance.

I'm standing on a giant ledge hacked out of the mountainside, shivering in my thin sweatshirt. "Yeah, I'm coming." I hurry across the expanse of decaying concrete, following the agents toward a gray windowless van.

As the sun rises above the eastern plains, we watch eight marines unload an extremely heavy object in a canvas bag out of the van. They wrestle the monster into a steel sling suspended from a professional grade engine hoist. The rig makes a moan of protest as it takes the load, but holds. When the men finish, they form a line, sweat forming dark shapes on their sandy T-shirts.

A tall, fit, thirty-something officer gives his men a curt nod. "At ease." The guy's dark skin is covered in tattoos, colorful shapes and lines snaking around his arms and neck: *The Illustrated Man.*

Agent Dick steps up to the van and adjusts his tie. "I'll take it from here, sergeant."

"With all due respect, Mr. Johnson, that duck weighs over 500 kilos, and it's going to steer like a tank."

Dick lowers his voice and glowers at the man in sandy fatigues. "I'm aware of that, sergeant. We'll handle it from here."

The marine officer pulls a folded piece of paper out of his shirt pocket, his face unreadable, and offers it to Agent Dick. With obvious disdain, the government man unfolds the paper, glances at it, and hands it back. "Okay, you come with us, but not the soldier boys."

A muscle in the marine's neck twitches.

*Even I know that marines hate to be called soldiers. How can a guy who works for the government not know that?*

Dick unbuttons his suit jacket and grabs onto the hoist, his tie flapping over his shoulder. "Let's get this inside quickly, Smith."

The tattooed officer raises an eyebrow. "They're marines, sir."

"What did you say?" Dick asks, his eyes narrowed into a frown.

The Illustrated Man's jaw tightens. "They're marines, Mr. Johnson, not soldiers."

"Yeah, whatever. They're done." Dick scans the sky, obviously expecting a battalion of enemy drones to attack, and then returns his attention to the hoist. He gives it a forceful shove.

Nothing happens.

*This guy is a laugh a minute.*

With practiced indifference, the marine officer turns back to his row of men. "Dismissed."

They salute and disappear into the maw of the gouged mountain.

The tattooed man turns back to the rig, his gaze coming to rest on the same lever as mine. He looks over at me, lifting his chin ever so slightly. I nod once. He leans against the van, his arms crossed and a slight smile on his lips.

I like him already.

Dick scowls at Junior, and the younger man jumps into action. He unbuttons his suit coat and lays his shoulder against the rig, adding his weight to the effort. The winch squeaks but refuses to budge, and I try hard not to laugh.

The marine catches my eye and nods again. I clear my throat. "Excuse me, gentlemen. May I be of assistance?" I walk over and release the hand brake on the hoist. As I'd guessed earlier, it's an expensive hydraulic rig and nearly perfectly balanced: one wheel twists sideways a centimeter and stops. I lower the suspension arm and let the cradle slide down almost to the ground.

Dick makes a move to stop me, but the marine sergeant leans over and grabs his arm. "Lowers the center of mass, Mr. Johnson, making it easier to steer."

Dick's eyebrows become lost in his thinning hair, but he recovers quickly. He leans his shoulder into the hoist, and with Junior's help, they start the duck rolling toward the mountain.

We watch, our hands shading our eyes from the rising sun, and then the marine officer turns and reaches out to me. "You must be the materials expert they hauled in this morning. I'm Sergeant Major Colton Richter. People on the project call me Picasso."

I shake his hand. "Professor Matt Hudson—friends call me anything but doctor. Nice to meet you." His grip is solid, but not pretentious.

"My pleasure, Professor Hudson. Welcome to the circus." He nods toward the government agents. "You just met the clowns."

I laugh.

We go back to watching the two suits wrestle 500 kilos of metal—the equivalent of four large refrigerators—across the uneven expanse of cracked and crumbling concrete.

Picasso shakes his head and walks over to shut the double doors on the van. He raps his knuckles against the side twice, and a uniformed arm waves from the driver's window. The vehicle makes a U-turn, passes through huge gates, and disappears down a narrow road carved into the mountainside.

"Where'd you work on car engines?" Picasso asks. He stands next to me, his hands in his pockets, both of us watching the rig weave and sway as Agent Dick yells inane commands at Junior.

"Plane engines, actually. I grew up outside London. Spent my free time working on Cessnas so I could afford to fly them. Never met an engine I didn't learn to love. Wish I could say the same about my interpersonal relationships."

He chuckles.

"How about you?" I ask.

"Been tinkering with engines since I first discovered that my father was afraid to get his hands dirty."

I glance at his ink-covered forearms and then up to his face. He has a strong force of personality and is well-built and smart, not the type I'd expect to be covered in tattoos. "Why all the ink, if you don't mind me asking?"

He takes his hands out of his pockets and turns them over in the waxing daylight. "Started adding them after my mother died, and my father told me he couldn't stand to look at me anymore. I guess I couldn't stand to look at me anymore, either."

"That must have been rough."

"I've seen more fucked-up shit than I care to remember," he says, "but I never saw anyone more terrified than my father when I told him I was going to quit law school and join the marines. Maybe that's why I did it."

I chuckle and turn back to the clowns, wondering if there's any chance the guy is gay.

Dick and Junior have stopped moving and are attempting to lift the engine hoist over some obstacle. We can hear Dick's angry shouts all the way across the expanse of concrete.

"Looks like our government boys have run into a bit of a snafu," I say.

Picasso rests his hand on my shoulder blade. "Come on, let's go help those pikers before they kill someone."

$$\infty$$

For the last two hours, white-coated technicians have been popping in and out of this bomb-proofed cave, running a parade of tests on the artifact, while I stand by and take notes. At this point, I wouldn't be surprised to find out that the damn thing has gallstones.

Now that I'm finally alone with it for a moment, I ignore the clamor of angry voices out in the hallway and run my fingertips across the cold metal enigma. The surface is perfectly smooth except for five raised symbols:

$e = mc^2$

The silver-gray, super-heavy tungsten alloy—ceramic, actually—doesn't have a scratch, nick, or dent anywhere on it. I rap my knuckles against it and listen to the sound, testing it like a ripe watermelon. I have a hunch that the center is hollow.

Agent Dick thinks it's a bomb, but I seriously doubt

that someone would go to all the trouble to forge a perfect sphere, carefully sintered with Einstein's equation, and use it to kill people—ignorant government goons excepted. Still, I'm a bit perplexed about why someone would launch it at super-sonic speeds into a landmark hotel, setting the better part of downtown Denver on fire.

The door bursts open and Agent Dick scurries in, his face contorted in anger, Junior on his heels.

He glances at the sphere and then pins me with a glare. "What is that thing? You've had two hours, and I want answers. The Pentagon doesn't want to start a panic, but you can imagine how much shit will hit the fan if that thing turns out to be a nuke."

I rub my eyes. "It's not a bomb—or any other kind of weapon, for that matter."

*I bloody-well hope I'm right.*

"What is it, then?"

"I don't know yet," I say, "but I think it's hollow."

He recoils. "Hollow? What the hell, Hudson? That thing weighs more than my car."

"Yeah, well, we'll know when the density numbers come back. My best guess is there's a small cavity in the center filled with inert gas."

Junior addresses me, his forehead wrinkled. "Can't we just x-ray it to see what's inside?"

"Unfortunately, no. It's tungsten carbide, nearly as hard as diamond and impervious to just about everything, including x-rays."

The kid glances down at his feet.

"But it's a good question," I add.

Dick glances at his watch. "How did it end up inside the Brown Palace Hotel?"

"I don't know."

"Who made it?"

"I don't know."

"Why is that damn equation on the outside?"

"I don't know that either."

He turns and slams his hands down on the desk. "What *do* you know, doctor?"

I try to keep my voice level. "A private company or a large university probably made it: people with money and access to special tools. It's not something you could whip up in the basement."

"Can you get it open?"

"Probably," I say. "Tungsten is strong, but brittle. Like an eggshell, the sphere could withstand extraordinary external pressure. But, if we hit it hard in one spot, it should fracture."

Dick looks over at Junior. "Do it."

I hold up my hands. "Whoa there, cowboys. Once you break it, there won't be any way to put it back together. Any information contained in the structure will be lost."

"Yeah, I'm feeling real sorry for Humpty Dumpty." Agent Dick turns to leave. "You can start gluing the pieces back together tomorrow morning."

"Tomorrow? What about my job—and my life? I haven't slept in thirty-six hours."

"Someone has been assigned to take over your responsibilities at the university, doctor. You are now on permanent loan until such time as the Pentagon says you are no longer needed on this project."

It's not as if teaching undergraduate physics is a particularly rewarding career choice, but still, it's *my* life. "Couldn't someone have asked me first?"

He shrugs and leaves the room, Junior trailing like a duckling.

I turn to a new page in my notebook and write:

*Why would someone take the time to put Einstein's equation on a tungsten sphere and then blow up a hotel with it?*

I stare at the page, unable to come up with anything that makes the least bit of sense.

*It was an accident? A warning? They got bad room service?*

The equation must be important: It's how I knew the thing wasn't a bomb. Any educated person would recognize those five symbols, no matter where they grew up.

I follow the logic a bit further. And whoever found it would assume that the near-perfect sphere was important, even if it was found in Ethiopia or Iceland. It's clearly more valuable than just the material it's made from. They'd call the police, who would notify the government.

Whoever created that sphere wanted to get the attention of an expert in physics *and* materials science.

*Me.*

"Bugger and blast."

Okay, so they have my attention, now what?

*It's some sort of message.*

I look over at the sphere, half-expecting it to start clicking or whistling.

"Who sent you, and what are you trying to tell me?"

The mysterious object remains silent.

$$\infty$$

Two hours later, I watch as the sphere is lowered into a robotic drill press that would make the MythBusters jealous. The contraption sits deep inside the mountain, crammed into a biometrically sealed and electromagnetically shielded blast room.

Picasso and his crew have rigged up a camera on a boom, and we're watching from the other side of the mountain, just in case.

The soft riffs of Junior's cell phone game are audible as we wait for Picasso to run a status check. A few minutes later, we hear a slight mechanical wheeze, and Junior puts his phone away. Picasso sits back in his chair. "Here she goes."

As we watch, the pressure gauge on the vice increases with agonizing slowness.

I shake my head, surprised that the sphere can withstand that much force.

Ninety seconds later, there's a single metallic pop, and the artifact shatters into tiny silver shards. A single slip of pink paper flits back and forth to the floor. It appears to have writing on it, but it's on the bottom side. The Geiger counter doesn't make a peep, and the indicators on the laser gas analyzer remain steady.

"Expensive way to send a valentine," Picasso says. He taps a few keys, and we watch a replay of it floating down in slow motion, but the handwriting is at a bad angle. "Looks like we'll have to wait until the artifact clears quarantine before we can read it." He doesn't wait for the next question. "That'll be at least an hour, probably two depending on the analysis of the enclosing gas."

Agent Dick leans in toward the monitor, pointing at a blue-green object the size of a small pocketknife. "What the hell is that?"

Picasso pans the camera across the gray metallic fragments and locks in on the capsule.

Junior whistles. "A thumb drive, sir."

Agent Dick glares at him.

The image zooms out, moves across the rubble, and stops on a dust-covered lump in the back, left corner. Picasso adjusts the camera angle and zooms in. A gray crosshatch pattern fills the display, sharp metallic shards poking into the weave at odd angles.

I recognize the close-up immediately. "Something made of cloth. Probably cotton."

Picasso raises his eyebrows.

"We used to look at stuff under the electron microscope when I was a grad student," I say. "Never dreamed it would prove useful."

Agent Dick shifts his weight. "Any idea what it is?"

Picasso zooms out to normal and shifts the angle again.

"A dirty sock!" Junior blurts out.

Agent Dick scowls. "What the hell would a dirty sock be doing inside an expensive metal sphere, Mr. Smith? Keep your mouth shut if you're not using your brain."

"Yes, sir."

"It *does* look like a crumpled-up athletic sock," I add.

Picasso pans the camera across more rubble, and I point at a thin, white disk leaning against one of the larger fragments. "How about that?"

Picasso taps some keys and the camera rotates. A button-shaped piece of white plastic comes into focus, a stylized apple with a missing bite etched on it.

Junior laughs. "I don't think they've invented that yet."

Agent Dick rounds on him. "That will be enough, Smith." He turns to Picasso. "I want to know what those things are, sergeant, and where they came from."

Picasso nods. "Don't we all, Mr. Johnson. Don't we all."

# CHAPTER 9

## *Diego: In a Pickle*

The moment I sit down, Anne pokes her head into my office, her long copper hair splashing around the doorframe.

"Hey, dude, you're late. The Water Project people are waiting for you in Mount Elbert. I started the video on the work we did for Frozen Ark, so you should be good for a few minutes." She stares at my closed fist. "You okay?"

"Yeah." I start gathering my proposal. "We moved into the cabin last week, and the drive took longer than I expected. Thanks for covering for me."

She nods, looking skeptical. "Oh, and I got a weird phone call this morning. Guy wanted to know how long you've worked here. Said he was with the US Immigration and Customs Enforcement. It sounded sort of fishy to me, so I told him if he left his number, I'd have someone call him back. He hung up." She crosses her arms. "You didn't go and piss off some oil sheik again, did you?"

"Not that I know of," I say, "but thanks for the heads up."

"No problem. Want to do lunch later?"

"Sure," I say. "Thanks again for covering."

"My pleasure." She disappears in another splash of red.

I get up and shut the door and then sit back down, my heart racing. I open up the desk drawer, take out my shell, and set it next to its twin.

*So if the one in the drawer is mine, where did this other one come from?*

For as much as I can tell, the two are *exactly* alike, from the shape of the spines down to the subtle pink coloring of the lip.

*What are the chances of that?*

My phone beeps with a text message.

*Now what?*

A friend in Legal wants me to stop by—but not until after the place clears out. I reply in the affirmative, stick the shells in my drawer, and rush off to the conference room.

∞

At a little past one, I walk with Anne to the sandwich shop on the corner. After we order, she excuses herself to use the bathroom. I sit down at a small patio table and watch the grade school kids across the street playing soccer.

There's only one girl in the mix, her long blond hair tied up in a ponytail and her red plaid skirt in stark contrast to the sea of navy blue shorts. As I watch, she crosses the ball and then sprints toward the goal. A boy with the same color hair steps up to her pass, fakes a goal kick, and then feeds the ball in to her though the confused defenders. She angles it into the back corner of the net for a goal. The twins exchange high-fives and then jog in lockstep back up the field.

Strong emotions well up inside me, and it takes me a moment to identify the heady mix: hope and longing.

*What an amazing experience it would be to have kids.*

Anne sits down with our sandwiches and glances over at the schoolyard. I've worked with her for a number of years and respect her both professionally and personally. She's young, attractive, and idealistic—and she has the organizational skills of a Chinese factory owner mixed with the enthusiasm of a Labrador retriever. But a few months ago, I made the mistake of allowing our professional relationship to cross the line, and things have been rocky between us ever since.

A teacher blows a whistle, and I scan the kids heading in from recess, trying to spot the soccer duo one last time. Anne fiddles with the chips next to her veggie-sub-with-extra-pickles and flushes when I look over at her.

"Diego," she says, tilting her head to the side and tossing her sheet of red hair back over one shoulder, her eyes focused on her sandwich. "I can't stop thinking about that night in Jan—"

My phone chimes, and I give her a weak smile. "Sorry. Let me see if it's urgent."

It's from Iz:

> **Big pow-wow with Stan at 6. Kelly said**
> **she'd give me a ride. Don't forget to buy**
> **ketchup.** ☺

Anne clears her throat. "Everything okay?"

"Yep. Just Isabel letting me know she'll be home late."

"Ah." Anne picks up her sandwich. "Must be nice to have someone to come home to." She takes a bite, and pickles squirt out onto her plate.

The smell of dill and vinegar hangs in the air. I remember that salty-sour taste lingering in my mouth after kissing her. "Yes, it is." I pick up my sandwich and then set it back down, not feeling hungry anymore.

"What about us, Diego?" She plops an errant pickle into

her mouth. "I thought you wanted to be with me—or, at least, you let me think you did."

I force myself to meet her eyes. "I'm sorry if I misled you, Anne. I honestly enjoyed the night we spent together, and I don't know what I'd do at the office without you, but it was never more than good friends for me. And I told you that at the time."

She glances down at her lap, tears in her eyes.

*Shit.*

I put my hand on her arm. "Hey, you're a beautiful, vivacious, caring woman, and I know you'll find the right guy: some young hotshot who will have his hands full just keeping up with you." I wait for her to look up. "But you're too much for an old fart like me."

*And my heart belongs to Iz.*

She swings her hair over her shoulder, avoiding my eyes. "Come on, Methuselah. Let's get back to saving the world."

∞

It's nearly seven by the time I make it up to Legal, but my friend is still there.

"Hey, Diego. Good to see you." After shaking my hand, he puts his arm around me, pulls me inside his office, and shuts the door.

"Uh oh. What's up?"

"I got a phone call about you today," he says. "A guy claiming to be a cop wanted to know if you're a citizen, who you're married to, and what your home address is. You in some sort of trouble?"

"Not that I know of, but Anne got a similar call this morning. Did you tell him anything?"

He claps me on the back. "Yeah. To show me the court order or stop wasting my time."

I laugh. "Thanks. I wonder what's going on?"

"Well, whoever it is, they're sloppy. I could hear freeway noise in the background and someone playing Letterpress on a cell phone—hope it wasn't the guy driving."

"You've got a good ear. Remind me not to get on your bad side, okay?"

He smiles. "Hey, I've got something else for you too." He pulls out a sheet of paper from his briefcase. "Have you seen this?"

It's a dark, poor-quality photo printed on too-thin paper. I study it for a minute, but can't make out much. "No. What is it?"

"A solid metal sphere about the size of a basketball. Some looters found it in the ruins of the Brown Palace Hotel a week after the fire. Which reminds me, how is Isabel doing?"

"Fine, thanks. Much better." I take another peek. Now that I know what it is, I can make out the large shiny ball next to a muddy high-top shoe. It does look rather impressive.

He takes back the photo. "You remember how no one could figure out how all those fires got started at precisely the same time in six buildings, blocks apart? No bombs. No arson. No nothing." He waits for me to nod. "Well, I made a map of where all those fires began and connected the dots. They're in a line with the Brown Palace, and that line ends right where the teenagers claim they found the sphere."

"Christ. So this is some sort of projectile that was fired into downtown Denver, blasted through a bunch of other buildings, and then demolished the hotel? How come none of this has been on the news?"

He holds the photo up by the corner. "Hank grabbed it off Instagram minutes after it was posted—you know what a night owl he is. When I went to look at it in the morning, it was gone, and I'll be damned if there's any mention of it on the Internet. Nothing. Like it never existed." He puts the photo back in his briefcase. "Hank dug up the address of the original poster and sent him an email, but he never heard back. Here's the best part: Hank's laptop was stolen from his car while he was in Starbucks that morning. He thought he'd just left it at home until it showed up that afternoon."

"Let me guess, the photo was gone."

"Yeah, and all references to the guy who posted it. But I renamed the copy I had on my computer, did some light editing in Photoshop so the digital signatures don't match anymore, and then printed it. Unfortunately, I don't have any idea who actually took the shot, or I'd ask him what really happened." He walks over and opens the office door. "Well, I should get going or Hank will worry. In any case, I'm glad you're not in any hot water. But you might keep an eye out, if you know what I mean."

"Yeah, I will. Thanks for the heads-up."

"Sure," he says. "Give Isabel my best."

I shake his hand again. "Will do. If you hear anything more about the sphere, let me know? And tell Hank I owe him one. Those solar panels he recommended are perfect."

"Sure thing." He locks his door and heads toward the back stairs. "See you tomorrow."

I stop by my office to grab the shells, take a moment to text Isabel that I'm on my way home, and then head out into the falling night, grateful that it's Friday.

# CHAPTER 10
## *Isabel: All the Facts*

"What a crock of shit," Stan says under his breath.

I consider pretending I didn't hear him, but it's been a long week, and my patience is shot. I set the dry-erase marker down on the conference table and cross my arms. "Did you have something constructive to add, Stan?"

Everyone in the conference room turns toward him.

He takes a slow drink of his soda and sets down the can. "Nope."

Stan Perkins heads up the business side of the company, and our relationship has always been strained. I do science for the sheer joy of it; he pimps my work for the money.

I fix my face into a bemused smile. "From your colorful remark, I can only assume you don't agree with my analysis. Or perhaps you didn't mean to say 'What a crock of shit'?"

My boss kicks me under the table.

I ignore her. "I know you're a very busy person, Stan, but perhaps you could spend a minute enlightening us on what you find so ridiculous?"

Stan pushes back from the table and stands up. "I've heard enough. If you had your way, this company would go belly up in a matter of weeks. For all your degrees and titles, you can't predict the future any better than the rest of us."

"You are quite correct," I say. "Oslo and Adelaide also ran the statistical analysis, and I simply told you what we *all* found: The volcanic ash in the lower atmosphere is collecting around the equator due to the Earth's Coriolis effect. The polar ice is melting at an accelerating rate due to greenhouse gases. If you put those two pieces together, like the popular press is doing right now, it would seem that they cancel each other out. But that's a logical fallacy. It's like watering your vegetable garden with boiling water and ice cubes: the *average* water temperature is perfect, but you'll end up starving anyway."

There are murmurs around the table, and I wait for them to settle.

"The Tropics are going to get cooler and the Polar Regions are going to get warmer, and the changes in *localized* temperatures are going to wreak havoc: Droughts occurring every year, category five-plus hurricanes, snow in the tropics, and massive heat waves in polar regions. And any *one* of those would mean mass extinctions. You can put your head in the sand as to whether it's human induced or not, but you can't ignore the hard data."

I look over at the director of marketing and then down at the CEO. "If our goal is to preserve and record diverse biomes, now is not the time to be moving resources over to Sales. We should be collecting as much data as possible, before it's too late."

The room fills with chatter.

I sit down, suppressing a burp from the excess stomach acid that's been plaguing me since I started back to work.

*Maybe it is time for a job with less stress.*

I slip my vibrating phone out of my pocket. It's nearly 7 P.M., and I assume Diego's already on his way home. In the weeks since I came back to work, the long hours and constant struggle to keep ahead of the disappearing genotypes have been wearing me down. I read his text and then close my eyes, imagining being in his arms.

*God, I'm looking forward to making love with him tonight.*

Kelly stands and quiets the room. "I know what Isabel is suggesting will impact the bottom line, but even Stan can't sell biomes he doesn't have. If we manage to collect some key organisms before they become extinct, that could turn out to be very lucrative." She looks at Stan. "Wouldn't you agree?"

The door to the conference room flies open, and Kelly's male secretary gapes at us. "Something terrible has happened! A nuclear bomb has been launched, but no one is sure who did it, or where it's headed." The cell phone in my hand makes a loud shrieking sound, followed by every other phone in the room. "The President is scheduled to make a broadcast in a few minutes, but they say we need to get down to the basement as quickly as possible." His handsome face is distraught. "My partner is on a business trip in Europe."

Stan crushes the soda can in his hand. "Goddamn towel heads got their hands on a nuke, and now we're fucked."

Kelly jumps up. "Let's not panic before we have all the facts." She nods at her secretary and then moves her gaze around the table. "The video production lab is below ground, and it has a TV with cable. Contact your loved ones, grab your things, and meet me there in five minutes. If you need to leave now, please let someone know. I'll be down just as soon as I check that we have everyone. Let's go, people!"

# CHAPTER II

## Matt: The Magic Kingdom

It's nearly seven when Picasso and I finally make it to the small cafeteria. I haven't eaten a meal in two days, and I'm famished. On top of that, I'm a terrible cook and mostly consume things that come frozen in small cardboard boxes, so everything looks great. When we sit down at the table, I notice that Picasso has skipped the main course. "Something I should know about the beef in here too?"

"No," he says with a sad smile. "My wife was a vegetarian, and I guess I never felt the need to go back to eating meat after she left."

"I know the feeling. My ex-wife sends me bleedin' self-help books every Christmas." I cut the steak and take a bite. "What happened with your wife, if you don't mind me asking?"

*So he's not gay. Damn. Then again, maybe he's like me and got married by mistake?*

He tips his head and stirs his applesauce with a fork.

"Things were always a bit fiery between us, and a couple years ago, she left me for a doctoring gig in some godforsaken hellhole."

"Ah, that's a pisser."

"I never could understand why she felt compelled to help people who wanted to kill her." He pushes peas around on his plate. "She told me she'd check back in a few years to see if I'd grown up."

"So maybe she'll be back? You seem to be pretty mature to me."

He takes a slow breath and lets it out, his eyes on his plate. "She was killed two years ago. Some dickhead rolled an IED into the tent where she was operating. There weren't any pieces big enough to send home."

"Bollocks, I'm sorry."

"Yeah. Me too. And she was also one hell of a surgeon."

We eat in silence for a bit.

His phone buzzes, and he glances at the display and then puts it away.

"What's up?" I ask. "Do they know what's inside the sphere?" I stick the banana in my sweatshirt pocket.

He watches me polish off the brownie. "When you're done, we'll go find out."

After dinner, we walk through a maze of hallways, deep into the heart of the mountain. We pass two guards with rifles, standing at attention on either side of a door with *SSO* engraved in gold foil. Picasso nods at them.

"Sergeant Major," they say in unison, but don't move a muscle.

We continue on to a door with an elaborate arrowhead insignia and the letters MARSOC on it. Picasso uses a badge to unlock it and then holds it open for me. Agent Dick is already inside, but Junior is conspicuously absent.

*Probably past his bedtime.*

I sit down in a chair, but Picasso remains standing.

Agent Dick doesn't bother with formalities. "Dr. Hudson, does the name Diego Nadales mean anything to you?"

I glance at Picasso and then at Agent Dick. "Yeah, sure. Diego used to live down the street from me. Nice guy, smart and friendly, late thirties, writes software for a living." I shrug my shoulders. "Likes the Dodgers."

The corner of Picasso's mouth twitches.

They wait for me to continue, but I don't know what else to tell them. "Uh, he did some computer work—consulting stuff—for the physics department a couple years ago. Knows a lot about quantum mechanics for a guy who's not a physicist. Why?"

Picasso looks at me. "His name was on the paper in the artifact."

"Diego's?" I blink a couple of times. "Anything else?"

"No." Agent Dick stands up. "It was handwritten on pink paper that had been cut into approximate fourths using dull scissors. The ink matches that found in a disposable pen. The handwriting is female, left-handed, standard Palmer cursive: probably attended public schools. There are indentations in the paper that indicate the woman wrote the name over and over on stacked sheets of twenty-two pound printer paper."

"No coffee stains?" I ask.

Agent Dick jerks around and stares at me. "How did you know that?" He looks suspiciously at Picasso.

Picasso's lip curls up slightly. "Educated guess, I'd say. Anyone who stayed up all night writing the same three words over and over was probably drinking coffee."

Agent Dick scowls at me. "Do you know his wife?"

I think back to the last time I saw Diego. "No. That is, he's not married. But he has a new girlfriend. I met her a few weeks ago, right before they moved in together."

"What do you know about the girlfriend?"

"Well," I say, "he seems to be quite smitten by her—Isabel, I think. I don't remember her last name. Come to think of it, she was almost killed by that explosion in the Brown Palace—the one started by the Einstein sphere. Diego managed to pull her out of the burning building right before the roof collapsed."

The two men look at each other. Picasso crosses his arms. "Where and when did you see her last?"

"At Starbucks, a number of weeks ago," I say. "They were having a heated discussion about micro-evolution—more like a wrestling match, actually. And I think she was winning."

"Anything else about Nadales that might be *relevant*, doctor?" Dick asks. "A connection to illegal metals manufacturing? Or atomic weapons? Terrorist organizations? Involvement with a rogue foreign government?"

I let out a snort of disbelief and glance over at Picasso, but his face is carefully blank.

Dick shifts his weight. "Well, doctor?"

*Stop calling me doctor.*

I let my gaze wander slowly around the room. "No. And Einstein's equation is not a recipe for an atomic bomb, Mr. Johnson. It describes the relationship between matter and energy, and it's not the least bit illicit, unpatriotic, or nefarious."

Dick glares at me. "Answer the question."

I let out an annoyed sigh and sink back into my chair.

"Dr. Hudson," Dick says. "I would like to remind you that this is a grave and time-sensitive government investigation, and your full cooperation is expected. What else do you know about the suspect?"

"The suspect? You mean Diego?" I respond. "He's a Tico—grew up in Costa Rica. That wasn't illegal last time I checked. He does occasionally import coffee beans for me, and given the sod you serve in here, maybe you should recruit him."

Dick pushes his chair back and starts stuffing papers into his briefcase. "Thank you, Hudson. You can go now. I'll have Smith drive you home."

"Wait a minute," I say, glancing back and forth at the two men. "What about the thumb drive? And the button thing? Can't you even tell me if it was a sock?"

"It's classified, doctor." Dick's voice contains a hint of glee.

Picasso gives him an exasperated look and then addresses me. "It *was* a sock. And Cyber Ops thinks the thumb drive contains instructions for building a computer, along with the source code to control it. We have people looking at it right now." He stops for a moment to check his phone. "There are two folders on the—"

Agent Dick jumps to his feet. "You do not have the authority to release that information to a civilian, sergeant."

The marine pulls an ID out of his shirt pocket and slides it across the table. "It's sergeant *major*, Mr. Johnson, and I have been formally assigned by PCAST to lead this project. Professor Hudson's clearance came through from SSO ten minutes ago. If you have a problem with that, take it up with the President." He turns to me. "As I was saying, the first folder is labeled 'Time Portal' and the main document is entitled 'Black Holes'. Given your research in that area, I've asked that you be shown the files."

"A time portal? That uses singularities? My god, why would someone send us instructions to build a time machine?"

"That's what we're here to find out," Picasso says.

For a moment, I don't know how to respond.

*This is the opportunity of a lifetime*

"Wait a minute," I say, "what was the name of the other folder? And what is that white plastic button with the apple on it?"

"The other folder is labeled Trans-Temporal Viewer."

Dick slams his hands down on the table. "You've told him enough. For chrissake, he works for a public university."

Picasso ignores his outburst. "We believe the button device is some form of compressed data similar to the thumb drive. Unfortunately, the technology used to read it does not yet exist."

"Hudson was brought in to evaluate the artifact, soldier. He's done that." Dick's voice is icy cold.

A look of distaste flashes across Picasso's face and disappears as quickly as it came. There's a knock on the door, and two marines with rifles step into the room, one holding a folded piece of paper. Junior is right behind them, and by the expression on his face, someone just blew up the White House.

Picasso takes the paper, glances at it, and pushes it across the table. "Professor Hudson will be consulting on this project for the foreseeable future. In the meantime, we're all moving into the secured area. A national emergency was declared three minutes ago, and I am officially taking over this project on the orders of the President of the United States."

He addresses the marines. "Escort Misters Johnson and Smith to retrieve their things, and then deposit them at the checkpoint. No need to babysit them."

"Yes, Sergeant Major." The two men salute and step apart.

"Dismissed."

Agent Dick is fuming. Picasso brushes past him. "Please come with me, professor. I believe you already have the required clearance, but there are a few things we need to take care of before we can cross over."

"Cross over? To where? What's happening outside? Why is there a national emergency?"

"I am not at liberty to disclose that information, but I will fill you in as soon as possible. In the meantime, we are moving to a safe area deep inside the mountain."

∞

Dick and Junior are standing in front of a huge blast door when we arrive, Junior playing a game on his phone. Picasso walks by them and types something on a keypad next to the sealed portal.

A female voice says, "Special Clearance Required to Proceed. Please identify."

Picasso inclines his head. "Sergeant Major Richter. Clearance code: Woden Umbra."

"Thank you, Sergeant Major. What is the first treble clef note in Beethoven's 'Moonlight Sonata'?"

"G sharp," Picasso replies.

"Thank you. Please identify your other companions, starting with the tallest."

Picasso nods at Agent Dick who clears his throat.

"Agent Johnson. NSA clearance bravo victor tango twelve forty-one."

"Thank you, Mr. Johnson. What was your undergraduate degree, and where was it conferred?"

Dick's face flushes. "Hospitality Management from the University of Missouri at St. Louis."

"Thank you. You must be accompanied by Sergeant Major Richter to proceed."

The muscles in Agent Dick's jaw constrict but he says nothing. Junior glances at me and stands a bit straighter.

Picasso turns toward the younger man. "Agent Smith. Clearance identical to Agent Johnson's."

"Mr. Smith," the computer says, "please state the name of your childhood pet and the color of your first car."

Junior looks flustered. "Ah, Poopsie, and, um, orange."

"Thank you, Mr. Smith."

A smile flickers across Picasso's face. "Matt Hudson,

PhD," he says, nodding at me. "Physics Chair at the University of Colorado, Boulder. PCAST clearance pending."

"Working," the disembodied female voice replies. "Professor Hudson, what is a black hole?"

"What you get in a black sock."

Picasso gives me a droll smile.

"Thank you, Professor." The light above the door changes from red to yellow. "The portal will open three seconds after these instructions finish. It will remain open for eight seconds. Once inside the secured area, you will not be able to leave without proper authorization. In the event of an emergency, you must return to this location for clearance to exit. Do you understand? Please state yes or no."

We all respond in the affirmative, although I'm starting to have second thoughts.

"Thank you," the computer says. "You are cleared for entry."

The yellow light above the portal begins flashing and then turns green. The door slides open, and we step through. A few seconds later, the door slides shut and a red square with a hand outline flashes next to it. The sign above it reads: "In case of an emergency, place palm on panel and wait thirty seconds for activation."

*And hope to hell there's not an armed terrorist chasing you.*

We follow Picasso past a second door, which opens automatically, and file into a large freight elevator. I struggle to keep my heart rate steady as the walls of the tight space press in on me. Picasso watches my face but says nothing. When the floor begins to fall away, he takes a step closer and puts his hand under my elbow. I recite a limerick under my breath, trying to focus on the silly wordplay.

*There was a young lady named Bright,*
*Who traveled much faster than light.*
*She set out one day,*

*In a relative way,*
*And came back the previous night.*

After far too long, the doors slide open, and we step out into another world.

I stand there with my mouth hanging open. "Sweet Fanny Adams." Buried deep inside the mountain is a huge underground city.

Down a gentle slope, buildings, some as tall as three stories, line a lake with a fountain in the middle. Trees and grass fill in the open areas, and a wide pathway marked with glowing street lamps lines the edge of the water. There's even a bowling alley. Hundreds, perhaps thousands, of people could live and work inside this vast man-made cavern.

I look up. The fake night sky is dotted with stars, but there's no moon. The whole place gives me the creeps, and it takes me a moment to place my misgivings: the constellations are all wrong! "Well this pretty much explains the national debt."

Picasso chuckles. "They roll up the sidewalks pretty early, so let's get you over to the hotel before the lights go out."

We take two electric golf carts to one of the larger buildings and are escorted to private rooms by men who appear uncomfortable in civilian clothing. Sitting inside the door to my room is a suitcase I own but didn't pack. A fake window looks out onto stars twinkling in the phony sky behind the Eiffel Tower.

"Blimey, these people are daft." I step inside and the lights come up.

My lab computer is on the desk, the screensaver plotting distant galaxies in false color.

*These guys are over-the-top: they snuck back into my house and loaded up my suitcase, then broke into my lab and made off with my laptop, including the monitor and all the cables.*

I'm starting to get a bad feeling about this.

Picasso appears in the doorway behind me, flanked by two marines. "Home, sweet, home, at least for now. Meet me in the lobby at oh-seven hundred for breakfast. If you need something, just pick up the phone."

"Sergeant Major Richter?"

"Yes, sir?"

"Is all this stuff real?"

He dismisses the two other men and then turns back to me. "You mean the city, Dr. Hudson?"

"Yeah, the lake and trees, all the buildings. And please, call me Matt. Every time someone says doctor, I'm left wondering who died."

His face softens. "Sure, Matt. And like I said, call me Picasso."

I shake his hand again. "It's a deal." I glance over at the fake windows. "So, *is* any of it real?"

"There's water in the lake, all right, but I wouldn't drink anything that didn't come out of a sealed container. This place was built about the same time as Disneyland, and I think they might have gotten the plans mixed up."

"That's encouraging."

"Don't worry. You'll have plenty of time to ask questions tomorrow." He turns to leave and then looks back. "And if I were you, I'd hit the sack—and not spend too much time wondering about the trees, if you know what I mean."

"Yeah. I'll try. Goodnight."

He shuts the door, and I listen to his footsteps fade down the hallway.

I check the door handle. It's locked.

A seed of panic forms in the back of my head, but I focus on the window scene, and the fear recedes. I flop down on the bed and eat my bruised banana, wondering what epic disaster has occurred in the outside world—and how long I'm going to be locked up in the Magic Kingdom.

# CHAPTER 12

## *Diego: Wait for Me*

Just as I'm merging onto the freeway, my phone blasts a loud, jarring tone that sets my heart racing. It takes my brain several seconds to recognize the sound: a flash flood warning.

I glance out my window into the clear twilight sky.

*Or maybe an Amber Alert?*

"Hey Siri, read my notifications."

"You have one new notification from Emergency Alert. It says: Possible nuclear attack imminent. Take shelter now. Presidential address soon. This is not a test."

*What the hell? A possible nuclear attack?*

I consider pulling over to reread the message, but decide the best thing to do is get to Isabel as quickly as possible. I take the next exit, cross over the freeway, and get back on going the opposite direction.

"Hey Siri, tell Isabel I'm on my way and to wait for me."

"Ready to send?"

"Yes."

I look into the frightened face of the woman driving next to me, and then change lanes and accelerate, fifteen exits—and a lifetime—away from Isabel.

I flip on the radio, but the same message is being repeated there: take shelter; don't panic; the President will address the country in a few minutes.

I force down my growing apprehension.

*What the hell happened? A nuke launched from the Middle East?*

"They don't have the capability—at least, I don't think they do."

*Maybe a suitcase bomb—or something like 9-11?*

If the President of the United States sent out an emergency alert, it would have to be something big, and he would have to be pretty damn sure it wasn't a red herring.

*Maybe the Russians had some sort of coup, and a panicked comrade launched a handful of ICBMs?*

Somewhere in the back of my brain, I remember that it takes about thirty minutes for a missile to get here. I do the math and then slam my hand against the steering wheel.

*I won't get to her in time. Please let it be a false alarm.*

When I get off the freeway, there are police everywhere, stopping cars and telling people to take shelter. After being delayed twice, I wave them off and keep driving toward Isabel. The traffic is getting worse, and at one point, I have to run a red light and cut across a lawn to avoid a long line of stopped cars.

*Wait for me, Iz.*

It takes longer than I want, but I manage to get to her building in just over thirty minutes. The parking lot is almost empty, but I see a white Porsche with the license plate "Stan T Man" parked across two spaces, and let out a sigh of relief.

*She's probably still here.*

I pull up next to the entrance, kill the engine, and jump out of my car. The main doors are locked, and there's no one at the guard station. I bang on the heavy glass portal, knowing it's futile, and then step back and force myself to think.

*Try the easy stuff first: call her.*

I do, but the lines are jammed, so I type in a text message telling her I'm outside. It takes a couple of tries, but it eventually goes through.

*Okay. Now what?*

A creepy sense of déjà vu comes over me.

*Well, at least this time the building isn't on fire.*

"At least not yet."

I take a look around. Her office complex is a glass and steel behemoth with high-tech security on every door. It would take me weeks to break in. And I have no reason to believe she's in any more danger inside. My best bet is to stay here and wait until she comes out.

I glance up at the sky.

*If she comes out.*

"Don't go there."

I jog back to my car and switch on the radio, but there's nothing new, so I lean against the door and wait. The fall evening is mild, a slight breeze blowing out of the south, the crescent moon hanging low in the west. I gaze up into the falling darkness, searching for god-knows-what, but don't see anything except the glowing contrail of a jet heading over the mountains.

*At least I'm not up there, with her stuck down here.*

And then I remember the note. The first line says "Prepare for the worst." I stare at the large packages of toilet paper, over-the-counter drugs, and various other items in the back seat—the last few things on my shopping list. I stopped this morning—it's what made me late for work.

*Cutting it a bit close on the timing, mae.*

Even if the "possible nuclear attack" turns out to be a false alarm, everyone will be spooked, and it will take weeks, if not months, for the repercussions to subside. Supply lines will be interrupted, prices will soar, and frightened people will start hoarding everything from flour to guns to, well, toilet paper.

And if, god forbid, there *is* an attack on the US. It will all be over before you can say "mutual annihilation." Even if it turns out to be an accident, the hawks will be demanding that we bomb the Middle East back to the stone age—and take out North Korea, Russia, and Africa just in case. And the rest of the world is not going to just sit around and wait to be murdered by faceless drones.

*Any way you slice it, things are going to get ugly, and fast.*

I look out into the city around me. Despite the order to stay inside, the streets are packed with cars. Flashing lights are everywhere, and the cool evening air is filled with the sounds of wailing sirens, skidding tires, and blaring horns. I imagine the grocery stores and camping supply outlets have already been overrun.

I walk back to the entrance and sit down on the cool tile floor, my back resting against the windows. I study the sliver of the moon as lights around me wink on.

*Maybe you're wrong, mae. Maybe people will remain calm and face the future with thoughtful compassion. Maybe everything will be okay.*

The wind shifts and I smell smoke, probably from the fires in Denver, or maybe even Albuquerque or Kansas City. After "extinct" volcanoes started erupting all around the world, people started listening to the doom-sayers, and the insanity spread quickly.

*A thoughtful and compassionate future, my ass. We're screwed.*

My phone beeps, and I almost drop it as I jump up and wrench it out of my pocket. It's from Isabel:

97

**One US nuke launched by mistake.**
**Attempting to dump in ocean. Possible**
**retaliatory nukes in flight. Wait for me!**

Just as I'm sticking my phone back in my pocket, I notice a group of people moving into the lobby. Isabel is not with them.

The woman at the head of the group sees me and gives me the OK sign. As the others gather around the TV at the guard's station, she hurries across the large lobby and lets me in. "You must be Diego. I'm Kelly, her boss." We shake hands. "I'm sorry we didn't get up here sooner, but I wanted to make sure we heard the whole news report before people left." She puts her hand on my arm. "Don't worry. Isabel will be down in a minute. She went up to grab her laptop. You know how she is."

"Yeah, I do. Thanks." The panic I'm feeling drops a notch.

She leans in, her voice low. "I know you two have a long drive home, and given the circumstances, you are welcome to stay with me tonight."

"Thanks for the offer. I'll ask her when she—"

Isabel steps out of the stairwell carrying her laptop bag and three large tackle boxes. She scans the room, her face worried.

"Excuse me." I push though the crowd.

When she sees me, she drops everything, and rushes toward me.

I sweep her up into my arms and hold her, unable to speak.

She clings to me, her face buried in my neck. "Thank you for coming."

I can feel her heart pounding, and an overpowering need to protect her fills me. "No need to have worried, hun. You knew I'd come. I always will." I hold her head against my chest, stroking her hair and kissing her until her heart rate slows. "But given the option, I am never letting you out of my sight again."

She laughs and starts coughing, tears streaming down her face. "We have to stop meeting like this or it's going to kill me."

I wipe a tear off her cheek. "Kill both of us."

Another alert tone sounds, and we crowd around the TV.

The news is not good: The US nuke detonated when it hit the water. The West Coast, from Seattle to San Francisco is being evacuated, with Southern California and the Pacific Islands put on high alert. Reports of three retaliatory Russian nuclear launches have been confirmed, one of which detonated in its silo in Siberia, and two of which are now being recalled.

Stan slaps the side of the TV. "How the hell do you recall ICBMs? They'll have to detonate them in the upper atmosphere or dump them in the Arctic. Either way, it's going to be a nightmare. Goddamn trigger-happy Russians."

Someone calls out, "And how the hell do you launch a nuke by mistake? Goddamn trigger-happy Americans."

The crowd shushes them.

North Korea and Pakistan are threatening to launch first strikes if the US doesn't immediately locate and disarm all five thousand plus warheads, and the rest of the nuclear states have their collective fingers poised over red buttons. If someone slips up and presses one, life as we know it will be over.

The President has issued a state of emergency but asks all citizens to remain calm and stay indoors. Any military personnel are to report immediately. Schools and all non-essential government services are suspended until further notice. A list of the cities and counties being evacuated scrolls up followed by FEMA websites and phone numbers, and then the message repeats.

Kelly glances around the circle of worried faces. "All of you are welcome to stay here for the night. If you don't live close by, you might consider waiting until the morning to brave the hordes. Those that do leave, please check the company website for updates on when we plan to reopen for business. In the meantime, stay safe and don't take any unnecessary risks."

Stan turns and jogs out the main door, followed by most of the others. A few people head back inside the building or pull up chairs in front of the TV.

Kelly comes over to us. "Would you two like to stay with me tonight? I don't live far, and the liquor cabinet is stocked, if not the refrigerator."

"Either way is fine with me," I say, looking at Iz. "I have a full tank of gas, but things are a mess out there."

Isabel leans against me. "Let's go home before it gets any worse." She reaches out to Kelly. "But thank you. Would you like to come with us?"

"Thanks for the offer, but I'm a city girl through and through. I'll take my chances with the hordes."

"Okay." Isabel gives her a hug. "I'll be in touch."

"Sounds good." Kelly looks a bit wistfully at me. "Take care of her, Diego."

"I will." I pick up Isabel's stuff, and we head out into the dark, moonless night.

## CHAPTER 13

### *Diego: The Long Way Home*

The roads are jammed, and it takes us more than an hour to get out of the city. When we finally get to the old highway and start climbing up the canyon, we both let out a sigh of relief. The traffic is heavy, but not as bad as I expected.

Isabel glances in the back seat and then puts her hand on my thigh. "I can't believe you went shopping this morning. Thanks." She looks over at me. "I thought you were crazy when you bought all those dried beans and rice, but I was wrong. How did you know this would happen?"

I put my hand on top of hers. "I didn't. I was just being prudent."

"Prudent, my ass. You're a terrible liar, Diego. Did that guy who works for the Feds tip you off—you know, the one who had the photo of the sphere?"

"You mean Hank? No. I told you, I was just planning ahead—particularly now that I have someone else to worry about. It doesn't take a genius to put two and two together:

between the volcanoes, the riots, the bombings, and a world full of aging nukes, something was bound to go wrong eventually. Hopefully, it'll all blow over in a week or two—although I'm glad we're not living in California now." I squeeze her hand. "If you want something to eat, there are some dried mangoes in back."

She leans over the seat, pushes on the overhead light, and rummages around. "What's this?" She pulls a shiny gold box of condoms into the front seat, along with the bag of dried fruit, and then turns off the light and puts her seatbelt back on.

I attempt to make my voice sound nonchalant. "Impulse purchase. You know how guys are."

"Right." She tears open the bag of mangoes, and sets it between us.

"Thanks." I take a handful and then drive in silence for a bit.

"Talk." Her voice is flat, but I can hear the pain behind it.

There aren't any streetlights, and the old highway is dark and narrow, our headlights pushing back the blackness as we cut though the steep canyon.

"Okay," she says. "So we're done taking chances. Is that what this means?"

I let out a heavy sigh, trying to decide what to say.

She gazes out her window into the night. "Well, to be honest, I'm grateful we don't have to worry about taking care of a baby right now."

I glance over at her. "I agree, and I think we should keep it that way. But as soon as things improve, we can go back to trying. Okay?"

She tosses the box of condoms into the back seat. "Sounds like you've got it covered."

"I love you, Iz."

She leans her head against my shoulder, tears running

down her cheeks. "Ditto."

I kiss her hair. "Thanks for saying you'll marry me."

She wipes her face on my shirt. "It's not like I had any choice after you rescued me from a fire, snuck my kitten into the hospital, and presented me with a stolen wedding ring. How romantic is that?"

"About as romantic as you breaking into a burning building to see if I would come after you."

"Hah." She runs her hand up the inside of my thigh, across my groin, and into the waistband of my pants. "I saw the ketchup in the back."

"Easy there, Miss Sanborn, I'm trying to drive."

"Yes, I detect a certain stiffness in you."

"You do make it hard."

She puts her hand back on my thigh—and then lets it wander a bit.

I turn on the radio to see if there's any news, but the canyon walls are too steep, and the signal keeps cutting out—at least I hope that's what's causing the static. I switch over to Isabel's playlist. She slides her fingertips across my jeans and sings along with the music, her mellifluous voice and feather-light touch filling me with warmth and anticipation.

We speed on into the dark night, strangely calm in a world teetering on the edge of disaster.

A few minutes after we drive through a deserted mountain town, I veer off onto the dirt road that leads up to our property.

And then slam on the brakes.

We skid to a stop, dirt from the road creating a small cloud around the car. I switch off the music, and the sudden silence is disconcerting.

It takes a few seconds for the breeze to clear away the fine powder.

Less than a meter in front of the car is a heavy metal gate, one that has never been closed before.

"What the f—"

Isabel opens the door and hops out. "I got it."

I roll down my window. "Be careful!"

Cold mountain air pours in, and I shiver.

I put the car in reverse and inch backwards, the crackle of tires on gravel loud in the still night. I point the headlights on her and put the car back in gear, watching her untangle a heavy chain wrapped around the post. She's wearing a skirt and heels, her bare legs stark in the harsh light and her breath visible in the cold mountain air.

But before she can finish, a figure emerges from the shadows and grabs her from behind. I reach for the door handle just as she lets out a muted cry.

The intruder wrenches her around in front of the gate and puts a knife under her throat, his eyes on me. "Put your hands up where I can see them and get out of the car."

I glance over at the glove compartment.

*Why didn't I expect something like this? I should have been ready.*

He forces Isabel to take a step closer to the car and presses the knife against her neck.

She lets out a frightened shriek.

I hold my hands up. "Okay. Take whatever you want, just don't hurt her."

"Do what I say, and no one gets cut." He lifts Isabel's chin with the knife. "Now!"

"Okay, okay. I'm getting out." I push the car door open with my foot.

And then everything happens at once.

The heavy chain unwinds from the post with a loud clanging noise, and the massive barrier swings open.

It hits the guy in the back, and he lurches sideways out of its path, dragging Isabel with him. The gate pushes past them, groaning with disuse and picking up speed, and then it crashes into the hood of my car.

In one motion, Isabel grabs the guy's arm, twists around, and knees him hard in the groin. The bastard lashes out with the knife as he doubles over in pain.

I jump out. "Get away from him!"

The car is still in gear, and the moment my foot leaves the brake, the vehicle lurches forward.

Isabel shoves the guy into the dirt and kicks the knife away. "You bastard. You messed with the wrong woman." He makes a move toward the weapon, but she scrambles into the middle of the road and picks it up before he can.

I take a step toward them and then realize I can't get there in time. "Watch out for the car!"

She looks up into the approaching headlights, bright red blood visible on her thigh. She stumbles backwards just as the gate plows into her doubled-over attacker. The heavy metal bars push him through the dirt, and then the gate bangs against the post, stopping the vehicle not six inches away from Isabel.

"Get in the car!" I run up, leap into the driver's seat, and slam on the brakes.

The guy reaches out for her ankle, his shirt covered in blood, but she slips through the railing, and jumps back in.

I lock the doors and put the car in reverse, easing backwards until the gate swings all the way open. "How badly are you hurt?"

She takes a ragged breath and drops the knife on the floor. "I'm okay. Let's get out of here!"

"Are you sure you don't need a doctor?"

"Yes, damn it! I'll be fine until we get to the cabin. Go!"

The guy is still rolling around in the middle of the road.

I lean my head out the window. "You've got three seconds to get out of the way, and then I run you over." I set the back of my hand on Isabel's uninjured thigh. "There's a gun in the glove box, and it's loaded so be careful. Hand it to me, please." I hear her sharp intake of breath as I watch the guy attempt to crawl out of the way.

A moment later, she sets the cold metal weapon in my hand.

"This is going to be loud, so you may want to cover your ears." I twist sideways so I can get my right arm out the window and then lean my head out too. "If I ever see you again, I'll kill you." I release the safety and fire one shot into the dirt a few feet away from Isabel's attacker.

He limps up the steep embankment and disappears into the brush.

I roll up my window, engage the gun safety, and set the warm firearm between my thighs. "Put your seatbelt on, please." I hear her do it, and then I put the car in gear and drive through the open gate, thankful that the cabin is still eight long miles up the canyon.

## CHAPTER 14
### *Isabel: Right As Rain*

Iigh above me, a peregrine falcon circles over the ravine, her warning cry cutting through the stagnant air. I take a shallow breath and release it, feeling queasy. Even after nearly two months, the gash on my leg hasn't healed properly, and I feel like I have a low-grade fever.

Or maybe it's just the oppressive heat.

*God, it's hot.*

I'm alone on the deck looking through old medical journals for studies on natural infection fighters, but the words evaporate the moment I read them. Diego's off helping the neighbors repair their roof and won't be home until dark, and I have something I need to tell him—something I *have* to tell him.

I scoot my chair into the dwindling shade and gaze out into the forest. Pine trees stand motionless in the blistering sun, untouched by even a hint of a breeze. This time of year, afternoon thunderstorms usually break up the heat of the day, but there hasn't been a single drop of rain since the rogue nuke detonated.

And that's not the worst of it. No one knows how many people were killed by the resulting tsunami, but the wall of seawater managed to make its way into the Central Valley, wiping out crops and poisoning the soil with salt. It'll take decades for the US food supply to rebound—if it ever does—and a lot of folks will be going hungry in the meantime.

On top of that, no one knows what happened to the Russian ICBMs—some say the missiles never made it out of the silos, and others, that they were dumped in the Arctic Ocean or even Australia. Diego has a ham radio, and he gets most of our news that way, but so far, there hasn't been any talk of radioactive fallout. I guess we're lucky it hasn't gotten any worse.

I drop the magazine and shut my eyes—and hear the lock in the front door turn.

"Isabel?" Diego's voice is filled with trepidation, and my heart races. "Where are you? Seamus has been hurt!" Seamus is the ten-year-old boy who lives with his grandmother in the cabin that Diego has been roofing.

"I'm out here!" I say, wincing as I stand up.

*The infection in my leg is getting worse.*

Diego jogs out on the deck, breathing hard and sweat trickling down his face.

The knot of dread in my chest twists tighter, pushing bile up in my throat. "What happened? Are you okay?"

"Yeah. I'm fine. Just winded from running uphill. Seamus fell off the roof and broke his leg. I told Mrs. Malloy I'd bring you over in the car. Do you feel up to going?"

"Yes, of course. Could you grab the box of medical supplies in the basement, please, and I'll get my bag."

∞

Diego has been hiking back and forth to the Malloys, so it's been weeks since we took the car anywhere, and the roads have definitely gotten worse. Between the huge pot-holes, the heavy dust, and the sweltering heat, I'm worried we won't make it. But thirty minutes later, I sit down next to a red-haired kid who looks like a skinny Ron Weasley.

"Hey, Seamus," I say. "I hear you were playing Quidditch and got knocked off your broom."

"Fraid it wasn't quite that spectacular, miss. I fell off the roof."

"I won't tell, if you won't." I smile and then check his pupils. "How hard did you hit your head?"

"Not very. It's mostly my leg that hurts."

I glance at Mrs. Malloy, a nurse midwife, and she nods in agreement.

"Okay if I take a look?" I ask him.

"Sure."

I lift the bag of ice and move my hands gently across his cool skin. His leg is bent in a way it shouldn't be, but no bones are sticking out. "I'm guessing it's a greenstick frac-ture, but I can't be sure without an x-ray. We should take him to a hospital."

His grandmother shakes her head and pulls Diego and me out into the hallway. "I spoke to a man on the short-wave a week ago. He drove all the way to Cheyenne looking for heart medication for his wife. Said all the hospitals are burned or looted. On the way back, he got trapped in a dead end by a gang of looters and nearly lost his truck—and his life. All in all, he spent four days and eighty gallons of gas and came back with nothing but a smashed windshield and a bad taste in his mouth."

Diego gives me a worried look. "So no x-rays."

"You're a doctor. What would you do if Seamus were your son?" Mrs. Malloy asks me, her face lined with worry.

"Straighten his leg and put a splint on it. He's young and healthy, and I think he'll be fine."

She nods. "Tell me what I can do to help."

"I'll get the box out of the car," Diego says, and I go to the kitchen to wash my hands.

"Alright," I say to Seamus when we walk back in, "I'm going to give you a shot that will help with the pain, and then I'm going to straighten your leg. It's still going to hurt, but I'll try to be quick."

"Yes, miss." His face is pale. "I'll hold real still."

I give him a shot of morphine and then realign the bone. It's not as difficult as I expected, and when it's back in place, His grandmother helps me put a splint on it.

"All done," I say, clasping my hands together to keep them from trembling. "You were very brave, Seamus."

"Ah, it didn't hurt that much." He smiles for the first time, his eyes glossy. "Thank you for fixing me up."

"You're welcome." I put a pillow under his leg and re-apply the cold pack. "Keep it elevated and continue icing it twenty minutes on, twenty minutes off until tomorrow night." I turn to Mrs. Malloy. "Keep an eye on his toes—make sure they stay pink. Do you have over-the-counter pain meds to give him?"

"Yes, plenty. Thank you so much. I don't know what I'd do without the two of you."

"We're happy to help," I say and give the boy a kiss on the forehead. "You're going to be just fine, Seamus. I'll send more books with Diego tomorrow so you have something to read while your leg is healing."

"That would be awesome, Miss Isabel."

Mrs. Malloy, who has a milk cow and chickens, insists that we take cheese, butter, and eggs, and we gratefully accept. She asks about the wound in my thigh, and I tell her not to worry. "I wash it with saline solution every night."

She and Diego exchange looks, but neither of them comment.

"I'll talk to you this evening at eight," Diego says as we get in the car. "See how Seamus is doing."

"Thank you, Diego. I'll look forward to chatting with you." She watches us turn the car around and then waves. "Drive safe."

I spend the next thirty minutes attempting to tell Diego my news, but no matter how hard I try, I can't seem to get the words to come out.

∞

The sun is setting as we drive up to the cabin. Diego parks in the garage and then writes the mileage and gas level in a small notebook. I give him a concerned look and he laughs. "No worries. I just want to keep track, so I know how much we have left."

I do the same with the medical supplies while he takes a shower.

A few minutes later, he joins me out on the deck. "Can I get you something to drink? Wine? Beer?"

"No, thanks. I'm good with just the water."

"Okay. Be right back." He disappears into the kitchen and returns with bread, cheese, and a glass of wine. After he sits down, he tears off a chunk of bread, sets a piece of cheese on it, and hands it to me on a napkin. He does the same for himself and then leans back, and we watch the dusk settle across the mountains. The falcon is soaring below coral-tinted clouds.

*Tell him!*

But I can't say it. "Who would have thought that a hundred thousand tons of volcanic ash could look so beautiful?"

"It does make for a nice gloaming." He winks.

I sniff the cheese, and my stomach turns.

111

"Are you sure you're alright?"

I set it on his napkin and bite into the bread. "Yes, I'm fine, thanks. Just not hungry for cheese."

"Okay. Sure I can't get you a glass of wine? You look like you could use it." He shakes his head. "I still can't believe you just bent Seamus's bone back into place. And, by the way, that's one excellent bedside manner you have. Seamus is madly in love with you already."

"He's a nice kid. I hope his leg heals properly."

We sit in silence for a bit, watching the falcon hunt.

I swallow the bile collecting in my throat and force the words out. "I have something I need to tell you."

"Okay." He takes a sip of wine. "What's up?"

I drop my gaze and fight back the urge to cry.

"What is it, Iz?"

"I'm pregnant."

He tries to set down his wineglass, but it grazes the arm of the chair and shatters in his hand. "Shit." He looks down at the mess and then at me, red wine dripping from his open palm. "I don't mean 'shit, you're pregnant', I mean 'shit, I broke the glass.'"

I laugh uncomfortably.

He stares at my stomach, his eyes big, and then he glances at his hand. "I'll be right back." He returns with a broom and starts sweeping up the glass shards. "How could you be pregnant, Iz? We've been using contraception for weeks. Months, in fact."

"I was already pregnant."

He stands there with his mouth open.

A wave of nausea overwhelms me, and I rush to the edge of the deck, vomiting into the dirt ten feet below. I feel dizzy, and it's all I can do not to pass out. I lean over the railing, my whole body shaking, and spit the vile taste out of my mouth.

*Oh my god, what am I going to do?*

112

He puts his hand on my back and offers me a cool, damp washcloth. "I guess I don't have to ask if you're sure."

I wipe my face and take a shaky breath. "Watch out, or I'll barf on your shoes."

He laughs. "I've had worse." He takes the washcloth and hands me a cold ginger ale. "You want to sit down?"

I nod, and he helps me back to the chair and then perches on the ottoman in front of me. I take another drink of the ginger ale, feeling a little better.

"How far along are you?"

"Ten weeks, possibly more. I've been feeling sick for a couple of months."

"Shit, I'm sorry." He leans over, puts his elbows on his thighs, and takes my hands in his. "I should have been paying more attention. I knew something was wrong, but I had no idea you were pregnant. Christ, I'm sorry."

"It's not your fault, Diego. We both wanted to try." I choke back a sour burp. "So what do we do now?"

He looks down at his hands, and I turn away, afraid to guess what he's thinking.

"Hey. It's not like that at all, Iz." He waits for me to look at him. "Mrs. Malloy told me there's a flea market down at the old Walmart, first Saturday of every month if the weather's good. She says they mostly barter for food and guns, but I'll go check it out next month. See what I can find."

"I'm going with you. I don't want to be here alone anymore." A tear runs down my face, and he wipes it away with his thumb.

"Okay, we'll go together. We'll need diapers and baby clothes and—" He holds my gaze. "And your leg is taking a long time to heal, so we'll find some antibiotics too."

I nod, my eyes filled with tears.

A breeze rustles through the aspens and tousles his hair. We watch it gust up the ravine, picking up speed as it crests the pine-covered ridge, a puff of air transformed into a tempest.

"I'm sorry," I say. "I should have told you sooner, but I was scared." I choke back a sob. "Scared you wouldn't want to have—"

"Shh." He takes the glass out of my hand and sets in on the deck, and then he pulls me up into a hug. "I love you, Iz, and that's all that matters."

I give up and cry against his chest.

"Everything is going to be all right, Isabel." He leans his head against mine and strokes my hair. "Mrs. Malloy is a midwife, for chrissake, and Seamus will be thrilled to have someone to play with. We'll figure it out, hun. "

A minute later, a raindrop hits the deck with a *spat*, and we both turn toward the sound. The drop of water evaporates at once, leaving a reddish-gray stain on the wood.

"Come on," he says. "Let's get inside."

A moment later, it's pouring.

## CHAPTER 15

### *Diego: Second Chances*

Isabel lies naked in my arms, both of us gazing out the bedroom window at the full moon. Between work on the cabin, finishing the Malloys' roof, and taking care of Isabel, the days fly by. If it weren't for the dire state of the world, I'd say I've never been happier.

Still, the infection in her thigh has me worried. She insists that it's normal for deep wounds to take a long time to heal, especially with the added stress of pregnancy, but I'm not sure I believe her, especially after three months.

I just wish I knew what to do about it. It hasn't stopped raining since she told me two weeks ago, and even if we could just drive down to the local clinic and pick up some antibiotics, there's no way we could get the car out in all this mud.

She snuggles against my chest, and I kiss the nape of her neck and then run my fingers lightly across her bare back. As we watch, the pale goddess of the night dips into the soot-choked lower atmosphere and is bathed in blood.

*Not a good omen in anyone's book.*

"It was six months ago tonight that you saved me." The warmth in her voice shatters my gloom.

"*Mierda*, you almost killed me." I nuzzle her hair, breathing in the scent of lavender soap mixed with sweaty sex—and feel myself getting hard again.

*I might end up being keen on this 'nobody gets to come' thing we have going.*

"At the restaurant?" she asks, her tone amused, "or in the fire?"

I kiss her nose. "Both." Her dark brown hair has strands of silver, and there are laugh lines around her eyes, but I adore every bit of her. Despite everything, the last few months have been the best of my life.

"Well the first time around, *you* almost killed *me*, Captain America." She rolls onto her back. "What a fiasco! We were so young and stupid."

She says *we*, but she means *you*.

I bite back a quick retort and caress her hair, letting an errant curl slide through my fingertips. I've learned a bit about dealing with her in the intervening years, and this time around, I find it easy to manage, even enjoy, these moments.

*Or maybe my armor is just thicker.*

I lean over and kiss her on the mouth, but she pulls away. "Why were you so apprehensive the first time around?"

"I was only twenty-four. Iz. And I wasn't apprehensive, I was scared stiff. Painfully stiff."

She ignores my innuendo. "I kept trying to make things work and you kept panicking. Good grief, you were afraid to walk me to my car."

"And for good reason. What was that guy's name, the one you played all the sports with? He kept trying to run me over in the parking lot."

"Kevin. And he never would have done that."

I nuzzle her ear.

*Yes, he would. He would have done anything to keep you, just like all the other guys—me included.*

"I had forgotten about him." Her voice is wistful.

"Yeah?" I say. "Well, if you ask me, the guy was clueless."

"So, why did you give up so easily?"

I pull her back against my chest. "I tried to make it work the best I knew how, Iz, but you got so damn impatient. Big surprise there."

She gives me an annoyed look.

"*Now* I understand what you wanted—what I wasn't able to give you—but back then I suffered just as much as you did. Perhaps more."

"Wasn't I worth fighting for, at least a little?"

"Isabel, my beautiful and mistaken love." I push her over on her back and trace the soft curve of her breast with my fingertips. "I fought with everything I had, and some things I didn't. I tried to be all that you wanted, sometimes losing myself in the process. It nearly killed me when you told me you wanted to go out with other guys—and I had only just met you!"

"Well, why didn't you say so?"

"I'm sure I did." I glide my lips across her shoulder and down between her breasts.

"No, you didn't. I remember that specifically, because I wanted you to. I wanted you to step up and be The Guy, but you just went with the flow, until the course got too rocky and then you bailed out."

I turn my head to the side and rest it on her shoulder. "I did not *bail out*, Iz."

"And, in the middle of everything, you stormed into my office and accused me of high treason for playing basketball with some short guy whose name I can't even remember."

*Damned if I do, and damned if I don't.*

She takes my face in her hands. "If you were so jealous, why didn't you just learn to play basketball, for godsake?" She releases me and stares out the window. "You never gave us a chance."

"Uh huh."

"Even before you got on that plane, I felt abandoned, Diego. I told you I couldn't take any more of the roller coaster ride." She has this uncanny ability to remember things nearly word-for-word, and the roller coaster bit rings true. "I needed someone to be there, and I wanted it to be you. God, I wanted it to be you."

I wrap my arms around her. "I love you, Isabel Sanborn. I have loved you since the first time I held you in my arms all those years ago." I sweep an errant lock of hair away from her face. "But I can't change the past, so the here and now will have to be enough. And for once in my life, I think it will be."

"Me too."

I slide my fingertips across her shoulder, down her arm, and leisurely around her still-flat belly. Earlier today, Mrs. Malloy used a portable ultrasound to determine that Isabel is fifteen weeks pregnant, and that we're having twins: a boy and a girl! I press my palm against her belly, knowing it's too early to feel anything, but still hoping. "Twins, huh? I should have known you wouldn't go for anything average."

She nips me on my shoulder.

"Ouch!" I run my fingers across her soft skin as rain spatters against the window and darkness falls. "What do you say we name them Nicholas and Alexandra, or Tristan and Isolde? I think Romeo and Juliet might be a bit much, but Tristan and Juliet has a sort of ring to it."

"They're siblings, Diego, not lovers."

118

"Oh, all right. You can name them Jaime and Cersei for all I care, but the first thing I'm getting for them is a soccer ball. One for each."

She brings her mouth up to mine, a smile on her lips. "How very practical of you."

# CHAPTER 16

## *Diego: Get in Line*

I dab Isabel's forehead with a cool washcloth, feeling next to useless. She lets out a whimper that slowly builds to a wail, the agony visible on her face. "Isn't there something we can do? A morphine injection like she gave Seamus? Or liquor, even?"

Mrs. Malloy puts her hand on my arm. "Anything we give her will only delay the inevitable, Diego. Now that the labor has started, her body needs to finish it."

"I can't stand to watch her suffer, Molly."

She squeezes my arm. "I know it's tough, but the miscarriage may be for the best. Carrying twins is an enormous strain on a woman's body, even when she's healthy."

"So there's no hope for the babies?"

"I'm sorry, but the little ones went off to Heaven before the bleeding started. I know it's not much consolation, but most women can get pregnant again within a few months. Once Isabel recovers, you could always try again."

*Hell no. Why would I put her though this another time?*

I wipe my face on my sleeve and turn back to Iz. She has her eyes shut and her hair is matted with sweat. Instead of gaining weight, she's lost it, and her cheeks are sunken and pale. The high fever started a week ago and Mrs. Malloy—Molly—and I have been unable to bring it down for more than a few hours. I know it's because the gash in Isabel's thigh is infected, and I also know that no amount of saline solution and topical salve is going to cure it. She needs antibiotics, and fast.

*Why did it take me so long to see that? If I had done something sooner, maybe I could have saved the twins.*

"If she'll let you," Molly says, "keep sponging her face and chest. We need to keep that fever down as much as possible. I wish I could do more, but as sick as she is, she should be in a hospital."

Isabel lets out a whimper, her face contorted with pain and her hands gripping the sheets so hard that her skin is ghostly white.

"I'm sorry, hun. I wish there was something I could do." I dip the sponge into the tepid water and touch it to her forehead.

She convulses with the strain of the contraction, spilling the basin of water onto the floor. "Please, Diego. Make it stop! I don't want to lose my babies. I'd rather die than lose the twins."

Mrs. Malloy catches my eye, shakes her head, and then mouths the words: "It will pass."

I get a clean towel off the stack on the dresser, wipe up the mess, and then go to the kitchen to refill the basin. Over the last few months, the twins have become a powerful bond between Isabel and me, a hopeful force pushing us toward the future. But now that they are gone, I'm scared that Isabel will stop fighting, and the infection will kill her.

121

*Now. You have to go now and get help before it's too late.*

Outside, freezing rain has been pouring down for weeks and the roads are impassable. I've let that—and the fact that Isabel keeps begging me not to leave her—be an excuse not to act. But there'll be no more excuses. I can't save the twins, but I can try to save her.

I swallow hard and go back in with Isabel.

Mrs. Malloy is trying to get her to sit up, but not having much success. "Please put the basin down and help me, Diego." Her voice has an edge, and it scares me. "If you sit behind her and help her stay upright, the contractions will do more good. She's close to exhaustion, and we're going to need her to push."

I lift up Isabel's head and shoulders—she weighs almost nothing—and then slip in behind her, letting her back rest against my chest. She collapses against me, tears streaming down her cheeks. "I'm sorry, Diego. I tried to save them, but—"

"Shh. It's going to be okay, Iz." I stroke her hair as lightly as I can, afraid that I might hurt her.

Mrs. Malloy places her hand on Isabel's swollen abdomen. "We're waiting for the next contraction, dearie, and then I'm going to need you to push hard. It's going to hurt, so don't be afraid to raise your voice."

"I can't," Isabel says. "I'm too tired. Please. Just let me sleep."

The midwife looks up at me, her eyes pleading.

I kiss Isabel's hair, my heart breaking. "I love you, hun. And I need you. Don't give up on me now."

A minute later, I feel the contraction seize her body. She lets out a cry, her whole torso shaking with the exertion. Molly nods at me, her face pale.

"Push, Isabel," I say. "Push as hard as you can."

She grabs onto my wrists and presses back against my

chest, her eyes squeezed shut. Sweat drips down her face, and she lets out a high-pitched wail that morphs into a shriek.

The sound goes on for longer than anyone should have to be in pain.

And then she collapses against me, sobbing and trembling, and I see a small head slip out of her body.

"Good work, dearie!" Mrs. Malloy says, looking very relieved. "The second one will be easier." She lifts the tiny infant, cuts the umbilical cord, and wraps it in a small, hand-knitted blanket.

Isabel reaches out. "Let me see my baby... please?"

Mrs. Malloy gives me a concerned look and then hands the small bundle to Iz. "She's a beautiful little girl, but she's an angel now."

I can feel another contraction take over Isabel's body, less than a minute from the last! She closes her eyes and then cries out as she bears down, her whole body shaking. Another head appears.

"Good girl! We're almost done now, and this last part shouldn't hurt." Mrs. Malloy wraps up the second baby and lays it in Isabel's other arm. "Perfect little boy, God rest his soul."

For a moment, the clouds part, and a ray of late-afternoon sunlight falls across us.

"Her name is Soleil," Isabel says. "And his name is Lucas. I want you to bury them by the outcropping of rocks where they will be in the sunshine."

Tears stream down my cheeks. "Okay, Iz. I will." I stare into the small faces and then run my fingertip across the girl's tiny chin. "She has your eyes."

Isabel picks up the boy's little hand. "And he has your fingers."

Mrs. Malloy lets out a soft sigh as she attends to the afterbirth. "They are beautiful babies."

Isabel collapses against me, still holding the twins in her arms. "I'm sorry I couldn't save them, Diego. I tried as hard as I could." Her eyes flutter shut.

I wrap my arms around all three of them and lean my head against Isabel's. She's asleep in a matter of seconds, but I lie there on the bed as the light fades, her feverish body pressed against mine, and cry.

When the room is dark, I carefully get up, tuck the blankets in around Isabel, and tiptoe into the kitchen to talk with Mrs. Malloy.

The next morning, I get up at first light and get dressed. It's still raining, but that can no longer deter me. I take the small bundles from the kitchen, stop by the garage to get a shovel, and then hike over to the point. Huge boulders loom above the swollen stream twenty meters below, and from here, you can see for miles.

I set the tiny bundles down and begin digging.

And after I finish, I sit down on the rocks overlooking the stream, rain soaking through my clothes, and stare up into the stormy sky, angry at the whole damn universe.

*Just this once, let me do the right thing and save her.*

I head back to the cabin, change my clothes, and throw some things in a backpack. Mrs. Malloy pushes a bowl of oatmeal across the table to me. "Eat. It may be the last hot food you see for a while."

"I'll be back as soon as I can, Molly. Thank you for staying."

She hands me a sandwich wrapped in a hankie. "For later. We'll be fine, Diego. We have everything we need, and Seamus will be over to check on us as soon as the rain lets up."

"I can't thank you enough... for last night and for..."

"Go. And come back soon. She needs you, Diego." She motions with her head toward the bedroom. "But don't leave without saying goodbye. You owe her that."

I sit down on the bed next to Isabel and run my hand across her feverish face, frightened by how frail she looks. "Hey, beautiful. I came to say goodbye."

Her eyes flicker open. "You said you'd never leave me, Captain America."

"I have to, Iz."

She turns away.

"But I'll be back. I promise. Wait for me. Please. Say you'll wait for me."

Her eyes fill with tears, and then she looks up at me. "I miss the twins. I'm sorry I wasn't strong enough to—"

I take her in my arms. "It's not your fault, Iz. And it doesn't matter now. All I care about is you getting well." I stroke her hair. "Once you're better, we can always try again."

She lets her head fall against my shoulder. "I think I would like that."

"Me too." I place her gently back down on the bed and then adjust the pillow. "I'm going to be gone for a few days, maybe even a week, but Mrs. Malloy will stay with you until I get back."

She takes my hand, her pallid skin hot to the touch. "Please don't go."

I smile at her through my tears. "I have to, hun. I have to try and get help." I stand up, but she holds onto my hand.

"I'll never see you again."

"Don't say that, Iz." I bend over and kiss her on the forehead. "I will always come for you."

She squeezes my hand. "Don't take too long."

I kiss her palm, and then steal one last look at the only woman I've ever loved—and force myself to walk out the door.

I use the spare key to turn the deadbolt, put it back underneath the third stair, and then pull the hood up on my poncho and jog out into the downpour, feeling exhausted and morose. I stop at the graves and place a small, fuzzy *futbol* next to each pile of stones and then start hiking down the mountain.

The freezing rain continues all morning, reminding me just how screwed up things have gotten: it's December, months past when the snow usually starts, and we've had nothing but torrential rain.

*Somewhere there must be one horrendous drought.*

At the bottom of the ravine, I stop to get a drink, still frustrated that all my plans to handle an emergency turned out to be so useless. The SUV has a full tank, plus I have forty gallons of gasoline in the garage. But even with snow cables on, I couldn't get the car to go ten feet without sinking up to the axles in mud.

I take one last look at the rocky outcrop and then continue down into the canyon.

I hike for an hour in the pouring rain, and when I get to the bottom of the ravine, I realize that the stream is too high to cross.

*Shit.*

I end up wasting an hour searching for a tree to push over, and then another hour backtracking up the canyon, trying to find a place where I can jump across—and every minute feels like a lifetime.

*Wait for me, Iz.*

I finally find a narrow section of the stream where I can jump from boulder to boulder, but the icy torrent is deep and fast moving in between the huge stones, and if I slip and fall, it will be all over.

*If I don't get across soon, it won't matter anyway.*

At least the damn rain has stopped. I take a run for it and vault over to the first rock, but my backpack is heavier than I anticipated, and its momentum nearly pushes me into the cold water. I balance on the slippery boulder and take off the pack, and then load the essentials into a small daypack and put that on. I heave the backpack over to the opposite bank, but it lands short and is quickly swept downstream.

*Shit. There goes my clothes and sleeping bag.*

I manage to cross to the opposite side, but not without landing waist-deep in the icy current and being forced to scramble up the muddy bank on my hands and knees. I peel off my jeans and attempt to wring them out, shivering the whole time. I consider starting a fire, but I don't want to waste any more daylight, so I put my pants back on, change into dry socks, and hike up the other side of the ravine, the cold, damp cotton chafing against my skin.

By the time I get down to the highway, my mud-caked clothes are almost dry, but the light is fading fast. I start trudging down the cracked asphalt, trying to guess how far I am from town.

*Maybe seven or eight miles?*

An hour later, I see a sign: "Aerie Town: 21 miles."

*It's going to take me all night.*

I'm getting a blister on my heel from the wet boots, so I sit down in front of a burned-out Walmart and dig out my last pair of dry socks. I don't have any idea what phase of the moon it is, or if it will even matter with all the cloud cover, but now that I've stopped moving, I'm freezing.

*Where is everyone?*

I could hole up in the Walmart for the night, but I decide to keep going—and just hope that the weather holds. I take out Mrs. Malloy's sandwich and then put on my daypack and start walking. The wind kicks up, and the charred pages from a catalog blow across the empty highway. One snags on my ankle, and I pick it up and stare into the happy face of a chubby baby. I stuff the paper into my pocket and continue on, unable to get the image of that first shovel of damp earth on hand-knit blankets out of my head.

*Why did she have to have Isabel's beautiful green eyes?*

I'm going to see those tiny faces in my nightmares for the rest of my life.

Ten minutes later, it starts raining again. I pull up the hood of my bright yellow poncho and keep walking. As the subdued light fades to black, the miles go by in a slow, soggy monotony—alarmingly hot skin and pale, hollow cheeks pushing me forward.

And then I see headlights.

The memory of the incident at the gate fills me with dread, and I consider hiding.

*What if it's a carload of looters? Or worse?*

"Or it could be my last chance to save Isabel." I reach inside my poncho and check the gun, and then stand out in the road and wave my arms.

The massive SUV stops ten feet away, the headlights blinding me. A male voice calls out in the rain. "Who are you?"

"I need a doctor. My fiancé is sick and needs antibiotics or she'll die."

"Put your hands up where we can see them."

I do as I'm told, convinced that if they were murderers, they would have just run over me.

"What's your name, sir?"

I let out a sigh of relief at the honorific.

*They must be military.*

"Diego Nadales. I need help. Please." I lower my hands. The SUV inches forward and stops next to me, the huge engine loud in the rainy dark.

Someone shines a flashlight in my face. "Shitty night to be out walking, Mr. Nadales."

"Tell me about it."

The light goes off. "Hand over your weapon and get in."

I stare into the passenger-side window at two men in white shirts and ties. "I don't have anything except food and wet socks."

The driver leans over to get a better look at me. "If you want to save that woman of yours, I suggest you follow orders, sir."

I hold up my hands again. "Okay, okay. I have a sidearm. But I want it back when this is over."

The guy riding shotgun snorts. "Yeah, and I want to ball Miss America. Get in."

After I hand over the gun, I duck into the backseat and toss my stuff into the cavernous rear. The moment I shut my door, the lock engages. Warm air buffets my face as I rub my hands together in front of the heater vent. "Thank you."

The guy in the front seat turns around. "Actually, we've been looking for you, Mr. Nadales."

"You have?" I can't keep the surprise out of my voice.

"I'm Mr. Johnson," he says and then gestures toward the driver, a guy who appears to be just out of diapers. "And this is Mr. Smith. We work for the government."

*Oh, shit.*

Mr. Smith glances over the seat at my muddy boots, and then meets my eyes, his mouth tight with a fake smile. "Mr. Nadales." He puts the car in drive and makes a U-turn.

"Where are you taking me?" Panic leaks out of my voice.

Mr. Smith accelerates hard into the downpour. "To get a doctor, sir. Just relax. We'll be there soon."

I sit back and look around. The inside of the SUV is immaculate: black leather seats that still smell new and an expensive-looking GPS system that is bigger than my computer.

"Nice wheels you have. Where'd you get the gas?"

"That's classified, sir."

An odd feeling comes over me, but given all that's happened in the last twenty-four hours, I'm not sure what to make of it. My emotions are a mess, I'm exhausted from the trek down the mountain, and I'm running on two hours of sleep. I brush off the uneasiness and settle back into the leather seat, staring out at the raindrops racing sideways across the tinted window.

We head down the pass, the heavy rain and drenched roads eerily silent inside the massive vehicle. I close my eyes and try to rest for the thirty minutes it's going to take, hoping to get back to the cabin tonight.

∞

My upper body shifts as the car goes around a tight curve, and I open my eyes. I must have dozed off, and it takes me a minute to realize where we are—or rather, where we aren't.

"Hey?" I say. "We passed the town. I need to find a doctor and get back to the cabin." I try to keep the desperation out of my voice. "Tonight."

"Don't worry. We'll be there soon, sir."

I lean over the front seat, attempting to see what's on the computer. "Where are you taking me?" There's text on the display but no map.

The guy picks up a three-ring notebook and tosses it over onto the seat next to me. "Like I said, we work for the government, Mr. Nadales, and you have been selected to assist in a top secret project of grave importance to the American people."

"Screw the American people. I'm a citizen of Costa Rica, and I need to get back to Isabel." I shove the notebook onto the floor. "Stop the car. I'm getting out." I reach over into the cargo area, drag my backpack onto the seat next to me, and then kick mud all over the back of Mr. Johnson's pristine seat. "I said stop the goddamn car."

The guys exchange looks. "We can't do that, sir. You're part of the project now, and our orders are to take you

130

directly to the mountain. We have the authority to do it by force, if that's what it takes."

Johnson jingles a set of plastic handcuffs over his shoulder. "If you would read the first few pages of the report, you'll understand why the mission is so critical."

I yank on the door handle. "Let me out of the fucking car!"

"Calm down, Mr. Nadales, and then we'll see what can be done to save your wife."

"God, I wish she was my wife—you goons destroyed the world before I had a chance to marry her!"

The driver glances over at Johnson, and he nods. The young guy peers at me in the rear-view mirror, his pale skin making him look like a vampire. "In exchange for your full cooperation, we will request that a medical team be dispatched in the morning, sir. Antibiotics, IVs, painkillers, the works."

I slam my hands down on the back of their seat. "She could die tonight, you assholes. I'm not going anywhere until I know she's okay." I lunge for my gun, but the guy slams *his* pistol into my face, and I fall back in a daze, blood trickling down from my nose.

He glances over his shoulder at me. "Sorry about that, but I did advise you to calm down. We've been searching for you for weeks, Nadales, and there's no way we're letting you out of the car tonight. Our orders are to get you inside the mountain, and that's what we intend to do."

"If I'm that goddamn important, then send a helicopter with antibiotics up to the cabin tonight. I'll give you the GPS coordinates." I wipe the blood off with my sleeve. "Save Isabel, and I'll do whatever you want."

The guy who calls himself Johnson types something into the computer. "I'd say the chances of that are negative zero, but I'll put in your request."

A few minutes later the console beeps and Johnson reads the response. "Holy shit, you must have some powerful friends in high places." He turns so he can look me in the face. "You give me your word that if we get medical attention to her tonight, you'll cooperate fully?"

"Yes. But if I find out you lied to me, I will hunt you down and flay you with a rusty penknife."

"Yeah, get in line."

The driver chuckles. "Like that's any worse than what's already coming down the pike."

## CHAPTER 17

## *Isabel: Out of the Blue*

I'm awakened by a loud thumping noise, and it takes me a moment to realize that it's not coming from inside my head. The windows are dark, but lights flash across the ceiling and walls of the bedroom. I lie there in a feverish stupor, the sheets sticking to me, and wonder why an alien spaceship would be hovering over the cabin.

Just as I close my eyes, I hear male voices in the hallway, and my heart beats a little stronger.

*He's back?*

The bedroom door opens, and a bright light blinds me. "Are you Isabel Sanborn-Kirkland?"

I stare up into the dazzling brilliance. "Diego?"

"Don't worry, ma'am. Your husband is waiting for you at the hospital. We have orders to transport you there immediately." The light shifts, and I hear more footsteps. "Get an IV started and then give her five cc's of clindamycin. When you're done, move her to the Black Hawk and start oh-two.

I'll get the laptop and meet you there. Once we're airborne, you can take vitals. I don't want to be on the ground a minute more than required."

"Yes, sir." Someone with cold hands lifts my wrist. "Just relax, ma'am. We're paramedics."

There's a poke in my arm, and the sound of tape being torn. A minute later, I'm lifted onto a gurney and rolled out the front door. I hear Mrs. Malloy's relieved voice. "Thank goodness Diego got to you in time."

Cold raindrops spatter against my face as the men jostle me toward the bright lights. I notice two small piles of stones casting long shadows over by the rock outcropping and wonder who did that, the aliens?

I'm lifted into the helicopter and the door slides shut.

"Get us out of here, lieutenant." Someone puts an oxygen mask over my face and covers me with another blanket. The sound of gravity being beaten into submission blocks out the rest of the world, and I drift off into oblivion.

Sometime later—hours or perhaps days, I can't say for sure which—I dream I'm back in the hotel fire, the smashed piano resting next to me on the hard atrium floor. In the back of my mind, I know that Diego will be here soon, and once he finds me, everything will be okay. So I force down my apprehensions and lie there in the dark, watching the flames leap closer.

"Isabel?"

I try to reply, but in the dream, I'm mute. My heart races. *What if he can't find me?*

And then I remember that I need to press the piano keys. If he hears them, he'll know I'm alive. I try to reach out, but my arm is tangled up in something.

*Diego! Don't leave me!*

"Isabel? Can you hear me?" I feel him lift my hand, and relief washes over me.

The dream fades…

"Hey, princess. How are you feeling?"

I open my eyes, trying to clear the cobwebs in my brain, and stare up into Dave's smiling face.

"Welcome to the world of the living."

I let out a startled cry, fully awake.

He laughs. "Nice to see you too."

I lie there for a minute, trying to put all the pieces together, and then glance around the hospital room. "Where's Diego?"

"How the hell should I know? He dumped you just like he did the last time—hung around long enough to get you pregnant and then high-tailed it out of the country, the bastard."

I try to sit up, but my arm is tangled in the IV. "You tricked me!"

"No," he says, "I just saved your ass. Maybe you could show a little appreciation."

A pretty nurse walks in carrying a small tray. She nods at Dave and smiles at me. "Good evening, Mrs. Kirkland! How are you feeling?" She sets down the tray and holds out a small cup of pills and a glass of water. "Oh, you look so much better already."

*Mrs. Kirkland?*

Dave takes the cups out of her hands. "My wife is still a bit disoriented, but I'll see that she takes these before I leave."

"I'm not his wife," I say, "and I'm not taking any more drugs."

The nurse raises her eyebrows.

"Thank you, lieutenant—" Dave glances at her badge. "Wilson. That will be all for now."

"Yes, Mr. Kirkland. I'll be back in twenty minutes to check on her, sir." The nurse walks out, Dave's eyes glued to *her* ass.

I round on him. "Why did she just call me Mrs. Kirkland, and why did you just say that I'm your wife? We're divorced,

Dave. Remember?"

"Will you give me a minute?" He sets the medicine down on the nightstand and runs his hands through his thinning hair. "Or shall I just get you a flamethrower?"

I roll my eyes and try to sit up.

"Here. Let me help." He lifts up my shoulders and stuffs two pillows behind my back. "What the hell possessed you to go live in that shack in the woods, Isabel? You should have come here months ago—both of you. Bad shit is coming down, and I can't protect you out there." He fluffs the pillows and softens his tone. "Better?"

"Yes," I say. "Thank you. Where are we?"

"In a military hospital on Powers Air Force base. You've been here for almost two weeks, but the doctor kept you sedated until your fever broke this afternoon. Between the blood loss, the deep gash on your thigh, and the sepsis, we weren't sure you were going to make it."

I untangle my IV and slide my hands under the covers. My breasts are tender to the touch, but my stomach is squishy and flat. The revelation bubbles up panic in my chest, and I can feel my heart pounding. "Where are the twins?"

He rubs the back of his neck.

"I was pregnant, Dave, with twins." I force the words out. "Where are they? I want to see them."

He meets my gaze, the self-assured look on his face wavering. "You had a miscarriage, Isabel. Before I could get to you."

And then it all comes flooding back… the pain, the blood, the tiny lifeless fingers.

"Oh god, no." I cover my face with my hands, the two piles of stones casting long shadows vivid in my memory now. "They died, and Diego buried them. I've… lost the babies."

"Yes. I'm sorry. If you had come to me sooner, it could

have turned out differently." He strokes my face and hair. "I can't believe that bastard abandoned you when you were pregnant and dying. If I could get my hands on him, I'd wring his useless neck."

I push him away. "He didn't abandon me, Dave, he went for help."

"Yeah? Well, he waited too fucking long." He holds my shoulders and looks into my face. "But you're going to be fine now, princess. Just fine."

"Thank you for sending the helicopter." I pull away from him and lean back into the pillow. "I do appreciate all you've done for me, Dave, but I want to go home."

"Take your meds, and we'll talk in the morning." He holds out the cup and pills.

"Why did you tell the nurse I'm your wife?" I ask, still not putting all the pieces together.

"I had to use all the resources at my disposal. Jet fuel is nearly impossible to get, and it's dangerous to fly in remote areas." He tucks the covers in around me. "So I exaggerated a little."

"How did you know where to find me? And that I was dying?"

"Now, princess. Long story, and you don't need to worry about that right now. The important thing is you're safe."

I force my brain to work. "Diego told you, didn't he? He made it down the mountain and got help."

*It all makes sense now.*

"You know, Isabel, I still love you. I'd be willing to call it all off if you'd stay here—"

"Don't start, Dave. All we did was fight. Since the first time you tried to jump me."

"Yeah, but the sex was always good."

I let out a cynical laugh. "You don't love me. You just want me in your harem." I glance away. "I want to go home.

Please."

"If that's what you want, I'll see what I can do."

"Thank you." I look more carefully at him. "So what are you doing at an Air Force base?"

"Kirkland Enterprises is building a biodome here, and I'm supervising the project. We've been recruiting street kids with brains and good survival skills and then bringing the best of them here to train. You'd be perfect to head up the research lab, what with your biodome expertise and your medical background."

I give him a disbelieving look. "With all the shit going down, you must be a very popular man."

He taps me on the nose. "Well, I don't spend all my time rescuing headstrong women from certain death, if that's what you mean." He lifts up the meds. "But feel free to throw it all away."

I resist the urge to roll my eyes. "Okay. I'll take the pills."

"I need your help, Izzy-Bee." He watches me swallow the tablets. "We're almost done building the biodome, but we can't seal it unless we get it balanced: plants and animals, oxygen and carbon dioxide, worms and bird shit—your area of expertise. That's turning out to be the tricky part."

"Uh huh."

"Like I said, Isabel, things are getting pretty fucked up out there." He's struggling to keep the annoyance out of his voice. "And if I can make this biodome viable, people will be begging me to build them all over the world. Lots of people. I could end up saving mankind."

I can almost see the dollar signs in his eyes. "Okay. So what do you want from me?"

"Your patents—and all your research data."

I let out a cynical laugh. "If I agree, will you take me back to the cabin and leave me in peace?"

"You should stay here where it's safe and live with—"

"I want to go home, Dave."

"Well, if you insist on going back to that shack, I'll drive you there myself." He reaches out to stroke my face, but I pull away, and he closes his hand into a fist. "Right. I'll have my attorney stop by in the morning with the paperwork."

"And you'll take me back to the cabin tomorrow?"

"Why don't we give it a couple of weeks to make sure you're healthy?" He takes my empty glass and stands up. "You might actually like it here, Isabel. I call the shots, and I can get almost anything: books, clothes, even coffee and chocolate. You could continue your research—we could work together. The rest of the world is going to hell in a hand basket, but if you stay with me, you can live like a queen."

"Thanks, Dave, but I'm not really the type." I slide back down under the covers. "The cabin is my home. It's where my children are buried, and where my heart lies."

"He's not coming back, doll."

I look up at him, my teeth clenched. "Yes, he is. He's probably there now."

"If he's not, you owe me a six-pack."

I roll away from him, my eyes full of tears.

A moment later, the lights go off, and I hear the door shut. I fall asleep imagining Diego's arms around me, the twins napping next to us.

*Yes, he is.*

In the morning, I insist on getting dressed before seeing Dave's lawyer. After the nurse removes the IV, I take a shower, and she goes in search of clothes. I'm weak and a bit wobbly on my feet, but otherwise, I feel fine.

When she returns, I get dressed and then eat breakfast: scrambled eggs, melon, and coffee with fresh cream. It's divine, and I feel much better after eating something. "Thank you."

"You're welcome, Mrs. Kirkland. If you're ready, I'll let

the attorney know."

It takes me ten minutes to sign away my life's work.

*Not much chance I'm going to use it anyway, and maybe it can do some good.*

As the lawyer is putting the documents into his brief-case, he asks, "Could you give me the password for your hard drive, please? I've been informed that the research data on it is encrypted."

I start at him. "How did you get my computer?"

His face reddens. "It was brought with you when you were airlifted to safety."

"It was, was it. More like you stole it from my cabin."

"Your computer contains information that is critical for the success of the biodome project, Mrs. Kirkland. It would have been irresponsible to leave it behind."

"I see. You sent a helicopter to get my computer and brought me along as an afterthought."

"As I understand it, Mr. Kirkland's intervention saved your life." He pushes a pen and a sheet of paper across the small table. "If you want to go home, I suggest you give me the password."

"And if I don't?"

"This is a military base, Mrs. Kirkland. You'll be nice and safe here."

I scribble my password on the paper, and he tucks it into his briefcase. "Thank you. It's been a pleasure."

"When do I go home?"

"You will need to speak to Mr. Kirkland about that, ma'am. Good day."

After he leaves, I pack up the small ditty bag from the bathroom, read through my chart, and then walk out to the nurses' station. "Thanks for everything. All of you have been very kind, but I'm ready to go home."

The two nurses look at each other and then the older

woman speaks, "We've been given instructions to keep you here until your doctor is available to see you."

"Okay. How long will that be?"

"I'm not sure. Possibly a week or two. He's away on a training mission."

I narrow my eyes. "And you only have one doctor here at the hospital?"

She gives a forced laugh. "Of course not, but *your* doctor is away."

"Could you get *another* doctor to check me out, please?"

"Yes, ma'am. Let me make a few calls and see what can be arranged." She gives the other woman a nervous glance and then picks up the phone, taps a button, and speaks into the receiver. "Get me Mr. Kirkland." She covers the bottom half of the phone with her hand. "If you would be so kind as to wait in your room, please."

"Of course." I walk back and then peek around the door, listening to the phone conversation.

"Yes, Mr. Kirkland. I understand completely. We can't have her running off with things the way they are. I'm sure she'll learn to like it here."

*He's not going to let me go.*

I hurry over to the bathroom, lock the door, and then shut it from the outside.

*It might buy me a few minutes.*

I go back to my eavesdropping.

"Of course," the nurse says and laughs self-consciously. "We'll see that she stays here until Dr. Zaius returns next month." There's a pause. "Yes, sir. I'll let her know you're on your way."

"Like hell you will." I sneak across the hallway, creep down the corridor, and duck into the elevator. I almost press the lobby button, but decide to look for a side exit instead. A minute later, I step out into the basement and follow the narrow hallway until I come to the employee coat room. I put on a civilian trench coat and a stocking cap—and then remember the hospital slippers on my feet.

*Life is a daring adventure or nothing at all.*

I take the stairs up a floor and find myself in the crowded hospital lobby. "Damn."

Out in front, Dave's Tesla pulls up to the loading zone. He jumps out and waves to the armed guard by the revolving front door.

"Shit." I tuck my hair up into the cap, pull it low onto my forehead, and start buttoning the coat. A group of women and children are walking toward the exit, and I hurry across the polished floor to join them. Just as Dave steps into the revolving door, I squeeze into the opposite side behind a large woman.

She glances down at my slippers, and then gives me a funny look.

"Sorry," I say. "I'm in a hurry to get home before the diarrhea starts."

Her eyes get big, and she steps aside the moment we exit the turnstile.

"Thanks," I say and size up the security guard.

He's helping an elderly man get out of a minivan. I wait until he turns away, and then walk over to the Tesla and open the door. Dave's cell phone is still seated in its cradle.

*Good thing his head's attached.*

I get in and shut the door, my heart still racing. The car smells of cheap perfume and Chinese takeout, and there's an unopened box of Godiva truffles on the passenger seat.

*He wasn't lying about living like royalty.*

I type in Dave's four-digit password, hoping that it hasn't changed, and let out a sigh of relief when the screen changes to the Tesla app.

I lock the doors and start the car. The dashboard lights

up, the number 214 in the center.

"Yes!"

I type in the cabin address, note that it's 167 miles away, and press go.

A warning chime sounds, and for a moment I think it's because the key is missing.

"Damn it."

And then I notice the seatbelt light.

I put it on, slip the car into gear, and ease out of the loading zone. The Tesla is so quiet that the guard doesn't even look up when I drive right behind him.

It takes three minutes to get to the main gate, and I spend the time trying to come up with something to tell the sentry. But when he sees the Tesla, he rushes out to open the gate, and I pass through without stopping, thankful for the tinted windows.

It's cold outside, and the sky is spitting gray slushy flakes as I pull out onto the empty freeway. The heater takes power that I might need later, so I turn it off. But after a few minutes, I'm so cold that I can't stop trembling. I crank up the thermostat and cross my fingers, hoping that the battery holds out long enough to get home. Dave's phone rings, and I reach over and power it off.

*Don't want anyone tracking me with GPS.*

Near the Air Force base, the roads are pretty good, but once I get closer to the city, there are abandoned cars and junk everywhere. The Tesla doesn't have a lot of ground clearance, and I don't want to accidentally run into something, so I force myself to keep the speed down.

As I'm driving through the city, I pass groups of people huddled around burning piles of rubbish. They look up at me, their eyes wide and their cheeks hollow, and then they go back to rubbing their hands and stamping their feet. All of the stores and gas stations I pass are burned or looted, their windows smashed and the parking lots littered with refuse.

*Once the world runs out of trash to burn, things are going to get dicey.*

After three hours of slow, tedious driving, I'm a little past halfway home.

The good news is I'm getting great mileage; the bad news is I have to pee so badly my eyeballs are floating. Just as I'm about to pull over, I come around a curve and see a roadblock in front of me. I slam on the brakes and come to a stop in front of a huge pile of old tires. Before I have a chance to think, men with knives and baseball bats come pouring over the barricade.

"Oh, shit."

Someone slams a bat into the windshield, and I scream—and then watch the heavy metal club bounce off the glass.

*Dave must have had the car armored.*

I put the Tesla in reverse and press the accelerator to the floor. The speed is limited to 20 MPH, but the acceleration is awesome. Bodies slide off the car. I twist the steering wheel around and brake hard. The pavement is wet from the half-hearted snowing, and the car whips around. I throw it back into drive and get the hell out of there.

*Next time I see Dave, I'll have to be nicer.*

I take a wide detour around the roadblock, and twenty minutes later, I get on the old highway and head west up into the mountains. Once I'm well into the canyon, I stop to relieve my bladder, my pulse racing the whole time, but I don't see or hear anyone else.

When the sun is low in the sky, I turn onto the dirt road leading up to the cabin and accelerate past the fateful gate where I was attacked. The temperature has dropped, and the muddy road is frozen solid, covered by a thin layer of fresh snow. There's still thirty-seven miles on the Tesla, and I let out a small whoop, grateful that Dave has good taste in cars and chocolates—and that tonight, I'll sleep in Diego's arms.

# PART TWO
## *The Magic Kingdom*

*I like a man who's good,*
*But not too good.*
*The good die young,*
*And I hate a dead one.*

Mae West

## CHAPTER 18

### *Diego: I Wouldn't Do That*

Johnson tosses the notebook down on the conference room table and turns to leave. "Read it, Nadales. I'll be back in half an hour to escort you into the secured area."

"You can go fuck yourself. I'm not doing anything until I talk to a lawyer."

Matt Hudson, a guy who used to live down the street from me, walks in. He smiles and offers me his hand. "Diego. It's good to see you."

"Matt? What are you doing here?" I shake his hand. "What am I doing here?" I glance around the room. "What the hell is going on?"

He smiles apologetically. "Sorry about that melodramatic abduction, mate. I tried to convince them to just tell you the truth and invite you to join us." He scowls at the agent. "But that would have been too easy."

"I'll leave you two alone for a nice little chat," Johnson says. "Be ready to take him in at oh-eight-hundred."

"That will be okey-dokey."

The government man shuts the door with a grunt.

"Arse. I think he actually enjoys kidnapping people." Matt pulls out a chair and sits down. "You look like hell. What happened?"

"Let's just say I had a rough night." I pour myself a glass of water from a sweating pitcher in the middle of the table and collapse into the chair across from him. "Do you know anything about Isabel?"

"I was told they sent a helicopter up to your cabin last night. Airlifted her to a military hospital."

"Thank god." I let out a relieved sigh. "What's going on, Matt? Why am I here?"

"Sorry about the kidnapping, mate. I'm not sure who ordered you brought in, but I can guess why." He fills me in on something he calls the Einstein Sphere. Turns out, it's the huge tungsten ball they found in the hotel fire that almost killed Isabel.

*That explains the Internet vanishing act.*

"It was hollow," he says, "and we had to crush it to get it open. Inside was a small electronic device that hasn't been invented in our world."

"Holy shit."

"There's more. It also contained plans for some weird kind of telescope that can see into other universes. And instructions to build a time machine."

A little alarm goes off in my head.

*With Einstein's help, you'll meet again.*

I pick up the glass of water. "So why did they kidnap me?"

"Uh, I wouldn't drink that, if I were you. Picasso—that's the buck who runs the show even though Dick pretends to—says they used to put chemicals in the water here to keep people cooperative. God only knows what might still be in it."

I slide the glass to the center of the table, leaving watery railroad tracks on the fake wood.

"As I was saying, you're here because of the note."

I give him a baffled look.

"It was also inside the sphere. Handwritten. Had your name on it."

"Me? Why would someone put my name inside a metal sphere?"

He shrugs. "Your guess is as good as mine."

"Can I see the note?"

"Yeah, sure—just don't tell Dick I told you all this." He grabs the notebook they keep telling me to read, flips through some pages, and slides it across the table. "There."

I glance at the photo, and my heart stops.

He scans my face, his expression worried. "What is it?"

"That's Isabel's handwriting... but my middle name is *Fernando*, not *Federico*."

## Chapter 19
### *Isabel: It Rings True*

Today is our wedding day. It's been more than a month since I escaped from the Base hospital, and Dave's Tesla sits hidden in the bushes at the bottom of the hill, the battery slowly losing power. After I escaped from the hospital, it took me most of the day to get home—and trudging up the last mile of snowy road in slippers was the worst part—but I made it.

To be honest, I don't think Dave bothered to come after me. He already had what he wanted: my laptop and the encryption key for all my research. I expect he'll eventually send someone to collect the car, but I don't care as long as he leaves me alone.

I take the beautiful white dress out of my closet and slip it on, struggling with the long zipper in back and sobbing. Mrs. Malloy brought it to me the day after I got back, and then she spent a week altering it while she made sure I was strong enough to live alone. That woman is an angel.

I stare at my hollow-cheeked reflection in the mirror, and then run my hands over my breasts and stomach, missing the two little lives that used to be inside me. Lucky sits on the bed watching as I fix up my hair and put on earrings. I try to add a little make-up, but I can't seem to stop crying long enough for my face to dry.

"At least I still have you, kitty girl."

She lets out a squeaky meow and then follows me out into the crisp fall morning.

Now that the Malloys' roof is done, they've left to find other family members, and I'm without any human company.

Still, I haven't given up hope.

*He said he'd come back, and I plan to be here when he does.*

The hem of the dress catches on the scrub oak as I make my way to the two tiny graves, tears streaming down my face. Heavy snow clouds threaten over the mountains, but bright sunshine still falls across the two small piles of stones out by the point.

I sit down on a large rock overlooking the creek and talk to my children, telling them about their father and how he saved me from the fire, and then from a raging infection, and finally about how he will be back to marry me.

*Don't make me wait too long.*

I have to keep clearing my throat and wiping my face on my sleeve until I finally run out of words and tears.

A cold wind blows up from the ravine, lifting dead leaves into the air and tossing them about. Lucky chases one for a bit and then jumps back up in my lap.

I stroke her soft fur and suppress a shiver. "Winter is coming."

She rubs her face against my hand.

"Thanks, kitty girl. I love you too." I stand up, still holding Lucky, and study the forest spread out below me, the plains visible in the distance. I scan the trees and rocks, the ridges and canyons, the shadows and light for any signs of life—just as I do every day.

*He always finds me.*

Kitty girl jumps down and trots back toward the cabin, meowing about the chilly breeze.

*He'll be back.*

I close my eyes and shout out, "I *know* he'll be back!" letting the whole damn universe know that I'm not giving up.

"Too bad he's not here right now." The gravelly voice comes from behind me.

I whirl around, accidentally treading on the dress and nearly falling over. The gaunt face of a man I've never seen before leers at me. A couple of his teeth are missing and his skin is covered with grime.

I take a step back, but I'm perilously close to the edge of the ravine already.

"Nice dress." He's no taller than I am, his clothes torn and dirty. "Unfortunately, I'm not the marrying type. But I'd be happy to do the honors anyways." He runs his gaze down my body. "Take it off."

"What?"

"You deaf or something? I said take the dress off, bitch." He pulls a thin rope out of his pocket. "Lover boy ain't gonna save you this time."

*Oh my god, he's the guy who stuck the knife in my thigh!*

I pick up my skirt and lunge toward the cabin, but he's quicker than I am, and he cuts me off after only a few strides.

"You fight, and it'll just go the worse for you." He takes a step toward me. "So I suggest you let me have what I came for."

I back away, shaking my head, and then turn and bolt in the opposite direction.

But I'm still weak and the dress is unwieldy. I trip on it and fall hard onto the cold ground.

As I'm struggling to get up, he grabs me around the waist and lifts me up. "I was thinking it would be more comfortable in that cute little cabin of yours, but I ain't gonna be too picky given how you've gone and gotten all gussied up."

I scream and try to get away, but he throws me face-down onto the ground and shoves his knee between my shoulder blades, pressing my chest and face into the dirt. "Shut up, bitch, or I'll kill you first and fuck you afterwards." He forces my hands behind my back and ties them together, the thin rope slicing into my wrists.

He lifts my hands and wrenches down the zipper on my dress. "Sweet Jesus, if you're not a sight for sore eyes." He pushes me over, my arms wedged painfully beneath my back, and straddles my torso. "Now that's better."

I spit into his face. He grabs onto the shoulder of the dress and laughs. "I like a woman with a little fight in her." I turn my head and bite his wrist as hard as I can.

"Shit!" He jerks his hand away. "You bitch." He slaps me hard across the face. "You do something like that again, and I *will* kill you." He takes a knife out and presses it against my throat.

I pull away, my cheek burning and the taste of blood in my mouth.

He forces my dress up, and I let out a cry. "Shut your mouth, or I'll gag you." He leans back and looks at my bare thighs, one corner of his mouth curling up. "So it is you! I gave you that pretty little scar." The smile disappears. "Right before that stupid boyfriend of yours tried to kill me."

I shut my eyes, my hands and arms already numb, and try to force down the panic enough to think.

He takes the knife away from my throat, and I hear him undoing his pants. "I been hankerin' to do you for a while now." He grabs the bodice of my dress. "Look at me! I wanna see the fear in your pretty green eyes." He yanks the fabric away from my chest and jabs the knife into it. "You be sure to tell him that I left him my callin' card, won't you?" He jerks the knife up toward my neck, cutting through the dress and exposing my breasts.

I scream and try to kick him off, but he's ready for me. He pins my throat with one hand, squeezing so hard I can't breathe. I stop struggling, and he lifts the knife over me, his lips pulled back from his teeth. "You're mine, bitch."

A mass of black and white leaps out of the shadows and closes its teeth around the man's wrist. The animal's momentum knocks the bastard off me, and I roll away. The guy gets up, yelling obscenities, his pants around his knees and the knife still in his hand, but the dog refuses to let go of his wrist. The animal snarls and jerks the man's arm around, trying to get him to drop the weapon.

The enraged man whips the dog around, dirt and spit flying everywhere. "Let go of me, you rabid mongrel!"

I struggle to get up, but with my hands tied behind me and the dress dangling off my shoulders, I keep stepping on the heavy fabric and falling. Finally, I manage to put my foot on the hem and wrench my body away, tearing off the bottom panel. I stagger to my feet and take a quick look at the mutt who saved my life, and then I stumble toward the cabin.

The sound of the man and dog fighting pushes up panic in my throat as I struggle to open the front door. Lucky comes racing up, meowing to get inside, but my hands are so numb I can barely feel the cold metal handle, and I can't see what I'm doing. When I eventually manage to get the door open, we rush though, and then I force it shut with my shoulder. I can't reach the dead bolt with my hands tied, so I use my teeth to turn the lock, and then collapse against the heavy wooden door and sob.

∞

A bit later, I get up and dip my wrists in cold dishwater. The moisture loosens the cords enough to work my hands free, and after I get the circulation back in my fingers, I change into jeans and a sweater, the bright red burn marks on my wrists a reminder of my stupidity.

I shut Lucky in the bedroom and grab a baseball bat from the hall closet, putting a canister of pepper spray in each pocket and carrying a third, the safety off and my finger on the trigger. I take a deep breath, unlock the front door, and slink out into the fading light.

But despite my trepidation, the man is gone, and it doesn't take me long to find the spot where I was attacked. A piece of my wedding dress is tangled up in the oaks, and a few feet away, I find the knife. There's no blood on it, and I let out a sigh of relief. The dog must have gotten the bastard to drop it before he chased him away.

I use the torn fabric to pick up his dull, rusty blade and notice something shiny in the dirt next to it. It's the sort of round metal disk people used to put on pet collars. I pick it up and turn it over.

It has one word on it, the lettering so scratched that it's barely legible.

I say the name out loud, forcing back tears. "Thank you, Tolstoy."

I hear something moving in the brush behind me, and I wheel around, but there's nothing there. I run back to the cabin and lock the door, and when my heart stops pounding, I make a promise:

*I will never be caught defenseless again.*

Tomorrow, I will hike down to the makeshift trading post at the burned-out Walmart and do whatever it takes to get a gun.

## CHAPTER 20
### Matt: The First Peep

All of us have been working sixteen-hour days for nearly six months, and the stress is showing. A guy on loan from the Air Force Research Laboratory yells at Cassie for deleting a file she's never touched, and Picasso steps in and tells the whole team to call it a night. We hurry out before Dick gets wind of us skiving off.

On the other side of the lake is a building everyone calls the Y, and we head over there. It's nothing but a room with a couple of ancient video games, a microwave that ticks ominously, and an old ping-pong table, but there's beer in the fridge and giant bags of stale popcorn in the closet. Picasso orders our newest conscript to come with us, and Diego mopes along behind, grumbling to himself.

I think he blames me for bringing him in here, but I didn't have anything to do with it. At first, he tried to get anyone who would listen to recruit his fiancée, but he seems to have given up on that now and spends most of his time brooding in his room—not at all the guy I used to know.

*Given what they did to him, I guess you can't blame him.*

Cassie, one of Picasso's conscripted grad students, tries to get Diego to join us for ping-pong, but he declines and slumps into a chair. Picasso opens a beer and sets it in front of him, but the guy doesn't even look at it. "Hey, Nadales. You play ping-pong with us, and I'll get you some photos of Isabel, prove to you that she's doing okay."

Diego glances up, his eyes narrowed, but before he can respond, Picasso tosses a pile of photographs on the table in front of him. "Those were taken two days ago by a drone. I need them back when you're done."

Diego picks up a picture, his eyes wide, and we gather around behind him to have a peek. I recognize Isabel immediately: she looks thinner than I remember, but well. There are two or three shots of her sitting on a deck reading—the healed scar on her left leg clearly visible—and a couple of her doing chores around a cabin with a red-headed kid in tow. The last one is of her sitting on some big rocks staring down at the forest floor, her face pensive.

Diego holds it for a long time and then looks up at Picasso, his eyes pleading.

Our fearless leader nods. "I think that one got mangled in the printer."

"Thank you." Diego slips the photo into his shirt.

"I wish I could do more, Nadales. I haven't given up trying to bring her in, but I don't hold out much hope. Someone on the inside doesn't want her involved. I'm sorry." Picasso reaches out to him. "Come on. Play ping-pong with us. Right now, there's nothing more you can do for her."

Diego stands, and Picasso picks up the open bottle from the table. "Are you sure you don't want this?"

"Yeah. And I suck at ping-pong."

"No worries, you're with me."

Cassie lets out a snort of disdain. "Fucking egomaniac."

We all walk back to the ping-pong table, Picasso holding the beer in his left hand. He pushes a paddle toward Diego. "Just keep it away from Cass, and you'll do fine. That woman likes to crush balls."

Cassie rolls her eyes. Not only is she a mathematical genius, she's lethal with a ping-pong paddle, and with Picasso trying to play with a bottle in one hand and Diego only swinging half-heartedly, we spank them twice in a row.

Picasso takes a long swig, sets the beer down, and nods at Cassie. "If you coded half as fast as you play ping-pong, you'd be done by now."

"Oh yeah? If you would tell me what the hell you're planning to do with the fucking time machine, maybe I could get it to work."

"Ah, that would take all the fun out of it."

She throws a handful of popcorn at him. "Bastard."

Despite all indications to the contrary, something is up between the two of them. I'd bet my last crumpet on it.

*I hope he has life insurance.*

Picasso gives her an injured look. "And besides, I convinced Johnson to show us the Peeping Tom. What more do you want?"

"Yeah," she says. "Because it can't do anything. And I've been telling you for weeks that something isn't right with the targeting math on the time machine, but no one listens to me." She screws up her face and says in a good imitation of Dick, "We didn't hire you to think, Miss Smith, we hired you to code."

Everyone except Diego laughs.

"Pinhead. Amazing the government has lasted this long with numb-nuts like him in charge. And I hate being called Miss Smith."

"You let us win this game, and I'll see what I can do."

Picasso winks at me.

"Fuck you." Cassie wipes her hands on her jeans and picks up the paddle and ball.

"Maybe when this is all over." Picasso takes another sip of beer.

"Will you put that goddamn bottle down and just play the game?"

"Don't get your panties in a wad, woman. My partner is having trouble seeing through that mop of hair he refuses to cut."

Diego's hair was already pretty long when he got here, but he refuses to let anyone touch it. Says it reminds him of how long he's been away from Isabel.

*That guy is hurting bad.*

Picasso turns back to Cassie. "Do you have a rubber band he can borrow?"

She gives Diego a sympathetic look and then starts digging in her pocket. A moment later, he pulls his hair back into a short ponytail.

It doesn't look half-bad on him.

Picasso claps him the shoulder. "No more excuses." He pins his eyes on Cassie. *"Now* we get serious."

Agent Dick bursts through the rec room door, Junior trailing behind him like a pull-toy.

We pretend not to notice.

"Speaking of pinheads." Cassie picks up the ball. "Zero-zero."

Diego nods, and she serves a rocket at him. He barely manages to get it back in play, and I lean in, ready to smash a winner off his weak return.

"Fault!" Picasso calls out, swinging his beer like a paddle. "It bounced on the wrong side of the center line."

"Are you goddamn blind?" Cassie stares at him with her mouth open, and I tap the ball weakly across the net.

Dick leans over and grabs it. "I hate to interrupt your playtime, but the Trans-Temporal Viewer Team just located a Type E Target. Update at the Rialto in three minutes."

Everyone stares at Dick.

"Holy fucking Barbie," Picasso says. "We have a peephole into another universe."

We drop the paddles and race out.

## Chapter 21

### Isabel: Gone to the Dogs

I lift the new Walther P-22 semi-automatic pistol out of my pack and hold it in my hand, still surprised by the deadly weight of it.

*That poor dog.*

I load five bullets into the magazine clip, check the safety, and place it in the pocket of my coat. Using my water bottle, I clean the vomit off my boots, and then rinse out my mouth and take a drink. The sun disappears behind the heavy snow clouds, and I shiver, anxious to get back to the safety of the cabin.

*If I ever see another Walmart, it will be too soon.*

I turn onto the old highway and start following it up the canyon, feeling the loaded handgun bump against my thigh with each step. The roadside is dotted with abandoned cars, their windows smashed out and the tires missing, but the world is strangely still and silent.

An ominous feeling slithers up my spine. I stop for a

moment and listen, looking for any signs of life.

*How will I know if there's radioactive fallout?*

I was hoping to get a little news when I bartered for the Walther, but after watching the dog massacre, I was too rattled to hang around and chat.

Still, I wonder what happened to all those nukes—and if more have been detonated.

*I guess it doesn't really matter. If there's radiation in the air, we're all dead.*

Twenty minutes later, I stop in front of a burned-out Seven-Eleven—my signal to take the shortcut Seamus told me about—and see a basset hound and a golden retriever cowering in the shadows, both of them matted with dirt and looking emaciated.

"Are you guys friends with Tolstoy?"

The basset hound struggles to his feet—one of his legs not working right—and wags his tail. They're both still wearing collars, and I can see a gash on the golden's shoulder.

*Poor things.*

I remember the bags of jerky in my pack and take one out, tossing each dog a large strip. A moment later, a couple of mutts slink out from the charred remains of the neighboring Starbucks, and I pitch some jerky to them too. Not surprisingly, none of the dogs will let me get close, but they are quick to gulp down the free food.

A few minutes after I stop hiking, Lucky comes trotting out of the forest. She skitters around the dogs and jumps into my lap, meowing up a storm.

"Kitty girl! What are you doing this far from the cabin?" I'm sitting on a tipped-over mailbox, and I offer her a piece of jerky, but she turns up her nose. "Not keen on eating someone else's kill? Can't say I blame you. God only knows what kind of meat it is."

I stay for another half hour, petting Lucky, chucking

out tidbits to the injured dogs, and waiting to see if Tolstoy appears.

I'm caught off-guard when it starts to snow. Huge flakes the same slate gray as the clouds float down and settle silently on the frozen earth. I've been so busy with the dogs that I forgot about the weather. I put on my pack, stuff Lucky inside my jacket, leaving her head sticking out beneath my chin, and call out my goodbyes to the bedraggled pets.

"Don't worry, boys and girls, I'll be back!"

Kitty girl meows, worried about the gathering storm or the abandoned dogs, I don't know which, but her plaintive cry sets my nerves on edge, and I quicken my pace, hurrying up the steep trail toward home.

I can hear the dog pack trailing behind me through the woods, but the flakes are falling thick and heavy, and after a short while, I am alone in the cold, dark forest. Fear creeps in for the first time: With this much snow, the path is nearly impossible to see.

The unwieldy handgun keeps bumping against my thigh every time I take a step, and I'm afraid it'll go off accidentally. Finally, I pull it out and put it back into the pack, wishing I had let Diego teach me how to use it. The moment I zip the pack shut an ominous chill creeps up my spine.

*What if my would-be rapist is following me, waiting for his chance to attack?*

I shudder and gaze out into the dark, snowy forest. I haven't seen any footprints, human or otherwise, so I force down my trepidation and tell myself that no one would be out in this weather if they had any other choice. And then I start hiking again, hoping I'm right.

After thirty minutes of uphill trekking, my legs are burning with the exertion, so I stop to rest and get my bearings. This time of year, it gets dark at four, so I have an hour or two of light left.

I haven't been able to find the ravine I followed on the way down, and with the clouds so low, all the usual landmarks are hidden. I unclip Diego's compass from my pack and find north. The arrow seems to point in the direction I expect, but I'm not sure which way the cabin is from here.

*I wish I had paid more attention when he showed me how to use it.*

I continue hiking uphill, slipping and falling to my knees in the deepening snow, and then struggling back to my feet. I keep looking for something I recognize, but I can barely see ten feet, let alone the outcropping of rocks on the ridge. After climbing a particularly steep incline, I stop to rest my legs and catch my breath again.

Lucky shifts inside my jacket and meows.

"I don't know for sure, kitty girl, but we've got to be getting close."

I take a drink of water from my pack. The snow is still falling, and I estimate that I've been hiking for over an hour. That would usually put me within spitting distance of the cabin, assuming I've been heading in the right direction.

*Big assumption there, Isabel.*

I have warm clothes, food and water, and a space blanket—thank goodness Diego insisted I keep it in the pack—but with darkness falling, that doesn't sound too comforting. Still, the temperature shouldn't drop much if the cloud-cover holds, and I have kitty girl to help keep me warm.

I unzip my coat and pat her head with my mitten, happy to have her company. She squeezes out and jumps down into the snow, and a seed of hope forms.

*Maybe she knows the way home.*

The white stuff is up to her chin, and her futile attempts to shake off the fluffy powder would be comical under other circumstances. She digs half-heartedly in the gray snow and relieves herself in the small clearing. When she's done, she meows and stretches her front paws up on my legs. I lift her up and stick her back inside my coat

She shakes the snow off her head, settles down inside my jacket, and starts purring.

"Easy for you to say, I'm doing all the hard work here." I gaze up into the falling snow, trying to gauge if it's getting any lighter. If the cloud-cover lifts, it could get very cold.

*Too cold to survive.*

I shift the backpack. "We should keep going for another hour and hope it clears enough to find the cabin."

I trudge on into the gathering darkness, the only sound the frosty air moving in and out of my lungs.

Thirty minutes later, I pause for another drink of water. The snow has stopped, and the temperature is dropping fast. Unfortunately, the clouds haven't lifted enough to recognize any landmarks, and soon it will be too dark to see. I shiver and stamp the snow off my boots. The wind is picking up, and if the snow starts again, I'll be lost in a blizzard.

*The chances of surviving that are grim.*

My stomach growls, but that's the least of my worries. In fifteen minutes, there won't be enough light to see the cabin, even if it's right in front of me.

*What would Diego do?*

*Build some sort of windbreak while there's still daylight.*

Lucky peeks out of my jacket and gives a squeaky meow.

"Sorry, kitty girl, it looks like we might be spending the night—" She tenses, the fur on her neck standing up.

I stop talking and listen.

With the wind swirling around us, it's difficult to tell which way the sound came from, but I definitely heard something too.

Lucky meows again and leaps down into the snow.

"Whoa, there, ma'am. It's too cold to go wandering off by yourself!"

She glances at me and then stares off into the dark, frozen forest.

And then I see him, the black and white dog, standing ten feet away from us. He appears to be a mix between a border collie and some larger breed, maybe a wolfhound. "Tolstoy!"

He wags his tail, his amber eyes glowing in the last of the light.

"Hey, there, boy! Did you come to help us?"

He barks, and Lucky bounds toward him through the deep snow.

"Wait! Kitty girl! Don't leave me!"

Tolstoy barks again, watching me, and then he turns and starts back the way he came.

I shiver and trudge through the snow to where the dog was standing. My toes are numb, and I'm losing the feeling in my fingers. I force back frozen tears and look around for Lucky, but don't see her. The wind grabs at my jacket, sandblasting ice crystals against my face and neck, and it burns like fire. I struggle to zip up my coat and then stumble forward, following the dog's footprints into the unknown.

## CHAPTER 22

### *Diego: The Peeping Tom*

The small movie theatre reeks of rancid oil and old smoke, but it's filled to capacity. I follow the gang in and sit down next to Cassie. The lead Peeking Tom scientist walks out on the stage wearing a Hawaiian shirt and a grin so big he can barely speak. "Ladies and gentlemen, we, the esteemed members of the Trans-Temporal Viewer Team—"

Someone yells out, "Peeping Toms!" and everyone but me laughs.

"—would like to show you seventeen seconds of images taken from another universe. One small peek for man, one giant photobomb for mankind."

The audience breaks into raucous cheers and applause, but pent-up anger and frustration fills my chest. I want to get back to Isabel. I don't care what they're doing, and I don't care if they make any progress. Isabel is trying to survive a harsh Colorado winter with nothing but a squeaky cat to keep her company, and here I sit inside an underground amusement park watching goddamn movies.

The lights in the theatre dim and a hush falls over the crowd. A black and white image appears on the movie screen. I distractedly watch a group of guys playing *futbol* on a beach. The video quality is poor, and the viewing angle is bizarre, as if we're watching from an unleveled tripod. I tip my head to the side, and a weird déjà vu feeling comes over me. Ten seconds in, the players race out of the picture, leaving one guy standing with his hands on his hips.

*That could be me from twenty-odd years ago.*

I blink a couple of times and take another look, the ball bounds back into view, and the frame fills up with the other players, all of whom I recognize from high school. A cold dread pours into my chest.

*What are the chances of that?*

The screen goes blank.

Someone asks, "How do you know it's from another universe?"

"Because the photons we're collecting don't exist in our universe."

"What universe *do* they exist in? And are we in it?"

"It's a timeline somewhat close to ours, although we don't know exactly when this happened. Once we figure that out, I'll be able to answer your second question with more certainty. But I would say, yes, we're all in that world, and we're all likely sitting in a smelly 1950's movie theatre, located a kilometer underground, asking self-centered questions."

People chuckle, but it gives me the creeps.

*If we're peeking into their universe, who's peeking into ours?*

"Our next goal is to find a universe farther away, one where we can verify that something is different from our own world: a street name that is changed or a landmark that is altered."

Agent Dick jumps up onto the stage before the guy can

say anything more. "Okay, folks. Show's over. As you can see, we've made some progress, but we're not there yet. We have two other teams with objectives to meet, and one of them has made almost no headway." He glances at the leader of the Hot Button Team. "And another group seems to think that playing pool is the best way to meet their goals." He scowls at Picasso.

Cassie stands up and starts marching up the aisle, her sneakers squeaking loudly on the sticky floor. Everyone turns to look at her.

"Glad to see you've decided to take your work more seriously, Miss Smith," Dick calls out after her.

Cassie lets out a snort of disgust and whirls around to face him. "It was ping-pong, you brainless prick."

Picasso grins from ear to ear.

Twice I lose the dog's tracks, and twice he comes back for me, barking and wagging his tail. I know we should be hunkering down someplace out of the wind to wait for the storm to pass, but he refuses to let me rest for more than a few seconds before bounding off again.

I keep catching glimpses of Lucky scrambling along behind the dog, struggling to keep up in the deep snow. And so I continue to lift one foot, drag it through the mounting drifts, and drop it ahead of the other, over and over, blindly following a half-wild creature through a raging snowstorm.

Eventually, the wind becomes so strong that I can't see my own feet. My eyelashes are nearly frozen shut—whether from the flying snow or my own tears, I can't say. I stop moving and cry out, hopelessly lost in the near-total whiteout.

*We're not going to make it.*

Lucky meows and scratches her claws against my frozen jeans. I reach down and pick her up, stuffing her unceremoniously back inside my coat. I can feel her heart pounding against my own. She complains at the rough treatment, but doesn't attempt to escape.

"Tolstoy! Where are you? Don't leave us!"

A moment later, something covered in shaggy ice brushes against my leg. I manage to slip my glove under the dog's heavy collar and hold on. He leads me, half-blind and exhausted, through the frozen maelstrom, our destination known to him alone.

Sometime later, my disembodied boot catches against a snow-covered rock, and I fall sideways into the deep powder, completely spent. Lucky shifts inside my down jacket, trying to figure out what's happened. I push my body up with numb fingers, and a warm tongue licks the snow off my cheek.

"I can't do it, big guy. It's too far. You take Lucky and go on without me."

He barks, his tail sweeping snow up into the air around us.

The wind has stopped, but the temperature has fallen precipitously. My jeans are frozen solid against my numb legs and my mittens are oval bricks.

Tolstoy barks again.

"Okay, okay. Give me a minute."

I focus on getting my hands to work and then push them down into the snow, trying to find purchase on the frozen earth. But it's no use. The ground is too slippery.

Lucky meows inside my coat and starts scratching to get out.

"Hold on, kitty girl. I'm trying."

I sweep my hands in the snow, looking for something to grab on to, and discover a flat surface, which turns out to be a step. Above it is another step, and then another. I crane my neck up, peering into the darkness, and let out a startled cry. I've fallen next to the front porch of the cabin. Somehow,

Tolstoy has led us home.

I reach up, wrap my exhausted arm around the railing, and pull myself up, breathing hard. My throat is burning from the cold air as I unzip the top of my down jacket and let Lucky out. She scrambles up the steps to where the snow is only a few inches deep and meows.

"Yes, ma'am. Let me find the key."

The frigid night is pitch black, no moon visible behind the wispy clouds, only the distant stars twinkling faintly in the velvet sky.

My elation fades a bit as I picture myself taking the key from its hiding place, only to drop it in the deep snow. Without a flashlight, I'd have no hope of finding it, and my mistake would kill us all. I imagine Seamus finding our frozen bodies, aghast that we made it all the way home, only to freeze to death on the front porch.

I brush the snow off the third step and collapse back down on it. I've done this a hundred times, but never in the freezing dark. I pull one glove off with my teeth and use my bare fingers to locate the metal hook under the third step. Even though my fingers are numb, the air feels biting cold.

*That's a good sign: no frostbite yet.*

I wrench my left mitten underneath the key in case it falls and then close my bare hand around the small treasure. I ease it carefully off the hook and then squeeze it as tightly as I can. "I got it!"

The metal is so cold it burns my skin.

I stand up, gripping the railing with my free arm, and step carefully toward the door. Shivering now, I pull the other mitten off with my teeth and drop it in the snow. Then keeping my hand horizontal, I try to open my fingers.

Lucky meows again, more emphatically this time.

"Almost there, kitty girl."

My palm must have been sweaty from being in the glove,

and in the sub-zero temperature, the moment the metal touched my skin, the moisture froze solid. I cannot open my hand without tearing off the skin.

"Damn, it's too cold!"

I stand there in the frozen dark, trying to think.

"I have to warm it up somehow."

I bring my hand up to my mouth and blow into it. The cold air burns my lungs, but eventually I feel the key dislodge. I fit the small treasure into the snow-encrusted lock and force the frozen bolt to move. Using the sleeve of my coat, I push the brass handle down and lean against the door. The heavy, wooden portal creaks open.

"Yes!"

Lucky rushes in, meowing up a storm.

I grab the flashlight I keep on a small table next to the door and slide it on. It flickers for a moment and then burns dimly, pushing back the night. I peer out into the still darkness, hoping the dog will come in, but he's already trotting off into the forest.

"Tolstoy! It's too cold to be outside tonight. Come back! You can stay with us."

He stops and turns, his tail wagging and his eyes glowing in the flashlight, and then he disappears into the frozen night.

# CHAPTER 24

## *Diego: Did You See the Blood?*

"Come on, people. Pipe down." Agent Dick strides across the small room like a Roman emperor. The time portal has taken over the Y, and a barbecue-shaped device dubbed the GrillMaster dominates the center, with various machines and power supplies stationed around it. Cassie's ping-pong table now straddles one of the lanes in the bowling alley next door, but the two vintage video games have been pushed back into a corner. Despite the fact that Matt told me this would be just a simple first test, it seems everyone in the Magic Kingdom is here.

Dick pauses with his hands on his hips, glaring at the crowd. "Can someone shut off those goddamn video games?"

No one moves.

He marches toward the ancient game consoles, a scowl on his face.

"Wait!" Junior scurries over. "I'll do it. If you power them off, I'll never get them to reboot." He pushes past people toward the games, and then reaches behind each machine and turns down the volume. The *bings* and *pew-pews* are barely audible above the hum of the huge exhaust fans that keep fresh air circulating in the Magic Kingdom.

Matt and I met with Picasso last night, and Cassie ended up joining us. We managed to convince Picasso that Isabel should be brought into the project, and he agreed to discuss it with the brass—if the time machine tests go smoothly. Afterwards, I offered to help Cassie run the final system software tests—beats sitting on my hands worrying about Isabel—and it turned into a long night.

I suppress a yawn and watch Cassie start up the time machine software. A minute later, she glances up at Matt. "We're good to go."

He steps up to the GrillMaster and clears his throat. The room goes silent. "This prototype is one-fifth the eventual size, but the time portal is otherwise exactly to spec."

I do the math in my head. The real time machine will have a two-meter long capsule.

*What idiot are they going to convince to crawl into that coffin?*

"What you see here today is mankind's first attempt at moving an object an instant *backwards* in time." Matt holds up a paperclip and then positions it inside the metal capsule. "If the time portal does what we expect, the moment Cassie starts the software, the paperclip will disappear from here," he shuts the pod lid, "and reappear here." He taps the shelf attached to the GrillMaster. "Ready?"

She nods.

He steps away from the time portal, and the crowd backs up a bit too. "Execute the code."

Cassie types in a command and hits return with a flourish. The lights in the room dim, but nothing else happens.

The audience groans.

Matt walks over to the computer. "Did you start the

program?"

"Yep," she says. "It ran without any errors."

Matt goes back to the GrillMaster, releases the lid, and opens it up. The paperclip is right where he left it. He reaches in and gingerly picks it up. "Not even hot." He doesn't try to hide his disappointment.

Phil, the head of the Peeping Tom team, is studying one of his instruments. "Well, it did something. It drew five-thousand megawatts in less than fifty milliseconds."

Matt whistles. "That's enough to light London for a week."

Picasso peers over Phil's shoulder. "Where did all that energy go? It can't just disappear."

"I don't know. I followed the time portal instructions, but I can't say I understand them. For all I know, the GrillMaster transferred electricity into a black hole."

Agent Dick crosses his arms. "So you think it worked?"

Phil shifts his weight. "I couldn't say. I vote to try again with something else. Maybe the time machine doesn't work with metal objects."

"Try something organic," Junior says. "Like in *The Terminator*: you can't send weapons."

Agent Dick glowers at him, but he takes a pencil out of his suit pocket. "Here." He hands it to Matt.

Junior rubs his hands together. "This is so cool. I bet only the wood part goes." He looks at his boss. "Uh, sorry, sir. Just trying to be helpful."

Matt sets the pencil in the portal. "Are we good to go, Phil?"

Phil holds up his finger for half a minute, his eyes on the battery gauge, and then points back at Matt "Yep."

Matt shuts the lid and engages the lock. "Ready, Cass."

Cassie types in the command, but the moment she hits the "return" key, the lights go out.

A moment later, they come back on. Something is on the landing pad.

"It worked!" Matt claps his hands together.

The room breaks out in raucous cheers.

On closer inspection, we discover that Junior was right: only the wooden part of the pencil was transported. The cylinder is very cold, but appears undamaged. The bar of graphite, the synthetic eraser, and the small metal band are still in the pod, surrounded by thin flecks of yellow paint.

Agent Dick turns to Picasso. "Let's try something bigger. Something alive."

Someone in the back hollers, "Why don't you go?" and someone else adds, "It wouldn't be a fair test, he's already dead."

The crowd laughs, but Dick ignores the jibe and addresses Junior. "Get me a mouse from the genetics lab."

Junior trots out.

"Let's get things set up, people, so we're ready when Smith gets back with the test subject."

I watch Cassie reset the software.

*Would it be possible to send something back in time and save the twins? Prevent Isabel from getting stabbed? If so, why didn't the note warn me? Instead of telling me to "prepare for the worst," why didn't it tell me to buy antibiotics?*

The answer hits me like a truck: because I had to come here—or HIS universe gets screwed up.

*Shit.*

I wait until everyone is finished. "Did you guys move the pencil to a different time or to a different location?"

Picasso looks at Cassie, and Cassie looks at Matt, and Matt looks at Phil.

"I don't think that question makes sense anymore," Phil says. "The time machine simply pushed the wood to a different place in four-dimensional space-time. From our frame of reference, the pencil seemed to jump to the landing pad because you don't remember it being there."

"But doesn't that break the laws of physics?" I glance from Cassie to Phil, and then back at Matt. "What about causality and time travel paradoxes?"

"Yeah, good question," Matt says. "We need to do more tests."

"You *can't* change your own past," Phil says. "So *this* pencil must have come from another universe. And ours went somewhere else."

"What?" Cassie says. "All at the same instant? You mean there's somebody in another universe running the exact same tests?"

"And probably having the exact same conversation."

She lifts up her hands and stares at them. "That's creepy."

The door bangs open, and Junior jogs into the room carrying a small cage. "Good luck, little buddy." He hands it to Matt. "Remember that it started with a dream and a mouse."

There are a few snickers.

Matt places the frightened mouse in the portal, shuts the lid, and locks it. "Go."

Spatters of blood appear on the landing pad a moment before the lights shut off.

Cassie lets out a yelp. "What the hell?"

Absolute darkness descends, the smell of burning circuits filling the air.

We hear the equipment power down, and for one very long moment, there is complete silence, not even the low rumble of the ubiquitous air exchange fans.

And then an alarm goes off, and the overhead sprinklers start spraying water all over half a billion dollars worth of computers and electronics.

Picasso's voice booms out over the gush. "Mr. Smith, can you get to the control panel and shut off the damn rain."

180

"I can't see a thing, sir."

Cassie's voice hails from in front of me. "Use your cell phone as a flash light."

Small pockets of light appear around the room, the bodies of the owners hunched over their phones to keep them dry.

Picasso's voice is calm but compelling. "Do it now, Smith."

Someone can be heard tripping across the equipment toward the back of the room.

"Everyone else, stay put. They should have the power back on—"

The lights come up, and *bings* can be heard all around the room as the computers reboot. Matt scrambles across cables and around desks and flips the master power switch before we're all electrocuted. The computers and all the equipment fade to black. He catches my eye, his face white, and then glances at Cassie, silently asking: *Did you see the blood?*

We both nod and then gape at the empty landing pad: no blood, no mouse, no nothing.

Once the sprinklers shut off, we can hear the whine of the air exchanger as the giant fans spin back up. The water on the floor is a quarter-inch deep, and everyone in the room is soaked.

A creepy voice in the back of the room hisses: "Beware, I live."

The stunned crowd parts as everyone looks for the source. Junior steps in front of the *Sinistar* game console and smiles weakly. The display behind him shorts out with a loud crack, and the smell of ozone fills the air again. He flips more control panel switches and the games go silent.

Matt walks back across the room and releases the seal on the GrillMaster. Everyone leans in to see. There are spatters of blood all over the inside of the metal capsule, but nothing else.

Cassie says what I'm thinking, "Explosive decompression. The poor thing was probably half-way between universes when the power failed."

"Christ," I say, looking up. "What poor fool are you planning to force into that deathtrap?"

Everyone is staring at me.

## CHAPTER 25

### *Isabel: He's Dead*

I'm on the ladder clearing snow off the solar panels when I first catch sight of him.

*Goddamn it! Why can't he just leave me alone?*

I crouch down behind the peak of the roof, my heart racing, and watch him skulking up the ravine a hundred meters away. He's keeping to the shadows, stealing furtive glances at the cabin and outcropping of rocks, but moving quickly toward the graves. I push down the panic in my chest, pat the loaded gun in my jacket, and climb down, taking care not to slip.

Once I confirm that Lucky is safely inside the cabin, I slip out the front door and turn the deadbolt, zipping the key into my coat. I pull the Wally out of my pocket, check that there is a round in the chamber, and make sure the safety is on.

I've only fired the gun a handful of times, but I'm no longer afraid of it. I know how to aim and shoot—and kill, if need be. I jog into the forest, the gun in my hand and adrenaline pumping through my veins.

It takes me a minute to circle around to the creek, staying hidden in the trees, and then I follow the stream down to where the rocks jut out over the rushing water.

I creep up behind the largest boulder and peek around it.

A minute later, I see my attempted rapist take a huge bowie knife out of his backpack and then slink through the trees toward my hiding place, his eyes on the cabin. Something about how he's dressed sets off an alarm in my head, but I ignore it.

*Focus on the task at hand, Isabel. It's you or him.*

I lean against the boulder, my forearm resting on a small ledge. I calculate how far away my target needs to be for me to get off three or four rounds—just in case the first two don't take him down—and then I mark the spot in my head and wait.

Doubt pushes up bile in the back of my throat, but I swallow it down and concentrate on the terror I felt when he cut off my dress.

*Either I shoot him now, or I live in fear—and danger—for the rest of my life.*

The choice is obvious, if brutal.

Still, I can't bring myself to gun him down in cold blood.

*Give him one chance to leave, and if he doesn't, shoot to kill.*

I glance at the scars on my wrists, focusing my fear and rage, and then shout, "Drop the knife and get off my property!"

It takes him a moment to find me behind the rocks. "Hey there, beautiful. Got yourself a gun, did ya? I came back to see how your honeymoon was going." He starts walking toward me. "Sorry about the dress. I got carried away, but you can't really blame me, you being so provocative and all."

I aim at his chest. "You take another step, and you're dead."

He stops and scans the woods. "Where's that rabid monster of yours? If I put down my knife, I'll be defenseless."

"You have one minute to get the hell off my property. If I ever see you again, I'll shoot you in the back."

He raises his hands, one wrist bandaged. "Okay, okay. Just let me keep the knife, and I'll skedaddle."

And then I realize what set off my alarm: He's wearing Diego's clothes.

"Where did you get that shirt?"

"It belonged to your boyfriend, did it?" He starts walking again. "I thought so. But you didn't know he was dead." He takes off the pack and holds it out to me. "His things are still in here: razor, compass, maps, even a cute little photo of you. Maybe we could make a trade?"

I release the safety on the Wally, but he keeps moving toward me.

"Ah, come on now. You're not going to shoot me, are you?"

"Stop! Or I swear I'll kill you!" Tears stream down my face.

He ignores me, and I fire a warning shot in front of him.

Bits of dirt jump up into the air and hit him in the chest and face.

He drops the pack and zigzags across the clearing, covering the space between us faster than seems possible. I fire two more shots, but he's too quick and both of them miss. He vaults over the rocks on the grave, his eyes wild, but catches his foot and stumbles to his knees.

He rises in a single motion, a leering grin on his face, and I pull the trigger three more times, point blank, and each shot finds its mark.

His body lurches forward, the momentum carrying his twitching hand within an arm's-length of my boots.

I stare down at the back of Diego's torn and bloody shirt, and then I let out a wail of despair so deep that no comfort could possibly reach it.

## CHAPTER 26

### *Diego: Tenpins With the Devil*

I sit in my underground jail and peer out the fake window at the Great Pyramid. I still don't understand why they plan to send me. Matt is a world-renowned physicist, and an expert on both black holes and material sciences. Cassie is some sort of mathematical super-genius, and Picasso is a mild-mannered Rambo who could single-handedly take down a small country.

I'm a nobody. If some asshole hadn't found my name in that sphere, I would be home in bed, curled up around Iz.

I take out the photo that Picasso gave me and stare at Isabel's face. She's sitting on the rocks overlooking the twins' grave and gazing out into the distance, almost like she's searching for me. The breeze is blowing wisps of her shoulder-length hair across her cheek and lips, and she's wearing one of my sweaters, the soft curve of her breasts visible beneath it. I close my eyes, blinking back tears, and imagine putting my arms around her—

There's a knock on my door.

It takes me a moment to get my emotions back under control. "Come."

Matt peeks around the door. "Hey, mate. The computers are all down for a security update, so I thought I'd see if you wanted to chat for a bit? Maybe play a round of tenpin?"

I hesitate.

"You and I got off to a rough start, and I was hoping you'd give me a chance to apologize." The guy's wearing flip-flops and lounge pants that are too long for him.

"Yeah, sure, Matt. No worries. I'm sorry I've been such an ass. I know you're not responsible for the fact that I'm here, but I'm having a rough time of it, knowing that Isabel is out there all alone."

"And rightfully so. Come on. Let's grab a bevvy first."

We stop off at the Y and get a couple of beers.

"Do you have any idea why they're sending me, Matt?"

"You mean other than because your name was in the sphere? No. I think they were hoping you could tell us."

We walk over to the bowling alley next door.

"Why won't they let me contact Isabel?" I ask. "She thinks I abandoned her."

"I'll ask Picasso if something can be arranged. I don't think they'll let you out, but maybe you can send her a letter."

"That would be awesome, Matt." I set the beers on a small table and pick out a bowling ball. "I'd be very grateful."

He lifts a sparkly green ball off the rack and swings it up to his chin. "Yeah, well, save the gratitude until after he says yes." He grunts and sets the ball back down and picks up another one.

"Do you have any idea what they want to change, Matt?" I watch him swing a kid-sized purple and yellow ball.

"I don't know any more than you do, mate, but I do know that we can't go mucking around in our own past. Quantum physics forbids it." He wrenches his fingers out of the tiny holes. "Bollocks!"

"So why build a time machine?"

"Good question. My best guess is that it would allow us to go to a *different* universe and attempt to change something there. But that's pure speculation."

"What good would that do us?"

He swings another ball and puts it back down. "I think they're hoping it'll have some sort of domino effect: we change another universe's past; it breaks off into new branches; one of those new branches changes our world."

He sets a blue and red ball down on the ball return, and then looks at me. "Aren't you going to play?"

I nod at the plain black ball next to his. "Just waiting for you, *mae*."

"Sorry. I'm not very good at this. By the way, what does 'my-ee' mean? Is it Spanish?"

"No, Costa Rican slang. Sort of the same thing as 'mate' in England."

"Ah."

I open the beer bottles. "So, do you know what they're hoping to change? In the other universe, I mean?"

He glances at a surveillance camera, and then turns away and lowers his voice. "No, but the event would have to be something very subtle, or things would rapidly spiral out of control."

I give him an uncomprehending look. "What do you mean?"

"Say, for example, we send someone back to prevent Lincoln's assassination. That would cause *huge* changes in the target universe, and there would be almost no possibility the modified universe would be anything like ours: no Magic Kingdom, no time machine, maybe even no United States—which means that Lincoln's universe won't even know we exist, and there's no way they could help us." He takes a sip of his beer, wipes his hands on his pants, and picks up the ball. "So it would change things in their universe, but not in ours."

I sit down in a chipped plastic chair. "So what sort of change *could* we make?"

Without preamble, he swings the ball back and tosses it hard onto the ancient wooden bowling alley. We watch it bump down the lane, clip a single beat-up pin on the left, and disappear.

"Well, if we make some sort of subtle change in the universe that sent us the sphere," he says, "maybe we end up saving *them* from the apocalypse, and in return, they do something to help us. And yeah, I know it's a bleedin' long shot, but what other options are there?"

"How could anyone figure that out?"

He holds his fingers over the hand dryer. "Beats me, but I'm betting that whoever sent the sphere knows a lot more than we do."

"Except their targeting is off. Assuming they didn't intend to torch five square miles of downtown Denver."

The bowling ball rolls up from the underground shoot and circles around.

"Let's nitpick once we manage to get something working, okay?" He picks up the ball for his second try. "Did you hear they made progress on the Hot Button?"

"I heard rumors."

"Turns out, it's some sort of 3-D display device. *iFlick* they're calling it. Some guy figured out how to fix the battery, and the rest was easy. It projects a hologram of a woman, clear as day, just like she's in the room with you."

"Don't tell me she said 'Help me, Obi-Wan'?"

He chuckles. "No, she says the button contains instructions for building a 'bionano,' sort of a mechanical cell." He tosses the ball down the lane, and it wobbles a bit, threatening to fall into the gutter. "There was more on the device, but it got melted by the fire."

"You said it was a hologram of a woman?"

"It wasn't Princess Leia," he says, "and it wasn't Isabel." We watch the ball knock down the pin on the other side. "The spooks have face-recognition software working on it right now, but so far, no matches."

I nod, more disappointed than I'm willing to let on. "Do they know what the bionano is supposed to do?"

"That's the million dollar question." He turns and picks up his beer. "But they do have the woman's first name." He scrunches up his nose. "Blast, I can't remember. Something French, I think. I'm sure Picasso will ask you about it."

"It's not... Soleil, is it?"

"Yeah, that's it! How'd you know?"

I see those beautiful green eyes in the lifeless face and feel an icy hand grip my throat.

"You okay, mate?"

"Yeah." I set my beer down in a pocket of the cracked Formica counter-top. "One of the stillborn twins was named Soleil. Painful coincidence, I'm sure."

He watches me pull the damp label off the bottle. "You know, Diego, one of the reasons they won't bring Isabel on board is because they need her as leverage—just in case you misbehave."

I look up at him, unsure what to make of his revelation.

He turns his back to the surveillance camera again. "Agent Dick flew off the handle when you initially refused to join the project. He thinks you're a loose cannon. And you have dual citizenship, so that makes you suspect. If you ask me, it's all a crock of shit, but nobody cares about my bloody opinion."

"A loose cannon? Why the hell did they kidnap me?"

"Easy, mate. They're probably watching us now." He

takes a slow drink of his beer. "They had to bring you in because your name's on that sodding note, although they can't decide if you're supposed to save the world—or destroy it. Dick wanted you placed under guard, but Picasso overruled him."

"Christ."

Matt sets the bottle down and rubs his hand across his mouth. "If I were you, I wouldn't talk too much about Isabel. You might end up regretting it."

We glance over at some guys from the Peeping Tom team. They haven't sent any balls down in a while and seem to be in a heated conversation, their voices getting steadily louder. One of them sees us looking over and motions with his head for us to join them.

Matt nods at him. "Let's go see what's up."

Here in the Magic Kingdom there's a two-caste system: government slash military personnel, and private citizens who have been conscripted to work on the project. Most of the latter were brought in under false pretenses, and we take every opportunity to ignore the "no talking about the projects" directive. What are they going to do, fire us?

We drag a couple of chairs over and shake hands all around.

The forty-something guy wearing a Hawaiian shirt over a Stanford T-shirt—Phil, I think his name is—lets out a heavy sigh. "You guys hear the latest about the Peeping Tom?"

Matt looks at me, and we both shake our heads. "No, what's up?"

The red-haired kid with a freckled face answers. "I figured out how to peer *forward* in time."

"Wow," Matt says. "No shit?"

"It's not as earth-shattering as you might think—time is just another dimension like width and height."

"But still. Peeking into the future. How far can you see?"

"Somewhere around five hundred days, and I had to view universes pretty far away to do it, so there's no telling if things will play out the same way here."

The balding guy in a JHU sweatshirt looks down at his hands. "Tell them the rest, Sam."

The kid glances up at the camera and then nervously around our circle.

"It's okay," Phil says. "Mr. Johnson, or whatever-the-heck his real name is, can't do anything more than impound the bowling balls." He puts his hand on the kid's shoulder. "They need us. Otherwise, they'll never figure out what causes it. And if there's any way to stop it."

"Stop what?" Matt scoots his chair in. "What are you guys talking about?"

"Doomsday. Mass extinction. The end of the world." The young guy stares at a bowling ball that comes out of the return shoot. "We've got somewhere between twelve to eighteen months before everything on the evolutionary tree above a cockroach bites it."

I look at Matt, asking with my eyes if he knows anything about this.

"How do you know it's going to happen here?" he asks. "You just said you couldn't see *our* future."

Sam jerks his head around, his eyes slits. "It happens in every universe I've seen, every single one, and I've checked out hundreds of them. We haven't been able to find *any* that escape. You want to bet against it? Go ahead, man. Me, I'm going to figure out how to get out of this hellhole and spend the time I got left drinking fifty-year-old scotch and bedding equally-expensive women."

He stands up and kicks the leg of his 1960s-era chair, sending it skidding across the floor.

The JHU guy gets up and retrieves the errant chair. "Take it easy, Sam. We knew something like this was coming—that's why they put this project together. Your job is to figure out what triggers it, so we can figure out how to stop it."

"You think it's some sort of super virus?" I ask.

"Possibly," Phil says, "but more likely some sort of man-made vaccine that goes rogue."

"And it kills more than one kind of animal?" Matt asks, his voice soft but with an edge. "Most viruses are species-specific."

"It's not too fucking difficult to see all the dead bodies," the kid says. "Everywhere you look. And it's not just humans feeding the vultures, it's everything with fur: dogs, cats, horses, rats, you name it."

Matt recoils. "Crikey Moses! Is there anything to be done?"

The kid shakes his head. "It's too damn late."

The JHU guy glances up at Matt, his eyes pleading. "What's the status on the time machine?"

"Well, we should have the full-sized version ready in a few days. And we've built a decompression capsule as well. It'll make the trip a bit more comfortable for Diego."

Everyone stares at me.

"That thing is an execution chamber," Sam says.

"No, it's not." Matt looks hurt. "The problem was the power supply, and we've fixed that now."

"Any idea where you're going?" Phil asks. "Or when?"

"We were hoping you guys could tell us."

"Believe me," the kid says. "I've been searching for a universe that doesn't go belly-up, and it doesn't look good."

We all sit staring at our hands.

And then the pieces fall into place. "That's what the bio-tech plans are for!" I say. "Somewhere, in some other universe, people figure out how to survive. They create the Einstein Sphere and use a time machine to send the plans back to us."

Phil thinks for a moment. "Then why send instruction to

build a time machine?"

"Maybe they want us to send the plans on to someone else," I say.

"Yeah. Sort of a domino effect," Matt adds. "But in any case, we may have been concentrating on the wrong project. We need to figure out how to build the biotech device. That may be more important than anything else."

Relief and hope flood into me. "Isabel. She's a geneticist. My god, it's her handwriting on the note." I look pointedly at Matt. "She's the one who figures out how to survive and sends us the bionano plans."

"Sweet Fanny Adams, you're right. They'll have to bring her in now."

The Peeping Tom guys stare at us, not following. "Who's Isabel and what's a bionano?"

Matt stands up. "Possibly our last chance to save the human race. Come on, we need to find Picasso. I'll fill you in on the way."

## CHAPTER 27

### *Matt: Pretty Nasty Stuff*

So here I sit deep inside an underground bunker outside Washington DC, Picasso pacing in front of me like a caged tiger. Everything in here looks eerily familiar, right down to the Empire State Building outside the fake window, the cheap imitation wood tables, and the beastly coffee. I remind myself not to drink the water.

After nearly an hour of twiddling my thumbs, I can't take it anymore. "Bloody hell, mate, can you stop with the pacing, please?"

A month ago, Air Force One was shot down over the Amazon rainforest, probably using a surface-to-air missile system sold to the terrorists by the US Government.

*If it weren't so god awful, it would almost be funny.*

Hours after the plane went down, an ex-Hollywood action hero was sworn in as the President. Turns out, the guy is a religious fanatic who promises to "bring back the real America." Apparently, the best way of doing that is by declaring martial law, offering huge tax incentives on gun purchases, and canceling all government services.

But that's not the worst of it. Only a couple of days after we figured things out, our funding was cut pending the new President's personal approval—personal as "in person." So here we are, locked inside an underground cell watching the clock tick.

*Why is it always cold, dark, and cramped? But I suppose it beats snakes.*

The door swings open, and we are escorted into a large conference room just as four elderly men are shown out. Picasso gives them a nod and then turns to me. "Ex Star Wars guys." I give him a blank stare, and he adds, "Now working on a city-sized force field, but they haven't made any real progress in decades."

The President, who is eating a chocolate-covered donut, is wearing a gray T-shirt with "Pro Life. Pro God. Pro Gun." on it. He's sitting at the head of an oblong table surrounded by what appears to be an impromptu Halloween party. On his right is a scantily-clad redhead with breasts the size of Montana. She's reading some sort of glossy fashion magazine and doesn't even glance up when we enter. Next to her is a short Asian man in a cowboy hat. To the President's left is a balding blond guy in a Hawaiian shirt, and next to him is a middle-aged woman wearing a white fedora and holding a small dog. Of the seven people seated at the table, there is only one person wearing anything close to business attire: a black woman in a dark blue suit.

The President licks chocolate off his fingers. "Well then, what's up?"

I take a seat, and the woman in a suit jacket reads out the title of our project.

Picasso, who is in dress uniform and pinned with enough medals to open a pawnshop, remains standing. "We have a working time machine, Mr. President, and we need your approval to use it on a matter of national security."

"A time machine? You mean like a TARDIS?"

"Yes, sir."

"That's the craziest thing I've heard all morning," the President says. "But definitely cool."

The well-dressed woman shifts in her chair. "Assuming that you *have* built a time machine, what do you intend to do with it?" She glances at the sheet of paper in her hand and adds, "Sergeant Major Richter?"

"Madam Secretary, we have not yet tested the theoretical limits of the machine, but the instructions we obtained from the Einstein Sphere call for a Faraday Cage large enough to carry a single human passenger. Upon arrival in the past, that time traveler would complete a prearranged mission, and any changes would propagate to us."

"You plan to undo some grave screw-up, I presume?"

"In a word, yes."

"And who decides and approves these actions?" the woman asks.

"We have a cross-discipline team approved by the National Security Agency, the CIA's Special Activities Division, and the DOD's Defense Clandestine Service."

"I see." The woman adjusts her reading glasses. "And you intend to strand this time traveler in the past?"

"Yes, ma'am. We don't have the ability to bring him back, and we don't expect him to survive more than a few days."

The guy in the cowboy hat gives a cynical laugh. "Poor bastard."

She motions toward the project sheet. "If I read this correctly, your Achilles heel is access to electricity. What are your specific power requirements?"

"I would need to check on exact numbers, but given our current mission parameters, a ballpark estimate would be six hundred megawatts."

She sits up straighter. "So this time machine of yours will require more electricity than a nuclear reactor produces in a year?"

Picasso nods once. "Yes, ma'am. That is correct."

Chatter breaks out around the table.

She speaks over the noise, visibly annoyed. "And what is the largest object that you have successfully sent back in time, Sergeant Major?"

I look up at Picasso, but he doesn't hesitate. "A pencil, Madam Secretary."

Her eyebrows rise. "And how far back in time did you manage to send this pencil?"

"A few milliseconds, ma'am."

The President, who has been doodling on his briefing papers, glances at his watch and makes an exasperated noise. "Can't you just tell me why we should fund this Doctor Who thing?"

Picasso shifts his weight. "Yes, sir. We plan to send one man back twenty years in the past. If his mission succeeds, the looming pandemic will be avoided, saving millions of American lives."

The President looks bemused. "Seriously? What pandemic are we talking about here?"

"I assume you are aware of Hemorrhagic Fever outbreaks in California, and now Texas and Florida?"

"Yes, of course. Strain of Ebola. We have a team putting out those fires right now."

"Well, it's going to get worse, much worse. The virus is going to mutate, and billions of people will die. There won't be enough manpower left to bury all of them, let alone keep the lights on and the tap water flowing. And you know who history will blame, sir. You."

The well-endowed redhead glances up from her magazine

and addresses the President. "He could be right, Maverick. If the virus becomes highly infectious, it could spread around the world in a matter of days. You know the Black Death in the 1400s killed sixty percent of Europe's population, and that was before air travel." She taps a red fingernail on his paper. "Pretty nasty stuff, darlin'. Maybe we should fund this one."

"That," Picasso says, "is a very astute analysis, ma'am."

The redhead nods at him and goes back to reading her magazine.

He turns to the President. "To put it succinctly, how much money would the government spend to save billions of lives, sir?"

"I expect we'll do whatever it takes." The leader of the free world gives the buxom woman a pat on the thigh and then nods at us. "Thank you, boys. We'll get back to you." He clears his throat. "Now then, who's next? Let's get them in here quickly. I was supposed to tee off ten minutes ago." He picks up another chocolate donut and takes a bite.

As I follow Picasso toward the door, the next group files in, and we step sideways to let them pass. A middle-aged guy with a name tag that reads David Kirkland brushes past us. He's carrying an expensive-looking poster of a city inside a bubble.

"I thought the force-field guys already went?"

"Must be something else," Picasso says. "And I think that's the CEO of Kirkland Enterprises, the guy who was planning to build the Mars habitats back before things went all to hell."

We watch a train of servicemen lug heavy cardboard boxes into the room. The last guy stumbles over the raised doorframe and spills the contents of his carton across the floor. Mr. Kirkland barely glances at him.

Picasso and I bend down to help the guy pick up the mess.

The President smacks his lips. "Let's get started."

The woman Picasso called Madam Secretary reads from the next brief. "Biodomes to Protect Cities from Infectious Disease, Environmental Threats, and Biological Weapons."

The King of Donuts lets out an exasperated groan. "Holy God in Heaven, doesn't anyone do research on nice things? With all these doom and gloom projects, you'd think we were all going to die."

## Chapter 28

### *Isabel: Heads or Tails*

I wake up to the sound of metal clattering on frozen ground. I can see my breath, and the floor is covered with a dusting of snow, tiny cat footprints leading from the open window to the bed and back. I pull the covers up over my ears and shut my eyes.

*Diego is dead. The babies are dead. I want to be dead.*

The annoying racket continues.

*Goddamn it! Just let me die in peace!*

I force myself to get out of bed, tiptoe across the frost-covered floor, and peer out the window. Except to use the bathroom, I haven't been out of bed in days, and my legs are wobbly.

The world outside is covered in a tattered blanket of old snow, but I don't see any signs of life, not even any footprints.

Lucky peeks out from the covers and meows.

"Yeah. I hear it too." My voice is gravelly from disuse.

There is more banging and clattering.

*God almighty, who is making all that racket?*

I shove my toes into old tennis shoes, put on Diego's robe, and shuffle out into the living room, careful not to step on any half-frozen mouse carcasses.

*Lucky's been bringing me food.*

Something about that thaws my frozen heart just a little.

After another minute of the banging and crashing, I unlock the front door and wrench it open, ready to face whatever awaits.

Two amber eyes gaze up at me, and then the black and white dog wheels and lopes away.

"Tolstoy?!"

I shiver in the icy draft. There on the porch is the empty water bowl.

I fill it up from the crock in the kitchen and carry it back to the front porch, Lucky on my heels. "Okay, Tolstoy. Here's your water." For half a minute I stand there, trembling in the cold, but nothing in the forest moves. "Damn." I whistle a couple of times.

A basset hound limps out from the garage, his head down and his tail wagging.

I smile for the first time in weeks. "Good boy! Come get a drink." A moment later, the dog is lapping up the water.

"Wanna come in?"

He wags his tail and takes a tentative step, then turns and looks back.

The golden retriever is peeking from behind the garage. I pat my thigh and she comes slinking forward, followed closely by one of the other mutts. The golden's shoulder is caked with blood and dirt, but she wags her tail when I call out encouragement.

"Wasn't there another one, kitty girl?"

Lucky peers up at me and meows.

"I thought so too. I wonder what happened to him."

A few moments later, the water bowl is empty, and I have three wagging tails on my front porch. I hurry back into the bedroom and pick up Lucky's half-frozen mice. I hold up one by its tail and call out in a stern voice, "Sit!"

Three dog butts hit the deck.

I give each dog a mousesicle and then spy Tolstoy watching from the edge of the trees. I call out to him too, but he won't come any closer, so I go to get more water.

All three dogs follow me into the kitchen, their toenails clicking on the hardwood floor. The Bassett plops down on the rug and shuts his eyes. The two other dogs sit next to him, their ears back.

"It's okay, guys. I won't hurt you." The golden wags her tail, slides her paws forward, and places her head on her feet. The beagle curls up next to her, and I notice that one floppy ear is torn and infected.

"You're safe now." I refill the water bowl and set it back down in front of them. The beagle takes another drink and licks my hand. I pat him on the head, careful not to touch his injured ear. "It must have been rough out there for you guys."

There's a scratching noise behind me, and I turn to find the missing shepherd pawing at the front door. Her beagle pal gets up and trots over to greet her, and then they both stare at me, their heads cocked.

"Sure. Come on in. The more, the merrier." I refill the water dish and take it back outside. Tolstoy is waiting at the edge of the trees. I take a couple of steps toward him, but he turns to go.

"Wait!" I set down the water dish, but he doesn't come any closer. "Okay. Take your time. After all that's happened, I don't blame you one bit."

He sits down in a bit of sunshine.

*What do dogs really love?*

I rummage around in the hall closet until I find an old can

of tennis balls and take one out. The shepherd lifts her head, watching me.

"I'll save one for you, girl."

She wags her tail for the first time.

I slip through the front door and bounce the ball on the porch.

Tolstoy barks, so I toss the ball into the forest. He bounds through the trees, retrieves it, and drops it on the first stair, his tail wagging.

I step down and pick it up. He backs away as I approach, but doesn't bolt. I toss the ball again, and while he chases it, I move the water dish down and then sit on the top step.

He retrieves the tennis ball, sets it next to the bowl, and takes a long drink.

I stay very still, smiling so hard my face hurts. "Thanks for saving me, Tolstoy. Twice, so far."

I throw the ball once more and then take the bowl back into the kitchen, leaving the door open a crack. I start water heating in the teapot, and then go back into the bedroom and shut the window, put on some warmer clothes, and brush my teeth.

When I tiptoe back to the kitchen, all five dogs are stretched out on the floor, four of them sound asleep. Lucky is lolling between Tolstoy's front paws, batting one of his ears and licking his face. He thumps his tail when he sees me and glances hopefully at the tennis ball next to the water dish.

"Later, big guy. Let your friends get some rest first."

He lets out a long, low sigh and puts his head back down.

I walk over to the front door, push it gently shut, and then make myself a cup of tea.

## CHAPTER 29
### *Diego: Out of Time*

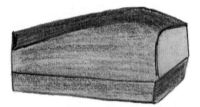

It's nearly midnight, and I'm sitting alone in my underground room, the stars twinkling outside my window at exactly the same spot as they did last night—and every other night since I was taken hostage. I'm scheduled to go back in time tomorrow morning, and to be honest, I'm glad to finally be done with this whole frustrating charade.

A couple of guys from PSYOPS have been prepping me on what to tell my parallel self, but I think Cassie gave me the best advice so far: Follow your heart. The guy's going to fall in love with Isabel just like I did, so teach him how to make it last.

*Maybe I should just tell my younger self to hunt down Dave Kirkland and stick his body in a dumpster.*

The thought is oddly appealing. Still, there's a part of me that hopes Dave is watching over Isabel, keeping her safe.

I swallow hard and stare out at the fake stars.

*I miss you, Iz.*

There's a knock on my door, and Matt peeks in. "Can I come in?"

"Sure. What's up?"

He sits down in the desk chair, rubbing at the back of his neck. "You know, I'd go in your place if I could, Diego. There's nothing keeping *me* here."

"Thanks, but Picasso is right. This one has my name written all over it."

He forces a smile. "Speaking of Picasso, I told him you wanted to get a message to your Isabel, but he didn't seem keen on the idea."

"No worries," I say. "Anyway, it doesn't matter now. I just wish she knew the truth."

"After all this time, she must think you're dead, mate. She's gone on with her life, maybe even found a new man. I know that's a hard one to swallow, but given your... situation, any contact now would only cause her more pain."

I know he's right, but it tears me up inside just thinking about it. "I want her to know that I didn't abandon her, Matt, that I did everything in my power to get back to her."

"Bloody hell." He lets out a weary sigh. "Write a note, and I'll do what I can to get it to her. What are they going to do, ground me?"

"Thanks, *mae*. I'd appreciate it."

We sit in silence for a bit.

"There's something else." I take the shell out of my pocket and turn it over in my hands. "I wasn't supposed to tell anyone, so I'd be grateful if you kept it to yourself unless..."

"The shit hits the fan?"

"Something like that."

"Okay, Shoot."

"A bit over a year ago, I received a handwritten message, possibly from the same guy who sent the Einstein Sphere. I think that person is me. Well, me from another universe."

"At this point," he says, "I'd believe just about anything."

"I left the original note at the cabin, but I have it memorized: Prepare for the worst. When things are darkest, give Isabel the shell and let her go. With Einstein's help, you will meet again. Tell no one or risk losing everything!"

"Blimey. So you think the ball is the Einstein Sphere?"

"Yeah," I say. "And 'Einstein's help' must be the time machine."

He considers my words. "So why are you telling me?"

"Because after tomorrow, I will have lost everything."

"Christ, Diego, I'm sorry."

"Thanks, but I know it's not your fault. In any case, the note appeared in the glove box of my car along with a seashell *exactly* like this one." I toss it to him.

"Don't tell me it was stuffed inside a dirty sock." He turns the shell over in his hands.

"How'd you know that?"

"There was a sock in the sphere too." He hands it back to me. "Where'd you get this one?"

"You know the clip the Peeping Tom guys showed us in the theatre, the one with the boys playing *futbol* on the tropical beach? I was in it. It happened twenty years ago. The same day I found this shell."

"Crikey Moses. Are you sure?"

"Yeah. I recognized all the other guys too. I don't know how or why, but I'm the one who connects all this together."

"So that's why you agreed to go?"

"I didn't really have much choice, but yeah. The only problem is, 'let her go' could mean that *Isabel* is the one who needs to go, not me. The shell is for *her* to use."

"Why didn't you say something sooner? Maybe we would have had more luck convincing the brass to bring her on board if they knew about this."

"Because the note was very explicit about keeping quiet,"

I say. "I didn't know where the hell I was supposed to go, or how I could ever get back to her, but I didn't want to mess it up."

"I probably would have done the same thing." He exhales. "Does she have the other shell?"

"It's at the cabin. I left it inside a wooden puzzle box in the bottom drawer of the desk. The note is there too."

"Did you tell Isabel about them?"

"No, you're the only one who knows. Like I said, I took the *keep it secret* warning seriously. That and I didn't want her to think I was crazy."

"We're all bleedin' crazy now."

I stand up and get a small silver bag out of my daypack. "I brought this to trade for the antibiotics, and I've been saving it for god knows what. It's whole bean, so you'll have to find some way to grind it." I hand him the bag of Costa Rican coffee. "Think of me when you drink it, okay, *mae?*"

He stands up and gives me a hug. "Thanks, Diego. And I hope the part about getting back to Isabel comes true. And I hope to hell there's someplace to come back to."

∞

On the way to breakfast, I hear raised voices coming from down the hallway, but when I step into the cafeteria, the whole place turns into a morgue.

I grab a tray and load on hash browns and fake eggs, and then address the room. "So, who died?"

Sam, the redhead kid on the Peeping Tom team who likes expensive scotch, stands up. "For the past few nights, I've been running tests with the coffin." He blushes bright red. "I mean the time portal. Anyway, I've managed to send a mouse back in time and locate it on the Peeper twice now."

"I didn't think we had that much control." I walk over to the nearest empty table and sit down facing him. "Or that

209

much power."

"The power part was easy," he continues. "I just ran the tests in the middle of the night. With all the crap that's going on outside, it'll take them months to trace it. And last week I came up with a new algorithm using a trick from cryptography that Cass suggested—she's been helping me run the tests."

He glances at Cassie, and she nods encouragement.

"We figured out a way to detect the ripple made in the space-time continuum. It's still a crap shoot, but the odds are a bit more in our favor now." He swipes his hand through the air. "But the important part is what happened to the mice."

A murmur goes around the cafeteria.

"The first time," he says, "we tried to send the mouse back a year. The targeting on the time machine is flaky—just like Cass has been telling everyone—but this time it did work, and we managed to pick up the mouse on the Peeper. It was dead the moment it arrived, all blood and guts. I thought the new decompression armor had failed, but Cass didn't think so. She said it looked like a fetus, and she guessed that it had aged backwards, even past the point when it was born, and *that* killed it."

"And the other mouse?" I ask, struggling to keep my voice level.

"I had to look around for an older one, but I found a male in the genetics lab who was just over three." The kid scans the room, his eyes coming to rest on Cassie, and she nods again.

"Anyway, I sent that mouse back to the same place and time, and just like Cass predicted, he got younger, and acted younger too, running around and humping everything." His face reddens again. "And then right before our eyes, he started to age. It was like watching a horror movie. His hair started falling out, and he started staggering and gasping for breath. In a matter of minutes, he collapsed and died."

There is a collective taking-in of breath.

"If I had to guess, I'd say he died of old age, but Cassie thinks it's radiation poisoning. Either way, time travel is lethal."

The guy sits down, and whispers ripple around the room.

I release the fork I've been clutching for the last minute and address the kid. "Thanks for doing the research—and for letting me know."

"Yeah, sure."

Cassie sits down next to me, and necks crane around to watch us. She glances over at someone I recognize but have never spoken to and gives him a scathing look. The guy turns away.

"The bio team," she says, "thinks *that's* what the bionanos are for: to repair cellular damage caused by the side-effects of time travel, not some magic bullet to fight off Hemorrhagic Fever."

"What? You mean it's *not* a vaccine?"

"Why would someone send us instructions for a time machine if the vaccine was all we needed? Besides, Dick's been ordering the guys in the lab to infect mice with various strains of Ebola and then inject them with the bionano. They all die in a matter of minutes."

"Shit." I pick at my breakfast while Cassie peels a black-market orange.

Picasso strolls in, grabs a cup of coffee, a bowl of apple-sauce, and some toast, and then sits down across from us. "You heard about the vaccine?"

I nod. "You heard about the mice?"

"Yeah. Field's team thinks it's crazy to use you as a guinea pig, and I'm leaning that way." He sips his coffee. "And the test subject died last night."

I drop the tasteless eggs I've been holding on my fork.

"What test subject? You mean someone volunteered to test the bionanos?"

Cassie glares at Picasso, her eyes full of accusations. "Smith. He wasn't playing video games last night."

"Johnson coerced him into volunteering," Picasso says, "and he had some sort of allergic reaction—"

"You killed him." Cassie spits it out.

Picasso ignores her. "The tech lead was up all night running tests, and he thinks the bionanos are designed to work on a specific genotype, perhaps on a single individual." He looks pointedly at me.

Cassie pushes back her chair. "Don't listen to him, Diego. They don't even know if all the data was recovered from the device, let alone that they synthesized it correctly. It's a death sentence."

"Or the key to staying alive." Picasso doesn't look up.

She grunts and gets up, knocking her chair over backwards. "You're pretty fucking generous with other people's lives, Mister GI Joe." She storms out of the cafeteria.

"I'm leaving it up to you," Picasso says. "Your name was in the artifact and your past is the key. The bionanos must be meant for you." He picks up Cassie's unused knife and lets it slide through his fingertips. It makes a sharp *rap* on the table each time it drops. "I can delay your trip for a day or two, give us some time to run more tests, and give you some time to think about—"

Cassie rushes back into the cafeteria, followed by Agent Dick and a gaggle of marines with rifles. "It's started!"

Picasso stands up. "What's started? What's going on?"

"The pandemic, Colt. The virus mutated. Half the population of Los Angeles is dead." She glances around the room. "Turn on the goddamn TV! The military is broadcasting some sort of emergency message."

Someone switches on the monitor in the corner, and we

stare up at a grim scene: bodies lying in the street, bodies slumped over steering wheels, bodies piled up in the back of trucks.

The room breaks out in panicked chatter.

*Oh my god. Isabel is out there alone!*

Dick slams his hands down on the table. "Everyone shut up!"

A hush falls as we strain to hear a male voice above the static. "...uncertain if Chicago and Philadelphia have been infected ... I repeat, if you live in or near a major metropolitan area, seek shelter immediately and remain indoors. All medical personnel are requested to ... working around the clock..."

The power goes off, immersing the cafeteria in the eerie glow of the emergency lamps. A moment later the lights flicker on, but the TV remains silent.

I look at Picasso. "Let's do it."

Five minutes later, he uses his badge to open the door to the genetics lab, and Cassie and I follow him in.

Agent Dick rushes in behind us. "She's not supposed to be in here, sergeant."

Picasso doesn't even glance at him. He rests his hand on my back. "Are you sure about this, Diego?"

"Yeah. Let's get it over with."

Picasso nods to the lab tech and then turns to Agent Dick. "Get the fuck out of here."

Johnson takes a step back, his eyes wide, and then leaves. Picasso waits for the door to click shut. "Over there, Diego, and take your shirt off."

I follow directions and then lie down on the exam table.

Picasso turns to Cassie. "If he has a reaction, it may get pretty ugly in here."

She nods, looking pale.

The lab tech prepares a syringe and then brings it over.

213

"This is going to sting a bit." She rubs alcohol on my arm, preps the needle, and glances at me. "Ready?"

Picasso rests his hand heavily on my shoulder, and Cassie puts both of hers on my thigh.

I swallow hard. "Yes."

The woman injects the needle. A burning sensation spreads out from the insertion site, and I can feel my heart racing. She withdraws the syringe and presses on the spot with a cotton ball. "Done."

Cassie rubs her hands over my thigh. "Are you okay?"

"Yeah. Just stings, as advertised."

Picasso watches the clock for sixty long seconds, keeping his hand on my shoulder. "Smith was in anaphylactic shock in less than a minute." He turns back to me. "Feel anything?"

"You mean besides scared shitless?"

He laughs and everyone in the room visibly relaxes.

"No. I'm fine." I sit up and put my shirt back on, feeling a bit light-headed but otherwise normal.

We give it fifteen minutes, and then head over to the time portal lab.

The new time machine is inside the gutted bowling alley, and the place is crammed with people, including a few I've never seen before. A hush falls over the crowd when we walk in.

Matt gives me a once-over. "You doing okay, mate?"

"Yeah, fine," I say. "A bit embarrassed by all the attention, actually."

He pats me on the back and then holds up a thin cotton towel. "As you know, every ounce counts, so you're going to have to strip down."

"Yeah." I stand behind them and take off everything, wrapping the thin towel tightly around my waist and tucking it in. I remember to grab the shell out of my pants and then amble over to the coffin.

Cassie opens the cover of the decompression armor for me. "You don't have to do this, Diego. You could wait a few days to make sure you're okay—and insist that they test the machine with something bigger than a mouse."

Picasso steps up behind her. "Cassie's right, but in another day or two, we might not have the power to run the time machine. I know it's risky, but I think this is our last chance."

I attempt to climb in, still holding the seashell and trying to keep the towel from falling off.

Cassie steadies my arm. "It's okay to be scared. It means you're about to do something really, really brave."

I settle back into the coffin. "It doesn't count as bravery if it's the only option." The armor is cold, and I shiver, clutching the seashell tighter.

"There are always other options, Diego. Always. It's not too late to call this off."

I shake my head, not meeting her gaze.

Cassie and Picasso exchange a look, but neither comments.

She taps her finger on the red circle directly above my chin. "Remember: You need to pop the lid before the oxygen runs out. One good bang right here should do it." She straightens the towel around my hips and then pulls her hand away, looking embarrassed. "Let's hope Douglas Adams was right about the towel."

I force a smile. "So long, and thanks for all the fish."

She leans in and kisses me. "For luck."

"Thanks, Cass. See you on the other side."

She gives me a shaky smile and closes the lid.

I can see shapes moving around outside the translucent sarcophagus and then the cover of the metal portal comes down, and I'm plunged into perfect blackness.

I lie in the dark, my senses on overdrive. I can hear muffled voices calling out the final system checks and a

215

computer-generated voice calling out the countdown. "Nineteen, eighteen, seventeen..."

I force down panic and bring up an image of Isabel asleep in my arms, her soft breath on my cheek.

"Six, five, four..."

*Goodbye, Iz. I love you. I have always loved—*

Outside, an alarm goes off, the pulsing whoop of the siren alternating with the calm countdown of the computer.

I hear Cassie's frightened voice, high-pitched and panicky, shouting above the melee. "Wait! There's something wrong. The targeting is off! Shut it down, goddamn it! Shut it down or we're going to lose him!"

And then it's perfectly silent.

Before I can breathe a sigh of relief, the coffin becomes icy cold and a crushing weight presses down on my chest, forcing the air out of my lungs. I try to yell, to pound my fists against the frozen lid, but my arms are too heavy, my body crushed by the terrible forces of a black hole.

And then, mercifully, the monster slams me down into dark oblivion.

## CHAPTER 30

## *Matt: If I'm Wrong*

Right after we lose Diego, Cassie locks herself in her room, insisting that it's her fault he's dead. Unfortunately, there's plenty of blame to go around, and we all tell her so, but she won't listen to reason. Picasso says to give her some time, but I can tell that it's tearing him up inside. Last night, he tried to use the master key to get in, but she had bolted the door. Seems she had the hardware smuggled in and installed it on her own. I don't think anyone was too surprised.

Picasso's been trying to talk sense into her all morning, and things out in the hall were pretty tense an hour ago, but I think Cassie got tired of yelling "bastard."

*That woman is a force to be reckoned with. I hope Picasso can handle it.*

It's been months since I had a day off, and now that the time machine project is stalled, I don't know what to do with myself. Phil has been busy with the Peeper, so I've been spending most of my time trying to stay out of his way, and that's been tough.

I stare out the fake window at the Eiffel Tower, wondering how bad things have gotten in Paris.

*Probably not as bad as Los Angeles.*

Half of California is under water from the nuke-induced tsunami, and the epidemic is spreading like wildfire there, although Picasso says it's just a bad Ebola strain, and it's not killing anything except humans—as if that's a good thing.

*And yeah, we rushed to send Diego back on a false alarm.*

In any case, the Peeping Tom guys are leaving, and they're taking their equipment with them.

And I imagine Phil's leaving with them.

I lie on the bed, gazing up into the half-light, feeling miserable. I guess I should go find out how long I have until he leaves.

When I walk out, I spy Picasso sitting outside Cassie's door with his head in his hands. "You okay, mate?"

He runs his fingers through his hair. "Yeah, I'm fine."

"You want to grab some chow?"

"No, thanks. You go ahead. I'm waiting for Cassie. She's gotta come out eventually."

I knock on her door and call out. "You want something to eat, Cass? I'll bring it up here for you."

We hear movement inside her room, and then the door opens a crack. She peeks out over a heavy metal chain, her eyes red and her hair a mess. "Yeah, thanks, Matt. And a couple bottles of water would be great."

"Sure you don't want to join me?" I ask. "A little change of stale air might do you good."

"Maybe in the morning." She sees Picasso and her eyes darken.

He's still sitting with his back to her, and for a moment, I think she's going to start yelling at him again, but she just lets out a heavy sigh.

He turns and gazes up at her, his expression tortured. "I'm sorry. I was wrong. It's not your fault. It's mine."

She swallows hard and starts to shut the door, but relents. "Why don't you ever listen to me, Colt? Is it because I don't follow orders, or you don't trust me, or what?" Her voice is defeated.

Picasso looks down at his hands. "No. It has nothing to do with any of that."

"Then what the hell is it?"

He shakes his head in frustration. "It's because of the way I feel about you, Cass. I'm trying to keep that from interfering with the job I have to do. So I overcompensate sometimes and—"

"You are seriously fucked up, Colton Richter."

"I'll just be off to the cafeteria, now," I say.

"I'll be down to grab something in a minute," he says and stands up. "But right now, I think Cass and I need to talk."

"Of course." I turn and walk down the hallway.

A few minutes later, I grab a stack of iffy-looking spam sandwiches—it's that or Iraq-era MREs—and head over to the lab.

Phil's team is in the process of packaging up the Peeper when I walk in.

He looks like he hasn't slept in days, but he smiles when he sees me. "Hey, Matt. Where the bloody hell have you been hiding?"

His comment leaves me feeling a bit off balance. Phil *never* swears. "Just trying to stay out of the way, actually, but I thought you'd be too busy packing to grab dinner."

"Thanks," he says and takes a sandwich. "You heard that everyone is leaving?"

"Yeah, I heard."

He steers me over to an empty workstation. "I've got something to ask you." He sits on the desk and looks up at me, his lips tight. "I... uh..."

"What? Just say it, Phil."

"Okay. I'll stay, if you want me to, Matt." His expression is carefully neutral. "I'll do what I can to help with the project, of course, but that wouldn't be the reason I'd stay."

Relief floods into me. "Sweet Fanny Adams, you're a wanker." I put my hands on his shoulders. "Please stay. I want you to stay."

He smiles. "Okay, I will."

I pull him into a hug, both of us still holding the sodding sandwiches. "Thanks, Phil."

A moment later, he glances around and then motions with his head toward a stool. "There's something else I think you should know." I pull it up to the desk and sit down. He sinks into the desk chair and leans closer. "Picasso's thinking about sending Isabel back in time."

"Bloody hell. I should have kept my mouth shut about Diego's note."

"And there's more." He takes a deep breath. "I didn't want to say anything with everyone around, but I found an anomaly in the data we collected yesterday on the timeline scans. It could just be a fluke, or even an error, but it was there: a ripple."

"A ripple?"

"Yeah, I don't know how else to describe it. It's a long ways away and not in the right direction, but it's a disturbance in the space-time continuum that matches the signature of an exo-object. I showed it to Sam—you know, the red-headed kid—but he thought I was imagining things," he says. "Maybe I am."

"You mean some other universe is sending out tungsten spheres?"

"Well, I suppose that's possible, but I was thinking that maybe Diego just ended up somewhere else, somewhere far away."

"We need to tell Picasso—and Cassie."

"I don't have any proof. The machine is in boxes, and the data was erased when we unplugged it."

"Ah, bugger that. Why didn't you print it out or something?"

"On what? Toilet paper?"

"I still think we should tell Picasso. Maybe there's some way to reproduce it, or… hell, I don't know, confirm that it's there."

"But if I'm wrong?" He stares at his half-eaten sandwich. "I'd be responsible for killing Isabel too."

## Chapter 31

### *Isabel: Precious & Few*

I glance up from my book at a sudden gust of wind, unable to shake the feeling that something is amiss. I'm out on the deck, surrounded by five exhausted dogs, Lucky asleep in my lap. The seven of us spent the day climbing the peak to take a look around, and even Sparky, the basset hound, managed to make it to the top.

A week ago, the air was laden with soot, black rain falling all across the Front Range, but tonight it's cool and clear. I doubt there's much left in the cities to set ablaze, so I suspect that a forest fire must be raging to the west, consuming trees that have been waiting a hundred years to burn. But even with binoculars, I couldn't see anything from the ridge, so I think we're safe for now.

Still I worry. This cabin and these animals are all I have left.

The sun has been out all week charging the batteries, and tonight I'm baking cookies—and dog biscuits. I can hear the drone of the generator in the kitchen.

Tolstoy stands and stares out into the darkening forest, the hair on his back standing up. I set down my book, turn off the flashlight, and pat the gun in my pocket. "What is it, boy? Can you feel it too?"

He growls, and then scans the dark house.

My pulse surges.

"Hello?" The disembodied voice comes from inside.

I let out a startled cry, slip my hand into my pocket, and slide the safety off. Tolstoy lowers his head and snarls. Lucky skitters off my lap and disappears into the cabin. The other dogs struggle to their feet with varying degrees of success.

The outline of the man's face is visible in the shadows, his eyes big. He sweeps his gaze across the motley crew. "Sorry. I didn't mean to frighten you. I knocked, but no one answered, so, I, ah, let myself in." He glances at me, his lips tight, and then gapes at Tolstoy.

"He won't attack unless he thinks you're going to hurt me, so I suggest you step out into the moonlight and keep your hands visible."

"Right-o." A man with thinning hair inches out onto the deck. "I'm sorry it's so late. It was rather a lot farther than I anticipated, and I got lost in—"

Tolstoy barks, his ears back and teeth bared.

I place one hand on the dog's shoulder, keeping my eyes on the intruder. "Who are you and what are you doing in my house?"

He's middle-aged and appears less grimy and better fed than most. He's wearing a leather bomber jacket over an oxford shirt and carrying a daypack. He clears his throat. "I'm sorry. I didn't mean to frighten you. It's just that I got lost, and when I saw your cabin..." He stands there in his high-top sneakers, waiting for me to speak, and when I don't, he continues. "I, uh, am looking for Isabel Sanborn-Kirkland."

223

Tolstoy growls.

The man lifts his hands like a statue of Jesus. "Please. I'm a scientist. A physicist, actually."

I shift in my chair, belatedly checking to see if he's alone. "Well you're no Einstein, that's for sure. What on earth prompted you to let yourself in? People who do that don't tend to live very long around here."

The flashlight slips from my lap and clatters onto the deck.

Tolstoy barks and takes a step closer. The man raises his hands higher.

"Do you have a gun?" I ask. "Now would not be a good time to lie."

"No, I'm unarmed." His voice is emphatic, almost desperate.

"Then stand very still, and he won't hurt you." I nod at Tolstoy. "Check him out."

The dog slinks across the deck, sniffs the man's shoes and pants, and then stretches up to smell the backpack. The guy holds his breath, his eyes huge.

A few moments later, Tolstoy returns to my side and sits, looking up at me.

I scratch his ears. "Good boy. Settle." He whines softly and slides down onto his belly, but he keeps his beautiful amber eyes trained on our guest.

"So you *don't* have a gun." I slip the safety back on the Wally.

"For the second time, yes, I'm unarmed."

"In this day and age, it pays to double check." I glance at the other dogs. "Excitement's over, guys. Settle."

They reluctantly go back to their down stays. All except Sparky. The basset hound rolls over on his back against Brontë, the golden retriever, and lets out a string of sorrowful yowls, his stiff leg sticking up like a ship's mast, but his tail wagging.

The man shifts his weight, apparently breathing again.

I pick up the flashlight and stand it up next to my chair. "Who are you?"

"My name is Matt Hudson. I'm a physics professor at CU—or rather, I was." He regards the resting dogs and relaxes a bit. "Are you Dr. Sanborn-Kirkland?"

I consider lying, but see no point. "Yes, but I'm divorced, and I never used the hyphenated name in the first place—despite Mr. Kirkland's forceful insistence and continued exasperation."

"Dr. Sanborn, then?"

I nod. "Who sent you, and how did you find me?"

"I have some things to discuss, and I've brought you a gift." He starts to opens his jacket, but stops when Tolstoy growls. "May I?"

"Yes, but I would advise against taking out anything that appears to be a weapon."

He swallows and pulls a small silver bag out of his jacket, pinching it from the top.

"Coffee?" The word tumbles out before I can stop myself.

Tolstoy looks at me and tips his head, unsure of my reaction.

The man's face softens. "Yes. Real coffee... Costa Rican." He holds it out with both hands, like an offering. "It's for you."

A minute later, I shut the heavy drapes in the kitchen, switch on a light, and start the electric teapot.

*Thank goodness for Diego's solar panels.*

I set the teapot on the table along with mugs, spoons, and a small jar of sugar. "Have a seat."

"Thank you." He hangs his jacket on the back of a chair and sits, his hands in his lap. "Nice place you have here. And very difficult to find."

225

A timer dings, and I take the cookies out of the oven, careful not to turn my back. "You seem to have managed. Where did you get the coffee?" It's *Tres Ríos*, Diego's favorite.

He watches me moving around the kitchen. "It was a gift, and I've been saving it." His face flushes bright red.

*He's lying.*

I set a plate of cookies on the table and sit down. Tolstoy flops down next to my chair, and Lucky leaps into my lap. I stroke her soft fur with a shaky hand.

"Why are you here?" Just as I finish speaking, the teapot whistles.

The man jerks his body around and knocks a mug onto the floor. "Damn it!"

Tolstoy jumps up snarling. After I convince Lucky to take her claws out of my thigh, I turn to Tolstoy. "It's okay, big guy. Settle." My protector lies down.

"Sorry about the cup," he says, "but couldn't you put the dog outside?" I can see the sweat on Professor Hudson's clean-shaven upper lip, and now that he's taken his jacket off, it's easy to tell that he doesn't do much manual labor. His hands are soft and uncallused.

*Where has this guy been for the last year?*

"Please, Dr. Sanborn. As I said, I'm a scientist. I mean you no harm. In fact, I came to ask for your help."

"Men are afraid that women will laugh at them, Professor Hudson, but women are afraid that men will kill them." I pick up the mug, check it for damage, and set it back on the table. "The dog stays."

He blinks, looking a bit pasty. "Of course. Please forgive me. As I'm sure you've deduced, I'm not much of a frontiers-man—or a rogue—and I'm very sorry I frightened you."

"No harm done." I reach over to the counter, pull out a drawer, and take out the severed end of a nylon stocking. I spoon coffee into it and set it in a cup. "So tell me, professor, what's happening in the outside world?" I pour hot water over the grounds and inhale the rich aroma.

*God, I've missed the smell of coffee.*

I push the cup toward him and make another. "Is it down to sticks and stones as Einstein famously predicted—or just styrofoam and plastic?" I take a sip of a world that no longer exists.

"Unfortunately, I don't really know. I've been holed-up inside a mountain for the last year, and not much makes it past the government censors. I did get a chance to fly to DC a couple of weeks ago, but the only stops we made were at military bases, and they didn't look much different to me." He takes a drink of his coffee. "Maybe people were a tad thinner than I remember. And the new President is a wanker."

"Have there been any more nuclear attacks? Or news of fallout spreading?"

"Not that I know of. The politicians are twits, but I don't think they're that stupid—at least, I hope they're not." He stares down at his hands.

"So what is it?"

He looks up. "There is a particularly nasty strain of Ebola spreading in the larger metropolitan areas. They're predicting *billions* of deaths in a matter of months, although I haven't heard of any outbreaks around here."

"Please tell me that someone is working on a vaccine."

"Actually, *we* are—in a manner of speaking."

"Is that why you're here?" I squeeze all the air out of the small silver bag, reseal it, and set it in front of him. "You do know that vaccines are not my area of expertise."

"Yes, I am aware of that, and that's not why I'm here."

"So tell me, Professor Hudson, why did you come all this way to share your precious coffee?"

"As I said, I've been working on a secret government project—" He shifts in his chair. "to build a time machine."

I let out a mirthless laugh.

"I'm afraid it's true. We've spent the last two years locked inside a secret underground facility searching for a way to avoid the looming apocalypse, and we've finally found the slimmest thread of hope: one change—twenty years in the past—that could turn out to save the world."

"Okay," I say. "So what's different in that universe?"

"You and Diego Nadales are happily married—and have been for nearly twenty years."

I drop my mug, and coffee splashes onto the table. "Diego's dead."

He peers into his empty cup. "Yes, I know."

I stand up. "I think you should leave now, Professor Hudson—or whoever the hell you are."

He stares at me, a pained expression on his face, and then he exhales and takes an envelope out of his pocket. "Please check in the bottom drawer of Diego's desk. There's a wooden puzzle box with a hidden compartment, and—"

My heart stops. "How do you know about that?"

"Diego told me about it before we bloody killed him." He drops his gaze. "Here." He holds out the letter. "He asked me to give you this."

## Chapter 32

### *Matt: Top of the List*

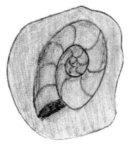

"What happened to Diego?" Her striking green eyes are red and swollen, but her voice is strong and defiant. "Where is he? What have you done with him?"

*She's a fighter, that's for sure. We should have brought her in sooner.*

I wait for her to sit down at the table. "We don't know. The time machine malfunctioned, and he's presumed dead."

She's quiet for a bit. "So who sent the shell and the note to him?"

"His parallel from another universe, we think."

She sets the seashell down on the table. "How did it get here?"

"Let me start at the beginning and tell you everything?"

Isabel nods once, her lips pressed together.

I take a sip of my coffee and begin. "Over a year ago, an artifact—a hollow tungsten sphere, actually—was discovered in the wreckage of a hotel fire."

"The Brown Palace. I was there the night it burned down."

"Ah, yes. I remember reading about your rescue—and Diego's subsequent arrival in the hospital. I think that was the world's most romantic marriage proposal ever." The cat looks up at me, flicking the tip of her tail. "And this must be the kitten you rescued from the fire? Lucky, isn't it?"

She glances down, her eyes squeezed shut.

"I'm sorry. This must be very painful for you." I give her a moment. "Shall I continue?"

She wipes her face on her sleeve and then nods.

"The sphere contained things from another universe—and possibly the future."

"The future? What was in it?"

I hesitate. "Information."

She gives me a scathing look, as if she sees right though me. "I thought you were going to tell me the truth."

"Yes," I say, "I'm sorry. It's a bit difficult to believe—and I've seen it with my own eyes."

"Try me."

"It contained an electronic device that hasn't been invented yet and some technology that may help us survive the impending disaster."

"Impending disaster?" Her voice is tight, and the dog lets out a soft whine and looks up. She pets his head. "You mean the Ebola pandemic? Or radioactive fallout?"

"No, something worse than either of those. Sometime in the next few months, an ill-conceived vaccine will mutate and turn out to be worse than the virus itself." I rub my eyes, fighting back exhaustion, and then reach down and pet Lucky on the head. "Even if we managed to shut down every hospital, university, and private lab, there's no guarantee that the vaccine isn't already out there just waiting to mutate. And whoever designed it wanted to eliminate future animal vectors for the disease too, so the vaccine was designed to work on all warm-blooded genotypes."

"Oh my god."

"Yeah. Between the virus and the vaccine, it's the end of the age of mammals." I glance at my hands. "By our best guess, we have nine months, perhaps a year."

"How could you know that?"

The cat jumps up into my lap, and I let out a surprised yelp.

"I can put her in the other room, if you like."

"No, she's fine. It's been along time since anyone wanted to sit in my lap, and I'll take it as a compliment." Isabel's expression softens little. I run my fingers across the cat's silky fur. "Have you ever heard of a Tesseract computer?"

"Back before things fell apart, Stanford University claimed to be building one. They planned to use it to confirm the existence of other universes, if I remember correctly?"

"Yes. Well, we've gone one step further. We have one that can see into other universes. A fortnight ago, we found a world, one out of tens of thousands, where doomsday is avoided. Either the vaccine isn't released, or it doesn't mutate—we don't know which." I look up at her. "Our best guess as to *why* that universe is different from ours—"

"You mean the thing that keeps the vaccine from mutating?"

"More like the first domino in a long and complicated string of dominoes, but yes."

"Okay. What is it?"

"Your relationship with Diego Nadales."

She rubs the back of her hand across her mouth. "How could you possibly narrow down the difference to two ordinary people? That sounds absurd."

"Well, it wasn't easy—that's for sure. Essentially, we scoured two movies to determine the place where they diverge, and then we tried to figure out what caused the split. Imagine trying to compare one day in our world with a nearly identical day in another." I shake my head. "We had to hope that something significant caused the split, something that would be noticed by lots of people."

"Someone important getting murdered," she says, "versus a frond falling off a palm tree on Fiji."

"Exactly. We concentrated on things you would read about on the front page of the *New York Times*, but we didn't find any differences, so we started looking at famous people who died and worked our way down to obscure individual deaths."

I run my hand across my scruffy face. "But, it turned out that those differences evened out: some people died a day or two earlier, and some a day or two later. It didn't seem to matter. Then we started over with births, and then marriages, divorces, and even adoptions. The task was gargantuan."

She takes a sip of her coffee.

"Finally," I say, "a very smart graduate student figured out a way to use the computer to do the compare, sort of like using sound waves to cancel each other out. She ran a whole day's worth of data in an hour, and we used those results to cancel out all the changes that didn't make a difference. After we had done that with thousands of universes, we were left with the critical events: the things that are different in the world that survives."

"And?"

"You and Diego are at the top of the list."

She pins me with her gaze. "So what do you want from me?"

"As I said, there's not much time left, and our resources are dwindling. We have made the decision to act now, even though the risks are high." I try to soften my tone. "The critical split in the multiverse happens at precisely the moment when you and Diego break up—that's how we know it's important. In the narrow stream of universes that lead to survival, that break never comes. For as much as we can determine, the two of you meet, fall in love, and remain together for the rest of your lives."

She shuts her eyes, tears streaming down her cheeks, and whispers, "So it *could have* been forever."

"Unfortunately, we know what needs to change, but not how to make it happen. We have been spending twenty-four hours a day, seven days a week, peering into progressively more distant universes, looking for a way to keep the two of you together."

"It's that bad?"

I smile. "Well, in most of the universes, you don't even meet. In a few, you meet but don't connect. And in a still smaller few, like our own, you meet and date briefly before things get dodgy."

She looks away. "You want me to go back in time and make our relationship work?"

"Yes—but there are a few things I need to tell you before you decide. We've addressed the problem with the time machine, so we're pretty sure we can get you there in one piece, but there won't be any way to get you back. It's a one-way trip."

Her expression doesn't change.

"And there are some, uh, side effects. We can't guarantee you will remain healthy for more than a day or two, but we do have a team working on that problem even as I speak."

She stares at me. "So you planned to kill Diego—even if the time machine hadn't malfunctioned."

"No. He was injected with a custom-made vaccine, and we were hopeful that it would protect him. The instructions for it were also in the Einstein Sphere. Diego knew the risks, and he choose to go."

She blinks back tears but doesn't speak.

"Unfortunately, the vaccine was designed to work on a single genome: Diego's."

"So you want to send me back in time, even though you know it's going to kill me?"

I can feel my face redden. "That's the worst case scenario, but it is possible."

"Why me, professor? Why not send a marriage counselor or a conflict resolution expert? For Pete's sake, send Oprah. Why do you need me? I already screwed it up once."

"Diego was our first choice, but..." I look down and pet the cat, unable to meet Isabel's eyes.

"So it has to be me."

"Yes," I say. "I can give you more details about the plan we've come up with, but basically, we want to send you to a universe very similar to ours. Once there, you would need to prepare a nineteen-year-old Diego to meet your future self. This scenario has the highest likelihood of success with the least likelihood of causing unwanted side effects."

"So if I managed to do it, would things here change? Could it keep Diego from..."

"Dying? I'm afraid not. You can change the past in another universe, but not your own." I watch her for a moment, feeling like an executioner. "But I can say: if you succeed, something in our future could change, something important."

"I see." She looks at me with those piercing green eyes. "But I would get to see him one more time, even if it's only for a day?"

"Yes."

She lets out a soft sob, and then leans over and hugs the dog. "How soon do I leave?"

*No wonder he loves her so much.*

# Part Three
## La Isla, Another Universe

*They say that time changes things,*
*But actually,*
*You have to change them yourself.*

Andy Warhol

## Chapter 33

### *Isabel: It Beats Taking the Bus*

I'm surrounded by total darkness, panic rising in my chest and choking me. It's bitterly cold inside the high tech sarcophagus, and icy numbness is spreading through my limbs like a corpse buried in an avalanche. I gasp for air, but try as I might, I can't move—can't exhale or shiver or even blink.

*This is what it feels like to die.*

Sometime later, diffuse sunlight falls across my eyelids. I lie there, my body trembling from the cold, and try to make sense of the flickering patterns of light and dark flashing across my retinas. Something is wrong. I know something is terribly wrong, but I'm so sleepy...

*Wake up, Iz! You're suffocating!*

Adrenaline leaks into my bloodstream, and I pound my fists against the translucent lid, my heart racing. Warm air rushes into my frozen grave, and for long moments, I lie transfixed, lungs burning, chest heaving, hand throbbing.

At last, the sublime sound of surf breaking on sand caresses my ears, and I take a breath from a quarter century in my past.

*Oh my god, I made it.*

I open my eyes and attempt to get out, but every muscle in my body shrieks in protest and my head spins. I fight down the vertigo and eventually manage to sit up. My left hand hurts like hell, and when I will my fingers open, an orange seashell drops onto my bare thigh, the sharp white spines flecked with scarlet drops of blood.

I stare at the gash in my hand and then use the flimsy towel to apply pressure to the cut while I look around. Condensation covers the cold walls of the coffin, but it's otherwise undamaged. I wish I could say the same. I feel like I was knocked down by a hockey puck and then run over by a Zamboni.

I pick up the shell and wedge my elbows against the slick, concave walls. My legs are rubbery, so I fling one foot over the edge and try to pry myself out with my arms. The pod shifts and I slip, landing hard on my shoulder. Sharp pain shoots across my back, and I vomit yellow bile against the translucent wall.

I shut my eyes, imagining Diego's arms around me, my head resting against his chest, his heartbeat in my ear.

*Somewhere out there, he's alive.*

And then I try again.

I flex my ankles to get the blood flowing, and then lever myself up onto the narrow rim using my elbows. I lower my feet onto the ground and then lean against the slippery coffin, shaking uncontrollably. There, half buried in the fine white sand, is a man's shoe. It's wedged under the pod, as if I landed in tropical Oz and accidentally crushed the wicked wizard of the tropics.

I watch a hermit crab scramble across the leather toe.

"Sorry, buddy. Looks like you'll have to do a bit more sole searching."

He waves his claw at me and scuttles away.

A warm breeze, soft as kitten's fur, tickles my bare back, bringing with it the cloying scent of plumeria and ginger.

*Toto, I've a feeling we're not in Kansas anymore.*

I reach into the capsule and grab the towel, and then attempt to stand. I totter for a step or two, but I can't seem to balance, and a moment later, the beach smacks me hard on the butt.

"Damn it all to hell."

I yield to the whims of gravity and lie back in the warm sand. Above me, towering palm trees buttress a deep blue sky, their fronds throwing emerald spatters of paint against a cerulean canvas. I lie still, waiting to die, or for my heart rate to settle, whichever comes first.

A few minutes later, I press my abused elbows into the soft sand and work my way up to a sitting position. The scene before me is exquisite: a white sand beach rimmed with verdant tropical forest nestles against a lazy azure sea. To the west, thunderheads bump against the jagged sides of steep volcanic peaks.

*Just another day in paradise.*

I take a couple of deep breaths and check that the strand of pearls is still around my neck. If the bank account number I have memorized doesn't work, I plan to pawn the necklace, but I'm hoping it doesn't come to that. Still, I can't wait to see the look on the teller's face when I walk in wearing only a towel and tell him all my belongings have been stolen.

I glance back at the coffin, drops of condensation still glistening on it in the sun. I consider camouflaging it, but decide against it. Time is of the essence, and the pod will disintegrate quickly if those thunderheads follow through.

I pick up the seashell and the sandy towel, and then slowly

stand, using a bit more caution this time. I wrap the thin cloth around my bare torso and do a double take: full perky breasts, flat tummy, and miles of smooth alabaster skin. Even my toes are cute. *Wow.*

It's just as they predicted, and that gives me hope, even though I know it won't last.

I peer up at the sky. It's already late afternoon, and I need to find a bank and a place to stay.

The distant sound of laughter startles me.

Down the beach, too far away to make out faces, is a group of guys playing soccer. Farther on, there's a small cluster of thatched-roof buildings and a three-story hotel, the windows reflecting the afternoon sun. I secure the towel and scan the low dunes for a rough-hewn beach cottage with a large porch. It's farther away than I imagined, but it's there.

I take a couple of tentative steps. My legs seem to have recovered somewhat, so I amble out from under the palm trees, pretending I've just been sun bathing.

*With 500 SPF sunscreen. Yikes! Look how white my skin is!*

Almost immediately, the bottoms of my feet are on fire. "Ouch!"

The dry sand is scorching hot, and the tight towel makes me shuffle like a geisha. After a moment of Asian Farce On Searing Coals, I hitch up the towel and lope toward the shade.

I stop when I reach the shadow of the cabana and hop from foot to foot, giggling.

*Add "slap-happy" to the list of time-travel side effects.*

When I manage to get back under control, I make my way up the cottage steps and lean against the heavy wooden railing, feeling surprisingly good. I watch the guys playing soccer and try to catch some movement that seems familiar. They're all dark-haired and skinny, their half-naked bodies gliding across the wet sand, laughing and calling out to each other in Spanish.

And then I recognize him.
*I died and went to Diego.*
"Well, it beats taking the bus."

## CHAPTER 34
### *Isabel: I Was Misinformed*

Droplets of seawater explode in fine flashes of late afternoon sunlight, tiny diamonds splashing up on his thighs and chest as I watch him jog across the wet sand and into the shallow surf. He plucks a soccer ball out of a wave, his movements fluid and relaxed, and then jogs back up the beach to rejoin his friends. I recognize him immediately: the dark eyes and bright flash of white teeth against olive skin. His hair is black, longish and wild, and he's younger than I've ever seen him—and I can't believe how skinny he is!

He returns to the game, teasing and bumping shoulders with his friends. I continue walking toward him, making futile adjustments to the ill-fitting bikini I bought and trying to stretch out the thin pink T-shirt the shop owner threw in.

*Beggars can't be choosers.*

A soccer ball comes shooting out of the mass of half-naked male bodies and flies across the sand. I take a couple of quick steps and trap it with my foot, willing him to come. His friends turn and look, but only he leaves the pack, loping toward me like a wolf pup—all legs, damp hair, and enthusiasm.

When he's ten meters away, he stops. *"Gracias!"*

I stare at him, unable to move, my heart pounding in my throat.

*Oh my god, it's him.*

He shifts his weight. *"La bola, porfa, señorita."* He glances at my feet, smiling. *"MUCHAS gracias."*

I flick the ball up with my toes, bounce it on my thigh, and catch it. I watch the surprise flit across his face—he taught me that move. I hold it out to him.

He glances at his friends and then strides across the sand toward me.

The delay in the game catches the attention of his buddies. One of them shouts, *"Póngale!"* and then switches to English. "Hey, *gringa*, come play with us. You can be on my team." The other guys all laugh.

"You must be Diego." I toss him the ball. He trips in the churned-up sand and almost misses the catch. "Gotta watch out for those sand snakes," I say, trying not to laugh.

He smiles sheepishly. "Do I know you?"

"You have a brother in the United States, right?"

His eyes are wide. *"Sí.* I mean yes. How did you know?"

One of his buddies calls out, *"Vamos,* Tego!"

He waves off his friend and then slides his hand around the sandy ball. "How do you know him?"

"From school. You look enough like him to be his twin." I allow my eyes to roam over his young, handsome face. "My name is Isabel Sanborn." I lean in.

He hesitates, and then steps closer and kisses me on the cheek, as I knew he would. "Nice to meet you, Isabel."

The sound of my name on his lips—mixed with the scent of his sweat and aftershave—grabs my heart, and for a moment, I can't breathe.

His friends whistle and call out, *"La bola,* Tego!"

"As you may have noticed, my very impatient friends call me Tego," he says. "Only my mom calls me Diego."

"Nice to meet you, Tay-go." The unusual word catches on my tongue, and I feel my face flush.

"But you can call me Diego, if you like."

I nod, feeling off balance. "Yes, I mean no." It's all I can do not to throw my arms around his neck. "I like Tego. It suits you."

*Don't blow it, Iz.*

I take a couple of steps and gesture with my head. "Would you like to join me? For a walk on the beach, I mean?"

He turns back to his buddies, and my heart jumps into my throat.

*What if he says no?*

"Sure," he says a moment later. "Let me give the ball to the guys, and I'll catch up with you."

I let out the breath I was holding, and watch him lope up the sand, my whole body filled with exhilaration. I glance down and place my toes into his footprint. A wave encircles my ankle, erasing all traces of him. Time, you fickle tease, giving and taking and giving back.

I look up at my teenaged lover, his feet leaving fleeting impressions in the damp sand, and resist the urge to cry out in joy.

*He's alive.*

I turn and start walking down the beach, my brain swamped with questions that begin with: How can it be possible…

Time travel, multiple universes, parallel selves, nineteen-year-old lovers resurrected from the dead?

My heart answers without hesitation: when he's standing right in front of me, the *hows* and *whys* don't matter anymore.

A few minutes later, I hear laughter and bravado, and

then his quick footfalls on the wet sand behind me. I watch him jog across the beach, aching to be in his arms.

*Easy there, Iz. Don't scare him.*

He settles in next to me, slightly out of breath. "So, what brings you to Costa Rica?" His accent is stronger than I remember.

"My health," I say. "I came to Costa Rica for the dry air."

He's quiet for a moment. "What dry air? We're in the tropics."

"I was misinformed."

He stops walking and looks at me, a sly smile spreading across his face. "I love that movie."

"I know—I mean—*Casablanca* is one of my favorites too." I turn away, trying to make it seem nonchalant.

*Good grief, Isabel, get a grip.*

He catches up with me. "Really. What brings you to *Nacascolo?*"

I tell him a story of flying south for the sun during winter break, trying to give enough detail to make it sound believable, but not so much that I get caught in a lie.

We walk in silence for a minute. He puts his hands in his pockets, keeping his eyes on the horizon, but furtively glancing over at me.

*He's interested, but worried about appearing too forward.*

I smile to myself.

*This is kind of fun.*

We take a few steps in silence, and then I give him an out. "How long are you staying here at La Isla?"

He stares at me. "I'm here for the week with friends, and then I have to get back to college."

I don't know how to interpret that look. "Am I keeping you from your plans for the afternoon?"

"No, I'm on holiday. I don't have any plans." He motions back toward his friends. "Besides playing *futbol* with those baboons." He gets that same unreadable expression on his face. "Where did you hear the name 'La Isla'? Everyone around here calls it *Nacascolo*."

Whoops, wardrobe malfunction. "Uh, I can't remember. It must have been your brother."

He raises one eyebrow but doesn't comment.

I notice his T-shirt for the first time: Love is Chemistry. Sex is Physics. "So, tell me, are you studying love or sex?"

He blushes, something I've never seen Diego do. "Neither. Engineering. But one of my hobbies is quantum physics."

"So then your answer would be 'quantum sex'?"

He stares at me for a moment, the corner of his mouth twitching, and I fight back the urge to wrap my arms around his neck and say, "Surprise! It's me, Isabel! We're lovers—remember?"

"I know this is weird," he says, "but I feel like we've met before."

"Nope. I'm pretty sure I would have remembered you."

He doesn't break eye contact. "Ditto."

I glance away, my heart racing, and spy an enormous crab poking around a tide pool. I take his arm and pull him over to look at it. He bends down to pluck the creature out of the sand, but it spies us and darts away. Tego grabs my hand and pulls me along, following the wild path of the crab. The curious animal stops next to a rock at the edge of the water, and I squat down to watch it dig a hole. Tego crouches down next to me and reaches over my thigh to snag it from behind.

"Gotcha!" I pinch his shoulder.

He loses his balance and falls over onto the water. The crab scurries away.

I lean in to kiss him and then remember where I am, who I am to him: nobody. Flustered, I jump up and jog across the sand, calling over my shoulder, "I bet you can't catch *me* either."

He bounds to his feet and chases after me, closing the distance with ease. I start running harder, testing my young legs, and then slow a bit to take off my T-shirt. I toss it down in the sand and race out into the surf, leaping over waves and kicking up rainbows in the late afternoon sun.

Just as he catches up with me, I dive over a wave and swim out into the warm, tropical sea. The bottom is nearly flat here, and the shallow water stretches out into the glistening horizon. I lengthen my stroke, in my element now, exhilarated to be so young again.

He follows, working to keep up.

I slow for a moment to adjust my too-small swimsuit, and he manages to grab my ankle and pull me back. I take a deep breath, twist out of his hand, and dive under the water. He lets go and stands, his shoulders just breaking the surface, watching me.

I spy a dazzling orange seashell nestled in the pristine white sand. It is *exactly* like the shell that cut my hand, the one I brought with me from another universe. I pluck it from the body of the sea and tuck it into my bikini top, my hand still tender from gripping its twin, and then circle back, still beneath the surface.

I reach out and grab his thighs, curling my torso around him.

He stands with his elbows out, watching me with wide eyes, his body awakening as I slide across his hips and stop with my chin pressed against his chest, looking up. Time stands still, our eyes locked. I have been holding my breath for a long time. A bubble of air escapes from my lips, breaking the trance, and he grabs my shoulders and lifts my head out of the water.

"You're a mermaid!"

I wrap my legs around his waist, run my hands through my hair, and then take out the shell and hold it up in the dazzling light. "A gift from the deep." I offer it to him.

"Thank you, oh, mystical sea creature." He says it with feigned awe, and then adds with sincerity, "It's exquisite."

*No, you are.*

He takes the shell from me and turns it over in his hands, stroking the spiral from the edge to the center. "May I keep it?"

"Well, you did capture me, so I suppose it counts as booty—"

"Aye, love. 'Tis the booty I want." He speaks in a low, raspy voice, making a goofy face and raising a hooked finger. "How long have ye been storing it in yer chest?" He motions with his head.

I shut my eyes, holding back tears.

*It's him. After all the suffering, tragedy and loss—it's him.*

He strokes the line of my jaw with his fingertip, and I gaze into his dark brown eyes, madly in love. "For an eternity you cannot imagine."

"Those are the best kind."

I glance down at the shell in his hand and clear my throat, struggling to control my emotions. "And given that the Jolly Roger is nowhere to be seen—" I scan the horizon with my hand shading my eyes and then lean in, daring him to replace the shell. "I'm guessing that you need to store it back in my chest."

Instead, he kisses me, and when I let out a yelp of surprise, he pulls away at the same moment I bring my arm down, and I whack him in the face with my elbow. "Ouch! Sorry! Are you okay?"

"I'm fine." He looks away, rubbing his jaw. "I... I didn't mean to startle you. Maybe I should get back."

I force down a twinge of apprehension. "I wasn't trying to discourage you, Tego."

He studies the beach, his shoulders still tense. I take his

chin in my palms and turn his head, waiting for him to look at me. "Really." It takes a moment. "It's just that you surprised me." His face feels wet and cool, the line of his jaw sharper than I remember. "But I like it... that you surprised me." I square my shoulders and raise my chin. "You have no idea how lonely it is being a mermaid, particularly after all the attractive pirates went into politics."

A flicker of amusement touches his lips.

I lean against him and slide my cheek up to his ear. I can smell traces of his aftershave, and my body responds to it like a starving man to the smell of baking bread. I let my lips brush against his ear. "Could I have another chance?"

He turns his head, our noses almost touching, and I lean back, my eyes focused on his lips. He pulls my mouth up to his and kisses me, soft and wet. I close my eyes, euphoria spreading out from where our bodies touch. A moan escapes the back of my throat, and he smiles, our lips still touching. I grab onto him, overcome with emotion, madly in love.

*If I die right now, it will have been worth it.*

I break the kiss and bring my hand up to my face to hide the tears. "Wow."

He smiles, wrenching my heart.

A wave falls over his shoulders, making his skin glisten in the fading sunlight.

I brush a lock of hair away from his lips, and let my gaze wander from his mouth to his chest. I couldn't bear to lose him again.

*This time, I'm dying on you, Captain America.*

I meet his eyes. "I have something I need to do this afternoon, but I was hoping you'd meet me for dinner?"

He doesn't hesitate. "What time?"

"Seven? At the open-air café just down the beach from the hotel, the place with the quaint gas lanterns and white tablecloths. You know the one?"

"Yes," he says, looking amused. "Rick's. It's the only café on this side of the island."

"Ah. Maybe your friends would like to join us after dinner?"

"My friends?" He lets go of my waist, and I slip down into the cool water. "Yeah, sure."

*He thinks I have an ulterior motive because I invited his friends?*

I remember this from the first time we dated. He took everything personally and didn't handle the competition well. I resist the urge to roll my eyes. "Hey. I figure if my friends like your friends, I won't have to worry about sharing you."

*Good grief, I'll have to convince the grad students I met at the boutique to come tonight.*

He glances down the beach and then places the shell in his pocket, *still* avoiding my eyes.

*Goddamn if he isn't a pain in the butt sometimes.*

"Tego?" I soften my voice. "Have dinner with me."

He turns back, his face unreadable.

"You're the one I want to be with tonight, okay?" I run my hand down his chest, sparks jumping between his skin and my fingertips. "Tell me you still want to be with me?"

His eyes get big. "Uh, sure. I mean—"

"Then I'll see you at seven." I motion with my head toward the soccer game. "Watch out for sand snakes."

"Right." He laughs and dives into a wave, using the swell to body surf back to the shore. A minute later, he shakes his hair like a dog and jogs down the beach toward his friends.

*Have I mentioned recently that I'm madly in love with you?*

## Chapter 35

### *Tego: I'm Not Going Anywhere*

When I get back to the *futbol* game, Beto gives me an inquisitive look, but doesn't say anything.

"I'll tell you later," I say.

He grins.

It takes a while for my pulse to stop racing.

Beto and I—and four buddies from high school—are all staying in a small, one-bedroom cabin a couple of blocks back from the island's main drag. It's crowded, but cheap, and we don't spend much time there anyway.

We continue kicking the ball around until the sun gets low in the sky and then head to a bar on the beach. On the way over, I tell the guys about Isabel's offer to bring her friends to the nightclub.

Tomás, who talks constantly about getting laid but has never been French kissed, lets out a whoop. The other guys tease him, but they're all clearly happy to have romantic prospects for the evening, particularly *gringas*: single American girls.

After one beer, I tell the guys I'm heading back to the cabin to take a shower. Beto asks me if I want company, and I nod, glad to have someone to talk to, but hoping he's not going to grill me about Isabel.

We step out into the fading sun and then cross the main road.

"She's got nice legs." Beto's tall and likes his women the same. He's also the best *futbol* player of us all—and the most popular with the girls. "So, she goes to school with Jorge? You're not horning in on your brother's girlfriend, are you?"

"Yeah, she does. And no, I'm not."

"She's at least five years older, *mae*, and she's going to have you by the balls in no time. Though that does have its merits, assuming she knows what she's doing." He grins at me. "What's she studying?"

"I have no idea."

"Shit, Tego. You ought to at least find out a little about her before you try to get her clothes off."

"Thanks for the tip, Beto. Speaking of clothes, did you bring any pants with you? All I've got is shorts."

"Trying to impress her, are you?" He claps me on the shoulder. "Good for you. 'Bout time you got laid, *mae*. And by an older women. That's fucking hot."

When we get back to the cabin, he pulls out black suit pants and a gray tie. "Too dressy?"

"Yeah, maybe."

"Let me see what else I have." He searches through his bag and lifts out a pair of tan linen pants. A moment later, he adds a black sand-washed silk shirt.

"Bingo." I hold the slacks up to check if they fit and Beto starts smirking. They're a couple of inches too long. "If I borrow these, what are you going to wear?"

"Shorts, Tego. I'm not trying to get laid. Claudia would

kill me. If she found out." He winks. "Let me see if I have any tape."

He rummages in a faded maroon duffel bag until he comes up with some white first aid tape and then looks over at the clock radio. It's nearly six thirty. "You better hit the shower. I'll fix the pants."

"Thanks. I owe you one."

As I'm rinsing my hair, he calls into the bathroom, "They're good to go. I'm heading back to the bar. See you at nine."

I shut off the water and step out. "Okay. Thanks for the loan—and the help."

"No problem." He tosses me a towel. "Maybe she has a twin sister."

∞

As the edge of the setting sun teases the surface of the ocean, I sit down at a small, linen-covered table that affords a perfect view of the sand and sea. I watch the lone waiter stroll around the open-air café, lighting Tiki torches.

Ten minutes later, a wave of paranoia washes over me.

*Did I get the time wrong?*

I glance around the café for the third time—an elderly gentleman, also sitting alone, nods at me and I return his greeting—but there's no sign of Isabel.

*Beto's right. I should have asked more questions.*

The waiter gives a theatrical cough. "May I get you something to drink, my man?" His skin is deep ebony, and he speaks English with a British accent.

Then I see her out on the beach, almost glowing in the last light of the sun. I watch as she floats across the sand, wind billowing her dress away from her body, her hair up. "*Ay, que bonita.*"

"A beauty, indeed." The waiter turns back to me. "I shall

return momentarily."

When Isabel sees me, she smiles and waves. Then, holding out her pale blue skirt, she twirls in the sand, strands of her hair blowing across her face as she gives a slight curtsy.

I stand up, searching for a way to get down to the beach. Behind me, the waiter coughs and tips his head toward the side of the café. I jog down four concrete steps, past a couple of palm trees, and out onto the beach, feeling awkward wearing shoes in the sand.

She reaches out to me. "Sorry I'm late."

"No worries." I take her hand and then kiss her on both cheeks, caught up in the intoxicating scent of her skin and hair. "You look beautiful."

She takes my offered arm, but something in her eyes is sad. "Thank you."

I remember that look from this afternoon. "Everything okay?"

"Uh huh." She squeezes my arm. "I missed you, Tego." When she says my name, my insides twist up in a way that could easily become addictive. I lead her past the palms, up the stairs to our table, and hold out her chair, my heart beating so fast I can barely breathe.

As I sit down, a twinge of pain flits across her face. "Are you sure you're okay?" The table is large for two, so I have to lean over to touch her hand. "Can I get you something?"

She glances down at my hand. "No, um, yes." She looks up at me, gazing long enough to make me feel self-conscious. "I'm fine now that you're here with me." Her voice is steady and reassuring. "In fact I'd be perfect if you weren't so far away."

Surprised but flattered, I try to scoot my chair around, but she doesn't let go of my hand. She lets her eyes roam across my chest, and when I manage to get the chair positioned next to her, she traces a line on my palm and then draws her fingertips up my arm, sending shivers across my skin. "Mmm. Better."

I watch her touching me, mesmerized, and the twisting inside me becomes more intense. I shift my weight and reposition my pants.

She goes back to stroking my palm. "How did you get the nickname Tego?"

I rest my arm on the back of her chair and run my fingers through the wisps of curls at the nape of her neck. "I played a lot of *futbol*—soccer in America—growing up, and I was usually the goalkeeper."

She nods and fingers the pearl necklace she's wearing.

"I once made a save that won us an important game, and afterwards, a couple of the guys started calling me *Protego*. That got shortened to *Tego*, and I guess it stuck."

She looks over at me, her face unreadable. "*Protego*. Protector. How romantic is that?" She bites her lip and peers out at the ocean, still stroking my hand.

For the first time, I have a chance to gaze at her without feeling self-conscious. Her skin is porcelain white, her eyes a stunning shade of green, and her lips full and soft.

*Mierda, she IS beautiful.*

We sit in silence, both of us enjoying the view.

She sighs softly. "It's lovely here."

"Yes. It's the most beautiful place in the world."

She continues gazing out at the waves, her lips parted. "Someday you'll have to watch the sun set over the Rocky Mountains."

"Will you take me?" I say it on a lark and then hope she doesn't think I'm being too presumptuous.

*Shit, I'm already in over my head.*

She glances at me, her eyes glossy. "Yes."

"Good." I run the back of my hand across her cheek, almost able to see the electricity jumping off her skin.

*I bet she looks great naked.*

The thought makes me excited and uncomfortable at the same time. We just met, and I don't want to push her or appear too desperate. I adjust my chair and take my arm down, trying to make it seem nonchalant.

She frowns and glances down at her hands. "Why did you take your hand away?"

*Ouch.*

She pins me with her gaze. "Hmm?"

"Uh." I look away. "It's just that I didn't want to—"

"Don't." She uses her finger to turn my head. "Don't take your hand away." She slides her fingertips down the line of my jaw and then places her palm against my chest, her eyes following. "Please." She meets my eyes. "God, you look gorgeous."

*Ay yai yai.*

I reach out and push a lock of hair away from her lips, and she closes her eyes and turns her head into my touch.

This time the passion rises in me like molten lava, and it's all I can do not to pull her into my arms and start kissing her right there in the restaurant.

*Get a grip, mae. You just met her!*

I slide my fingertips across her shoulder, down her bare arm, and then squeeze her hand. "Would you like to have dinner first?"

She laughs, a sound that I have already come to crave, and her eyes pop open. "As long as you don't stop touching me."

"I think that can be arranged."

Over dinner, our conversation jumps from how inept the UN can be, to how hard it is to train cats. We tussle over whether guys should pay on the first date, and if the people behind Anonymous are heroes or outlaws—or both. She keeps getting the names of public figures wrong, and when

I tease her about it, she reels off the winner of every Grand Slam tennis tournament for the last three years, and then tells me she can do the next three years as well.

I suggest she move to Las Vegas, and she laughs. "That's a good idea. Maybe I will."

By the time we get the main course, my face hurts from smiling so much.

She continues with a never-ending string of queries, but I find that if I stop and turn her questions around, she is willing to share her opinions with me, although it does seem that she has to work at answering instead of interrogating. She laughs when I call her on it, and then proceeds to ask another question.

*While stroking the inside of my thigh. Mierda.*

It turns out we both dislike shopping for shoes, but disagree about doing laundry: I think it's not that bad, but she thinks it's torture. She tells me she doesn't eat red meat, and when I ask what that means, she says, "I don't eat mammals out of professional courtesy."

I point out that there are plenty of mammals that don't share her sentiments, and then tell her about the game theory project I'm working on to predict wildlife population explosions. I'm surprised when she knows the terminology and even makes a suggestion about something I've overlooked.

*Ay, she's smart.*

I try not to be intimidated.

As we eat, she throws out an endless stream of questions, and I find myself enjoying her company more than I would have thought possible. That's the good news. The bad news is it's a challenge to stay with her intellectually, particularly when she keeps touching me like we're already lovers. The more we talk, the higher the bar moves, and the more I want to impress her—and the more difficult it becomes to think about anything except taking her clothes off.

*Shit.*

At one point, she sets down her fork and teases the threads at the corner of her placemat with her fingertips. "So tell me, are you seeing someone?" Her tone is casual, but she doesn't look up.

*That body language I can read.*

I move my left hand across the table and slip it under hers, caressing her palm and fingers. "Do I have a girlfriend? No, not really. I've been in a couple of relationships, but I'm not ready to make any long-term commitments." It's my standard reply.

She bites her lip, still playing with my fingertips, and then laughs.

"What's so funny?"

"I bet that's your stock reply." She makes quotation marks with her fingers. "Not ready to make any commitments."

I stare at her, feeling uncomfortable.

"Hey," she says, "no worries. It sounds like a great plan. My mother always told me not to make any big decisions until I was twenty-five, and that should be just about right."

"Just about right for what?"

"For you." One side of her mouth twitches. "And, well, me." She drags the back of one finger up the inside of my forearm, tracing the line of the muscle.

I have no idea what she's talking about, but my concern vanishes the moment she starts touching me.

*So what's new?*

Her caress is light, tickling me, and I squirm beneath her touch. "What about you? Are you going out with someone?"

She laughs, and I stare at her, bewitched by the way her face changes when she smiles.

She runs her fingernail back down my arm. "I forgot that you're so tick—" She blushes. "I mean, I forgot that someone could *be* so ticklish." She turns away, peering out into the lush tropical night, her fingertips gliding across my arm.

I study her profile, watching escaped strands of her hair swirl about her face. "So. *Are* you seeing someone?"

"No." She looks at me, a mischievous glint in her eyes. "And I'm dead certain about it."

I chuckle, trying to find a clever retort, but failing.

She slides her open palm up my arm to my shoulder and bumps my chin in a mock jab. "No one but you, that is."

My whole body responds to her implication.

*Ay! Maybe I am ready to make that commitment.*

She takes a drink of water, running her finger around the condensation ring on the table, her eyes downcast.

*She's going to ask me something risky again.*

I smile to myself and mentally brace for her next question.

She sets the glass down and leans forward, stroking the back of my hand. "Do you plan to have kids someday?"

"Yeah, sure. Not for a while, but eventually, yes. How about you?"

She holds up her finger, asking me to wait. "Hypothetical question, so there's no correct answer." She raises her eyebrows, and I nod. "Suppose you got your girlfriend pregnant when you were twenty-five and not ready to have kids—" I start to protest, but she cuts me off. "Through no fault of yours. Say the condom broke."

"Uh huh."

She moves the back of her fingers down the line of my jaw, her eyes following her touch. "So she's pregnant now, and somehow you know that this is your *only* chance to have kids."

"Okay."

"Would you choose to have the baby?"

I think for a moment. "Does she know it's our only chance?"

"No. Just you."

I pause for a minute before answering, trying to stay focused on her question instead of the way she's touching me. "That's a tough one, Iz. I guess it would depend on our relationship, if we were planning to get married or had already talked about having kids someday."

She runs her fingertips across my lips and then glances at my eyes. "So?"

"So, if the relationship was solid, and I was certain I wanted to marry her, maybe so. But a lot would depend on what she wanted too." I take her hand and kiss her fingertips. "What about you? What would you do if the situation was reversed?"

She slides her hand slowly up the inside of my leg. "Well, if *you* were pregnant, that would be a trick."

"Right." I say it with heavy sarcasm and then press her hand flat against my leg, not allowing her to distract me.

She looks up, her eyes big.

I give her the eyebrow. "That was pathetic."

She jerks her hand away.

*Damn if she isn't used to calling the shots.*

I make a show of placing her hand back on my thigh. "You have been demanding honest answers from me all evening, Isabel. Don't you think I deserve the same?"

"Touché." She stares at my mouth.

*Mierda, I want to kiss her.*

I force my brain to work. "So. What would you do if *you* knew it was your only chance to have a baby?"

She tilts her head and traces an imaginary outline on my leg, her finger moving within nanometers of my very attentive cock. "I'd have to give up most of my career aspirations. And it would be rough for our relationship: no savings, not enough money to buy a house, lots of new bills, and no time as a couple." She lets out a heavy sigh. "It would be a hard decision, but I *still* don't think I would have the baby." She pauses in her drawing. "And I asked you that because it's an area where we differ."

"Oh, really. I thought my answer was identical to yours."

"Well," she says, looking flustered, "I'm not really a 'right to life' type, and you are."

"Well, shit, I'd better get on that. I don't think I've saved a single life yet, unless you count the people in the train set I had as a kid. My mom tried to throw those away when I left for college, but I found them in the trash and stashed them behind the old Boogie Board in the garage. You never know when you might need miniature people."

She takes her hand away again, looking annoyed.

"Really, Isabel, why do you say that? I don't think abortions are a particularly good form of contraception, but I don't have any moral issue with them either. Besides, in your scenario, she *could* have the baby and give it up for adoption, if that's what she wanted to do. If she wasn't ready to be a mother, I certainly wouldn't try to talk her into it—even if I *was* planning to marry her."

"Now you tell me."

Something about her tone of voice gives me pause. "What do you mean by that?"

"Nothing. Nothing at all." She gazes out into the night.

We sit in silence, watching the waves break out on the reef, my body missing her touch.

I reach out and stroke her cheek. "Hey."

She glances at me, her eyes filled with tears. "God, I've missed you."

"I'm not going anywhere."

She shuts her eyes and then rubs her cheek against my fingers. "I just wish it didn't have to end."

I stare at her, uncertain if she's talking about tonight, this week, or the rest of our lives.

She places her hand back on my thigh, letting it wander.

"And I've missed him too."

"Him?"

She traces my erection with her fingertip. "Gus."

"Who's Gus?"

She slides her palm across my now very hard cock. "You know. Gus."

*Ay!*

Gus strains toward her touch, and it's all I can do not to moan. "Ah." I can feel my face getting warm. "I didn't know he had a name."

"He does now," she says. "So tell me, what are you and Gus planning to do after graduation?"

"I have no effing idea. You're making it too *hard* to think, Iz."

She smirks. "I'll stop if you want."

"Please don't." I place my hand on top of hers and entwine our fingers. "I love the way you touch me, and I want to return the favor."

"I'd like that."

My pulse races and my brain freezes.

"Um," she says, "how about we have a chocolate soufflé first?"

"Excellent idea." I motion toward a wooden loveseat hanging between two palm trees. "And eat it over there?"

The waiter sees us looking at the swing and mouths the word "soufflé?"

I nod, wondering how he knows what I'm thinking. This is the third time this evening he's done that.

Isabel stands up, pulling me with her, and then leads me into the flickering shadows, her hand warm in mine. Suddenly, nothing but being with her seems to matter.

We rock back and forth on the loveseat, holding hands and gazing out as the moon casts an alabaster glow on the breakers. A gentle breeze rustles through the palm fronds, making her eyes sparkle in the moonlight.

Ten minutes later, we dip our spoons into chocolate heaven, maybe even better than my signature chocolate cake. We eat and talk while the tables in the café fill and empty, and fill again.

When the waiter comes to clear the dish, I pull out my wallet.

"The bill has already been taken care of, sir." The waiter glances at Isabel and back at me. "Let me know if I can get you anything else." He returns to the café.

I look over at her, a bit taken aback. "Thank you. You didn't have to do that."

"I'd love to say you're welcome. But I didn't do it."

We both turn toward the café. An elderly man nods at us and then gets up to leave. He's the same guy who was sitting alone in the restaurant when I arrived, and he's still wearing sunglasses and a Panama hat—even though it's dark now. I wonder who he is, and why he doesn't want to be recognized.

Isabel blows him a kiss. "Thank you!"

The man gazes at her, his hands twitching at his side, and then nods in acknowledgment. I get that weird feeling again, like something isn't quite what it seems, and then he disappears into the night.

"How sweet," she says. "Is he a friend of yours?"

I shake my head, still trying to figure out who he might be, but coming up empty. "But I think he likes you. A lot." I trace my finger across her lower lip. "And so do I."

She cocks her head and slides her hand across my chest, and then notices that there's something underneath my shirt. "What's this?" She pulls out the gold St. Christopher medal I have worn since I was a child and studies the Latin inscription on the back. "What does it say?"

I remain silent.

"Tego?" She gives me a concerned look, wondering if I

didn't hear her question.

"It is better to keep one's mouth shut and be thought a fool, than to open it and remove all doubt."

She groans. "Right."

I give her an injured look. "My godmother gave it to me when I was eight, and I never really thought about it. She was very old at the time. We called her *Aunt Teak*."

She ignores my pun. "So you're Catholic?"

I shift uncomfortably. "Yes and no. It says that on my birth certificate, but it's not something I was given a choice about. And I don't recall what the back says."

"Really." Her voice is droll, but it cuts. "For all you know, it could say: this guy is an idiot."

"For all you know, it could be right."

She bursts out laughing and then tucks the gold disk back inside my shirt, letting her fingertips linger against my skin.

"Okay, you got me," I say, keeping a straight face.

She drops her hand to my forearm and gives me a quizzical look.

"It's a chick magnet. And a damn good one, if you're any indication."

"Hah." She pulls her hand away, but I grab it and kiss it, and then set it back on my thigh.

*And I hope to hell it keeps working.*

She draws her fingertip across my shirt, moving it around the buttons in exaggerated figure eights—and brushing both my nipples.

My body responds in spades, and I force down the almost-overwhelming urge to get her naked.

*Easy, mae, or you'll scare her away.*

When her finger bumps into my waistband, she hesitates and then places her hand flat against my chest, her eyes following.

I let out the breath I didn't realize I was holding.

She taps her finger. "Am I that intimidating?" She doesn't glance up. "Or is there some other reason you don't want to touch me?" There is the slightest waver in her voice, the first crack I've seen in her thick and shiny armor.

*So she's only pretending to be in control!*

I suppress a smile, but the voices in my head are yelling like drunken frat boys, whooping and shouting obscenities. I force myself to keep a straight face. "Well, to be honest," I wait for her to look up at me. "I'm gay."

She stares at me, her mouth agape. Then her eyes get really big, and she pulls her hand away.

I start laughing, and she whacks me hard on the shoulder. "You bastard—"

I reach out, grab her head, and kiss her, holding her the same way she held me this afternoon. For the first time all evening, I feel like I'm in control, and it's awesome.

She continues to call me names and threaten to kill me, but I don't let go of her.

And then she kisses me back, deep and hard, the need in her so intense that I could easily lose myself in it. Desire explodes in me, fiery shocks of super-heated electricity moving from where our mouths touch, deep into my core, making my fingers and toes—and other parts—tingle.

*Maybe there is a chance I could stand as her equal. The thought gives me—and Gus—courage.*

I break the kiss. "I don't imagine there's a guy in the world that wouldn't find you intimidating, Isabel. You're well-educated, athletic, and incredibly bright." For the first time, I don't feel self-conscious. "And on top of that, you have amazing force of personality, a biting sense of humor, and—" I glance from her eyes to her lips, and then lean away and let my gaze fall across her body. *"Curvas hermosas."* I study her face. "You're beautiful, Iz. How could I *not* find you intimidating?"

265

I'm unsure if she's going to hit me or hug me, and for once, I don't think she knows either. So I kiss her again, the frat guys in my head still whooping.

# CHAPTER 36
## Matt: Shell-Shocked

When the time portal shuts down, the four of us stand in the murky glow of the computer screen staring at the GrillMaster. The lab feels like a funeral parlor after everyone has filed past the casket and there's nothing left to do but bury the dead and try to go on living.

The emergency backup system kicks in and the lights come up. I listen for the soft hum of the air-exchanger, the panic in my chest growing with every passing second. Without that huge fan, this is the world's most expensive tomb.

A moment later, I hear the soft purr of life, and my heart starts beating again.

Picasso clears his throat and then nods at me. "You're up."

I step closer to the GrillMaster and place my hands against the ice-cold metal. It's covered with droplets of moisture, and my hands slip as I try to release the lock. "Shit." I wipe the handle with my shirt and try again.

*Crikey Moses, I hate this part.*

I lift the lid and look inside. "It's... bloody empty!"

"Bad choice of words, Matt" Phil says with a smile. "But I think we get the idea."

"Can we confirm that she arrived at the target?" Picasso asks.

Everyone looks at Cassie.

Ever since Picasso announced they were going after Isabel, Cassie's been working night and day on the targeting software, trying to pin down what went wrong with Diego and make sure it doesn't happen again.

Despite the official pronouncement that we lost Diego because of a glitch in the power supply, Cassie has continued to insist that the targeting is to blame: For reasons unknown, the software sent Diego to the wrong universe—one very far away from ours—and *that* caused the time machine to suck down more power than expected, overloading the circuits and shutting down the system.

Last I heard, she still had no idea what went wrong.

We wait for another minute while she curses and types on her keyboard.

Picasso shifts his weight, his face apprehensive, but doesn't rush her. She's steamed at him for lying to Isabel about what really happened to Diego—and for ordering all of us to keep quiet about it.

*Can't say I blame her.*

Cassie takes a deep breath and lets it out, blowing loose strands of hair off her forehead. She sets her hands in her lap and looks up at Picasso, then remembers that she's not talking to him and turns to me. "Isabel's no longer in this universe, and the computer says it put her in the right place and time." She glances at Phil. "I just sent you her last known coordinates."

Phil nods and starts typing on what little remains of a

prototype Peeping Tom the Stanford team discarded months ago. It's a hundred times less powerful than the machine we were using with Diego, but it's all we've got left. "Give me a minute to run a trace on her," he says. "If she made it, I'll find her."

Ten minutes later, Phil lets out an exasperated sigh. "Damn it." He kicks the metal box at his feet. "I would have found her by now if we had the latest hardware. This piece of crap is useless."

I place my hands on Phil's shoulders. "Can you find any trace of her? Any blip or wrinkle?"

He doesn't stop typing, but shakes his head, no.

We all wait in silence as the minutes tick by, Phil frantically trying to confirm that we didn't just kill Isabel.

Finally, he stops typing, his fingers still resting on the keyboard, his eyes locked on the screen. "I can't find her. She should be right here, but she's not." He smacks the monitor, frustrated that the computer won't give him the confirmation we all want. "I was certain we could trace her once we had the destination coordinates. Atoms from a foreign universe stick out like a sore thumb, even on this crippled Peeper, but it's been too long now. Once she starts breathing in air from another universe, the effect fades quickly."

"It's not your fault," Cassie says. "This is precisely what happened to Diego: the computer said the time machine worked, but it didn't." She pins her gaze on Picasso. "We shouldn't have sent Isabel until we figured out what went wrong—and fixed it."

Picasso has the decency to look chagrined.

"It was a death sentence," she adds. "And we all knew it."

He glances down at the dark blue robe Isabel was wearing and then back at Cassie. "She was aware of the risks." His face is etched with lines of stress. "And what's at stake."

Cassie snorts. "Easy for you to say. It's not your fucking

269

body being dismembered by a black hole."

Picasso winces, but she doesn't back off.

"We should have told her about Diego. And we should have told her we have no idea what the nanotechs are for." There are tears in her eyes but she fights them back. "And just for the record, I'm not lying for you ever again, Colton Richter, no matter how many Boy Scout badges you're wearing."

Picasso turns away. "You went along with it just like everybody else, Cassandra. Nobody held a knife to your throat..."

"What did you say?"

"Nothing. Fucking nothing."

Cassie jumps up out of her chair, murder in her eyes. "You bastard!"

"Whoa. Take it easy." I put my hand on Cassie's arm. "We're all on the same team here, folks. Arguing about who's at fault isn't going to help us find Isabel."

Picasso slumps down into a chair. "You wouldn't fucking know it by the way she keeps—"

"Bloody hell, mate. Will you put a sock in it?"

Picasso's shoulders rise and fall. "Okay. I'm sorry." He meets Cassie's gaze. "I'm doing the best I can, Cass, and it would be great if you could cut me a little slack."

Cassie bites her lip and then sits back down, mumbling under her breath. "I hope I don't choke to death on the damn sock."

A light bulb goes off in the back of my head, but it takes me a moment to realize why.

"Wait a second," I say. "The sock. There was a sock in the Einstein Sphere, and Diego said he found one in with his seashell too."

"I never heard about any socks," Phil says. "Why the heck would someone put a sock in the Einstein Sphere?"

"Good question," Cassie says. "But I bet it wasn't an

270

accident."

"Well," I say, thinking out loud, "cotton is organic, so it can pass through the time portal just like a living organism."

"But why a sock, for Pete's sake?" Phil asks. "It's not useful."

"Or we haven't figured out why it *is* useful," I say, the cogs turning in my brain. "The molecular structure of the sock is fixed, no cells moving around and dividing, so maybe they needed something organically stable."

"But," Phil says, "there were other non-living objects in the sphere: the thumb drive and the Apple button. I know they were made of some special biodegradable plastic, but why toss in a sock too?"

I sit down next to Phil. "Maybe because the sock is forever. The moment that biodegradable plastic touches the air, it starts oxidizing, mixing with molecules from the target universe and changing. But even in ten or twenty years, the molecular structure of the sock will be essentially the same. It might not glow in the Peeper forever, but it will definitely last longer than a living organism would."

"Well that's all great," Picasso says. "But in case you hadn't noticed, we neglected to put a sock in with Isabel."

"Right." I say, still looking for the connection. "But we did put in the seashell..."

"Because Diego's note told us to..." Cassie adds.

"Bloody hell, that's it! Instead of Isabel, we should be trying to track the damn mollusk."

"Of course!" Phil smacks himself on the forehead. "It was staring us in the face the whole time." He starts typing on the Peeper again. "Shoot. Why didn't we think of this sooner?"

"Because we're all exhausted," Picasso says and stands up. "Between getting Isabel ready and setting up the time jump, none of us have gotten more than a few hours of sleep in the last two weeks, and it's showing. Let's get some rest."

Phil holds up one hand, still typing with the other. "I'm okay. I took a nap while you guys were setting up the portal. Let me give it another hour, and if I can't find the shell, I'll turn in." He glances up. "I know it's a long shot, but I want to try."

"Okay," Picasso says. "We'll meet in the mess at eight. Until then, everyone else gets some shut-eye." He lets his gaze rest on Cassie. "I have something I need to tell you, but I need you calm and clear-headed."

For a moment, I think she might explode again, but she doesn't. She crosses her arms and sets them on the desk. "If Phil's staying, I'm staying." She looks over at him. "Wake me up if you need anything."

Phil nods. "Thanks."

Cassie puts her head down on her arms and shuts her eyes.

"Me too," I say. "We can sleep tomorrow."

Picasso gives a resigned shrug. "It's like herding goddamn cats."

He steps over behind Phil and squeezes his shoulder. "I need to talk with Matt for a minute, but we'll be right outside the door. Just give a holler."

Phil doesn't look up. "Will do."

I follow Picasso out into the empty courtyard. The air is still and lifeless, but the fake stars are twinkling above us. Everything non-essential is turned off, but the misaligned constellations can't seem to be snuffed out.

"So, what's up?" I ask him.

He studies my face for a moment and then looks away. "I have been attempting to complete the mission on my own." He glances back at the light streaming out of the lab door. "I got Phil to help me while you were away recruiting Isabel, but we couldn't get the damn software to run—it kept resetting at the last second. I think Cass put some sort of fail-safe

272

lock on it."

"You what?" I stare at him, unable to believe what I just heard. "Christ, you're an idiot. Even if we could get you there alive, you saw the numbers. Your chances of success are zero to three decimal places. You'd be throwing your life away."

"Like I said, we all know what's at stake. If that hemorrhagic fever virus mutates before we manage to get someone to the critical place in the past, we'll all be dead anyway."

"We don't know that for sure!"

"Damn it, Matt, it's all over the news. They're calling it the Doomsday Plague, and the death toll just here and in the EU has surpassed that of the Spanish Flu and the Black Plague combined. God knows how many millions have died elsewhere."

"So you think this could be it? The pathogen that's going to jump species and attack everything warm-blooded?"

He shakes his head. "I don't know. From what we saw in the other universes, all the bad shit goes down within a few days, a couple weeks at most. Doomsday just doesn't spread fast enough for that, and with the ban on international flights and the way they're isolating victims now, we might be able to contain it. But if I'm wrong, the consequences could be catastrophic."

"Bloody hell."

"And even if Doomsday isn't THE virus, Cassie got one thing right: no Marine worth a shit would send another person where he wouldn't go himself. I have to try to complete the mission while there's still time."

I narrow my gaze. "Is that what you plan to tell everyone in the morning, that you intend to commit suicide after breakfast?"

"No." He exhales slowly, his eyes downcast. "And I don't want Cassie to know what I've been up to. Things are bad enough between us as it is." He rubs his beard stubble with the palm of his hand. "They're closing us down, Matt—throwing us out. The orders will be here by the end of the week."

"Christ. What do they expect us to do, go camping?"

"That's what I wanted to talk about in the morning. I think you should head back to Isabel's cabin. From the sounds of it, there's food, water, and even electricity. Problem is, I won't be there to help, so I want to make sure the three of you are prepared to survive on your own." He puts his hands on my shoulders and looks me in the eyes. "And I need you and Phil to take care of Cass for me. Make sure she's safe."

"Yeah, of course. We're like family, mate. We'll stay together, but—"

"Damn that woman." He steps away. "I shouldn't be telling you this, but it's all so fucked up, and I need your help bypassing her code." He closes his eyes, pain and regret turning his handsome face into a grimace. "Can you do it, Matt? Can you crack Cassie's code?"

"Maybe if I had a couple of weeks, but in a day or two? Probably not. And even if I could break her code, I'm not sure I would. All I'd be doing is sending you to a certain—and rather pointless—death."

"I could order you to do it, just like I did Phil, but I'd rather not have it come to that."

"Right. I'm not going to put you in that death trap, and Cassie isn't going to kill you either—unless she strangles you."

He laughs and shakes his head. "I'm sorry, Matt. I shouldn't have laid all this on you, but I have no one else to turn to, and I'm running out of options."

"Is there any chance you can buy us more time?" I ask.

"I'll do what I can, see if I can get them to let us stay..."

I nod, but he's not very convincing.

Curses drift out over Cassie's soft snores.

I peek back inside. "Everything okay?"

"I can't find any Tyrian purple molecules," Phil says. "The shell Isabel took is a murex, and it contains a well-known crystalline structure used in purple dye. It has a very distinctive chemical signature, and with the coordinates Cassie gave me, I should be able to see it glowing in the Peeper." He thinks for a moment. "Unless the seashell is from the *same universe*, and all Isabel did was take it back..."

I walk in and pick up Isabel's robe. "She had a towel, too. Remember? And now that I think about it, the sock was cotton too. Maybe cotton has some chemical property that makes it stand out?"

"Or maybe it wasn't being used as a trace," Cassie says through a yawn and sits up. "Maybe we're still missing something."

"Cassie must be right," Phil says. "Cotton fabric is just cellulose. The processing takes out everything else." He gives a heavy sigh. "It would be a seriously bad choice for tracking in the Peeper."

He glances around at our faces. "But it's worth a try."

Picasso stands up. "I'm going to get some coffee. Anyone else want some?"

We all nod.

"I'll come with you," Cassie says. "The walk would do me good."

"Ditto. You okay on your own for a few minutes?" I ask Phil.

"Yep. Cream and sugar, please."

We're halfway around the lake when we hear Phil's voice. "I found her! She made it!"

I start running toward the rectangle of light coming out the lab door, Cassie following behind. Picasso calls out, "I need to tell the Brass. I'll catch up with you in a minute."

When I step through the lab door, breathing hard, Phil is

back at the computer typing furiously.

"So you found the towel?" I ask, bent over to catch my breath.

"Yes! It took a while, but it was glowing just like we hoped! I'm following the associated time stream now, running Cassie's comparison algorithms." He looks up at me, his eyes glossy. "There are changes that weren't there yesterday, Matt! Did you hear me? Things are different, and some of them are pretty darn big!" He goes back to his typing. "There's no way to know if Isabel succeeded, but she's definitely changing things."

Cassie comes sprinting into the room whooping like she won the lottery. She races across the room and pulls us into a hug. "You two are geniuses, fucking geniuses!"

Picasso peeks around the doorframe, smiling sheepishly. "So Isabel made it safe and sound?"

Phil nods. "I found the towel—and it's moving around like Isabel is wearing it!"

Picasso looks at me, and then at Phil and finally, at Cassie. "You guys did good. I'm goddamn proud of you."

Cassie releases us, runs across the room, and leaps up into the air. Picasso catches her, and she wraps her arms and legs around him, half laughing and half crying. "I am so mad at you, Colton Richter. If you ever order me to do anything else ever again, ever, I'm going to kill you with knitting needles. Do you hear me?" She glares at him through clenched teeth.

A smile inches across his face. "And I was just about to order you to kiss me."

"You bastard." She grabs onto his tousled hair. "You were right about sending Isabel. I'm sorry I gave you shit for it." She kisses him hard on the mouth, and a moment later, he takes her head in his hands and kisses her back.

Phil and I look on, feeling a bit like voyeurs. And then Phil pulls me against his chest, and I put my arms around him, wishing I had the nerve to just out-and-out kiss him.

He tips his head against mine, both of us in tears. "We did it, Matt. We bloody well did it."

## Chapter 37

### *Tego: Around Her Finger*

Beto and my friends show up right at nine, and we join them in the café, which has been transformed into a nightclub with a live band and a dance floor. A short while later, Isabel's friends arrive in a wave of bright colors and eclectic scents. We do introductions all around and, in a matter of minutes, everyone is chatting or dancing. As I help push tables together and collect chairs, Beto offers Isabel a seat next to him, and she accepts. I glare at my soon-to-be-ex-best friend and sit down across from them.

Beto turns his chair around and leans against the back, facing her. "Isabel, right?"

"You have a good memory."

"You're worth remembering." He grins like a shark.

She glances down at her hands, and he gives me a sly wink.

*I'm going to kill him.*

"Beto short for Alberto?" she asks.

"Uh huh." He wraps his arms around the back of the chair and flexes his muscles. "Can I buy you a drink?"

*Goddamn him.*

"Yes, please. Is there a local beer you recommend?"

"Yeah, but it's a German-style amber ale. Still want to try it?"

"Of course," she says, smiling. "That sounds great."

"Tego—" He knows I'm listening in. "—you want to go in on a pitcher?"

He also knows I don't like dark beer.

"Yeah, sure," I say.

Beto orders a pitcher of *Bavaria* just as the band starts playing "La Bamba." He hops up and grabs Isabel by the hand, pulling her to her feet and then bowing like a matador. She responds with a flourish of her skirt. I feel a sharp stab in my gut.

*I'm going to kill him—slow and painfully.*

I look around. The place is packed with people enjoying the warm tropical evening. "Not such a bad idea she had," I say to no one in particular. One of Isabel's friends catches my eye and nods toward the dance floor. Without even thinking, I shake my head and say, "Sorry. I don't dance." Tomás sticks his head into our line of sight and animatedly points to himself, and the girl nods.

They head up to the dance floor while I sit, brooding, and try to figure out a way to get Isabel back.

The next song is a medley of Latin Golden Oldies traditionally requiring a partner change at each segue. At the first change, Tomás takes Isabel away from Beto, and then gives her an injured look when another guy cuts in on the next switch.

Isabel catches my eye and mouths, "Dance with me?" just as the music ends.

But before I can respond, Beto takes her hand and whirls

her around. They stand on the dance floor chatting while the band decides on the next song, which turns out to be a slow ballad. Beto takes her into his arms while the guitar player sings about how much he wants to boff his best friend's girl.

*Mierda.*

I drink my beer, feeling sullen, until I notice that Isabel is looking at me. Every time she's facing me, we lock eyes, and I feel my insides twist.

When the song ends, she motions with her head toward the dance floor, and my desire to be with her wins out over my trepidation about dancing. She takes my hand, fingering the pearls she's wearing with the other. "I'm flattered. I know you don't like to dance."

*Was it that obvious?*

The lively music starts, but she refuses to release me, and instead, places my palm flat against the small of her back.

"Dancing is easy if you remember three things." She ticks them off on her fingertips. "One, stay on your toes. That way you won't step on anyone's foot. Two, maintain a strong frame, so I can trust your lead." She pushes my shoulders back and raises my arm, bending it like a wooden soldier's, and then tests to make sure it's solid.

I pull her closer, enjoying her attentions.

"And three, make sure you keep at least one hand on me at all times, so I know how to get back to you."

"Sounds like good advice for life in general."

She kisses me on the mouth—right there in front of everyone—and then walks me through a couple of dance steps, showing me how to lead with my right hand and slide my left palm across her back when she turns away. I follow her advice as best I can and discover that dancing is not that difficult, maybe even fun. She steps around me, swaying her hips seductively and wrapping herself in my arms, making it seem as though I'm a good dancer.

When the music finally stops, she leans against me, and I am flattered by her public display of affection until I realize that she is feeling faint. I put my arms around her waist, supporting her, and she grabs onto my shoulders. Her heart is racing, but her hands are icy cold.

I touch my head to her forehead. "Are you okay?"

She nods but says nothing, still leaning on me. After holding her for a few moments, I take her arm and help her back to the table. I have her sit in my chair while I go scrounge up another one.

"Are you sure you're okay?" I ask when I get back.

"Yes, thanks for catching me. I turned my ankle, but it feels much better now."

I raise an eyebrow.

"Really, Tego, I'm fine."

The band takes a break, and people return to the table.

She scoots her chair closer to mine and places her hand on my thigh. The soft fragrance of her skin and hair settles around me.

Beto calls across to Isabel, "So I hear you go to school with Tego's brother. What are you studying?"

I scowl at him, but he ignores me.

"Yes. He's in my calc class. I'm majoring in Biomolecular Engineering." Under the table, she slides her hand up the inside of my thigh, causing ripples of pleasure to wash over my body. "How about you?"

"Law at the University of Costa Rica."

Tomás, who's sitting on the other side of Beto, scoots his chair in and calls out, "He comes from a long line of sharks. I mean, attorneys. Be careful because he bites."

The whole group laughs.

The blonde next to Beto leans forward. "How do you tell if a lawyer is lying?"

Tomás pats Beto on the back. "His lips are moving."

"How do you tell if a lawyer is well hung?" Isabel pins her eyes on Beto.

Tomás snickers, and Beto gives Isabel a wry smile, enjoying the innuendo. "How?"

"You can't get your finger between…" She draws out the silence, "the rope and his neck."

Everyone groans, and Beto breaks out laughing and mock-tips his hat to Iz. "You know, it's the ninety-eight percent of the lawyers who give us two percent a bad name."

The whole table laughs.

Beto glances at me and shrugs, and then winks at the *macha* sitting next to him.

A moment later, Isabel and a couple of her friends get up to use the bathroom.

Beto slides across a couple of empty chairs, pours more beer into my mug, and leans in. "I like her. Not that you need my approval or anything, but she's smart and a great dancer. Too bad she lives half a continent away." The band starts to play, and one of Isabel's friends taps Beto on the shoulder. He grins. "Excuse me."

I nod and sip my beer.

When Isabel comes back, she stops to speak to the drummer and then tosses her shoes under my chair. "Dance with me?" Without waiting for an answer, she pulls me up and leads me to the dance floor.

The music starts, a wistful love song, and I rest my hands lightly on her hips, unsure of her intentions or her health.

She pulls my arms tighter around her waist, pressing our bodies together—and then recoils. "Ouch!" She looks down, frowning. "Hard is good, but sharp not so much." I start to release her, but she grabs onto my shoulders. "Keep your hands right where they are, Tego Nadales." She slides her fingers down my chest and slips them inside the pocket of my pants, the intimacy of her touch turning me to stone.

Beto glances over and gives me a lecherous grin.

I exhale, my whole body wound so tightly, it takes a conscious effort to breathe.

Isabel works the shell out of my pocket and then holds it up between us, leaning back in my arms and singing with the music, her lips wrapping seductively around the words "lover in the night."

I watch, wide-eyed, as she places the shell in her bra, rose-colored lace peeking out between the curve of her full breasts.

"Avast, me buxom beauty," I say. "My tremendous intuitive sense of the female creature informs me that you are trouble."

She laughs and melts back against my chest, her breath tickling my neck. "Between two evils, I always pick the one I never tried before."

I close my eyes and take her in my arms, holding her, surrendering to her, falling in love with her. She *is* a creature of the sea, but not a mermaid. She is a Siren. And I am her very willing prey.

∞

The moon moves across the dark sky and threatens to disappear in the wispy clouds hanging above the edge of the ocean. The crowd thins—a couple of my friends disappearing with her friends, including Beto and the *macha*. As the distant surf settles into darkness, the music dies and the band starts packing up.

"Walk me back to my cabana?" she asks.

"I'd love to." Anticipation courses through my veins like electric current, filling me with anticipation.

*I have never felt this way before.*

We stroll up the beach, holding hands and gazing up into the starry night, both of us lost in thought.

Provocative images flash through my brain: my hands sliding across her naked back, my mouth on her smooth white skin, her fingers clutching my tangled hair as her breath quickens. She's been teasing me all evening, but still I worry that I want too much, too soon.

*Mierda, girls are so complicated.*

At the steps to her cabana, she stops and turns to face me. Before I have a chance to feel awkward, she takes both my hands and wraps my arms around her waist. Then she swivels around, pressing her back against my chest and looking out at the sea. She tightens my arms around her and leans her head against my shoulder. I savor the exotic scent of her perfume and let the sublime pleasure of holding her in my arms wash over me.

We stand in silence, watching the last of the moonlight dance on the waves.

She snuggles against me, and when she speaks, her voice is laden with emotion. "Right now, *at this very moment*, the universe is…" She hesitates. "Perfect."

With one hand, I brush a strand of hair out of her face and then wrap my arms back around her, feeling exhilarated by everything about her.

She glances over her shoulder at me. "Standing here in the moonlight, with your arms around me, everything still possible."

I kiss her lightly on her temple, not sure about the *everything still possible* part.

She shudders and grabs onto my arm.

"Isabel—" I hold onto her. "What's wrong?"

She shakes her head, sliding her hands along my forearms, but doesn't speak.

I can feel her heart pounding. "I know you didn't twist your ankle earlier, and I want to know what's really going on." All sorts of horrible thoughts race through my mind—cancer, brain tumors, debilitating diseases.

She leans her head against my cheek, her hair tickling my nose and lips. "I'm fine, Tego. Just tired. Really. I'm sorry I worried you."

I twist her shoulders around to face me. "Why won't you tell me the truth?"

She places her arms loosely around my neck. "I got up way too early, spent far too long traveling inside a metal cylinder, and I'm beat. Okay?"

"Beat."

"Yeah. That means tired as opposed to—oh, never mind." She's quiet for a minute, studying my face.

"I don't believe you."

"Oh, Tego, there's nothing wrong with me that a little medicinal-only kiss won't cure." She gives a fake cough, catching it daintily, and then places her hands on my shoulders, lifts her chin, and closes her eyes.

I don't know if I should kiss her or call a doctor. I feel manipulated, frustrated by her endless games—but still very aroused.

I stare at her mouth, trying hard not to think with my dick.

She peeks at me with one eye and then runs her hands across my chest. "Mmm. You feel so good." She slips her thigh between mine and presses her hip against me.

It's as if she knows more about teasing me than I know about myself—and she's taking every opportunity to use it against me.

Just as I'm about to protest, she moves her hands back over my chest, flicking her fingernails against my nipples and causing bursts of hot pleasure to explode across my body and collect in my cock.

*Mierda that feels good.*

She slides her body against me, checking to see if her

touch has produced the desired result. "A hard man is good to find."

I give up and lean in to kiss her.

But when our lips are almost touching, she turns her head away, denying me.

Annoyance erupts inside me, mixing icy frustration with pent-up desire and trapping me in the middle. I know she's teasing, and I know there's not much I can do to keep my body from responding, but it still makes me feel manipulated.

*But in a very pleasurable sort of way.*

Her eyes pop open, and she puts her hands flat on my chest, pushing me away. Then talking to my chin and playing with my shirt buttons, she says with mock seriousness, "Gosh, I don't want to talk you into something you don't like. Medicinal kissing can be very demanding. Are you sure it isn't too *hard?*" She looks up, feigning innocence. "Do you have the proper *stiffness* training?"

*Two can play at this game.*

"Madam," I say, "although I have not yet received my advanced degree, I am well versed in the *ins and outs* of therapeutic osculation."

*Ay, I hope I said that word right.*

"So I believe *my standard* is *up* to yours." I hold her more tightly around the waist and lean in, for the second time, to kiss her.

Giggling now, she pulls away at the last minute. Each time I try to kiss her, she moves aside, until I'm forced to release her waist and take her head in my hands. Overflowing with the need to kiss her, I force her to hold still and then place my mouth against hers, my whole body focused on the meeting of our lips.

She grabs onto my hair and kisses me hard, like she's trying to take all of me inside her.

A minute later, she slides her hands across my shoulders,

puts her head against my chest, and kisses me in the hollow under my jaw. "God, you smell so good." Her voice is like a striptease.

I play with the curls around her ear and temple, crazy thoughts bouncing around in my brain. And then I notice that her hands are trembling. "Please, Isabel, tell me what's going on. Are you ill? Maybe I can help."

She doesn't respond, and a minute later, she pulls away and slides her fingertips down my arm and takes my hand. "Thank you for a wonderful evening."

I look down at the dark, sandy path, searching for words to express the emotions raging around inside my head. I try to find something to tell her that will bring her back, convince her she can trust me, but I am unable to speak.

She lifts my chin, the gesture subtle and yet intense. "Thank you, Tego." She glances back and forth between my eyes. "I *did* have a fantastic time." She pokes me in the chest. "But it's been a very long day for me, and I'll die if I don't get some sleep."

The biting cold steel of her dismissal stabs me in the chest, and I fall back.

She squeezes my hand, not letting go, and we stand there in the cool breeze. The moon has set, and the night is dark, the only light a weak glow from the porch of the neighboring cabana.

I can hear the sound of her breathing interspersed with the barely audible *ticks* of the breeze snapping the fabric of her dress. The smell of her skin and hair lingers on my skin, and the scent of her makes my heart race.

She turns, still holding my hand, and moves up the steps, releasing my fingers at the very last moment.

I watch her ascend the stairs, her long, pale legs moving seductively in and out of the shadows.

She opens the door without looking back.

"Isabel." My voice is laden with accusations. "Please?"

She wheels around, her movements no longer sensuous. "If I could, I would, Tego. Believe me. I'm feeling the same way you are."

I stare at her, unable to speak.

And then the volcano erupts, fiery magma pouring out through the wound she has inflicted. "Shit, Isabel, stop treating me like a child. I can handle whatever it is—whatever is wrong with you. You're more to me than just another girl, so don't blow me off." I look up at her, frustrated and hurt. *And in love.* "Please."

She gazes down at me, the breeze tousling her hair and dress. "Meet me here tomorrow at two. If for some reason, I'm not here... Oh never mind. It won't matter." She starts to turn and then looks back at me. "And please don't call me a girl again." Nothing but sadness remains in her voice. "It's important."

She disappears behind the heavy wooden door.

Stunned and demoralized, I walk away, loneliness settling around me like a cold, dense fog.

# CHAPTER 38

## *Isabel: Alone in the Dark*

I slam the door as tears roll down my face and drip onto the worn hardwood floor. A moment later, I rush to the bathroom and throw up in the toilet, blood and bile splattering across the white porcelain bowl. Tego's seashell slips out of my bra and rolls across the bathroom tile. I sit on the floor, crying and vomiting, until I have nothing left inside.

Walking away from him was the most perverse and disheartening thing I have ever done.

*He knows something is wrong, but what can I tell him?*

I get up off the floor and rinse my mouth in the sink.

*And he's going to think I'm some sort of fanatical feminist after the "girl" comment.*

I leave the light off and stumble out to the kitchen. It's nearly two in the morning. I peer through the open window as he trudges across the sand, his shoulders hunched, the magic all gone out with the moonlight.

I watch until the darkness swallows him.

"I can't imagine he'll be coming back for more of this."

I fill a glass with water and take a sip, still feeling nauseated. "They picked the wrong person to save the world."

Leaning heavily against the kitchen counter, I stare out into the empty darkness long after he has disappeared, my hands shaking uncontrollably and my insides heaving.

*I'm dying.*

I peer up at the stars, feeling the vast emptiness of space. "Please. Let me have one more day with him. Just one more."

I return to the bathroom and switch on the light. The face looking back at me in the garish glow of the cheap florescent bulb is ghostly white and aging rapidly. I pick up his shell and turn it over in my hands. If I manage to survive the night, I'll probably be ninety by tomorrow evening. He won't even recognize me, an old woman of no consequence.

*I would rather die than have to live through that.*

I don't think I've made any difference in his life, other than angering him, and he's going to get plenty of that from my stunt double. All I've done is make it worse.

Despite my exhaustion, I take a sheet of stationery and an envelope out of the kitchen drawer, write out the address, and affix a stamp. Then I grab a box of tissues and sit down at the small kitchen table, writing and crying my way through a letter.

Once I finish, I force myself to get up and stumble across the sand to the dark café, barely able to support my own weight. I slip the envelope under the door and manage to return to the cabana without incident. I set a bunny-shaped clock to wake me in eight hours, shut off the light, and collapse into the bed.

On the nightstand, the white edge of Diego's shell glows luminescent in the dark room.

*I love you, wherever you are. And I'll be joining you soon.*

## Chapter 39

### *Tego: In the Moonlight*

I make my way back to the one-room cabin, the tension in my jaw threatening to turn into a headache. There's a faint glow coming from the vacant café, but no other signs of life. I cross the deserted main street, cut through an overgrown yard, and slip through the unlocked door of the cottage. The place reeks of old pizza, sour sweat, and dirty socks. I open a window, hoping the mosquitoes won't be too bad, and then shuffle toward my bunk, tripping over backpacks and sport bags as I go.

I peel off my clothes, collapse onto the bed, and stare up into the darkness, resisting the urge to pick up my shirt and search for her scent on it. I lie there listening to the soft snores of my friends, but despite the fact that I'm physically and emotionally spent, sleep won't come. I can't get her out of my head: The breeze pressing her dress against her hips and breasts as she strolls down the beach. The way she bites her lip when she looks at me. The electricity that arcs between us when she slides her hand up my thigh.

I exhale and grab my shirt off the floor, annoyed with myself for being so desperate. I bring it up to my nose and breathe in the faint scent of her skin and hair, my whole body responding to the powerful longing it stirs up.

*Shit, I'm hopeless.*

Even though we just met, I want to know what's going on with her—and with us.

*And I need to find some way to deal with the overwhelming sense of despair I feel when she pushes me away, because right now it's killing me.*

The cabin door opens and shuts with a soft creak, and Beto makes his way into the cluttered room. He collapses on the last empty bunk, and after a minute, gets up and opens more windows. I can smell the *macha's* cloying perfume wafting off him as the cool breeze trips across the dark space. He strips and falls back into bed, and a few moments later, I hear his breath quicken, and eventually slow.

*I wish it were that easy to get her out of my head.*

Just as it starts to get light, I fall into an exhausted sleep.

> *She stands before me like a statue in a shaft of moonlight. My breath catches in my throat as she slides her hands up to her breasts, her mouth open and her eyes on me. She lifts her arms above her head and pulls out her ponytail. Her hair tumbles to her shoulders, dancing in and out of the shadows. She runs her fingers through the loose curls, her eyes shut and her nipples erect.*
>
> *I gape at her soft curves, a familiar ache twisting up my insides and filling me with heat.*

*As I watch, she slips her fingers into her mouth and then trails her hand down her body until it rests between her thighs. I let my gaze fall across her long legs, imagining them wrapped around my waist, pulling my hardness inside her.*

*A moan forms in my throat and escapes before I can stop it. She lifts her hair, a smile flitting across her lips, and turns away, rocking her hips to some slow, internal beat. I visualize kissing the nape of her neck, my hands moving down the curve of her back to her smooth, round ass. I stare at the white triangle drawn there by the sun, longing to drag my tongue down the center of that alabaster marker, searching for the center of her sex and making her writhe and cry out with pleasure.*

*She turns to me, her eyes glossy, and I reach out. But before I can get my arms around her, a stab of pain cuts across her face, and she falters.*

*I lunge for her...*

And bang my head on the top bunk.

"Shit!"

I fall back onto the damp sheets, my heart pounding. Harsh daylight pours in through the open windows, but everyone else is still snoring. I rub my forehead and try to fall back asleep. Eventually, I get up, take a shower, and go in search of coffee.

The morning is quiet, the streets empty except for a few locals. I buy a croissant at the café but have no appetite, and end up feeding it to the seagulls. No one's around to play *futbol* this early, so I flop in the sand and shut my eyes, wondering if she's still asleep, wondering if she's dreaming about me.

*Mierda, I'm dying to see her again.*

Around lunchtime, half looking for something to eat and half just killing time, I head over to the touristy shops crowding around the beach hotel. Behind a row of turtle magnets, dolphin mobiles, and beach mats, I spy a wooden puzzle box carved from a local hardwood tree. The wood is purple with white veins and is carved in such a way that there are no sharp edges, the top curving into the sides and bottom. I pick it up and run my fingers across the smooth surface.

*It's almost as beautiful as she is.*

I know it's too soon to be buying her a gift, but she's already under my skin, a drug that I crave and have given up all hopes of resisting.

I carry it up to the cashier and take out my wallet, the voices in my head clucking their tongues.

*This is not going to end well.*

# CHAPTER 40

## Matt: Throw in the Towel

There's a loud banging on my door, and Phil startles awake next to me, his arm still draped across my chest. "Who is it?" he whispers.

Out in the hallway, there's some sort of alarm sounding, and a voice repeating an unintelligible phrase that starts with "Attention!"

He starts to pull away, but I hold onto him. "I don't know."

Cassie peeks in the door. "Something has happened, Matt. Something bad. Picasso wants us in the mess ASAP." She notices Phil. "Oh, um... sorry."

"No worries," Phil says. "We'll be right there."

Cassie disappears, and we get dressed in hurried silence.

When we leave the room, the lights in the hallway are flashing, and a female voice warns: "Attention! This is not a drill. Proceed immediately to the secured area. Stay away from windows. In case of sudden blast, duck and cover."

"Duck and cover?" I say. "Christ, those instructions must

have been recorded back in the Fifties during the Cold War."

Phil glances over at me. "Well whatever happened, it can't have been good. Do you think it has something to do with that Doomsday Plague thing?"

"Christ, I hope not. And anyway, your team estimated we had at least another year to come up with a vaccine, right?" I open the door to the next building. "Maybe that idiot who runs the country ran out of chocolate donuts and called a national emergency."

He forces a smile. "I hope you're right."

We walk into the mess and sit down across from Picasso and Cass who are watching CNN on an iPad and sharing one set of earbuds. Picasso holds up a finger, asking us to wait for a second, and then returns his attention to the news broadcast.

There's a jug of milk, a bag of Toasty O's, and a stack of small bowls on the table. I reach for the cereal and then notice that Picasso is in the same wrinkled clothes as yesterday.

*He hasn't slept at all.*

Picasso turns off the iPad and glances over at us, his face carefully blank.

"What is it?" I ask. "What's happened?"

Although I've known about Cass and Picasso for months, other than last night, I've never seen a public display of affection between them. So it takes me by surprise when he reaches out and strokes a lock of hair back from Cassie's cheek.

Phil slips his hand onto my thigh, and I reach under the table and take it. Something about the way Picasso is looking at Cassie scares us both.

"As you all know, this is a high-security, nuclear-hardened facility," he says. "It's equipped with a variety of fail-safe sensors—both locally and internationally—to detect a range of nasties: nuclear fallout, killer asteroids, chemical weapons, and a hundred other atrocities perpetrated by man or God."

296

"Mostly man," Cassie adds.

"A little over three hours ago," Picasso continues, "a whole slew of those sensors tripped, and the automatic protocols kicked in, sealing us inside the Magic Kingdom."

Phil and I exchange looks. "Do we know what tripped them?" I ask.

"Well, reports are conflicting, but word is the Doomsday Plague virus mutated. They're saying it's airborne now, dispersed by the wind, and if that's true, it will spread around the globe in a matter of days. I don't have a lot of information yet, but that redheaded hotshot who saw Armageddon on the Peeper—""

"—Sam," Phil interjects.

"Yeah, Sam. Well, he pretty much nailed it."

"Oh my god." Phil's voice is barely audible.

"Yeah." Picasso takes a slow breath. "We're still in contact with most of the governments in the western hemisphere, and there are a smattering of reports from people in environment suits in Hong Kong, but mainland China and India are a black hole. The last official transmission from Beijing went out at 2 a.m. our time, and it wasn't good."

"What about Europe?" Phil asks and squeezes my arm. "Any news?"

"They've been handing out gas masks for a couple of months there, and they have some of the best civil defense systems in the world." He glances at me, his face pained. "But the reports from Berlin, Paris, and London aren't good. It seems people are collapsing in the streets, but it's difficult to tell if it's from the virus or all the panic."

"Christ," I say. "My parents are in London... were in London. Is there any good news?"

"Down Under, the government is throwing together positive pressure environments in large stadiums and such, and in Japan, they're handing out stockpiled Tyvek suits."

"Has it spread to the Americas?" Phil asks.

"I don't know." Picasso exhales. "It may have reached the East Coast in the last half-hour. Calls to 911 in New York and Boston are off the charts, but there's no way to know what's real and what's hysteria. All the major airports have been shut down, and people are being told to stay indoors, shut their windows, and remain calm. Unfortunately, the statistics for long-term survival under those conditions aren't good, but the CDC is marshaling all their resources. We'll know more soon."

"What about the bionano?" I ask. "Early on we thought it might provide protection from the virus. Surely someone is working on that?"

"Yes. The CDC has a whole wing investigating it, as do biodefense labs in Kansas, Texas, and Virginia. Last I heard, it was still killing the mice before they were even exposed to the virus."

"Shit." Cassie stands up, her hands clenched at her sides. "Surely there are other protected installations where people might have come up with a vaccine?"

"There are," Picasso says, keeping his voice level. "And as of a few minutes ago, they're all up and running. We'll know more in a day or two, but given the unexpected nature of the threat, most governments were caught with their pants down, and it seems ours was one of them."

Phil drags his hand across his mouth. "You mean we're all going to die? All seven billion of us?"

"No," I say and put my arm around his shoulders. "We'll figure this out."

Picasso nods. "Even if things go from bad to worse, there are a couple thousand people on nuclear submarines and a few thousand more in sealed environments like ours. I expect hundreds might be holed up inside protected bio labs or clean rooms, and it's reasonable to assume that a few lucky souls will have a natural immunity."

"Fucking wrong use of the word lucky, if you ask me," Cassie says, tears filling her eyes. "How long will it take for all of us to starve or go crazy locked inside metal tubes, plastic bubbles, and underground tombs?"

Picasso stands up and takes her into his arms. "I don't know, Cass, but we're safe for now. This place may not be the Ritz-Carlton, but it was built to handle something just like this."

"Are there any other people here?" I ask. "In the Magic Kingdom, I mean? Did anyone else manage to make it inside?"

He shakes his head. "There is a general call out to high-ranking military personnel and their families, along with foreign heads of state and such, so we should be expecting guests. But right now, we're it."

## CHAPTER 41

### *Tego: Crazy for You*

A couple of minutes before two, I head down the beach to Isabel's cabana, forcing myself to walk. She is waiting for me outside on the lanai, sitting in a porch swing built for vertically challenged guests. The bench is no more than a foot off the ground.

"Tego! You are a sight for sore eyes." Her voice falls on me like drops of rain in the desert. "Did you sleep well?"

"Yes, thanks."

She laughs. "You're lying."

"You got me. How about you?"

"Same."

She's wearing jean shorts and a bikini top, her long legs propped up on a gnarled piece of driftwood, toes wiggling as she speaks. Not knowing what she expects and feeling uncomfortable with my own intense desire, I stand there gaping at her in the absurdly low porch swing.

She reaches out to me. "Come here? I promise I won't

bite—unless you want me to."

*Ay, dios mio.*

I take the steps two at a time and lean over to kiss her on the cheek. The smell of her hair fills me with desire, and I have to force myself to pull away.

She pats the seat beside her and gazes up at me. Something about her seems subtly different, but I can't quite put my finger on it.

I turn the small package over in my hands and then hold it out to her, confident that it's the right thing to do, but still nervous about being too forward, wanting too much. "For you," I say.

"How sweet." She takes it and reaches out to me. "I missed you. A lot."

Relief floods in. I take her hand and sit down.

She leans her head against my shoulder, and the implied intimacy sets my pulse racing again.

Without tearing the paper, she unwraps the present and then gives a startled cry, tears filling her eyes.

"Oh, Tego. It's... lovely." She turns the box over in her hands the same way I did, stroking the smooth, heavy wood. She looks over at me, her eyes glossy. "Thank you."

"Welcome." I'm caught off guard when she slides forward out of the swing and leans her head against my thigh. She holds the box to her chest and stays silent for a long time.

I'm a bit overwhelmed by her response, but definitely pleased that she likes my gift. I stroke her hair and let my fingers float across the pale skin on her shoulders and back, feeling the electricity jump between us just like last night. She lets out a soft moan, and it pulls at my insides, twisting them into a knot.

*She is an enigma, a tempest, and a goddess all rolled up into one, and I could get used to having her in my life.*

I run my fingers through her damp curls and feel her

tremble. "Hey? Are you okay?"

She nods but remains silent.

I continue stroking her skin, content to just be close to her.

The swing sways slightly with her breathing, and I watch the sunlight play in her mahogany hair—and notice a gray strand. I look more carefully. There are quite a few silver streaks mixed in with her dark locks!

*Going gray in her twenties? Unusual, but not impossible.*

I push a curl back from her face and lean over to kiss her temple, taking in the smell of her skin and hair.

A few moments later, she sits up, her face flushed and damp.

"Anything I can do?" I ask.

She shakes her head, wipes her eyes with the back of her hand, and then produces my shell.

"*Ay!* Thanks."

"You need to take better care of it, or I'm going to charge you storage and recovery fees." She chastises me with her eyebrows.

"I'm sorry, Miss Moneypenny, but it wasn't my fault. Some diabolical dame picked my pocket. Given the *woman's* villainous technique, I was fortunate to get away with my clothes intact."

"Mr. Bond, any *woman* proficient enough to pilfer a paragon from your pocket without your permission…" She thinks for moment, "…could have purloined your pants as well."

"If I had not made the mistake of calling her a girl, maybe she would have."

She stands up. "Perhaps."

I take the seashell and put it back in my pocket, feeling off balance again.

She bumps me on the shoulder with her hip. "I hope you have your board shorts on because this time you *will* be losing your clothes."

Before I can think of something clever to say, my stomach growls.

She addresses my belly: "All right, all right. Let's get you something to eat first." She looks down at me. "Can't take advantage of you on an empty stomach." She grabs my hand, pulls me up, and leads me through the doorway.

Walking from the bright sunlight into the subdued darkness of the beach house blinds me, and I stop, waiting for my eyes to adjust.

A moment later, I see her washing her hands in a compact kitchen sink, a pink T-shirt over her bikini. In the corner is a bed, neatly made. On the opposite wall, a door to a small bathroom hangs open, her dress from last night draped over the top.

"What would you like? A sandwich?" She pirouettes to face me. "Coffee, tea, or me?" She raises her palm above her shoulder and twirls a tea towel with the other hand.

"Definitely you."

She turns back toward the small refrigerator. "Seriously, I'm afraid I don't have a lot to choose from, but you're welcome to whatever is here." She opens the fridge door and peers in. "Iced tea?"

"A sandwich and some iced tea would be great." I walk over to the sink. "What can I do to help?"

"Hmm." She starts taking things out of the fridge and setting them on the counter: an orange, a papaya, and a melon. "My first choice would be your chocolate cake, but we don't have the time, so how about a fruit salad?"

I stand and stare at her. "My chocolate cake? How do you know about my chocolate cake?"

"Lucky guess."

"Lucky guess, my ass."

She rolls the melon across the counter to me. "Fruit

salad?"

"Sure." I turn on the faucet. "Why did the cantaloupe go swimming?"

Still holding the fridge door open, she watches me washing the melon, then returns to her search. "Why?"

"He wanted to be a watermelon."

"How do you remember all that stuff?"

"I read *Increasing Your Brainpower* by Sarah Bellum."

She gives me a wistful look and then glances away.

"Hey, it wasn't that bad." I shut off the faucet and dry my hands, but she doesn't respond. I watch her bend over and reach into the bottom drawer of the fridge. The edge of her T-shirt slides up, revealing the curve of her butt, and I feel myself getting hard. I can't seem to get that pale triangle out of my head.

She turns back to me. "I'm afraid it's peanut butter and banana sandwiches—very exotic where I come from." She tosses a banana at me. "Here. Catch."

I'm still ravaging her naked body in my mind, and I barely manage to grab it. "Time flies like an arrow. Fruit flies like a banana?"

"Hah." She tosses me a papaya, a pineapple, a mango, a star fruit, and an avocado.

I manage to catch all of them. "Good thing I took *Fruit Tossing 101* last semester."

She shakes her head, but I can see that she's smiling.

"Are you sure about the avocado?" I hold it up like a gemstone.

"Hmm. Probably not. Better toss that one back."

I do. She catches it deftly in her left hand—very athletic—and sets it down on the counter.

I pick up the pineapple. "I bet you like to play a racquet sport, probably tennis."

She gives me a quizzical look and surreptitiously glances

304

around the room. "How did you know that?"

"I seek not to know the answers, but to understand the questions." I put the palms of my hands together and bow, and then add in my regular voice. "And you ask a lot of questions."

She rolls her eyes.

I enlighten her, showing off a bit. "You caught the avocado with your left hand, but I know you're right-handed."

"Really." Her tone is condescending, and that annoys me a little. She raises her eyebrows. "And how would you know that?"

"From the way you held your fork at dinner last night." I stick my tongue out at her.

"And what does that have to do with tennis?"

"Well, my young Jedi, you probably hold the racquet with your right hand and catch balls with your left."

She purses her lips. "I see."

"Am I right?" Just this once, I want her to acknowledge that I can be clever too.

"Yes." She glances down at my shorts. "At least the part about the balls."

I feel suddenly warm, but my stomach growls, and we both laugh.

She opens the freezer and takes out a loaf of bread, and I watch as she struggles to open the twist-tie around the bag, her hands visibly shaking. "Hey, are you okay? Let me help." I reach out, but she pulls away.

"I'm fine, thanks. Really." She manages to get the bag open and then gestures toward the cutting board with her chin. "Back to training the fruit flies?"

I nod, and she stands still for a moment, watching me rinse the pineapple. I peel and cut it, the sweet, tart smell making my mouth water. She starts opening cupboard doors and eventually takes out a large, blue ceramic bowl, the outside covered with brightly colored tropical fish. I scoot the golden cubes into it using the side of the knife.

She grabs a piece of pineapple and pops it in her mouth, lingering a bit with her lips around her fingers. "Have you ever been in love?"

I glance up at her mouth, watching her suck on her fingers, and then look back at the cutting board, my insides twisting again. I want to suck on her fingers and kiss her hard on the mouth and—

*Ay.*

The panic I felt after waking up from the nightmare floods back into me.

*Why do I feel so nervous?*

I force myself to concentrate. "Nope. Never been in love."

The only sound is the soft click of my knife hitting the wood. I slide the small, round slices of banana to the edge of the cutting board and pick up the star fruit.

She takes peanut butter out of a cupboard and spreads it over two slices of bread, then changes her mind and adds a third. After placing the bananas on top, she adds another slice of bread and cuts each sandwich corner to corner, then arranges the white triangles on a matching blue plate. She licks the dull knife and sets it in the sink. "Are you afraid of getting old?"

Over the course of the last few hours, I've had plenty of time to think about questions to ask *her*, but I just can't seem to get started. The lack of sleep combined with hunger and stress—and my frustration with my own lack of initiative—spills out, and I hear myself say in an annoyed voice, "I have no idea."

"Ouch." She gazes out the kitchen window at a grove of palms rustling in the breeze, then stops what she's doing and puts everything down.

She takes me by the shoulders and turns me to face her.

"Ay yai yai." I give her a tight-lipped smile.

She crosses her arms. "Okay, Tego, what's up? Have I asked too many questions? Am I dredging up deep, dark secrets? Do you hate peanut butter and banana sandwiches?"

I stand there, knife in hand, feeling sheepish. "Guess I'll *cut* right to the quick."

She doesn't smile.

"I'm hungry and a little tired." I continue with more resolve. "And I'm frustrated. I want to know what's going on with you."

*And what's going on with us.*

She bites her lip and scans my face. "Okay."

"Enough with the cloak and dagger shit, Iz. You know all this stuff about me, but I barely know anything about you." I look down at the half-cut mango. "I keep struggling to find the right moment to start asking, and when I finally do, you just blow me off."

"You won't believe me."

"I don't believe you now." I return to chopping the mango, stopping to toss the pit into the trash using more force than necessary. "What's the deal with you? Are you sick? Why won't you tell me the truth?"

She stands still, watching me wash and dry the cutting board. I take the bowl of fruit and the plate of sandwiches and place them on the small kitchen table, and then slide out a chair and sit down.

She glances away.

*That worked wonders.*

## CHAPTER 42

### *Isabel: You Have No Idea*

I take a couple of glasses out of a cupboard and put ice in them, my heart racing. "I'm sorry, Tego." I set plates and napkins on the table. "But I don't know what to tell you."

"How about the truth?"

I get a pitcher of iced tea out of the fridge, take two forks and spoons out of a drawer, shut it with my hip, and return to the table. "If I tell you the truth, you'll think I'm psycho."

"Try me."

I sit down and peer across the table at him, all pretense gone. "I'm from another universe."

He gives me a fake smile and then takes a couple of sandwiches, serves himself some fruit, pours iced tea into both of our glasses, and starts to eat. "I can see that you're sick or something."

*God, he's persistent.*

I take a sip of iced tea.

His eyes are on his plate. "Is it serious?"

I take a sandwich and some fruit and put them on my plate, still considering what to tell him.

"You're dying." He blurts it out, his voice tight, and then he clears his throat. "That's why you won't answer my questions, and why you're so forward with me. You have nothing to lose. You're just using me—" His voice trails off but the accusation hangs there.

"We're *all* dying, Tego." It comes out harsher than I intended. "You don't know how long you have to live and neither do I. And you're wrong about my interest in you. It's not just some last fling with whomever happens to be available."

He looks up from his plate. "You should have chosen Beto. This is more his sort of gig."

"I don't want Beto or anyone else." I pin him with my eyes. "I want you." I exhale, feeling adrift. "So *do* you feel used?"

He shakes his head and then turns away.

"Liar."

He doesn't bother to disagree.

I take a bite of my sandwich, emotions raging inside me.

He sets down his fork and puts his head in his hands, his elbows resting on the table. "Why are you doing this to me?"

I reach over and place my hand on his forearm, and then wait for him to look up.

He does, but then he sits back in the chair, pulling away from me.

There's a stabbing pain in my chest, and I feel like I'm standing on the edge of a windy cliff.

He picks up his fork and continues eating, his eyes distant.

I take a deep breath and jump off. "Well, despite what you think, I'm madly in love with you, and it's all I can do to keep from ripping your clothes off every time I *see* you, let alone *touch* you." I glance down at his open mouth. "Just looking at you makes me believe the world is worth saving—and that's saying something." It's a simple statement of fact.

He freezes with his fork suspended over his plate, his eyes wide.

I take a bite of fruit salad, feeling emboldened. "And every time you say my name or look at me that way, or god forbid touch me, everything else in the universe seems—" I glance out the window, "inconsequential. And trust me, that's not a good thing."

He stares at me, eyebrows furrowed, trying to make sense of the incongruous mix of words. And then he drops his hand—and his gaze—to the plate.

I smile to myself, enjoying his discomfort with the truth he's begged so hard to get. "Like I said, I'm from another universe, and we don't have much time. There are things I need to tell you, things you need to learn, important things, but I don't know where to start." I let out a heavy sigh. "And all I want to do is curl up in your arms and forget about everything."

*It's liberating to finally stop the charade.*

I watch him push fruit around on his plate.

"Oh," I add, "and I wasn't supposed to tell you any of that. I probably just blew up someone's Multiverse Doohickey and made a butterfly in China disappear." I uncross my arms and pick up my fork. "So yeah, I've got a lethal case of jet lag and no return ticket. Is that enough naked honesty for you?"

He pours us more iced tea and then continues eating, a whole dictionary of emotions playing across his face.

I set down my fork, no longer hungry.

He narrows his eyes. "So, how long do you have?"

"Does it matter?"

He takes a bite from the last quarter of his second sandwich. "At the risk of obliterating more Asian insects, can you tell me what it is I need to learn—what my glaring ignorance is?" The expression on his face softens. "And can you repeat the part about ripping my clothes off? I'm not sure I heard you correctly."

I wad up my napkin and throw it at him.

"It's not just a coincidence we met, is it?" He's on a roll. "What's really going on?"

"Let's see." I tick the items off with my finger. "I'm from your future. And we're lovers, kind of—"

"Kind of?"

"Well, if it wasn't for the fact that you ran off and got yourself killed, leaving me to face the collapse of civilization alone—which I'm still annoyed about, mind you—we still would be." I cross my arms. "And don't get me started on your damn seashell."

He looks nonplussed.

"Some government scientists spent a lot of time and money getting me and one skimpy towel into your universe." I nod at the limp cloth draped over his chair. "Just so I could talk to you. And I may appear twenty-something, but I'm way older."

A smile flirts with his lips. "Wow. You make a stunning cougar. Beto is going to be so jealous."

I ignore him. "My goal, however improbable, is to make sure that *after* you fall in love with my parallel in this universe, the two of you don't screw it up like we did in my universe."

He sits eating and nodding, giving no indication that he suspects I'm a lunatic. "Uh huh."

"And as I said, we don't have much time. Oh, and if I fail, mankind—and all the golden retrievers—are doomed."

"Of course. Nice to know we solved the Fermi Paradox, though." He raises an eyebrow. "So who *is* your parallel in this universe?"

"The Goddamn Queen of Sheba." I set my glass down and look up at him. "You don't believe a word of it, do you?" It's not really a question.

"Nope."

"Okay, I was kidding about the Queen of Sheba part. I don't even know where Sheba is. The rest is more or less true."

"Right. I'll go along with you, Agent 99, but you'll have to give me the secret handshake and tell me something that only my lover from the future would know."

I flip him the bird.

He laughs and starts stacking the lunch dishes. "When I accused you of using me, I was more thinking along the lines of sex slave, but I suppose signing me up to save the world technically counts."

I stare at him, watching the muscles in his shoulders and arms flex as he clears up the table. "Okay." I walk over to the nightstand and take my shell out of the drawer, and then bring it back and set it on the table. "Mine is *exactly* the same as yours, only it came from another universe. My universe."

He puts the dishes in the sink and then turns and leans against the counter, his face amused. "Is that all you got?"

"You dressed up as a cat for Halloween when you were six, a little heavy on the face paint but great moccasins. You hate black olives, but you love olive oil. You like to kiss with your eyes open. You toast the bread for your sandwiches." I give him a condescending smile. "And you like to have your nipples bitten." I blush."Or at least you will."

His eyes get big.

"You wear *Vétiver Carven* aftershave," I continue. "Your right index finger is slightly misshapen because you nearly cut it off as a child, and your father, who's a surgeon, sewed it back on. Your favorite holiday is Christmas even though you wouldn't know Jesus Christ from Attila the Hun. Your favorite perfume is *Arpège*, probably because your mother wears it, and your favorite author is—" I purse my lips. "Damn. I don't remember."

312

He stares at me with his mouth open.

"You don't like cats, but you will later. You and Gus like to make love with the lights on. Your favorite part of a woman's body is her thong-covered butt—smooth, white triangles, anyone? And you make the World's Best Chocolate Cake." I leer at him. "How am I doing?"

He gives an uncomfortable laugh. "This is getting weird."

"You have no idea."

He tips his head to the side. "Okay. So you *do* know my brother, and he told you a bunch of stuff about me, showed you a photo album or something. Is that it?"

"Ah, Tego, you're too quick." I raise my hands and let them fall into my lap. "Of course. I chatted with your brother, and he told me all about how you like to kiss, and the part about Gus,and your nipples. And the tan lines on my butt—he particularly enjoyed telling me about that."

He glances away. "I'll have you know, I almost never toast the bread for sandwiches—only if it's getting stale."

"Keep the bread in the freezer, dude. Your brother told me that too." I get up, feeling lost, overwhelmed by forces I don't understand and can't control. Even to myself, I sound like a raving lunatic.

*How can I possibly expect him to believe me? And if he doesn't believe me, how can I possibly change him?*

I gaze out at the tranquil sea. "Come on, let's go for a swim."

## CHAPTER 43
### *Isabel: Drowning in Regrets*

The late afternoon sun splashes brilliant vermilion across the scattered high clouds, sending dazzling shards of light careening off the water all around me. In another place and time, it would be the tantalizing prelude to a perfect tropical evening, but here and now, it only serves to remind me of the long, lonely night that awaits.

I stand chest-deep in the water, fighting back tears, and watch as Tego wades out of the surf and flops down in the sand, the diffuse light changing his skin to bronze. He's tired, he tells me, and needs time to think.

*Right.*

He glances up at the radiant light, and then begins gouging the sand with a stick, scooping it up with his hand, and tossing it out into the waves.

I scan the horizon, wondering where the other me is right now, but certain that she's not as exhausted and disheartened as I am.

Now that I've told him everything, I can't seem to stay focused. I'm tired of being strong, tired of struggling to convince him, tired of fighting to save a world I'll never see again.

I take a ragged breath, tears streaming down my face.

Since the first moment I saw him, I've wanted nothing more than to be in his arms, to make love with him and fall asleep with his body curled around mine. This whole absurd mission is just a ruse, an excuse to be close to him one last time, and he's seen through it.

I shut my eyes, trying to summon strength, and then open them again and gaze at my future lover. He stands and brushes the sand off his shorts, and then scans the beach for his soccer-playing buddies, his hand shading his eyes.

*I've lost him.*

I turn away, my heart breaking, and dive underwater, swimming out into the near-perfect solitude, my tears mixing with the vast depths of the Pacific.

*Stroke, breathe, kick, glide. Stroke, breathe, kick, glide.*

When the sea floor drops into the blue abyss, I flip over onto my back, drifting up and down with the swell, watching a lone seagull riding the air currents high up in the fading light.

*No, Iz, you didn't lose him. You never had him.*

I release the air from my lungs and close my eyes, sinking into the arms of the sea. The water cradles my body, rocking me like a lost doll in a sinking ship, the low murmur of the distant surf comforting me as I sink deeper into the Pacific's ever-colder embrace.

Something snags my wrist, stopping my descent.

I open my eyes and gaze up into a corona of sunlight filtering through the water above me. Tego wraps his arm around my waist and pulls me against his chest, and then kicking hard, he drags us both up to the surface.

*I didn't know he could swim that well.*

315

He faces me, treading water with difficulty and breathing hard. "Isabel." He takes a quick breath. "It's Gabriel." Another ragged breath. "García Márquez."

I give him a blank look.

"My—" He takes a deep breath and releases me. "Favorite author."

I let my head slip under the surface, sweeping the hair out of my face, and feel his tight grip on my arm again. I come back up, treading water. "I'm okay, thanks. Just tired."

He stares at me, his eyes wide, and then nods and releases me. "Yeah. Me too." He glances back and forth between my eyes. "Just because it seems impossible, doesn't mean I don't believe you, Iz. But do you think we could discuss it—" He motions toward the shore, "some place where I'm not so far over my head?"

I can't take my eyes off his mouth.

"Please?" He looks at me, his gaze steady. "I have no idea what you want from me, but I'm willing to try."

"I love you, Tego Nadales." I leap up out of the water and throw my arms around his neck, kissing him, sinking us both.

## CHAPTER 44

### *Matt: Signal to Noise*

For a month now, I've been spending my days—and some of my nights—in the communications room, using the radio to search for survivors.

For the first week, the four of us pretty much lived in here, eating and sleeping and hoping. Picasso taped a world map up on the wall, and we celebrated each time we made contact with someone new. We circled their city on the map, wrote down who we spoke to and how many people were with them, and then agreed on a time to talk the following day. Within twenty-four hours, we had heard from hundreds of people, and we estimated that millions were still alive.

But since then, people have started missing our appointed meetings, and when I don't hear a peep from them for three days, I make a red X through the city, visually tracking the spread of the virus on the map.

*It's crude, but efficient.*

After the first week, Cassie and Phil gave up, so it was

just Picasso and me. We'd take turns on the radio, trading off so that there was always someone listening, but now it's just me. I guess that makes me an optimist.

Picasso decided to explore the Magic Kingdom. He pointed out that none of us has any idea how our air is filtered, where the water is coming from, or even where our backup power is generated, and if we're going to be stuck inside here for a while, it seemed like a good idea to figure that out.

He's also appropriated a Tyvek suit from the biocontainment lab, and when I'm not manning the radio, I've been helping him rig up a backpack to carry oxygen. He plans to test the external airlock system as soon as he finishes his life-support survey so we have access to supplies and equipment stored in the low-security areas. Cassie thinks it's a bad idea to go outside before we have any hard data on the virus, and after she made us watch *The Andromeda Strain* a couple nights ago, I tend to agree. But there's no stopping Picasso once he gets his mind set on something. Matter of fact, you could say the same about Cass.

*Can't wait to see the fireworks over this one.*

I take a sip of instant coffee and then press the talk button on the mic. "This is Matt Hudson in Deep Springs, Colorado. We have food and shelter. Is there anybody out there?" I wait thirty seconds and then repeat the message. There's nothing but static on the channel. I check the log again and then verify that the radio settings are correct. I spoke with a woman on this frequency four days ago but haven't heard from her since.

*Maybe she's just busy right now, and she'll get back to me when the laundry is done. I'll just give her another day before I do anything rash like assume she and a couple thousand friends are dead.*

*Christ.*

I make a note on the log and switch to the next band.

While I've been searching for survivors, Cassie has been

taking an inventory of the Magic Kingdom. The place is huge, and it will probably take months to complete the survey, but it seems we have enough food to last for decades, centuries even. The place was designed to keep five hundred people alive for twenty years without outside assistance, and with only the four of us, it will last longer than we will.

Still, as Cassie so eloquently pointed out, I'm not sure if that makes us lucky or not.

Phil has been spending his time trying to glean information about Isabel via the movement of her towel. He hauled the Peeper up here, and we watched the cotton material change shape and move around for nearly a week, but it's only drifting through time now—which means it could be at the bottom of a pile of dirty laundry or crumpled next to her lifeless body.

The thought depresses me, so I go back to imagining the towel, clean and folded in a closet somewhere, patiently glowing in the dark, just waiting for someone to come get it.

After Phil managed to find Isabel's towel, he spent some time looking for Diego's. Unfortunately, we sent Diego before Cassie added the location metrics to the tracking software, so we don't have any idea where he went after he left our universe. Even after two weeks, Phil hasn't been able to turn up anything. When you think about it, it's not too surprising given the nearly infinite number of universes out there and how long it's been since Diego left. But it would have been nice to know we didn't just deposit him in the center of a supernova or something.

*Bloody hell.*

All this death and destruction is getting to me.

*That and the prospect of spending the rest of my life inside this godforsaken underground tomb.*

I don't have to look far to know that things could be way worse, but that doesn't seem to matter except in a purely intellectual sense: I'm impossibly fortunate to be alive, but the day-to-day reality of that "luck" is perversely morbid.

I take a deep breath and try to focus on the positive: I have food, water, shelter, electricity, safety, and even Scotch. On top of that, I haven't known Phil for long, but for the first time in my life, the relationship feels right to me.

*Why can't that be enough?*

The electronic lock on the door clicks, bringing me back to the present. I glance at my watch, but I still have more than an hour to go before dinner break.

Picasso walks in, Cassie and Phil right behind him. He tosses an old lab notebook on the desk and then collapses into a chair, letting his head fall into his hands.

"Bloody hell," I say. "What is it this time?"

Picasso waits for the others to scrounge up a chair and then looks up at me. "Turn to the last page and take a read."

I glance at Phil and he nods, his face drawn.

"Where did you get this?" I ask as I pick up the lab book, reading the name scrawled on the cover but not recognizing it.

"I discovered it behind a filing cabinet in the genetics lab this afternoon," Cassie says, stroking the chinchilla on her shoulder. She found the little guy a few days ago, happily eating his way through a giant bag of cornflakes, and she has been carrying him around ever since.

Phil exhales. "Looks like someone was running tests on the bionano we gave Isabel but didn't want anyone to know the results."

I flip through the handwritten pages until I come to the last one and then read it, my heart pounding. "Christ. Who would want to cover up something like this?"

Picasso says what we're all thinking: "Johnson."

"Agent fucking Dickwad," Cassie says. "He knew the bionanos would stop working within 24 hours, and Isabel would die."

Phil exhales softly. "I know it's not much consolation, but unless the guy really was a zombie, he won't be doing anything like that again."

I put my hand on Phil's thigh. "Any news on Isabel? Are there any more changes in the time stream?"

He shakes his head. "The only thing we're seeing are the side effects of whatever she did the first day or so."

"Well then that confirms it," Picasso says. "We have to assume she's dead."

"But she did make some changes!" Cassie says. "We know she managed to do something."

"Sure, but do you think twenty-four hours was enough time to make the critical change?" Phil gets up to leave and then turns around at the last moment. "I don't mean to be cruel, but look around you, Cassie... It clearly wasn't."

# CHAPTER 45

## *Tego: Rip Your Heart Out*

We sit in the sand watching the sun tease the surface of the glittering Pacific. It's the longest amount of time she's gone without asking me a question since I met her, and I'm enjoying the reprieve.

She shakes the sand out of her T-shirt and pulls it on over her head.

I reach over and pull her ponytail out from under her collar. "May I?" She nods and I release her hair, watching the loose curls dance around her shoulders.

She slides her knees up to her chin, wraps her arms around her legs, and leans against my shoulder.

I stare at her profile, mesmerized. The breeze has picked up, and it flutters dark strands of hair across her enigmatic face. Something deep in my core stirs. She has definitely gotten under my skin.

*Beto will be happy to hear that I have been cured of my infatuation with blonds.*

She seems lost in thought, in another world, and I allow my gaze to fall across her long, silky legs. The scene is perfect until I notice that her hands are shaking. I still don't have any idea what's wrong with her, but clearly something is.

The afternoon has been a roller coaster ride of questions and warnings and pithy sayings mixed with electric caresses and sexual innuendo. Unfortunately, I can't say that I've learned anything profound or life changing, despite her earlier entreaty.

*But it certainly hasn't been boring.*

She glances over at me. "Thanks for spending the day with me. Even though you think I'm mental."

"*Con mucho gusto.* It has been my pleasure. You are, by far, my favorite lunatic."

"Hah." She peers out into the darkening sky. I draw lazy circles in the sand and try to decide if I believe anything she's said, but come up empty-handed.

*It can't possibly be true. Why am I even considering it?*

She doesn't seem the least bit flaky, quite the contrary, and that doesn't make any sense. Maybe she's hiding something. Something so awkward that she can't tell me?

*Something more bizarre than what she's already said? That's a laugh.*

She's both beautiful and dangerous, and I have no hope of dragging the truth out of her if she doesn't want to tell me. It's frustrating to admit, but it is what it is.

She snuggles closer to me and slides her fingertips up the inside of my leg. Despite my emotional, mental, and physical exhaustion, my body responds to her touch, begging for more—and I'm disappointed when she stops.

She looks frazzled, in need of a hot shower and a little down time.

*You and me, both.*

I watch the waves break and exhaust themselves on the

sand. I imagine myself crawling into bed with her, kissing her hair and stroking her smooth white skin until she falls asleep with her head on my chest. I see myself wake up next to her and take a fresh look at everything.

The thought is very appealing.

We sit in silence, gazing out to sea, until she removes her hand from my thigh, crosses her arms, and gives me a glowering look.

"What?" I glance over at her, feeling slightly hurt. "You're annoyed at me, but I don't have any idea why."

*And I'm too tired for this shit.*

When she becomes convinced that I am at a total loss, she snaps up my hand and plunks it down on the inside of her thigh. "Talk." She says it flatly, her eyes pinned on me like a firing squad.

"Um. About what?"

She makes an annoyed huff.

"I don't know what to say. I don't know what you want."

She glares at me and tosses her hair. "How long were you planning to wait before touching me back?"

*Mierda. Damned if I do and damned if I don't.*

This is not turning out like I expected, and the erratic fluctuations between dysfunction and rapture are wearing on my nerves—and my confidence. I feel as if I'm stuck in a bell jar of her creation, on trial for some transgression I have yet to commit.

"Well?"

"*Ay*, Iz! I don't know." Annoyance spills from my voice. "I guess I didn't want to push you." My hand on her thigh feels severed from my body. "I was enjoying being close to you. It was enough for me." The words don't come out the way I intend. It sounds like I don't want to touch her, which is totally wrong.

"Damn it, Tego, you're killing me." She looks like she's

going to cry again. "Last night you were begging me to let you stay, and now you can't summon the strength to rest your hand on my leg?" She turns away, and I think she *is* crying.

Anything I say will be wrong, but I can't keep my mouth shut. "Am I your minion or something? Do you even care what I want? *Mierda*, Isabel, does everything have to be about you?"

The question hangs between us, frozen in time.

She uncrosses her arms, a very deliberate act, and leans back on her elbows in the sand. She speaks to the clouds, her hair cascading down onto the sand. "If I touch you and you don't respond, you're telling me you don't want to be touched *and* that you don't want to touch me. You're pushing me away."

She's lecturing now. "So, I'll give you space, and that will make *you* step back, which will completely crush the intimacy I've worked so hard to build. In no time, it will be over between us." She sits up and looks at me, her face miserable. "God, it's so obvious now."

I have no idea what she's taking about.

"I'm not saying you have to rip my clothes off every time I brush your arm, but if I touch you and you like it, you have to respond." For a moment, she looks ill. "Assuming you *do* want to touch me."

"Iz." I reach out to her.

She pushes me away and draws her thighs up to her chest.

I pull my hand back.

*Yeah, well, same to you.*

She sits with her arms wrapped around her legs and her chin on her knees. "I'm too old for this shit."

I close my eyes, resisting the urge to get up and walk away.

Minutes pass.

She wiggles her toes in the sand. "We have to communicate better. I know that for a fact. Both of us have to try harder." She looks at me for confirmation, and I nod because she wants me to. "Tego, we have to learn how to get what we need without hurting each other."

"What do you need, Iz? Why don't you just tell me?"

She gazes out at some hopeful surfer trying to catch his last wave of the day. "My god, this is hopeless. There's not a snowflake's chance in hell you're going to be able to put up with her, no matter what I tell you."

I have no idea how she expects me to respond to that, and I'm too tired to care. She's trying to cram too much into too small a space.

But amazingly—annoyingly—she doesn't give up.

"When you first get to know someone, there are lots of uncertainties flying about. The trick is to match them up so that both people are engaged and challenged, but not overwhelmed or lost. Set and meet expectations so that the other person has a balancing point. Don't give too much; don't ask for too much."

Given what's been going on all afternoon, I find that last bit too much to take, and I laugh—and then attempt to turn it into a cough."

"Are you even listening?"

"Yes, Isabel. Relationships require balance, and we're in sorry need of that right now." My tone is harsh, but I'm too annoyed to care. "But go ahead and finish with the lecture. I know you're going to anyway."

Anger flares in her eyes. "And don't say things that are only meant to hurt."

"Okay, I'm sorry." I put my hand on her leg, wanting to reconnect.

"The chemistry is important, but I know it will be there in spades. So you have to pay attention to the other things. Take risks, make sacrifices, learn when to push and when to let go. None of it is easy, and some of it is downright painful, but all of it is essential." She glances down at my hand on her thigh. "Does that make any sense?"

"Um, I think so." I tell her that, but I have no idea what she's talking about.

She looks away, and I return my hand to my lap.

Silence descends like heavy fog, chilling me and making me want to bolt.

I don't think this is coming off the way she intended. I know she wants me to step up, say something to make her feel better, but I'm working on only a couple hours of sleep, and I don't know what to tell her. I've been hard—painfully so—for almost twenty-four hours, and I'm annoyed that it doesn't seem to count in the positive feedback column of her spreadsheet.

*And anyway, the point is moot now.*

I can't deny the way I feel about her, but she's trying to mold me into someone I'm not, some ideal man she's dreamt up after reading too many vampire books. I feel over-whelmed, exhausted, even threatened, like a kid in trouble for something he didn't do and doesn't understand. I like her and all—and maybe it's more than that—but I feel like she's pressing me for a long-term commitment when I don't even know her last name.

I'm startled by her voice. "It's not just you taking a risk here. It's both of us. I have my own set of insecurities." She picks up a fistful of damp sand and flings it at the surf. "God, is that an understatement."

She rests her temple against her knee, peering over at me. "Try to see it from both sides, and don't be so quick to assume the worst. I know you see me as confident and controlling, but sometimes it's just an act. You need to be persistent and assertive, and it won't work if you drop the ball every time I make you uncomfortable." She glances away. "The things worth having are worth fighting for."

"Isabel—" I stop, unsure how to continue. Never in my life have I been awash in such a turbid sea of emotions: consumed with desire and battered by insecurities, entranced by her clever words and torn by her cutting jibes, challenged by her intellect and crushed by her indifference, enthralled by her erotic touch and threatened by her casual intimacy.

*Either this is an evil plot to destroy me, or I'm in love.*

*Probably both.*

She shuts her eyes. "I want you to touch me, Tego."

I stare at her lips.

"I want you to take me in your arms and hold me."

Her words catch me by surprise, and something inside me is undone by the distress in her voice, by the unguarded vulnerability of her need, and I find myself teetering precipitously on a cliff.

*Ay, if she's going to kill me, I might as well enjoy it.*

I reach out and turn her chin, waiting for her to look at me, and I understand the significance of that gesture, why she used it on me earlier. "I'm dying to touch you, Iz."

The next part is easy.

"I've thought about it almost constantly since you took my arm yesterday when we were chasing the crab."

I stroke her cheek and then twist a lock of her hair around my finger. "Most of the time I like taking risks, but around you—especially around you—alarms keep going off in my head: Don't push too much. Don't make a nuisance of myself. Be patient. Give it time."

She closes her eyes.

I take her hand and stroke the soft skin on the inside of her wrist. "Last night, at the end of the evening, I didn't want to let you go. Things were working for me—for both of us, I thought. You were encouraging me, making me want more. The intimacy and trust were there for me. And something I've never felt before, something very... powerful."

*Don't go there, mae.*

She doesn't move.

I stroke the back of her hand. "I put my arms around you, and the alarms were silenced. It was safe to fall in love with you."

She opens her eyes.

"And then you got mad and sent me home."

I'm trying hard not to let the frustration leak into my voice, but know I'm failing, so I quit trying and just call it like I saw it, spilling my guts on the sand. "Obviously, I wanted too much and you set me straight. I got the message, and I'm fine with taking it slower. I want the physical part, but honestly, if that was all I wanted, I'd be gone by now."

She studies my face, her lips tight.

I release her hand and look away. "And now you're telling me to jump right back into the fire, and when I show a little discretion, you chastise me for not being more resilient. I feel manipulated, and at a loss for what you want." I brush sand off my thighs. "But, hey, I'm still here."

"Oh, Tego." A tear falls down her cheek. "I'm sorry. God, what a mess I've made." She says it again, enunciating each syllable. "I. Am. So. Sorry."

I'm caught off guard by her untempered apology.

"I know you'll find this difficult to believe, but last night was worse for me. I *knew* what I was missing. Truly, I had no choice." She picks up a piece of driftwood and jams it into the sand. "I wanted you to stay, but it just wasn't physically possible. Please don't read any more into it than that."

I try to figure out what she's talking about, what she means by a physical impossibility, and it all comes back to her being sick or something equally menacing.

She gazes out at the horizon. "I've never met anyone else like you. You are unique in a way that fits perfectly with me." She shakes her head. "Why couldn't I see it back then? How

329

the hell did I end up married to Dave?" She covers her face with her hands. "He failed every item on my list—even his car embarrassed me."

"Was it a motor-mouth or just horny all the time?"

She makes an annoyed huff, but the corners of her mouth rise.

"And who's Dave? Give me his last name, and I'll have one of my brothers take care of him—tie his shoelaces together and push him into a volcano."

She stares at me, and then looks down and draws squiggles in the sand. "I know you don't believe me, but I came here to change you, Tego, show you how to make things work between us." She peers out at the waves, and I follow her gaze.

The lone surfer is gone.

She tosses a shell out into the surf and then wraps her arms around her legs and lets her forehead fall against her knees. "I am such an idiot."

I place my hand on her shoulder blade and stroke the long curve of her back. "Did you hear about the Zen master who bought a hot dog from a street vendor in New York City?"

She looks at me.

"He gave the guy a twenty dollar bill and said, 'Make me one with everything.'"

She rolls her eyes.

I brush the hair away from her face. "The man pocketed the money and handed the guru his order, and when the master inquired about his change, the vendor replied, 'Change comes from within.'"

She suppresses a smile, rubs the sand off a shell fragment, and tosses it into the water, following the movement with her eyes.

We sit there in silence for a couple of minutes, my hands twitching in my lap.

*Suck it up, mae, and just put your arms around her.*

But I can't bring myself to jump across the abyss she's created between us.

She glances over at me and waits until I meet her eyes. "There's no doubt in my mind that this relationship can work, Tego—that we have the potential to build something most people only dream about." She stops talking and spends a few moments studying me, thoughts racing across her face.

*She's going to hurt you, Tego. She's going to rip your goddamn heart out and chop it into little pieces. And you are going to happily let her do it. So you better start figuring out how to survive it.*

I reach up and stroke her cheek with the back of my fingers.

She closes her eyes and leans into my touch. "Your part is easy. Just trust your instincts when it comes to dealing with... her."

"Whoa, whoa. Wait a sec." I pull her chin back around. "You said *her*? Who are we talking about here, the Queen of Sheba?"

She scrunches up her face. "My stunt double in this world." Her eyes pop open. "You haven't met her yet."

I let out a groan. "As if one of you isn't enough."

## CHAPTER 46

### *Tego: In My Wildest Dreams*

She goes on as if her revelation makes perfect sense. "As I said, she'll like what she sees. All you have to do is demonstrate that you're interested—and committed."

"What if I'm not committed?"

She gives me an annoyed look. "Is that a serious question, Tego? Because if it is, I'm going to kill you right now and save her the trouble."

"Never mind. If what you're saying is true, I'll need to be committed—or, at least, heavily sedated."

She smacks me on the thigh. "Don't act aloof, but don't smother her either. Just be yourself."

"Maybe you *should* just shoot me."

"I would except you wouldn't be as much fun dead."

I laugh.

"Still, it's going to take some time to get close to her. She has to learn to trust you, and given her past, that won't be easy, so don't step back."

"What past?"

"I'm afraid you'll have to ask her that yourself."

"Righty-oh."

She glares at me. "This is important, Tego!"

"*Ay!* I'm listening."

She pokes me in the chest. "Don't..." she pokes again, "step..." she tries to poke me a third time, but I grab her finger and kiss it.

"Back," I add. "I got it. *Mierda*, I need more dance lessons." I toss sand on her feet and then stroke the inside of her leg, electricity flowing from her thigh into my fingertips. "By the way, what exactly do you mean by 'don't step back'?"

She lets out an exasperated sigh. "The next time you do it, I'll let you know."

"That's helpful. What about 'don't smother her'?"

"Actually, I don't think you need to worry about that one. You're not really the smothering type." She falls back onto her elbows in the sand. "But no matter how angry she makes you, don't withdraw your affection to punish her."

"No smothering, no retreating, and no punishing. That doesn't leave me a lot of underhanded tactics."

She rolls her eyes. "She's going to be a royal pain in the ass, Tego. But it's you she wants. Only you. The rest is just a test to see if you're going to hang around when the going gets tough."

"Hang around or hang myself?"

"A ship in the harbor is safe, but that is not what ships are built for."

"Whoever said that never stood on the deck of a sinking ship, Iz."

"Suck it up, Tego, because you'll have to get wet if you want to land this one."

"As long as she gets wet too"

She stops playing in the sand and stares at me, her eyes

glistening.

I reach over and stroke her cheek. "I'm looking forward to it."

She glances down, and I pull my hand away, feeling off-balance. "So," I say, "what else do I need to worry about?"

"Contraception. You absolutely, positively *cannot* get her pregnant."

I let out an appalled gasp. "What if we get married and want to have kids?"

She shuts her eyes, and I wonder if I've pushed her too far. "Hey," I say. "I was kidding." I watch a tear run down her cheek, frustrated that she's so volatile. "Iz?"

She wipes her face on the back of her hand and then looks at me. "Don't get her pregnant by *accident,* okay? And believe me, it's not rocket science—"

"Are you disparaging my rocket?"

She laughs. "And don't rush into having sex. Wait for the right opportunity. You may only get one chance, so take your time and make it count." She scoops up a handful of dry sand and lets it slip through her fingers. "And that's *definitely* going to be a test, so you'll need to stay in control of your own needs—"

"Whoa." I form my hands into a T. "Good grief, Iz, what does that mean?"

"It means, if you come before she does and then fall asleep on her, you will be history, sayonara, so long and thanks for—"

"All the fish." I hold up my hands. "Okay, I got it."

"I'm not saying she needs to orgasm every time, but she's going to be paying attention to any growing discrepancies, so I suggest you do the same."

"Shit. Does that mean I shouldn't come, or that I shouldn't sleep?"

She brushes the sand off her thighs and then looks up at

me. "I guess you'll just have to figure that one out for yourself." She softens her expression. "At least at first, try to make it be about her. I know it's not something guys your age typically pay attention to, but you might find you actually enjoy it."

"I think I would." I let my gaze fall to her mouth and linger there. "What do you say we give it a try later?"

She blushes, and I can feel my body respond.

*Mierda, what I wouldn't give for one straight answer.*

I smooth out the sand between us and then draw a question mark in it. "So how am I supposed to decide between the two of you?" I mean it as a joke, but she doesn't take it that way.

She's traces my mark in the sand, thinking, and then rubs it out. "There will be no need."

"What about the other way around? Given everything you've told me, it sounds like I'm the wrong guy for her. And jumping through all those hoops is going to drive me crazy. How sure are you about this?"

She draws a heart in the sand. "Positive."

"Really. I'm sheriff of the Step Back Posse, remember?" I write an "I + T" in her heart. "How did I win the cosmic lottery? Why me?"

"Good question. Maybe it's the way you stare at me when I'm dancing with someone else, or perhaps it's your athletic prowess: flying bananas are pretty hard to catch, although I did have a hand in, um, *getting it up.*" She runs her eyes over my shorts.

"That was terrible. Totally lacking in *appeal.*"

She glances back and forth between my eyes. "The truth is, it's your chocolate cake." She turns away, flicking sand with her fingertips. "But you haven't made one for me yet, so I suppose that doesn't count."

"Right. So, you won't tell me how I fit into the puzzle.

Can you tell me how long I have the pleasure of your company this evening? You know, set my expectations, help me find a balance." I lie back in the sand and place my hands behind my head. "Are you going to let me stay the night?"

She laughs, not taking any offense, and that gives me courage.

"Just FYI," she says. "Your Isabel isn't going to let you stay. At least not at first." She scans my face. "But don't take it personally. She's a light sleeper *and* she has to learn to trust you—and that's going to take some time."

I nod and pull her over in the sand next to me. "Okay, but what about you? What about tonight? You can have your way with me, or let me have my way with you—whichever you prefer."

She aims her fingers at me like a pistol. "That was very brave of you, sheriff. Aren't you worried you'll get shot down?"

"Well, that's a Smith & Wesson, lady, and you've had your six."

She straddles my hips, her toes digging into the sand, and leans over me, holding my wrists down. "Tego, my love, you are a terrible tease." She begins tickling the inside of my arm with her nose, her breasts brushing against my face. "And I don't know how much longer I can resist you." She looks gorgeous hanging there above me, her hair dancing in the golden rays of the sunset, her nipples hard inside her thin T-shirt.

I inhale the intoxicating scent of her—and then I remember what happened last night. "You didn't answer my question."

She bites me on the shoulder and then starts tickling me with her fingers. "You're wrong."

I try to stop her, but she has my wrists pinned, and it takes me a minute to free them. Once I do, I pull her down against my chest, but she refuses to be held, and we roll back and forth in the sand, struggling for control and laughing. When I finally manage to get on top, I lift her hands above her head and hold them down, my elbows resting in the sand beside her head. She continues to fight, but gravity's on my side, and she eventually gives up.

I gaze down at her mouth, wanting more than anything to kiss her, but she turns her head away and sighs melodramatically. "I guess this means you get to have your way with me."

I chuckle, still breathing hard. "I don't think anyone gets to have their way with you, Iz." I flop over on the sand next to her.

She lets out a frustrated yelp. "There. You just did it again. You stepped back. I know it's because you're uncomfortable even pretending to hold me against my will, but if you do that to her, she'll crucify you for withdrawing your affection."

*Mierda, does she just make up the rules as she goes?*

She glances away, her eyes damp. "Damn it, Tego. If you don't want things to get more intimate, now would be a great time to say so."

I swallow hard and look over at her, trying to figure out what she wants from me, and if there's any way I could possibly give it to her. "I just asked if I could stay the night, Iz. How can you not know what I want?"

"I just said yes, and then you pushed me away."

"Goddamn it, Isabel. Why is it always about *me* reading between the lines and bending over backwards?" I flop over on my back in the sand and gaze up at a seagull riding the updrafts in the fading light. "You want to change me into somebody I'm not, and it's not going to work. I'm done trying."

I hear her sharp intake of breath, but I force down the sea of emotions it stirs up in me.

"You're right, Tego. I came here to change you, teach

337

you how to please her. But the whole goddamn mission is pointless. Even if I did manage to transform you into Mr. Perfect—whoever the hell that is—it wouldn't make one bit of difference. She's going to blame you for everything, no matter what." She rubs her face with her hands. "I know that because I've spent my whole life blaming you for fucking things up, only to realize in the last two days that I'm the one at fault. And believe me, it's not a very flattering discovery."

I stare at her, unsure if she's kidding.

"It's not you who needs to change, Tego, it's me—her. But there's no chance of that. All I can do is try to make you more bulletproof."

"Great." I look away, still feeling the slow burn.

"She's going to hurt you, Tego, and make you really mad, but it's not your fault, so don't blame yourself. Forgive her, get over it, and come back."

The pain in her voice catches me by surprise, but I don't let it soften my anger. "So what's new. I'm the whipping boy."

"Please don't be like that."

My temper boils over. "You've spent the last two days lecturing me about how everything I do—every instinct I have—is wrong, Isabel, and now you're telling me it doesn't matter? Christ, I don't know what to think. Do we ever actually get it together in any of these millions of universes of yours? Or do I fuck it up every single time?" I let out a frustrated sigh. "I can't believe I'm talking about this bullshit like it's even remotely possible."

She sits up and dusts off her hands. "That bullshit is my life, Tego. What's left of it, anyway. It's why I came back, but I'm done trying to convince you." She glances down the beach at Rick's Café. "So go back to your soccer friends. Have a lite beer on me. Live long and prosper."

My heart is pounding in my chest, but I don't move.

"Look at me. Please."

338

I take a slow breath and then meet her gaze, drowning in her turbulent green eyes.

"I don't have any idea why our lives are intertwined, but they are. Across time and space—and even death. You just met me, but in your heart, you already know what's possible between us. I can see it in your eyes, and I have to believe you can see it in mine."

*She's right, as hard as that is to admit.*

"But she's going to betray you in the worst possible way, Tego, and break your heart. But you have to stay the course no matter how hard she tries to push you away, no matter how angry she makes you." She looks out at the dark sky. "I know it won't be easy, and I know there'll be times when you're sick to death of being the fall guy, but you have to keep fighting. You have to keep coming back."

"Shit, Isabel, you ask a lot."

She meets my gaze. "Don't do it for me, Tego, do it for you. Because if—against all odds—you manage to make this relationship work, it will be worth all the pain and suffering. A hundred times over, a thousand. For both of you." She turns away. "For the whole fucked up world."

I lie there in the sand, watching night fall and the first stars pop out. The breeze carries the scent of her skin, tugging at my heart and filling me with hope and fear and longing.

There are so many conflicting emotions bumping around inside my head that I am days, perhaps weeks, away from sorting them all out. I stare at her sitting in the sand, an arm's length away from me, her head on her knees and her shoulders rising and falling in the gathering darkness.

The moon rises out of the ocean, framing her in light, and I realize that my anger has burned out, and all that's left is emptiness. Yes, she's making me crazy with all her lecturing and warnings and demands, but the thought of losing her is worse.

*Way worse.*

I sit up and reach out to her.

But she stands up, brushes off her clothes, and turns away, the moonlight illuminating sparkles of white sand on the back of her thighs.

"Iz?"

She shakes her head and starts walking.

"Isabel, please! I'm sorry. Don't go."

She strides up the sand, hurrying toward her beach house.

I jump up and run after her, and when I catch up, I take hold of her arm and try to get her to stop. "Hey. Wait a sec."

But she pulls away from me, her eyes flashing in the moonlight. "Don't."

I step around in front and put my hands on her shoulders, forcing her to stop. "Please. I'm sorry. Give me another chance."

She looks up at me, her face unreadable in the falling darkness, and then she pushes past me. "I'm done, Tego. Go back to your friends."

Panic fills me with desperate courage. "Teach me how to be your lover, Iz. I promise not to give up, if you promise not to give up on me."

She freezes, her hair fluttering in the light breeze. I walk up behind her, afraid to breathe. "You can make me stand out here all night, Iz," I reach across the abyss and put my hands on her bare arms, "if that's what it takes." As gently as I can, I turn her around and then lift her chin so that our eyes meet. "But I'm not letting you go."

She falls against me, her head on my shoulder, crying softly. I put my arms around her, my own eyes damp, and kiss her hair, speechless. She slides her hands up my chest and then wraps them around my neck, and we stand like that, holding on to each other, for a long time.

Finally, she lifts her head and looks up at me. "From here

on out, I'm going to follow my heart." She fingers the collar of my T-shirt. "And so are you."

I put my lips against her forehead. "It would be my pleasure." A tear trickles down her cheek, and I wipe it away with my thumb.

She bites her lip. "And if I say or do something that makes you uncomfortable—if things get too intense, or whatever—just tell me, and we'll stop. Okay?"

"Yeah," I say, smiling. "More than okay. I want to make it work for you—make it work for us. Just don't say the word commitment." I wink and then kiss her on the nose.

"Assuming, of course, that I don't kill you first."

I laugh and run my hand across her cheek. "I'm new at this intimacy balance thing, so be patient with me. I'm trying." I tuck an escaped strand of hair behind her ear. "And you expect a lot."

Something in her face changes, some shadow lifts, and she laughs.

"What is it, Iz? "

She shakes her head, her eyes still sparkling.

"Tell me."

She glides her finger slowly across my lips, her gaze following her touch. "For the first time in my life, I believe we can be that one in a million."

I take her finger into my mouth and caress it with my tongue, wanting more of her—believing her.

She moans softly, and it fills me with heat and light.

"Come on." I take her hand and lead her up the sand.

∞

"Let's see," I say when I step into the dark room. "If I remember correctly, I like to have the lights on."

"Very funny, Tego." She brushes past me and turns on a small lamp. It casts a spell of warmth across the cozy space, illuminating the orange seashell on her nightstand. I reach into my pocket and finger its identical twin, wondering about the connection.

"Next?" She sits down on the bed and sand falls onto the floor—a lot of sand. "Yikes. Definitely a shower." She looks over at me. "So what's it going to be? Take a shower alone or with me? The bathroom is pretty small, so I'll understand if you want to have it all to yourself."

I step into the circle of light. "That was the easiest question you've asked, Iz."

She laughs and pulls her T-shirt off over her head—and then starts untying her bikini top. I stand there with my mouth open.

"Come on. Last one in is a decomposed germ cell." She turns away, grabs a towel off the chair, and disappears into the bathroom. A second later the shower starts, and she calls out, "Are you coming in, or did you just want to watch?"

I pad over to the open door. "Now *that* is a tough choice."

The bathroom *is* tiny, the shower tucked in the corner. An amber sconce casts a soft glow across the white sink and polished blue tile, giving everything a sepia tint.

I step in front of the shower, and my heart stops.

She is standing in the flow of the water with her eyes shut, her pale skin almost glowing. I watch in stunned silence as she lifts her hands above her head and runs her fingers through her hair, the water splashing over her upturned face. I let my gaze slide down her full breasts, slender waist, and soft hips to the dark triangle of curls between her legs.

*Ay, she looks great naked, even better than in my dream.*

Her eyes pop open, and I fall back against the sink, feeling like a voyeur.

"Well," she says, her eyes mischievous. "Did you decide?"

"Let me see, I can watch a beautiful woman bathe in the nude." I cross my arms. "Or, despite feeling awkward and

342

*way* over my head, get in and actually touch her wet, naked body. Shit, that's a tough one."

She grabs my elbow and pulls me in. "You have to be fast or the water gets cold."

I smile, my shirt and shorts getting soaked. "Been a while since I took a shower with my clothes on. Nice of you to offer."

"Hah." She runs her hands up under my T-shirt, lifting the waterlogged cotton away from my chest. "Off," she orders.

I hoist it over my head and then drape it across the shower wall.

She stands with her hands on her hips, staring at me.

"Um," I say, "that would be the 'over my head' part." I nod at my T-shirt. "And this would be where the 'awkward' sequence commences."

She laughs. "Maybe it *is* the wordplay that I love about you." She runs her hands over my biceps and across my chest. "No need to be shy, Tego. I've seen it all before. Remember?" She leans her head against my shoulder blade, her breasts pressing against me as the water pours over us.

And then she slips her hands inside my shorts, and I have to force myself to breathe. "But I haven't."

She lifts her head and looks up into my face, and for once, I can see that she's unsure.

"Yes?" I say, drawing out the s-sound just like she does.

She smacks me on the chest. "Okay, Mister..." she glances down at my swollen shorts, "Innocent."

The hot water runs out and she gasps, whirls around, and wrenches off the tap. She turns back to me and shrugs. "I told you it gets cold fast."

We stand in the half-lit bathroom, the only sound the water dripping off my shirt, and stare at each other: me in soaked shorts, hard as I get, and her, buck naked, wet nipples sticking straight out.

We both start laughing, and all the tension falls away.

I step closer and wrap my arms around her. "Best shower I ever took if you ignore the fact that my hair's dry, I didn't touch the soap, and I still have my clothes on."

She gazes into my eyes, her lips parted. "God, I've missed you." She pulls my mouth down to hers and kisses me, soft and warm, and it's all I can do not to explode with desire.

She pulls her mouth away, slides her hands between us, and starts undoing my shorts. I shut my eyes and move my lips across her ear and neck, my heart pounding in my chest. She squirms against me, and when she finally manages to get my shorts undone, she slips one hand inside and wraps it around my hard cock, making my whole body go rigid.

"Shit that feels good."

She smiles and pushes down on the sandy waistband, rubbing her breasts against me as she lifts the waterlogged fabric over my erection. When my shorts plunk to the tile floor, she kneels on them and looks up at me. "So. Is this your first time?" Her lips are almost touching the tip of my cock.

I exhale, my knees suddenly weak. "If you're asking what I *think* you're asking, then yes."

She smiles and then tugs on my ankle, and I step out of my damp clothes. She tosses them out of the shower and stands back up. "I was hoping you were going to say that." She grabs a towel and wraps it around herself. "But first, you have to wash those buns. They've got more sand on them than Waikiki Beach."

I turn the shower back on, my heart still stuck in my throat, and step into the deluge of tepid water.

She leans against the sink, wide-eyed, and dries her hair. "I should have known you'd do that."

I take some of her shampoo and lather my hair and chest, the smell of tropical flowers filling the small room. When I'm done, I rinse all the sand off, Gus still at attention, and then step out of the shower. "Thanks for waiting."

"I could watch that every night for the rest of my life."

I shrug and step back in.

She laughs and tosses a towel at me. "Oh no you don't. I've got plans for you."

I dry off, ignoring her lusty stare, and then wrap the thin cotton around my waist. "Shall we?"

She saunters out of the bathroom, and I follow, unable to take my eyes off her. But after a couple of steps, I stop and watch her walk across the room, trying to memorize the way her hips sway and the way her hair catches the light.

She shakes sand off the hand-made quilt, folds it back with the sheet, and then turns to me. "You still okay with this?"

"I have never wanted anything more in my life, Iz."

She tugs at the corner of her towel, and it falls away from her body. I let out an astonished breath, and she laughs. "I'll take that as a compliment."

"*Mierda*, Isabel. Even in my wildest dreams, I could never have imagined anything like this."

She reaches out to me. "Come here, you."

# Chapter 47
## *Isabel: All Is Lost*

Tego stands before me, the skimpy white towel wrapped low and tight around his hips and the outline of his hard-on clearly visible.

I glance up to his face. "Where were we?"

"Um, I was going to get started on that chocolate cake?"

I throw a pillow at him and grab another one. "Excuse me? I didn't catch that."

He scoops the cushion up off the floor and uses it as a shield. "Well, my second choice would be to kiss every millimeter of your body until you beg me to make you come."

I feel my face flush.

"If blushing is any indication, I'd say you're voting for the second one."

I take the pillow out of his hands. "So what happened to the shy, reticent guy who was so torqued at me out on the beach today?"

"Oh, he couldn't swim worth shit, so I swapped universes

with him. I think he had to untie you from some railroad tracks."

"Very funny, Tego. Good thing I wasn't actually drowning, or we'd both be dead."

"To be honest, you don't seem like the type to give up without a fight, so I figured you were just testing to see if I could handle being in over my head."

"I think you passed."

"Does that mean I get to keep you?"

I pat the bed. "So what made you change your mind?"

"Well, after you sent me home last night, I was feeling pretty manipulated, like you were toying with me." He sits down facing me, his eyes downcast. "And this afternoon, I felt like you were trying to cram a whole relationship into an hour—and you expected me to take notes." He draws his fingers across my hip and thigh, his gaze following his touch. "But I was still pretty hung up on you."

I close my eyes and bask in his touch. "You're right about the relationship thing. That's exactly what I was trying to do. And just for the record, I don't recommend it."

He slides his fingers underneath my damp hair, lifting it away from my face and shoulders and collecting it in his hand at the back of my head.

He gives it a tug, and I open my eyes.

"You're right about what's possible between us—and I can see it too." He tips his head to the side, studying my face. "Which is not to say that I'm totally comfortable or anything, just that it feels right to be here with you." He smiles. "You're pretty irresistible, Iz, and it's great to stop fighting the way I feel about you."

I entwine my fingers in his. "If you're not careful, Tego, I may not let you go."

The corner of his mouth twitches. "It may already be too late for me."

A powerful tightness grabs my heart, and I have to look away.

*He's not yours, Isabel. He belongs to a different world.*

I force myself to breathe.

*I know that, damn it. I know. But I'm madly in love with him just the same.*

"I hope I didn't just blow it."

I run my fingertips down the inside of his arm. "There you go stepping back again."

He lets out a disbelieving huff, and I lift his chin until our eyes meet. "I have been madly in love with you for years, Tego, so I don't think you have too much to worry about."

"Even though you just met me yesterday."

"Yeah. That part is particularly painful."

He gives me the eyebrow, and I laugh. "So where were we?"

"I was stepping back," he says, "and you were chastising me for it."

I chuckle. "Ah yes. So, given the imminent arrival of the posse, shall I take matters into my own hands, or do you have the proper tool for the job?" I kiss his palm and then glance down at the lump in his towel.

"Well, miss." His voice has a slight southern twang. "A skilled lawman knows how to choose the right tool for the job, and that—" He motions with his head, "—is not the one I plan to use right now. Sorry to disappoint."

"I hate it when you get cocky."

"No, you don't." He stands, unwraps the towel, and tosses it over the back of the chair, not the least bit shy.

I reach out and pull him down next to me. "You're right, I don't."

He rolls onto his side, his head propped up on his palm. "Where have you been all my life?"

"Stuck in your future." I push him onto his back and roll

over on top of him, enjoying his wide-eyed look. I place his hands behind his head and then slide my palm across the muscles in his arm.

He turns his head to the side, watching me touch him. "I thought you loved me for my chocolate cake."

I draw my lips across his chest, taking in his dark, masculine scent. "God, you look great naked."

His erection swells against my thigh. "Ah, to hell with it." He grabs my head and pulls my mouth down to his, his whole body rigid.

I let out a surprised breath and sit up on his hips, his hard cock between my thighs. "Golly, sheriff, you ain't thinking I'm that kind of girl, now, are you?"

He lets his gaze slide from my face down to my breasts, his lips parted. "I'm pretty sure you've fired a pistol or two in your time, missy."

I give him an exaggerated pout and run my fingertip down his chest until it bumps into the head of his cock. "I thought you were going to show me *your* six-shooter."

"Sure thing, little lady. I'll even let you fire it, if you like." He stares at my mouth. "An' I suppose you could ride my pony, if he's not too wild for you."

I break out laughing. "Bring it on."

He grabs my shoulders and tries to pull me back down against his chest, but I resist.

"You're going to have to try harder than that, shooter."

"*Mierda.*"

He grabs my wrists and throws his weight sideways, making me lose my balance, and I collapse against him. Before I have a chance to react, he wraps his arms around me, pinning my hands against his chest, and then he attempts to roll over on top of me. But I push him away and try to duck out of his hold. "I call the shots, Nadales, and you'd better get used to it."

He grabs my head and holds on tight. "Get used to disappointment." He kisses me, sucking on my lip and teasing me with his tongue, but not letting me kiss him back.

"Who the hell taught you that?"

"You did."

We wrestle on the bed, pillows flying everywhere, and I'm grateful we're not in a hotel room because the neighbors would be banging on the walls by now. He's much more comfortable with the mock fighting now, and despite my best efforts, he manages to get on top and pin down my shoulders with his hands.

I stare up at his full lips and dark brown eyes, both of us breathing hard.

*God, I've missed you.*

He slides his fingers into my hair and grabs on, holding my head still. I try to twist away, but he doesn't let go. "Nice try, Iz, but I'm calling the shots now."

"That didn't take very long."

He waits until I stop struggling and then strokes my cheek and places his mouth above mine. "So *are* you that kind of *woman?*"

I slide my hands across his flexed biceps and then run my fingernails down his back. He squirms against me, but doesn't let go. I gaze up into his face. "Seems your pony's a bit skittish tonight."

He lets go of my hair and lifts my arms above my head, holding them there with one hand. I try to pull my hands free, be he doesn't let go of my wrists.

"Yeah, he can be a real nightmare."

I laugh. "Damn, you're good."

"And you are very, very bad." He starts at my wrists, drawing his lips across my skin, kissing and nibbling his way up to my shoulder. I squirm beneath his touch, my pulse quickening.

350

"But I know just what to do about it." He slides his open mouth up to the crest of my breast. I twist my body, trying to get my nipple into his mouth, but he shakes his head. "Uh-uh. It's my turn to torture you, and believe me, I've been thinking about it non-stop since the first time you touched me."

"Well that explains why you weren't paying attention this afternoon."

He nudges my chin with his nose, tipping my head back and exposing my neck. "Shh." He puts his hand on my chin, holding me still, and then places his mouth lightly against my neck.

A soft moan forms in my throat and slips out my lips.

He lifts his head, gazing down at me. "Shit, you look hot." And then he presses his wet, open mouth into the soft hollow beneath my jaw and kisses me hard.

I writhe beneath him, sighing with pleasure.

He releases my hands, his lips still touching me. "Enough with the horseplay."

I smack him hard on the butt.

His gaze dances between my eyes and my lips. "I think you like to be dominated. In fact, I think you crave it." He strokes my face with his fingertips, not breaking eye contact. "Tell me I'm wrong."

I reach up and pull his head down very, very slowly. "You're wrong."

When our lips touch, he opens his mouth, waiting. "Oh, I think not." He slips his fingers in my hair. "And I'm definitely up for it."

My breath catches in my throat and it takes me a moment to respond. "So tell me, Mr. Grey, what is it that I crave?"

He tips my head to the side and places his lips against mine. "Oh, I'd say you're dying to be fucked. Deep and hard. Slow and wet. Gentle and desperate." He lifts his mouth away. "Did I miss anything?"

"Shit, you're good." I lift my lips up to his—and then push him over and roll on top, grabbing onto his hair and slipping my hand down onto his hard cock. "You got the deep, hard, and wet part right." And then I kiss him, sliding my hand over his hardness as I press my body against his, wanting him inside me.

He grabs my head and forces it down against his shoulder and then pins my hand flat against his belly, his body rigid.

I exhale, my heart still racing, and collapse against him.

He stares up at the ceiling. "Don't say it."

I wiggle out of his grip and kiss him on the shoulder. "I know why you just stepped back, but your Isabel is going to take that as negative feedback."

"Can't help yourself, huh?"

I smack him on the chest.

"That was not stepping back, Isabel, and you know it."

I try to keep the condescension out of my voice. "She'll think that you're tired. That you've had enough. That something about her turned you off."

"She'd have to be goddamn deaf and blind."

I poke him in the chest. "And all sorts of terrible things will flash through her over-active imagination, each and every one causing her pain—which she will cover by getting mad. At you."

He gives me a look of disbelief. "You're not serious."

"I'm dead serious. After what happened to her, you can hardly blame her."

"So what happened to her?"

"It doesn't matter. What matters is that you won't have any idea why she's torqued, so you'll back off, and she'll take that as confirmation that you don't want to be with her, and before you can say 'disastrously dysfunctional date'—poof—the evening will be over. Ten minutes later, you'll be driving home in the pouring rain, wondering what you did to make her cry."

"Ouch."

I draw my fingertip across his lips. "Of course, if you told her what was going on, then she'd be flattered rather than threatened. You are, after all, withdrawing your affection with no attempt at explanation, and if she did the same thing to you, I guarantee that you would take it as negative feedback."

He bites my finger. "Except that I've been hard for two days, and you know exactly why I stopped you from touching me."

"I do. But to be honest, Diego does the same thing, and it makes me uncomfortable."

His eyes get big. "You have a Diego?"

*Oops.*

"There's a *me* in your world?" He smacks himself on the forehead. "Of course there is." He flexes his biceps. "Is he as manly as I am?"

I roll my eyes.

"Can you at least tell me if I'm going to be rich and famous?"

"Did you even hear what I just said?"

"Yes, *his* Isabel. Sheesh, you're demanding." He gives me an annoyed look. "It's sort of embarrassing, not having as much control as I want. So, it's not something I'd want to call further attention to by talking about it."

"Well then, *her* Tego, you just need more practice." I nod in encouragement. "Go on, give it a shot."

"I thought I was trying to avoid that."

I smack him on the shoulder.

"Ouch! Okay, okay." He theatrically clears his throat. "Isabel, Queen of Sheba, I stopped you from touching me because I'm too excited. I can guarantee that it's not because

353

I dislike the way you're touching me or any other goofy idea you might have in that nefarious brain of yours involving me being anything except delighted with your overtures." He takes my hand, kisses it, and places it back on his hard cock. "Thank you for your attention. Carry on."

"Not bad, not bad. But I have a better idea." I prop my head up on one hand. "Make yourself come."

He gives me an incredulous look.

I pick up his hand and wrap it around his cock. "Seriously. On your mark, get set, go."

He remains motionless.

"It's not that big a deal, Diego. Simply apply up and down friction to your erect penis, causing ejaculation. Do you need me to show you?"

"No, I don't need you to show me."

I let out an exasperated sigh.

He gives me the Spock eyebrow. "You're kidding, right?"

"Just trust me on this, okay?"

He gives it a half-hearted stroke, and I stifle a laugh. The expression on his face takes a turn for the worse.

"Shut your eyes," I say.

His hand falls back onto the bed, and he glares up at the ceiling. "And only my mother calls me Diego."

"Oops. Sorry. It won't happen again, Tego. Please. Shut your eyes." I brush his eyelids down with my fingertips. "Perhaps I can give you a *head* start."

His erection regains a little of his zest, and a smirk ripples across his face.

I lean down and slip my tongue in between his hand and the hard shaft of his penis, letting the wetness from my mouth flow onto his cock. When his hand starts moving in time to some internal beat, I move my mouth up to his nipple and match his tempo with my tongue. He grabs my head and comes in a matter of seconds.

354

*Youth is wasted on the young.*

I give him a few moments to catch his breath. He looks gorgeous lying there with his eyes shut, still hard, his breath slowing. I reach over to the chair, grab the towel, and then wipe off his belly and chest, enjoying the bashful expression on his face.

He peeks with one eye. "Bedtime?"

"Did I mention that Lorena Bobbitt is a relative of mine?" I give his penis a knowing glance and pantomime scissors.

"*Ay!*" He wraps his arms around my waist and pulls me over on top of him. "*Mierda*, Isabel, I can't believe you talked me into that." He gathers my hair behind my head. "Of course, the best defense is a good offense." He pushes me over onto the pillows, rolls on top, and moves down my body.

I grab onto his shoulders. "Whoa there, shooter. We got another horse to break before you consider heading south."

He groans. "How about I head south and *then* you ride the pony?" I laugh, and he looks up at me. "I'll take that as a yes."

A wave of powerful emotion crashes over me. There is chemistry between us that is impossible to fight, impossible to ignore, and impossible to live without. I am hopelessly addicted to the euphoria I feel when I'm with him, but at the same time, terrified of all that I have to lose. After only a matter of hours, I'm madly in love with him, desperate for his touch, unable to imagine life without him.

*And I'm going to lose him all over again.*

I run my fingers through his dark hair, blinking back tears. "Come here."

He kisses my belly, and then lifts his head, his lips slightly parted. "Let me make you come first."

I gaze down at his upturned face and then stroke the line of his jaw. His facial hair is soft and fine.

*So young. So full of possibilities.*

"Thanks for the offer—and I mean that sincerely—but no."

"Why not?"

I force down the voices in my head. "Because I don't want to, Tego. But thanks."

He puts his head down on my belly. "So what's going on here, Isabel?" He draws his fingertip across my hipbone. "Are you testing me? Should I push you? Should I let it drop?" He lets out a frustrated sigh. "You've been lecturing me all day about returning affection and paying attention to *her* needs, and now you're pushing me away?" He glances up, his jaw set. "So, help me out here, because I'm at a complete loss."

"It's not like that at all, Tego. Can you please just let it go?"

"No, I can't."

I pull on his shoulders, already in too deep, knowing I'm going to drown, but unable to stop myself. "Please."

He hesitates, his lips tight, and then moves up next to me and props his head up on his hand. "I want to know what's going on, Isabel. You owe me that much."

I tussle his hair and look away, trying not to cry.

"Hey." He kisses my palm. "You just made me come, and I'm not complaining, but now I'm in some sort of temporary limbo where my body and my brain are strangely disconnected, so maybe you could trust me enough to let me return the favor."

"No." I take a ragged breath. "I don't want to talk about it, Tego."

"Well, I do. And I think I deserve an explanation."

"It happened a long time ago, but the scar is still fresh."

"What are you talking about? What scar?"

I glance away. "It's nothing like that. As far as I know, there isn't anything physically wrong with me."

"*Mierda*, Iz. That sounds ominous. Just tell me what

356

happened."

I stroke his face, not meeting his eyes. "Patrick happened." I spit the name out like an obscenity.

"Okay," he says. "Married to Dave the Asshole, scarred by Patrick the Bastard, and saved by Tego the Hero. When should I expect the bastard to barge onto the scene?"

"Never. It's already too late—even in this universe." I trace the muscles in his forearm. "But you will definitely have to deal with the fallout."

"Fair enough. So tell me what he did."

"I can't, Tego. I've spent a lifetime trying to forget it. I never even told Diego."

He kisses me on the shoulder. "Well, then teach me what I need to know." He raises his eyebrow. "I assume this involves making you come?"

I close my eyes, unable to speak.

He leans in and wipes an escaped tear off my cheek. "Iz?"

I open my eyes and stare at his mouth, my heart in my throat. "I don't know what to teach you, Tego." I swallow and look away. "Just thinking about it terrifies me—and it's going to be even worse for her."

"Forget about *her*, Isabel. I want to make it work for you."

"Well I don't even know where to start."

He leans over and kisses me, slow and soft. "Okay. Then we'll figure it out together."

I scan his handsome face, my pulse racing. All along, my mission has been to ensure that things will work between Tego and some other woman. Someone I happen to know a lot about, but still, another woman. Now, a fierce and intoxicating thought forces everything else out of my head.

*What if I don't let him go?*

I move my gaze across his full lips, the sharp line of his jaw, the long eyelashes and dark brown eyes—hopelessly in love.

"Say yes." His voice is warm and gentle.

I shut my eyes, holding back tears. "Yes, but—"

He puts his finger up to my lips. "Shh. The journey is the reward. Remember?" He pulls me over on top of him and wraps his arms around me, kissing my hair and holding me while I sob into his chest.

*All that I came for is lost, but I am found.*

When I manage to get my emotions back under control, he lifts up my chin and wipes a tear away with his thumb. "Have I told you recently that I'm madly in love with you?"

I grab onto his head and kiss him, passion and need and hope pushing out everything except the exquisite pleasure of being in his arms.

# CHAPTER 48
## *Matt: We're Domed*

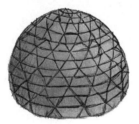

I stand up and tear Picasso's world map off the wall. Everyone else gave up on it weeks ago, but I just couldn't bring myself to let go until now. It's been almost a month since we heard from anyone, and the map is drowning in red ink.

"Enough with those bloody X's."

We're still receiving the date and time from a station in Ft. Collins—and the buzzer tones from UVB-76 in Russia are right on schedule—but other than the six people starving to death on the ISS, it seems we're alone.

I grab the useless mic, ripping the plug out of the receptacle, and throw it across the room. Four people on the whole bloody planet: one super-intelligent women who hates taking orders, one thirty-something Rambo who can't stop giving them, and two middle-aged gay men. If it wasn't so tragic, it would be funny.

I sit back down and continue with what I know will be a

fruitless search, wondering just how much longer we're going to keep up the charade.

We could survive for fifty years, maybe longer if Cass and Picasso had kids, but in the end, mankind is doomed. We'd need at least a hundred people to have any chance of survival, and the odds of that have become increasingly grim.

I push the button to start the automatic sweep through the next band, letting the computer search for a signal. It clicks as it scans through each frequency, listening at the weakest possible setting for any signs of life.

I get up and fish four aspirin out of a five-pound cardboard drum I hauled up from the dispensary. There are six more where that one came from, and given the amount I've been drinking, I may need all of them. I dry swallow the tablets and then collapse into my chair.

Phil had some sort of breakdown. He stays in his room, watching old TV shows on his computer. Every morning he begs me to stay, and every morning I leave earlier. We had a fight a couple of days ago, and I've been sleeping up here ever since. I care for the guy more than anyone I've ever met, but I don't know how much more I can take.

At first Cass and Picasso tried to help with Phil. We ate meals in his room and took turns sitting with him, trying to convince him that things weren't as bad as they seemed, but it was all a charade, and everyone knew it. Eventually, Cassie and Picasso came up with some excuse to be busy for a couple of days, and never came back.

They haven't said as much, but they think I'm wasting my time in here. I can see it in their eyes when we eat dinner together, which is hardly at all these days.

*At least they have each other.*

The radio makes one long, low beep and stops searching. A number appears on the screen, the words "Signal Detected" flashing in red next to it.

360

*Probably some satellite.*

I pick up the list of known autonomous signals and attempt to match the number, but it's not on there. I check twice, and then plug in the headphones and crank up the volume.

"...Q, calling C-Q. This is the Kirkland Biodome in Denver, Colorado calling at twenty meters and standing by..."

I scramble to reach the microphone and end up ripping the headphones off as I lunge to grab it up off the floor. After I retrieve the headphones, I shove them over my head and plug in the mic. The blood is pounding in my head so loud, I'm not sure if I'm imagining things, but the voice sounds like a woman's.

I stab the talk button with a shaky hand and speak out loud for the first time in days. "Kirkland Biodome this is Matt Hudson inside a bloody government mountain about forty miles south of Denver. There are four of us here, and I can't tell you how glad I am to hear your voice."

There is noise on the other end... no, not noise: voices. Human voices!

"Well I'll be a halfwit mooker. Damn nice to hear from you, Bloody Mountain. I copy your location and number of survivors. How's your food and water supply?"

"We have enough rations, electricity, and beds to house five hundred people for twenty years, Kirkland. How many are you?"

"Just short of two hundred, Bloody Mountain, but we're running short of—"

His voice cuts off, but comes back a moment later. "Please stand by, Bloody Mountain, I have someone here who says he knows you."

I sit in my chair, staring at the flashing "signal detected" for five long seconds, and then nearly die of a heart attack.

"Matt, is that you in the Magic Kingdom? It's Diego...

Diego Nadales."

"Diego? But how..." I realize I'm not pressing the talk button and start over, but there is so much shouting going on in my head, that I can barely think above the fray. "How did you..."

"Matt. *Mierda*, I can't believe it's you. It's a long story, *mae*, but I brought the vaccine back with—."

"What vaccine? What are you talking about?"

"The bionano. I have a version that works against the mutated virus, but we don't have the facilities to produce it here. We had to seal the biodome in a hurry, and we ended up losing the hospital and all the medical labs. In any case, we have the people and the know-how, but no tools or supplies. And we're running out of food."

I take a deep breath, my headache gone. "Bloody hell, we have labs, food, and empty beds coming out our ass. If we can figure out some way to get you people over here, we could start working on the vaccine tomorrow."

There's cheering on the other end, and then Diego's voice again. "Hey, Matt." He clears his throat. "I know it's a long shot, but is Isabel there with you? Did she make it?"

*Oh fuck.*

"Uh, yeah. She made it, or rather she wasn't outside when the virus mutated." I can't bring myself to tell him the rest.

"So is she there? I heard there are only four of you. Is that right?"

"Yes, only four. And Isabel's not here."

"Christ, Matt, where is she?"

"I'm sorry, Diego. After we lost you, we sent Isabel. She's in another universe, mate, and we can't get her back."

There is silence, and I wonder if I've killed him, broken his heart.

But a moment later, Diego's defiant voice comes back across the ether. "Then you'll just have to send me there too."

"Don't tell me goodnight." She blurts it out, her voice laden with angst.

I snuggle against her back and slip my arm around her waist. "Is *buenas noches* out too?"

She tries to pull away, but I don't let her.

"Hey. It's okay, Iz. I'm not going anywhere." I sweep her hair to the side and kiss her shoulder. She's ticklish there, and she wiggles against me as I move my lips up to her ear, inhaling the intoxicating scent of her. "I'm yours. For as long as you'll have me."

She lifts my hand, kisses my palm, and holds it against her cheek. My fingers comes away damp with her tears.

*Okay, so maybe we're both in a bit over our heads.*

I slide my fingertips across her skin, enjoying the velvety softness of the inside of her thigh, the smooth curve of her ass, the sensual line where her breasts emerge unannounced from her ribs. "Go to sleep, *mi amor*."

She sighs with pleasure as I touch her, and the sound fills me with a powerful need to protect her, to stay close to her, and to make her happy.

"I'll be right here when you wake up."

When her breathing slows, I leave my hand on her thigh and drift off into a deep and welcome sleep, happier than I can ever remember being.

∞

In my dream, she presses her breasts against my back and kisses the hollow between my shoulder blades, her open mouth soft and wet. Warm desire flows into me as she glides her palm across my biceps, over my shoulder, and up to my lips. She slips one fingertip into my mouth, and then rubs the cool wetness across my nipple, sending sparks of electricity down to my cock.

I lie perfectly still, afraid of falling out of the compelling fantasy.

She slides her palm down my chest and wraps her hand around my awakening cock. It stiffens in her encouraging grasp, and I let out a moan, my whole body flush with desire.

And then realize I'm not dreaming.

She places my hand between her thighs, making my heart race, and then pushes my fingertips inside her.

"Mmm," I say. "You're so wet." I turn over, keeping my hand pressed against her. "*Mierda*, you make me hard fast."

She bites me lightly on the shoulder and pushes her hips against my hand, forcing my fingers deeper inside her. "I want you."

"You had me from the first smile, Iz."

She pulls my hand away and rolls over on top of me, tossing the covers off both of us.

I put up no resistance, simply pushing locks of her hair back from her face. She places her lips against mine, and I open my mouth to her, caught up in her deep, wet kiss and provocative scent. She moves her mouth slowly down to my chest and teases my nipples with her tongue. My erection swells against her well-placed hip.

She drags her tongue leisurely down my chest, eventually settling with her shoulders between my thighs. I stuff a frog-shaped pillow behind my head and then stroke her face and hair with the other hand, captivated by the sight of her kissing me.

She slips the head of my penis into her mouth and runs her tongue around the line of my foreskin. I let out a soft moan as my cock swells beneath her wet caress.

Moving a little at a time, she slides her lips down the shaft until the crown bumps against the back of her throat, and then she reverses the action, pressing her tongue and hand against my cock as she draws her mouth up.

"*Mierda*, that feels good."

She moves her hand to the base of my erection, and then repeats the motion, slowly accelerating.

Almost immediately, I reach down and grab her head, forcing her to stop. "Easy there, *mi amor*." There's a smile in my voice. "Or you'll make me come." I fight down the desire to ejaculate. "And did I mention how absolutely magnificent that feels?"

She laughs and plants wet kisses around the crown of my very hard cock—which pushes me right to the edge again. I grab onto her shoulders and pull her up onto my chest, ignoring her protests. I cradle her head in my hands and kiss her with a passion—a need—that I have not felt before.

When I release her, she places my swollen cock between her thighs, the anticipation of being inside her almost palpable.

"You still okay with this?" Her voice is guarded.

"No."

She stares at my mouth. "Seriously?"

"Seriously." I pick up her hand and kiss it. "Actually, I'm *way* past being okay with having sex. In fact, I'm rapidly approaching being unable to think about anything else. But not tonight. I want another chance to make you come first."

"It would be my pleasure, Tego. Really."

I slide my fingers into her hair and let my gaze wander around her face. "I've been enjoying my pleasure all night, Iz. And if I have to enjoy any more pleasure, I might die of exhaustion, despite what Gus thinks." I bump my hips against her.

She smacks me on the chest. "Don't make me tie you up, Nadales."

I give her a stunned look. "Were you planning to?"

She repositions her thigh with the tip of my penis pressing against her wetness. "Say yes."

"I'm already way too excited, Isabel, and being inside you is going to make me come in ten seconds."

"Is that a yes?" She pushes against the tip of my very hard cock.

"Make that five seconds, possibly less."

"Hah. Then you better make it good."

"Yes."

"Say it again."

"Yes, I want to have sex with you."

She sits up and settles onto my erection.

I let out a gasp and grab onto her hips. "But what about all that stuff you told me—"

She places a finger over my lips. "Shh. Let me give you this one gift. Please."

I close my eyes, dangerously close to the edge, and try to focus on the most physically demanding work I can think of: chopping wood.

*Ay, I'm going to get a hard-on every time I see a dead tree.*

366

She bends over and takes one of my nipples in her mouth, and then begins moving her hips against mine.

"*Mierda*." I force her to hold still. "That's cheating and you know it." I pull her hips forward. "What about contraception?"

She laughs. "That would be a hoot."

"Not so much."

She glances up at the ceiling and waves. "What would the Peeping Tom guys think if I got pregnant?"

"Given all the things we talked about this afternoon, you have me a bit confused."

"Well you shouldn't be." She tosses her hair over her shoulder. "I don't think there's a snowflake's chance in hell you could get me pregnant, and a day from now the point will be moot."

"Isabel, women say stuff like that all the time. And then turn up pregnant."

"How would you know?"

I laugh. "With you it would probably be twins."

She freezes, her eyes dark and far away.

"Hey. Protection should be worn on every conceivable occasion."

"Yes, but this is not a conceivable occasion." She rolls away from me and then pulls me over on top. "I don't want anything between us. Just this once. It's important to me."

"*Mierda*, Isabel."

She shuts her eyes. "There are condoms in the drawer of the nightstand. You can get one if you want."

I take a deep breath, trying to decide what to do.

She exhales and then opens her eyes. "Trust me, okay?"

## CHAPTER 50

### *Isabel: One Last Time*

He gazes down at my face for a moment, and then slips inside me.

My breath catches in my throat. "Oh god that feels good." I slide my hands down his back and pull him deeper, but he resists, so I grab onto his shoulders and try to move against him.

"Uh uh." He pins my hips, refusing to cooperate.

I smack him hard on the butt. "Damn you. Stop teasing me."

"I am not moving until you explain the 'point will be moot' part."

I grab his shoulders and try to push him over so I can get on top.

"I'm serious, Isabel. I'm not letting you up until you tell me everything."

I flop back into the pillows. "I did already. There's nothing more to tell you, Tego." I try to keep my voice level. "I wish it were otherwise. You can't know how much I wish it were otherwise."

He starts to slide out of me, and when I resist, he rolls onto his side, taking me with him, our legs entangled.

He props up his head and places his other hand on my hip. "*Are* you dying?"

I close my eyes and move my lips across his chest. "Yes."

He takes hold of my head and waits for me to look at him. "And you only have a few days to live?"

I glance from his mouth to his eyes. "Yes. Possibly less."

"How can that be?" His voice is full of disbelief. "You seem fine—well, mostly fine. Maybe a little weak now and then, but, *mierda*, Isabel, how could you be dying?"

"It's part of the bargain I made with the devil—the devil of black holes and quantum physics. He owns me, and he will be taking me back very soon."

The look on his face is dark and tormented.

I let my gaze run over his shoulders and face, taking in as much of him as I can. "It doesn't change anything, Nadales. If I had a whole lifetime ahead of me, I would have done things exactly the same—only you can be damn sure I wouldn't be telling you about some other woman." I move a lock of hair away from his eyes. "I know you're finding all of this difficult to believe. *I'm* finding it difficult to believe, and I'm the one who got squeezed through a black hole."

He rolls onto his back, pulling me over on top of him. I rest against his chest, listening to his heartbeat, taking in his scent, and trying to make up for a lifetime without him.

"I'm in love with you, Iz. You can't die on me."

"Sorry, gorgeous, it's my turn."

He takes my head in his hands and stares at me. "You can't mean that."

I slide my fingers along the line of his jaw. "And you will love her just as much. Perhaps more." I tell him that, knowing

369

it's true, breaking my heart.

He moves his thumb across my lips. "You're wrong."

I look into his dark eyes. "I don't know where the physics gods are taking me, but you will always be in my heart. Always." I kiss him, and he responds with his whole body, focusing the entire universe, just for a moment, on that one kiss.

I can feel him getting hard against my thigh, and I slide down, taking him deep inside, and begin moving against him, finding the rhythm. An uncontrollable passion takes hold, sweeping us up into a place where nothing else matters, all time and space disappearing into the perfect fusing of our bodies.

Minutes turn into hours, and lifetimes into moments. Universes are created and destroyed with nary a pop. What was saved, no longer exists. What was lost, no longer matters.

## CHAPTER 51
### Isabel: Left for Dead

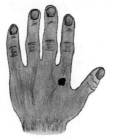

I startle awake, gasping for breath and my head pounding. The sheets are damp with sweat, and my whole body cries out in agony.

And I am very, very thirsty.

I lie there, trying to remember where I am.

Heavy rain is beating on the roof, and the first hint of dawn is creeping in through the water-streaked windows. It is a terrible and bitterly harsh light.

*Tego.*

He lies next to me, his arm still draped across my thigh, his breathing deep and regular. I reach out to him, but stop short. Even in the dim light, I can see the wrinkled skin on the back of my trembling hand.

Moving very slowly, I slide out from underneath his arm, and then crawl to the edge of the bed and let my feet drop to the floor. I'm so drained by the effort that I can barely push myself up to a sitting position.

*Come on, Isabel. You can do this.*

I grab onto the headboard, fighting vertigo, and close my eyes, concentrating on my breathing. Every cell in my body is dying, self-destructing, screaming in pain at each tiny movement. But it is nothing—*nothing*—compared to the torture of my heart breaking.

I force my eyes open and, clinging to the bed frame, pull myself up. The room starts to spin, and I force down the urge to vomit. My head feels like it's on fire. I take a deep breath, blood pounding in my ears, and push down the panic.

*I'm dying.*

I shuffle across the tiny room, grabbing on to the chair, and then the table, and then the doorframe of the bathroom, a sick old woman unable to walk without support.

Tego sighs in his sleep and turns away.

I stare at him for a moment and then slip on my dress, my muscles screaming in protest at each movement. When I twist my damp, tangled hair back in a knot, my shaking hands come away covered with gray strands.

Through a deluge of tears, I struggle to write out a note and then place it on the table underneath his wooden box. I sit for more than a minute staring at our seashells on the nightstand, trying to collect the strength to do what I know I must.

Finally, I stand, forcing myself not to cry out in pain, and totter over to pick up my shell. I place it between my breasts, and gaze, for the very last time, at my lover asleep in my bed.

*Goodbye, Tego. I'm sorry. I'm so very sorry.*

I shuffle out the door, down the steps, and out into the pouring rain, sobbing uncontrollably in the dull gray predawn light. I have no idea where I'm going, only that I don't want Tego to wake up next to my cold, aged corpse. Rain beats down on my head and chest, soaking me to the bone. I shudder and force my feet to keep moving.

Lightning flashes over the ocean, filling the distant sky with ragged shards of light, and that decides it for me: back to the sea. For courage, I bring up the image of Tego asleep in my bed, and then force my legs to carry me down the slope of the sand into watery oblivion.

But I only manage a couple of steps before I realize that the beach is covered with snakes, hundreds of them slithering down toward the surf. I recoil, and then lose my balance and collapse onto the writhing mass, but the snakes are gone, replaced by rivulets of water.

*What's happening to me?*

I cannot lift my head, let alone stand, so I curl up there in the damp sand, raindrops striking my neck and back. Tremors wrack my failing body, but I'm too dehydrated to cry anymore. I roll my head to the side and let the cool beads of water run down my cheek and into my mouth.

*I'm so thirsty.*

I smell freshly cut grass and hear the notes of a Bach concerto rise from the waves. Something about that is wrong, but I don't have the strength to think about it.

The sun will be rising soon, but it will be too late to save me.

*Nothing can save me this time, not even you, Diego.*

I shut my eyes, feeling the watery snakes slither across my skin, and let the universe fade to black.

## CHAPTER 52
### *Tego: To Hell & Gone*

My sleeping brain grimaces but refuses to respond to an incessant chirping, subconsciously hoping someone else will shut the damn thing off. I wait until I can no longer ignore the sound of innocent rabbits being tortured, and stretching across the bed toward the annoying racket, grope around until I find the bunny-shaped device and maul it into silence.

I realize where I am—and that I am alone. "Iz?" I wait for a few moments and then call out again, louder, "Isabel?"

Lying very still, I listen for the sound of the shower, and then for any sound at all. I can hear rain falling outside, but nothing else. Maybe she got up early and went for a swim? I turn over and look at the White Rabbit. It's almost ten. I have no idea what time we went to sleep, but I can't believe I've been asleep for more than a few hours.

*Where is she? She can't have gone far.*

I get up, wrap a damp towel around my waist, and peek

into the bathroom. Empty. Her bikini is in a pile in the corner, her toothbrush by the sink, but her dress is gone. The kitchen appears unchanged: dishes stacked in the sink, the lone avocado still sitting on the counter next to the fridge.

I drop the towel and pull on my damp, sandy shorts, and then cross over to the nightstand to get my seashell.

*Mierda, her shell is gone too!*

I walk out onto the covered lanai. It's raining hard, and the sky is filled with dense, low-lying clouds. The tide is out, and there is nothing on the vast expanse of sodden beach except for an old man walking along the shore under a red and white umbrella.

*Loco.*

I put the shell in my pocket and go back inside.

*Where is she?*

I take another look out the kitchen window at the umbrella man and then pick up the avocado and toss it back and forth between my hands, trying to think where Isabel would have gone.

*To get breakfast? Maybe she left me a note?*

Certain that after everything that passed between us last night, her absence must be temporary, I go over to the table, and sure enough, there's a note tucked under the Nazareno box I gave her.

I snatch it up and fall through thin ice.

*Tego, My Love-*

*A thousand tears, falling like the rain,
can't wash away the pain of goodbye...*

*I know you don't believe my story, but
regrettably, it is true. You will find her,
and it will be a challenge to make things*

work. For both of you. (What a pain in the ass I can be, no?) Find the balance. Be strong and patient. Make the first time count. Trust me, she's in love with you even if she doesn't know it yet.

Thank you for the beautiful gift. Please keep it safe for me. Where I am going, I can take only the sublime memory of lying in your arms, and I live by the thread of hope that by some quirk of space and time, I will do so again.

The journey is the reward,

Isabel

# Epilogue

## *Don't Stay Away Too Long*

"Isabel?"

The voice comes from far away, and it takes all my strength to open my eyes.

"Oh my god, Isabel!"

I peer up into the rain. The world is tipped on its side, but I can make out Mary Poppins. She's hurrying toward me with her red and white umbrella held aloft. The snakes pay her no attention, so neither do I.

I take a labored breath and let my eyelids slip back down.

"Oh shit! I should have come sooner."

Someone strokes my back, and I know it must be Mary Poppins, but I'm confused by the obscenity. Mary Poppins would never swear. Perhaps the snakes have scared her? Adam and Jamie say it helps to swear when you're afraid.

A cool hand touches my cheek. "Christ, you're burning up."

The snakes are still crawling across my arms and legs, and

it makes me shiver. They must be attracted to my body heat. "It's okay. The snakes aren't poisonous. They're just cold."

"You're hallucinating, Iz, but it's going to be okay. I'll get you to a doctor."

The hands grab hold of my shoulders, and I am grateful for their warmth.

"Can you stand?"

Pain shoots through my neck and back, and I cry out. "No. Stop. Please. I have to get to the water. I don't want Tego to find my body."

"Tego?" The voice becomes soothing. "It's okay, hun, I'll get you some water. But first I have to lift you up. It's going to hurt a little, but then it will get better. Okay?"

I take a labored breath and close my eyes, too tired to fight.

"Don't leave me, Isabel!" Strong hands slide beneath me and lift me out of the cold, damp sand. It hurts to move, but I know Mary Poppins is trying to help me, so I don't cry out. "You have to stay awake, Iz. Please."

Raindrops spatter against my face and chest, and I shudder.

Mary lifts me like a child, holding me against her warm body, and strides through the rain. She smells like sandalwood and fresh soap, and the scent fills me with a strange euphoria. I settle against her muscular chest, listening to her heart pound, and then reach up to touch her damp face.

She kisses the palm of my hand. "Almost there, hun. Hang on for just a little bit longer."

I laugh because her face is so rough.

Mary Poppins has beard stubble!

But before I can think too much about it, there are more startled voices, and the sounds of people running and doors banging. I want to see where we are, but I'm too exhausted to open my eyes, so I rest my head on her shoulder and try not to cry.

Lights come on and then go off, and I can feel the world shift beneath me. Mary Poppins-with-a-beard must be flying with her umbrella.

At last, she sets me down on something soft. Tremors wrack my body as gentle hands remove my wet clothes. A moment later, I'm covered with a warm blanket, and then I hear footsteps and more voices. I can't understand everything they're saying, but I keep hearing an apprehensive voice say, "vaccine" and "syringe."

Someone lifts my head and presses a cool glass against my lips. "Here's the water, Iz." I try to say that I've been misunderstood, that I wanted to go *to* the water, but the cool liquid tastes so good that all I can do is swallow.

When the glass is taken away, there's a jab in my arm, and I can no longer hold back the tears. Mary Poppins will think I'm a baby, but I can't seem to stop crying. I force my eyes open, to show her that despite the tears, I'm not afraid of dying.

She takes my hand and places it against her cool cheek, and I realize that she is crying too.

"Christ, I hope it's not too late." Her voice is almost angry.

I try to smile. "I don't mean to be rude, Miss Poppins, but you need to shave or people will think you're a man."

She laughs, deep and resonant, and then strokes my face. "I'll remember that for next time, hun."

I close my eyes, grateful for her tender touch, but wishing it were his lips I felt kissing my forehead as I drift off into the long night.

## ACKNOWLEDGMENTS

My life changed the day my fourth-grade teacher started reading *A Wrinkle In Time* to our class. I was transported to another world, and I never wanted to come back.

That day marked the first step of a journey that led to this book, and my life is richer because the voyage took me through the worlds of Clarke, Asimov, Vinge, Card, Le Guin, Heinlein, Morgan, Rowling, Steinbeck, Moore, Willis, Simmons, Vinge, Brin, and many others.

So now, welcome to my universe! If there is the tiniest glimpse of brilliance in these pages, it is because I am standing on the shoulders of giants, and the view is magnificent.

∞

I would also like to thank my grandmother who believed I could change the world and told me so, my mother who encouraged me to write, Weronika (who loved the book even if she couldn't sell it), Sue and Annie at *Etopia Press* and the fine folks at *BookTrope* who all offered to publish it (you were very kind), and finally, you, gentle reader, who spent your precious time living and breathing in my world. Thank you.

∞

I wrote fifty thousand words that didn't make it into the final draft because my editor, David Stafford Taylor, thought I could do better. (In all my life, I have never worked so hard to please a guy, Dave, and I'm still amazed that you could see the diamond in the rough. But you were right. You were always right. Thanks.)

If you, gentle reader, find a turn of phrase that sparkles or a plot twist that cuts like a blade, it's because Dave's firm but gentle hand carved and polished it.

> *There once was an Irishman, Dave,*
> *Who worked as a manuscript slave.*
> *But instead of a hook up,*
> *He picked my book up,*
> *And made all the bad prose behave.*

∞

Lastly, I would like to thank the people who taught me about relationships, intimacy, and love. I am in awe of the intellect, passion, and talents you shared with me:

For David, who shared his Twinkies and his doctoring skills (to his mother's chagrin); and for Brent, who taught me to see the possibilities in a broken toaster—and strong hands.

Each of you for a summer: Gary, our noses cold, but your lips warm and soft; John: touching me, touching you and then done too soon; Randy, you were right about back rubs but not the rest; and Pat, all's well that ends well.

**R**emember our pact, Dale? Friends with benefits before anyone called it that. And enigmatic Lance, I lived to see your smile and was sad when I found out why you wouldn't go with me. Sweet sixteen, Chris: we swam in a lake, skied a glacier, and sat at the top of the mountain with the wind in our faces. You only kissed me once, but I remember.

**N**ights that turned into days, talking, touching, falling in love. There's a part of my heart that fits perfectly in your hands, Richard, and always will.

**A**nd Drew, Pierre, Dave. Bruce, Gary, Jubal. John, Michael, Tim. Bill, Jack & Guy. (If you're looking for your name here and didn't find it, no worries. Trust me, you're in there too.) I might not have given you what you wanted, and sometimes not even what you needed, but that doesn't mean it wasn't good. The fault was always mine.

**N**ow I look back and see that you saved me too, Rob. That night. The moment you stepped through the moonlit doorway, and I heard your breath catch in your throat—and I knew the truth.

**D**ays turn into weeks, and weeks into years, and I find that love is the most important thing, and that it *does* transcend time. Which leaves me with...

**O**nly you, Nano. Each of the others was a thread woven into a tapestry, a magic carpet that brought me into your arms. Thanks for waiting for me. The journey *is* the reward.

## ABOUT THE AUTHOR

D. L. ORTON is a graduate of Stanford University's Writers Workshop and a past editor of "Top of the Western Staircase," a literary publication of CU, Boulder. The author has a number of short stories published in on-line literary magazines, including *Melusine*, *Cosmoetica*, *The Ranfurly Review*, and *Catalyst Press*.

Ms. Orton lives in the foothills of Colorado where she and her husband are raising three boys, a golden retriever, two Siberian cats, and an extremely long-lived Triops. Her plans include completing the five books in this series followed by an extended vacation on a remote tropical island (with a Starbucks).

When she's not writing, playing tennis, coding, or helping with algebra, she's building a time machine so that someone can go back and do the laundry.

# LOST TIME

*(Preview)*

# D.L. ORTON

*Between Two Evils Series*
*The 2nd Disaster*

ROCKY MOUNTAIN PRESS

# CHAPTER I
## *Diego: Out on a Limb*

I lie in greenish half-light, my lungs on fire, panic forcing out any rational thought. And then I remember where I am. Or rather where I am supposed to be. I pound my fists against the translucent coffin until I manage to hit the release lever. The lid pops opens and frigid air rushes in, smelling of damp, rotting leaves. I gasp for breath.

I lie still for a few moments, inhaling the clammy air and waiting for my pulse to stop pounding in my ears. The last thing I remember before everything went black is Cassie's panicked voice shouting to abort the mission. Stop the count-down because…

*Shit. I can't remember. But it definitely wasn't good.*

I lift my head and a blinding pain stabs me in the fore-head. I take a forced breath, pushing down the urge to vomit, and open my eyes. All my body parts seem to be attached, but my skin is unnaturally wrinkled, like I stayed in the ocean for hours.

I collapse back into the cold capsule and notice the blood spattered across the lid. Now that I think about it, I can feel the cut in my right palm, probably from the sharp spines of the damn seashell.

I wipe my bloody hand on the flimsy towel and shudder. The air is too cold and damp for the beach. Where the hell am I?

I take a deep breath. It doesn't smell like the beach, either. Maybe I missed the target by a bit and landed in the cloud forest?

*At least I didn't arrive underwater.*

I lie still, listening for the sound of the surf, but hear nothing except a low-pitched groan. The capsule is tipping ever so slightly. I gather my strength and kick the lid off. It bangs and crashes as it falls away from the pod, taking a long time to land.

I force my near-sighted eyes to focus. Above me, massive coniferous branches fan out, fog rolling in just beyond the treetops. This is definitely not Costa Rica.

I heave myself up high enough to see over the side of the capsule, now shivering uncontrollably in the damp, chilly air. The pod is lodged in the upper boughs of a giant tree, perhaps thirty meters above the blurry fern-covered forest floor.

*God, I hate heights.*

The soft groan becomes louder and the pod shifts beneath me.

*Shit. Let's do this.*

I rush to get out before it gives way, but my muscles aren't working very well, and it's harder than I expect. I manage to wrench myself out on the third try, but as I climb over the edge of the pod, my towel slips off and lodges in a couple of limbs below me.

*Just perfect. Now I'm completely naked.*

2 (Preview)

I put my bare feet down on the moss-covered bark and grab onto a higher branch, Gus and the boys uncomfortably exposed. I glance down at my shriveled privates.

Given my current predicament, maybe I should say "man-root and the nuts."

I look up and shiver. There's a cold breeze blowing and the fog is getting thicker by the minute. If I don't get down before it gets dark…

*Let's not go there just yet.*

I shuffle sideways along the slippery branch until I reach the relative safety of the trunk, and then take a moment to look around. The world is green as far as I can see. The only exception is what must be a blue body of water floating where the hills meet the horizon. There is not a person, house, car, road, or other sign of human life anywhere.

Something moves at the edge of my vision, and when I look more carefully, the trees seem to be crawling with giant bugs! I blink a couple of times and realize that they're not insects, but large, black birds—hundreds of them perched in every tree. I shut my eyes for a moment, pushing down vertigo, and then start climbing down, naked and shivering, trying to figure out how the hell I ended up in Alfred Hitchcock's nightmare.

I believe the trees are redwoods, but I'm not particularly good with plant identification. It occurs to me that Isabel would know, and a wave of despair sweeps over me. I try to shake it off and concentrate on the problem at hand. In any case, they are definitely not the sort of trees that grow in the tropics—at least not in my time. Now that I think about it, it does look a lot like the Jurassic forests you see in dinosaur movies.

*Mierda.*

I look out across the forest again, dread creeping up my exposed back. My whole body is shaking, and I feel weak.

No tyrannosaurs or brachiosaurs; nothing but green—and all those birds! Birds descended from dinosaurs, so I probably don't need to worry about being eaten by velociraptors, but I can't remember if there were ever giant, man-eating dodos.

The redwood is huge, and I have to shinny sideways around the trunk to find foot and hand holds, causing my naked front side to bump and scrape against the rough bark.

Note to self: *The Hitchhiker's Guide* was wrong. When time traveling, shine the towel and wear some boxers.

As I move painstakingly down the tree trunk, the black birds start returning, hundreds of them, and I get an uncomfortable feeling, like something sinister is watching me.

*Why are there so many birds?*

I hear a loud snap and look up to see a black explosion of wings. A moment later, the translucent sarcophagus comes barreling down the tree branches like a bobsled on a spiral staircase, heading straight for me. I force myself to look down for the first time, trying to gauge if I'm low enough to jump.

Before I have a chance to decide, I notice a flash of red moving through the ubiquitous green vegetation. There's an astronaut right out of *2001: A Space Odyssey* standing on the ridge watching me!

*What the—*

"Diego!"

I whip my head around. There's a woman at the base of the tree staring up at me!

*Isabel?*

The damn towel drops over my head, covering my face, and I lose my balance.

*Shit!*

My foot slips, pitching me backwards, and for a sickening moment, I know I'm going to die. Then the back of my head strikes a branch. Pain shoots through my neck and shoulders as I tumble sideways into nothingness.

THANK YOU FOR READING!

If you enjoyed the book, please leave a review.
(I read every single one.)

If you would like to be notified
when the next book in the series
is published, please visit:

*www.BetweenTwoEvils.com*

CPSIA information can be obtained at www.ICGtesting.com
Printed in the USA
LVOW11*0532190116

471180LV00012B/514/P

May 2016 LIU